What's Good for Gara

A COMIC MYSTERY

Robert Sanchez

To Roger !
Hope you enjoy!

RS

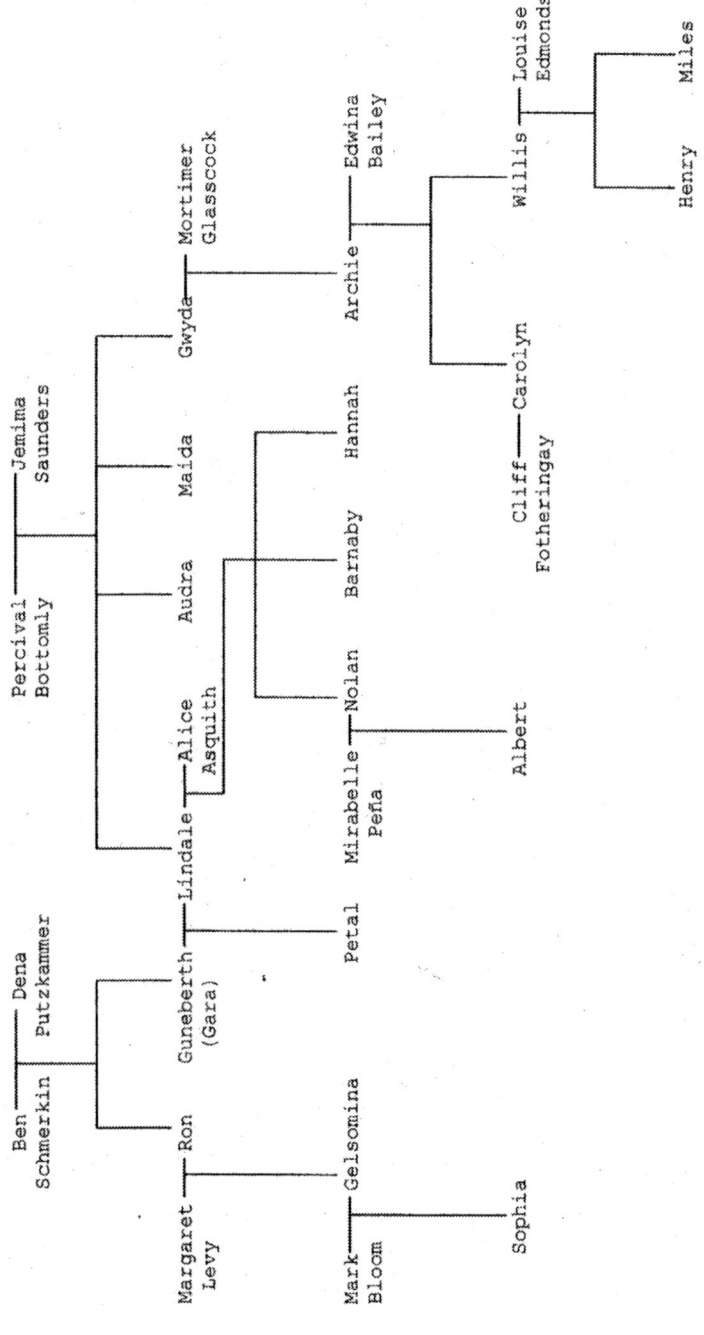

CHAPTER 1

You don't know who Gara St. James is?

"*Ker-plop*! That's the sound of jaws dropping across the country after news that two of Hollywood's biggest stars have left their spouses and are now declaring that they're in love. Industry insiders are wondering if this scandal will jeopardize the opening weekend box office of their upcoming summer blockbuster, *Huge Miscalculation*. For more information, let's go to our entertainment reporter, Gillian Armstrong."

"Thanks, Richard. Everyone's been thrown for a loop by this news. The lovebirds are reportedly keeping a low profile in –"

"Mom! Don't change the channel! That's important news!" Sophie wailed as Mina aimed the remote at the TV in the breakfast nook.

"Sweetie, that's hardly news," Mina quipped, searching for morning television's more intelligent offerings (a difficult prospect amid the flood of celebrity interviews and sketchy "in depth" special reports on the dangers of too much exercise or medical research on babies smoking).

"That's supposed to be the biggest movie this summer," Sophie grumbled.

"I'm sure it will be, although they might want to change the title to *Huge Publicity Stunt*. Why have the morning news shows become more gossip than actual news?" Mina asked, sailing past channels of vacuous talking heads and reality show marathons.

"Well, I think it's news," grumbled Sophie.

"No, this is news," Mina replied, stopping her channel-surfing at BBC America. "Let's see what's going on in the world. Might be good for you to hear some actual news, since you'll spend the rest of the day texting your friends and listening to your iPod."

"It's summer, I'm supposed to waste time and have fun," Sophie countered, taking a bite out of her waffle.

"Don't I know it. Funny that I'm on vacation, too, but I'm supposed to chauffeur you to the mall, soccer practice –"

"Some mothers are glad to do stuff for their kids. I saw a story about a woman who sacrificed everything for her kids, who didn't complain about doing things for them, who didn't -"

Now where did you see that one? Couldn't have been the news because that sounds more like science fiction."

Mina Bloom smiled as they continued breakfast. The two of them enjoyed a comfortable existence in their Connecticut town where Mina taught cultural anthropology at a small liberal arts college. Life hadn't always been ideal, as when her husband Mark died of cancer when Sophie was five. But internal fortitude and a wry sense of humor had served Mina well over the last eight years, and personal setbacks were navigated with a style and aplomb that Elizabeth Taylor would envy.

And despite her apparent disdain for things entertainment-related, she was connected to Hollywood in more ways than she would like. How often had her father been compared in appearance to Robert Mitchum, both tall and dark and handsome in a rough way. And her mother had been told on many an occasion that she bore a resemblance to Deborah Kerr. It was almost a surreal experience to watch *The Sundowners* or *Heaven Knows, Mr. Allison* (the latter film an especially odd viewing experience, with the double entendre of watching one's parents playing a Marine and a nun on a deserted island). And then there was Aunt Gara ...

But while her parents might have resembled great stars of Hollywood past, Mina didn't view herself in those terms. She might have inherited her dad's helpful nature and her mother's red hair, but she didn't see herself in Nicole Kidman or Amy Adams (and the world is a better place for such common sense).

Sophie was physically a lot like Mina, with red hair and a peaches and cream complexion, but her hazel eyes were like Mark's. It had been just the two of them for such a long time, and familiarity was a comfortable place. An interruption in their daily lives might result in both distress and excitement, not unlike James Stewart meeting Jean Arthur's eccentric onscreen family in a screwball comedy. But life had a way of upsetting the familiar ...

"And the Prime Minister had no comment on the statements from the press conference," the anchorman reported blithely on BBC America, shaking Mina back to reality. "We have sad news to report; Lord Lindale Fotheringay Bottomly, affectionately known as 'Laddie,' has died at the age of 107."

"Oh, no," Mina sighed.

"Lord Bottomly was known as a man-about-town during his marriage to Alice Asquith and later became a minor matinee idol in two Hollywood films," the anchorman continued as a glossy still of Laddie in his heyday was displayed onscreen. "His amorous antics in the film capital were more commonly known and included romances with actresses Yvonne DeCarlo and Arlene Dahl, as well as marriages to the mother of former starlet Barbara Lamont, and to fellow minor contract player Gara St. James. The Bottomlys will gather at the ancestral home Brownmoor in Flemshire, with funeral details to be announced later."

"Who's he?" Sophie asked, her curiosity piqued with Mina's reaction to the news item.

"He's your – rather, *our* cousin Pet's father. Do you remember Pet? You haven't seen her since you were six or seven."

"Not really. She's in one of the pictures in the hall, isn't she, the tall lady with the curly hair?"

"That's right."

"Pet – is that short for something?"

"Yes, Petal. The two of us had that in common when we were kids, both with weird names."

"Weird? What do you mean, Gelsomina?"

"Watch it, I almost named you Tziporah. Anyway, Petula Clark was popular then, so they called her Pet, like Petula was nicknamed."

"Who's Petula Clark?"

"Smart. Don't worry, one day your kids are going to be asking, 'Who's Miley Cyrus?'" Mina commented.

"Heck, I'm asking that one myself," Sophie snarked. "Gosh, Lord Bottomly was really old. He was one hundred-and-seven?"

"I guess that's right. He must have been in his sixties when he met Aunt Gara," Mina recalled.

"Oh geez, Great Aunt Gara. Does that mean 'The Creature from the Yiddish Lagoon' is going to make an appearance?"

"Now, Sophie, you shouldn't call her that."

"Why not? *You* call her that."

"I've earned the right to call her that. When you've put up with her as long as I have, then you can call her whatever you like."

"Well, I know you don't consider it news, but sometimes I run across goofy items at online gossip sites about her. Lately she's like Britney, Paris, and Lindsay all rolled into one," Sophie joked.

"I can only imagine," Mina replied as she picked up the telephone and started dialing. "I'm calling Pet. Now that her dad has died, she'll be sharing quality time with Aunt Gara, *if* that pleasure hasn't already begun."

Someone who knew what quality time with Gara meant was

Barbara Lamont, the actress whose mother, Myrtle Dempster, had once been wed to Lord Bottomly. At present, Barbara's concentration was on more physical matters.

"God, Joey, it's so hard," Barbara moaned, prostrate on the floor.

"Keep it up, we're almost there."

"My butt can't take it much more!"

"Keep it up, ladies, I know you can do it!" Joey Daytona yelled from the TV screen. The latest "workout coach to the stars" held classes at the most exclusive gym in Los Angeles, but cost-conscious, ever-so-slightly mature actresses (and the general population) had to settle for purchasing his workout DVDs in the hopes of getting flat tummies and arms free of underside flab.

"Ugh. Love ya, Joey, but that's it for today," Barbara protested, flopping over one last time. Satisfied with her workout goal, she reached toward the coffee table and spread Boursin on a toasted rosemary cracker.

"Babs! Barbara Jr.!" she bellowed, patting her forehead gently with a Kate Spade towel. "Could you scramble up some eggs for your precious mother?"

Confident her daughter was seeing to her request, Barbara stopped the DVD. Joey's muscle-flexing was replaced by a cable newscast.

"– as well as marriages to the mother of former starlet Barbara Lamont, and to fellow minor contract player Gara St. James. The Bottomlys will gather at the ancestral home Brownmoor in Flemshire, with funeral details to be announced later."

"Oh my God, Lord Bottomly's dead?" Barbara exclaimed. She remembered the more important detail of the news. "How dare that little bastard call me a 'former starlet,' like I'm yesterday's news, like I'm not still a star in the cinema firmament. I shouldn't complain too much. After all, they only called Gara a 'minor contract player.' Although that bitch shouldn't have *that* good a description."

Barbara picked up the phone and dialed.

"Hello?"

"Gloria? Gloria! He's dead!"

"Barbara, it's only a nightmare. Shake it off and wake up, dear. I don't understand why you get those dreams, you weren't even there when it happened," soothed Gloria Prescott, Barbara's closest friend and fellow actress.

"No, you don't understand –"

"If anyone should have nightmares, it's me. *I* was the one who saw the gardener blast my husband with the industrial leaf blower, and the resulting echo caused a shower of glass shards in the greenhouse, killing them both. That's what happened, all right. And I without a scratch. A *milagro* for me, not so much for Donald and Jorgé."

"You're not listening, I wasn't having a dream. But you know, perhaps I have those nightmares not over your scandalous tragedy, but more about your designer dress narrowly escaping damage. I'll mention that to my analyst next time. Anyway, that's not what I'm calling about. Lord Bottomly's dead."

"I thought he died a long time ago. Whose funeral was that we attended in England back in '98?"

"Dear, that was Linda McCartney. Don't you remember the favors they passed out, those packaged vegetarian dinners and invitations to join that charity group of theirs?"

"Oh yeah, that was sad. Remember the parties back in the old days when we'd have those sing-alongs and Ringo would wink and call us 'dirty birds?'"

"Gloria, back to the present, dear. This means we'll have to go to England for another funeral."

"Why? Your mother divorced him *años* ago."

"Yes, but she always said she had stuff on him that ensured she'd be in his will." Myrtle Dempster had been (and was still) a tough customer, whether doing her best Mama Rose imitation as manager to her daughters Athole and Barbara's kiddie vaudeville act, or going into overdrive when her girls sought adult screen stardom. More than one studio head had quaked in fear of Myrtle's vicious blackmail attempts or outright punches to the gut in the quest to get Athole and Barbara's names in lights.

"Lord Bottomly's estate is sure to be *grande*," Gloria whistled. Mexican by birth (although Hollywood by vocation), the actress couldn't resist sprinkling her speech with Spanglish. "Does your mother already know?"

"Not yet, she's still asleep."

"How easy is it to wake her up in that sleeping chamber? Like rousing The Mummy from his pyramid?"

"I better do it myself. I didn't give the new nurse the security codes to get into the third chamber yet."

An alarm suddenly pierced the air, and then screams and desperate beseechments to God.

"Mother must have broken out again and frightened the nurse. I hope she hasn't set off that extra security feature, you know the one, the statues that shoot poison darts. God forbid we have another incident like that one years ago, when we lost those hospice workers." Barbara placed her hand to the phone's speaker. "Binky? Binky!" she yelled.

A slim fory-ish man with fluffy blond curls, wearing an aqua satin dance costume and holding a color-coordinated assault rifle, raced by. "I'm on it, Mother!" he called as he skipped upstairs.

"Can Binky handle her? Should you shut yourself in the panic room?" Gloria asked.

"It's not the first time he's had to take her down. But he may need Barbara Jr. for cover. Babs! Get your handgun and give your brother backup!"

"Perhaps I should let you deal with the household drama. While your kids are securing the east wing, why don't I have my Didums start looking into flight arrangements."

"Good idea. Remember, first class for you and me. The children are better at dealing with those teensy seats in coach. How many of those little liquor bottles do they give away? Can we bring our own? Maybe I should have Mother tranquilized and have her shipped. Tell Didums to check with Fed-Ex. Anything to make this easier on my frazzled nerves!"

"No, oh my, no, that won't do at all," Peony Lipschitz squeaked into the phone. "We need better flight arrangements than that. Don't you realize whom we're talking about? Gara? Gara St. James?"

Peony was silent for a moment before a shocked gasp escaped her lips. "You can't be serious. You don't know who Gara St. James is? The greatest star there ever was? The star of *Kissimmee Kate*? *The Branded Cowgirl*? *Dowdy Henrietta*? The woman Ronald Reagan named as his favorite actress? And you're supposedly an American? You wouldn't want to disgrace the memory of our greatest former President, would you?"

Peony paced as she negotiated with the airline. A loud crash from upstairs interrupted her work. "An extra seat! Make sure to get an extra seat for my ball gowns!" boomed a loud voice from faraway.

"I'm working on it, Miss St. James!"

"I won't have them wrinkled or catching odors from cheap luggage! Do you know how hard it is to get the smell of the lower classes out of chiffon velvet?"

"Yes, I remember that ruined Halston two-piece in 1976!" Peony returned to the phone. "We need an extra seat in first class for Miss St. James's gowns! I don't care about the cost. Well, actually we do care about the cost. Can we use some frequent flier miles for that? Oh, and don't forget the seat in economy for me. I'll fly in baggage, if necessary!"

"Of course we'll be there, Pet. We're family, even if we don't get the chance to see each other often. I'm on summer sabbatical, and of course, Sophie's out of school right now, too," Mina said as she talked to her cousin across the country.

"I appreciate it. I wish we *did* have the chance to get together more often, and not for events like this."

"I was telling Sophie the last time she saw you was at her grandfather's funeral."

"Uncle Ron was so wonderful. You had a terrific dad. He was the only one who could keep my mother in line to any degree."

"That's the truth. *Bubee* Dena always indulged her, even as an adult. I guess it was hard to impose rules on her; she was the family breadwinner all those years."

"Too true. When Momsy does crazy things, I try to give her some benefit, within reason. Although we both know she's often a million miles from reasonable."

"Are you flying out with her?"

"No, Momsy has to take care of some things in L.A. first, plus she's flying with her assistant. I've got a flight out this afternoon from San Francisco."

"You still can't stop calling her Momsy," Mina teased.

"Give me a break, you know how I've tried to curb that habit," Pet groaned. "She was in competition with every actress in Hollywood. If Joan Crawford had her kids call her 'Mommie Dearest,' she had to have me call her 'Momsy-Womsy.' I only managed to get rid of the 'Womsy' when I went to college!"

"Just giving you a hard time. Okay, Sophie and I fly out tomorrow and we'll see you there. You keep holding up. Love you, bye-bye."

"Bye, and thanks for everything."

"So, we're going to London?" Sophie asked, barely able to contain her excitement.

"Yes, we are. Brownmoor's just to the east of London, in Flemshire, so we'll fly into the city and drive out."

"Is it a big house?"

"Yes, it was one of the most celebrated homes in England, an enormous manor house on hundreds of acres. One of the wings and some outlying buildings burned down some thirty, forty years ago. But it's still supposed to be impressive."

"How many Bottomlys are left?"

"I'm not sure. There's Pet, of course, and Nolan, he's Pet's half-brother from Laddie's first marriage."

"How many times was he married?"

"I think that newscaster mentioned three or four. And there were Nolan's brother and sister, Barnaby and Hannah. They both died in that fire a long time ago. I think Laddie's sister, Gwyda, is still among the living, and has children and grandchildren. I'm sure I remember that. I haven't been to Brownmoor since I was a kid."

"Did you spend summer vacation with Pet?"

"Yes, we spent several summers there. Pet and I were close in age. Nolan was already an adult, so were Barnaby and Hannah. The guys ignored us, but Hannah was sweet. There were a couple of other cousins around our age, I believe. Now that I think about it, we were there the summer of the big fire. I didn't get to see Pet much after that."

"That's weird. What really happened?"

"I don't know. Mom and Dad were glad for an excuse for us to return to the States. Your grandmother couldn't stand Gara. She always referred to her as 'a good excuse for the return of silent films.' Although Dad could usually rein her in. All it took was a good talk with your granddad and Gara would apologize or do whatever it took to make things right. But when he died, she lost any restraint she may have once had."

"I thought she never had *any* restraint. I read some old gossip about her online once. She said and did whatever she felt like saying, didn't she?"

"She never was afraid of burning bridges. You know, she does have *some* admirable traits. She'd hate to be called a feminist, but she did believe a woman had to look out for herself. But like everything else, she'd take it to ridiculous lengths. Like the time she did that awful Italian vampire movie in 1977, *The Nun Also Rises*, along with a couple of other old-timers. The producers ran out of money and couldn't pay the cast and crew. So Aunt Gara stormed the office and held the producer over the balcony until she got her money. 'I might be just a girl, but don't think I'm gonna let you screw me over and not pay me for the privilege,' she said more times than I can count."

"Maybe she's not as bad as you've built her up to be all these years," Sophie teased.

"Sweetie, you have no idea. People like her, who were famous and live in Hollywood – it's a different reality. They get used to a ridiculous fantasy life and have a hard time relating to the real world. Don't say I didn't warn you."

"I can't believe they almost bumped us from first class for those reality show people," Gloria groused, settling into her seat.

"Well, they didn't and we're here now," Barbara replied as she shrugged off her mink coat.

"Who the hell are Heidi and Spencer, anyway? Is that what passes for stars nowadays?"

"Sadly, yes. It's a good thing the rest of the 'old guard' didn't live to see this sorry state. Marilyn, Jayne, Carroll Baker ..."

"You know Carroll's still alive."

"She is? Oh, so it's just her career that's passed on."

Gloria opened her cell phone and dialed. "Didums, *mi hijo*, did we pack my fox scarf and muff?"

"Ma'am, you shouldn't be using a cell phone at this time," a flight attendant reminded.

"Ma'am? Goodness, you make me sound like something out of a book by those Brontë cousins. And how else can I ask my Didums a question? Unless you'd care to be a dear and ask him for me. He's back in Row something-or-other. You can't miss him, he's the one with aubergine hair in the Chanel swing coat. Ask him if he packed Mother's fox scarf and muff," Gloria said, sending the attendant on with a wave of her hand.

"You're *so* concerned about that muff of yours."

"Paying attention to one's muff is a surefire way to get ahead in the business. Besides, those English estates are always drafty, like Cary's old place in Bel Air."

"Cary's place was cold because he was a cheapskate with the heating bill. He preferred other ways to keep warm, if I recall correctly."

"Only you and Randolph Scott would know for sure," Gloria said, checking her makeup in an ornate hand mirror.

"Don't be so flippant, darling. You had firsthand knowledge yourself, lest we forget that *Confidential* headline, 'Gloria Prescott Wears Out Cary, Gary & Larry.'"

"Oh, that awful tabloid media. I hope we aren't hounded when we reach London."

"I just hope Mother weathers the trip," Barbara said as she inspected her manicure.

"She'll be fine. What a stroke of luck you were able to check her in as cargo with her hyperbaric chamber."

"It's better than having to put up with her, even in coach. She's never been a good airplane passenger, especially after that incident in 1972."

"Known worldwide as 'Myrtle's Pan Am Pandemonium.' I understand that's the reason flight waitresses now wear flame-retardant uniforms. Anyway, it's probably impossible to check her in as a passenger. Undoubtedly her name is on some terrorist watch list nowadays," Gloria observed.

"That'd be all I need. How long is this flight anyway?" Barbara craned her neck. "And when do these stewardesses start serving martinis? I have a feeling we'll need our own pitcher."

The flight attendant spied one purple-haired head in coach, seated between a sleeping man wearing a great deal of makeup and a blonde woman with hot pink streaks in her hair. She bent down and spoke softly, "Excuse me, miss, your grandmother asked that I give you a message."

From behind a pair of Dolce & Gabbana shades, two shockingly arched brows and jet black eyes appeared. "Oh sir, I beg your pardon. I mistook you for a –"

In an amusing but deadly and rather operatic voice, Didums trilled, "Excuse *moi, et tu,* Karen Black?"

"Monsieur, I am not fluent in the language."

"*Quel* beeyotch!" he glared at the attendant.

"The lady in first class is concerned about her muff."

"Finally we get there. That's not a lady, that's my mother, and she isn't just any old bag. She happens to be a glamorous star from the Golden Age of Hollywood. Ever hear of it?"

"Sir, I didn't –"

"I don't wish to underline any one's ignorance further, but do the names Gloria Prescott and Barbara Lamont mean anything to you?"

"Barbara Lamont? I thought she died in Portugal."

"So did we but they dried her out, or was it re-hydrated her? Rather like those powdered Sea Monkeys ... they added water to her, and she perked back up," Babs interjected.

"Er, if you don't mind I need to begin the drink orders," the flight attendant protested.

Binky sat up, awakened from a self-induced mini-coma. "By all means, bring me a double Naughty Kitty ... and don't be stingy with the vodka," he purred and arched his back in anticipation.

STRANGE INTERLUDE 1

The Baby Gara doll ... yours for only $1.65!

Chicagoland Temple Sinai of Flossmoor Community News, May 12, 1934
Happy news for Benjamin and Dena Schmerkin, who welcomed a daughter, Guneberth Amaleah, on May 4. She was also welcomed by her big brother Ron, 2. (Ron can't pronounce Guneberth, and calls his new sister Gara, or rather, "Ga-wa". Isn't that adorable?) Please congratulate them and offer your help with food, gifts, and promises to babysit. The baby's grandmother, Galenka Rosenthal, reports that her grandchild is a sweet little *pisk* [loudmouth]!

Jeweled Toes Dance Academy Newsletter *The Weekly Diamond*, Miss Polly's *What's Shining* column, October 21, 1935
Last week's Autumn Recital was a big success for our students and instructors. Special mention goes to Guneberth Schmerkin. Little Gara, as she's called, was the star of our Baguette Division. Gara performed her routine like a Denishawn Dancer, and actually moved from the back row, over two little friends who had apparently tripped, to front and center in time for the finale. Maybe our Little Gara ought to head out West and take over for that adorable Shirley Temple!

Turner Classic Movies Schedule, July 22, 2004
Spotlight on Baby Gara
8:00 P.M. EST - *Collected Baby Gara Shorts*. Three film shorts featured on the new DVD collection *Baby Gara in a Box*, which collects the one- and two-reelers actress Gara St. James did when she was but a tyke and billed as Baby Gara. Featured tonight are *Baby's First Torah* and *Gesundheit, Gara!* (both 1936). The talent and charm which helped her bridge the path to stardom in feature films is apparent even at this young age. Also debuting tonight is the amusing three-reel *Gone With the Wind* spoof *Baby Gara ...*

Rhymes With Tara (1937). Released to capitalize on the huge success of the Margaret Mitchell novel, it's amusing to spot comparisons to the later MGM epic. Especially funny is Gara's double duty as "Scarlett O'Gara" and "Gammy;" you'll chuckle at the sight of Baby Gara in blackface and heavily padded, bellowing, "Miz Scawlett, I know you said you wuzn't gonna go hungry no mo', but you ain't left no tater tot casserole fo' de rest o' us!"

8:45 P.M. EST - *Little Miss Sweet Knees* (RKO, 1937) Directed by Alfred E. Green. Starring Warner Baxter, Glenda Farrell, Leila Hyams, Eugene Pallette, Baby Gara, Henry Stephenson, Ned Sparks, Louise Beavers. Showbiz impresario Baxter, smarting from failed affair with leading lady Farrell, discovers talented foundling on penthouse doorstep; promoting toddler as star leads to success and new romance with sweet Hyams. A step above other programmers of the same period due to the presence of Baby Gara, who swipes the spotlight from seasoned costars. The film's highlight is a musical number featuring Baby Gara in "Dance of the Dodo Bird."

10:30 P.M. EST - *Crawling Back to Broadway* (MGM, 1937) Directed by Norman Z. McLeod. Starring Baby Gara, John Boles, Gloria Stuart, Guy Kibbee, Isabel Jewell, Paul Lukas, Wayne Morris, Mary Boland. Lawyer Boles and girlfriend Stuart's circle of pals put on Broadway show. Boland's daughter Baby Gara wows with a Garbo impersonation, performing to The Inkspots's "Your Feet's Too Big," and is deemed the salvation to their fledgling show. Rival producer Kibbee aims to ruin everything and has the talented tot kidnapped. Of course, the show goes on to great success, when Baby Gara manages to, yes, crawl back to Broadway from the bumbling kidnappers's hideout in Battery Park just in time to shine onstage.

Excerpt from *Kiddie Stars from Our Gang to Hannah Montana* by Allison Macready

Although Shirley Temple dominated the '30s, other performers shone in their own ways. Jane Withers was spunkier than Shirley and not afraid to appear bossy. Freddie Bartholemew had a soulful gaze and fortitude that belied his young age. Adorable Judy Garland was wistful and had that amazing voice.

One child star who created her own niche was Gara St. James, then billed as Baby Gara. Although Baby Gara could be charming, she wasn't afraid to go beyond spunky into loud and overbearing. She could pull pranks and do things that average kids couldn't get away with. Children found wish fulfillment in watching Baby Gara's obnoxious onscreen antics.

In the two-reeler *Baby Gara vs. the Classroom Crime Queen* (1936), Baby Gara organizes her nursery schoolmates to retaliate against the evil teacher forcing them into a sweat shop producing wallets and purses for upscale department stores. Kids cheered when Gara hit the teacher with a well-aimed bean bag from a slingshot; they cheered even louder when the meanie fell through the factory machinery and came out stitched up and easily carted away by an alerted policeman.

Shrewdly playing the studios against one another, the star's mother negotiated short-term contracts. This resulted in bidding wars at the end of contract periods and helped Baby Gara become a high-earning kiddie star.

Vehicles were created for the star in a thoughtful manner. They alternated scenarios where she might be a tomboyish, miniature hellion in one film (like *Lizzie Borden's Tea Party*) and then play a charming, orphaned tap-dancer in the next (like *Black Mary Janes and Silver Sequins*).

Shirley's career was considered the gold standard, and there were attempts to mirror Gara's screen roles. Shirley portrayed plucky Southern girls in *The Little Colonel* and *The Littlest Rebel*; Gara played dual roles in the antebellum spoof *Baby Gara ... Rhymes With Tara*. Shirley appeared in films derived from classic children's literature like *Heidi* and *The Blue Bird*; Gara appeared in *The Yiddish Garden* and *The Magical Dutch Oven*.

Shirley Temple was more famous, Jane Withers was more spirited, and Bonita Granville was more feminine. But Baby Gara was an original: a gutsy, sassy Cinderella who'd learned a trick or two from those evil stepsisters.

Louella Parsons's column, April 5, 1938

Hello, film fans! I had a delightful afternoon yesterday with one of your favorite stars. I'm speaking of that delightful movie moppet Baby Gara, star of the upcoming feature *Urchin in Mink*. Since landing in the film capital, Baby Gara has graduated from film shorts to her own features. Little girls buy Baby Gara paper dolls and starstruck mothers style their daughters's hair in frizzy layers, just like Gara's.

I had tea yesterday afternoon with Baby Gara and her dolls, as well as Gara's pleased-as-punch mother, Mrs. Dena Schmerkin. Mrs. Schmerkin served petit fours and Cambric tea for her daughter's little party. Dena beamed like the always lovely Marion Davies in a divine close-up in her latest cinematic triumph, *Ever Since Eve*.

Gara's talent at tap dancing led the family to trek from Chicago to Hollywood in pursuit of a dream, the dream of millions of my devoted readers. She stood out in extras casting calls and making the studio rounds. She began appearing in one-reelers, then as a headliner for Columbia's *Dumpling Delights* shorts, a modern version of the *Baby Burlesks* films that brought Shirley Temple to everyone's attention. (And we'll get around to Shirley in our interview shortly!)

Gara grabbed her big chance when poor Jane Withers was felled by food poisoning and couldn't start filming *The Little Nipper Toddles Home*. Baby Gara had just met her cinematic rival Withers the day before at a luncheon where Hollywood mothers brought their girls for a special mother/daughter fashion show.

"Same cake," Gara gurgled charmingly.

"Yes, dear, these are the same cakes as we had at that very luncheon," Dena agreed.

"What a shame that Jane Withers got sick that afternoon, but it allowed you to slip into the role for your big break, didn't it?" I asked the star.

"Piece a' cake," she giggled; pleased with her own pun, she couldn't stop laughing in such a cute manner. "Of course, darling, you may have another piece," I agreed.

Of course, this leads us to the biggest star in Hollywood, Shirley Temple, who once shared the screen with Jane. Might Gara one day do the same?

"Gara was up for the part of Klara in *Heidi*," Mrs. Schmerkin revealed. "But Shirley was threatened by Gara's talent and nixed that idea. So they stuck some nobody in the part." (That "nobody" was sweet Marcia Mae Jones, who was menaced so memorably by Bonita Granville in *These Three* last year.)

"Now, Mrs. Schmerkin, surely you don't think Shirley would do something like that?" I pressed, hoping to get more tidbits from the celebrity mother more than one contemporary has steered clear of as far as bragging rights go. "Didn't Shirley and Gara play together at the Fourth of July party on the Fox back lot this past summer?"

"Gara was just playing cowboys and Indians, that's why Shirley had those ropes around her arms. Just playing, that's my Baby Gara," Mrs. Schmerkin beamed.

Next up for Baby Gara is a proposed children's version of the Garbo success, *Camille*, to be written by Mercedes de Acosta. That's sure to be terribly interesting!

Ad in *Picturegoer* magazine, October, 1940

You've enjoyed her in countless film successes ... now you can have her for your very own!

The Baby Gara doll ... yours for only $1.65!

You loved her in *Orphan in the Sahara* and *The Kid from Poughkeepsie*! Here's your chance to own a Baby Gara doll! So lifelike you'll swear she's in the room with you!

Genuine rooted hair in Baby Gara's famous frizz! Comes dressed in a replica of the ruffled dress she wore as *The Minor Mayor of Milwaukee*. Also included are a pretty nightgown for sleepy-time and a sparkly costume for her dance numbers.

Run, don't walk, to be the first of your friends to own a genuine Baby Gara doll!

Be sure to catch Baby Gara in *Little Bonnie Parker*, a prestige offering from RKO Studios next month at your local theater!

From *Leopold Maltby's Movie & Video Guide*

The Littlest Stenographer (RKO, 1942) Directed by Anthony Mann. Starring Jean Arthur, Ralph Bellamy, Baby Gara, Phil Silvers, Charles Coburn, Helen Broderick, Hans Conreid, Grant Withers. Arthur, as prim efficiency expert hired by Coburn to evaluate his company, clashes with his son Bellamy. To ensure her failure, he concocts a scheme whereby the company must hire Baby Gara as Coburn's executive secretary. Film marks the first Baby Gara film to lose money. Her acting can no longer hide behind infantile charm. An otherwise talented cast tries but can't overcome a foolish script with scenes of Gara fumbling with an adding machine and getting entangled in an out-of-control typewriter ribbon. The film squeezes in a musical number for Baby Gara in "When the Red Red Robin Comes Bob Bob Bobbin' Along," but it lays an egg.

Hedda Hopper's column, June 23, 1944

I had quite a day yesterday, dear readers, without a moment to myself. Luckily, I managed to gather tasty tidbits of both the dietary and gossip variety!

Had a smidge of breakfast yesterday morning at the Universal commissary with some adorable moppets. The vaudeville act Dainty Athole and Her Little Sailors performed a cute Andrews Sisters takeoff for a Henry King musical short.

Athole's mother and sister were also onset and made an impression, as well. Mother Myrtle Dempster almost shoved Henry King out of a two-shot featuring darling Athole! And little sis Barbara, as one of the sailors, danced a bit too energetically, displaying moves more befitting a burlesque chorus girl than a Navy gob!

Had lunch with Gara Schmerkin and her mother, Dena. Surely you remember those Baby Gara films of yesteryear. But babies grow up, and they don't always adjust to growing pains. Take Shirley Temple, who suffered a setback when she grew out of those adorable roles. But Shirley's talent will pull her through as you'll see when you catch her in the magnificent *Since You Went Away*. Everyone's marvelous in it, and keep a hanky handy for the tearjerker scenes.

But for every Shirley Temple, there are a dozen "Our Gang" kiddies who fade away. Gara's at that crossroads now and her options are on shaky ground. RKO released her from contract and acting offers have dried up. Recent films have been failures as the cute baby turned into an awkward young lady.

But Gara and her mother remained confident. "Those geniuses in the front office wouldn't know a star if it fell to Earth right in front of them," Dena boomed. "We'll shine again like we always have, won't we, my Baby Gara?"

Gara, perhaps having a little headache, sniffed a loud "harrumph." Actually, she did this more than a few times during our lunch. If she keeps that up, we may take to calling her "The Harrumph Girl!"

Dena confided that Gara was recently at MGM to audition for *Lassie Come Home*. "She was perfect for that part, but for some reason, they picked that Taylor kid," complained Dena, referring to the angelic Elizabeth Taylor. "I don't see how we failed. I even rubbed a little steak juice behind Gara's ears, but that lousy mongrel whimpered whenever he came near my darling baby, piddled on her shoes, and made a beeline for that English girl with the purple eyes! That's not normal! There's probably witchcraft in her ancestors."

Well! As lunch drew to its conclusion, Dena and Gara remained confident that luck would shine their way again. "There's a terrific part as a good Midwestern girl in *Our Vines Have Tender Grapes*. After all, that's what Gara is, deep down inside!" Dena enthused as Gara offered one last, "Harrumph." Keep up that good attitude, girls!

CHAPTER 2

He nearly killed her, but managed to only tear off her arm.

Mina closed the *Daily Mirror* after reading the same story about Lord Bottomly for the third time. She'd only been a child during summers at Brownmoor, and so had dim memories of a mildly sinister old man who paid her little mind, like Uriah Heep relegated to an ineffective maître d' position. But as usual, the truth was more complex.

His exploits as a jet-setting dandy involved countless affairs as well as four marriages, the first to Alice Asquith, daughter of a tin magnate, who bore him three children: Nolan, Barnaby, and Hannah. Subsequent marriages to Myrtle Dempster (the manager mother of Barbara Lamont), Gara St. James, and Jenny Menzies (a former magician's assistant) brought no peace to the fun-loving Englishman.

But peace was perhaps the last thing Laddie had ever wanted out of life. He was stagestruck at an early age, due to a boyhood crush on Sarah Bernhardt, a friend of Lady Jemima Bottomly and frequent visitor to Brownmoor. As the oldest and the only boy (his sisters were, in order, Audra, Maida, and Gwyda), the Bottomly women stroked his ego and made all females objects of interest, particularly those painted ladies of stage, screen, and naughty postcards.

That affection for stage ladies continued throughout his life, and contributed to the breakup of his first marriage, when stories of his affair with chorus girl Winnie Potter became fodder for the columns. Only after the fact was it discovered Winnie had borne him a daughter, Evie, who had been killed in a bomb fire in 1941 during the blitz. Unable to face further humiliation, Alice initiated divorce proceedings, to which Laddie acceded.

He abandoned England for the sunny shores of Hollywood where he was surrounded by glamorous actresses impressed by European titles. He even starred in two minor films, *The Bayou Blossom* (a Civil War melodrama with Janet Blair) and *Sun Valley Soufflé* (a frothy musical-comedy with Adele Jergens).

It was there he met and wed Myrtle Dempster, a marriage that lasted two years and was accompanied by numerous gossip scandals. Once free of Hollywood's constraints, he remained on the move for years, flitting from Buenos Aires to Monte Carlo to Hong Kong and points in between. It was in Barbados he met Gara and started a whirlwind romance, leading to marriage and the birth of Pet. But things eventually soured between the pair, as they always did, and they separated not long after the tragic fire at Brownmoor which killed Barnaby and Hannah.

That fire so long ago ... there was something about it that now gnawed hamster-like at the corners of Mina's mind ...

"Mom, is this line ever going to move?" Sophie asked, rousing her from her private thoughts.

"Sorry, sweetie, customs isn't designed to move fast in this day and age. We'll get through it okay. Pet sent a car for us, and we'll drive out to Flemshire."

"How far is it outside London? Will we still be able to go shopping?"

"We'll make time for that later. The most important part is for us to be there for Pet," Mina reminded.

"I'm sorry, you're right. I wonder what the family's like, and how the house will look."

Mina wondered the same thing. Vague images of the house stirred the drama of her thoughts, which reimagined Brownmoor as a mélange of Manderley, Bleak House, and the Chicken Ranch. Only later would she realize the bizarre farrago had contained some truth.

"Didums, are you sure this is right?"

"Yes, Mother, we change planes in Newark and continue on to London," he assured a concerned Gloria.

"Ugh, don't let anyone know we were stuck in Newark. Sounds like years ago, do you remember, when we toured in *Mame* and hit all those little towns?" Barbara interjected.

"Don't remind me, I almost broke my neck on the staircase in Baton Rouge. Oh, for the old days, when burly teamsters put the sets together, and not under-aged volunteers from local acting workshops," Gloria shuddered.

"Ooh, those brutish teamsters!" Barbara brightened at the memory. "You know, a touch of the brute never did a willing lady any harm."

"Don't I know," Binky added as he perused a hunky baggage carrier transporting a cart through the airport.

"Where's my handbag? I need one of my vitamins," Gloria said.

"Is that what they're called?" Barbara emitted a coy smile as

Didums produced the bottle from Gloria's purse.

"Don't start, or I'll have to mention that special flask of 'white water' in *your* clutch," Gloria averred.

"Wouldn't one of Mother's special white water Mai Tais be nice while we wait?" Barbara cooed, licking her lips. "The one useful thing Mother picked up during her affair with that Oriental warlord. Well, when they weren't trying to undermine the Japanese economy with that financial scheme. Wait a minute, are they're going to transfer Mother to the right plane? Babs! Ask that flight hostess to make sure they'll put Myrtle on the right plane."

Babs and Binky attended to the request as Barbara smoothed out her fur coat. "How long is the delay? Do I have time for a little nappy?"

"Within the hour," Didums replied, checking the time on his antique locket worn on an ornate, jeweled Robert Whiteside bracelet.

"Just enough time for a quick *siesta*," Gloria said as the two stars settled into their seats and snuggled against sable. "Wake us, sweetie, when that infernal airline is ready to serve us again."

"Mrs. Dutton, are we quite prepared? Some of the guests will be American and may have odd requests. We should try to be accommodating, within reason. I apologize in advance for unreasonable demands you're sure to encounter."

"Mrs. Glasscock, I remember Miss St. James quite well. I was already a downstairs maid at Brownmoor when Lord Bottomly brought her here," the housekeeper reminded.

"Yes, of course. I wish I could forget that dreadful harpy's complete existence. Perhaps time has tempered her banshee temperament ... but I shouldn't count on it," Dame Gwyda Glasscock sniffed.

The elderly Dame was still a formidable presence, whether addressing a lecture hall of terrified students, making dinner party small talk with international dignitaries, or hiking across Britain's rugged terrain. Tall and rangy with oversized, hawklike features, she spent her life barreling forward, minus concern for the opinions of others, save necessary social protocol. That attitude served her well professionally; she rose to prominence in wildlife circles, a David Attenborough with dried-up ovaries.

Her marriage to Mortimer Glasscock, noted thimble enthusiast and scion of a silversmithing fortune, was no exception to her dominant inclinations. Her bulldozer personality and his sparrow-like nature seemed to mesh perfectly in a happy union. They were married almost 60 years until his death from lead poisoning. (On the death certificate, the coroner ruled that Glasscock succumbed to blood poisoning after an accidental injury involving an antique hatpin, noting in the margin that death was caused by an "unfortunate prick.")

Gwyda continued, "In any case, we're expecting Pet's cousin Gelsomina and her daughter Sophia this afternoon. She's an intellectual, so we can expect her to behave well, for an American. Not so sure about the child."

"Mina and Sophie won't be a problem whatsoever. Sophie's a well-behaved young lady. She's about the same age as your great-grandsons," Pet said as she entered the kitchen.

"That's all for now, Mrs. Dutton," Gwyda dismissed the housekeeper and turned to Pet. "I'm sure you're right. I'm only trying to minimize any suffering on the staff's behalf."

"I know my mother isn't going to be easy. She never is. I appreciate everything you've done, and will have to deal with, in the coming days."

Gwyda allowed a measured smile to cross her face. "Of course, my dear. And if I haven't said it yet, I'm happy to have you here, even under sad circumstances." She studied Pet's features for a moment. "Your father's eyes," she observed.

"Nolan would disagree."

"Just his selfish desire to keep everything to himself, not even sharing one physical trait with you, much less Laddie's affection. Your father loved you, you know that. Yes, those same eyes. Who knows where your dark complexion comes from. Gypsy blood, I shouldn't wonder. We really must do something about your hair one of these days. Too bad *that* you inherited from your mother."

"Are you aware, Miss ... Brenda, is it? Brenda, are you aware that we're expected at a state funeral? Well, not a state funeral, I don't think they have states in England. But Miss St. James must be on the next plane," Peony implored the harried clerk at the reservation desk.

"I understand, and will do everything within my power to make this happen for you," Brenda replied crisply.

"Don't worry about me, I'm nothing. You have to ensure this is fixed to Miss St. James's satisfaction. She's a star and expects certain treatment. I still don't understand why we had to land in Chicago."

"There's a storm surge moving down from Canada through the northeast as we speak. But we'll do everything we can to ensure that you're on the next available flight," Brenda said, a touch of irritation peeking through.

Peony's cell phone interrupted the negotiation. "Excuse me," she apologized. "Hello?"

"Peony? Aren't those airline people supposed to feed us when these things happen? Tell them I want one of those chicken strip meal deals from Burgerville, and a bottle of red wine."

"Right away!" Peony snapped to attention, glancing at the back of Gara's head three feet away. "Miss St. James's blood sugar has dropped, she needs sustenance immediately! A chicken strip meal and a good bottle of shiraz, pronto!"

"There are several restaurants on this concourse, Miss Lipschitz," Brenda snapped, placing a slight emphasis on the second syllable of Peony's surname. "You may feed your boss at your convenience."

"That's hardly convenient! Are you aware the Bush White House – the father, not the son – kept a special dining set specifically for Gara St. James? A deep dish plate and mug designed by the Franklin Mint? Would you expect a national treasure to schlep her own tray?" Peony gasped.

Peony's cell rang again. "Yes, of course we're in your beloved hometown. Special Chicago-style hot dogs instead? Right away!" She glared at Brenda again. "Thank you for your complete lack of assistance! I'm going to get Miss St. James some hot dogs *myself*, and when I get back I hope you know our revised flight information."

Peony turned and glanced at the back of her boss's head. "I should have touched up Gara's hair before we left," she mused. "Thank goodness I packed those boxes of 'Bronzette Lilith Dye #7.' Maybe I can go up to first class and touch-up her roots."

Again, the cell phone interrupted Peony's boss-worship. "Do I gotta go kill and skin some hogs myself? Oy, I haven't prepared kosher meat myself in ages! And don't forget extra relish!" star-shrieks pierced her assistant's ear, and the less accustomed ears of adjacent fellow travelers.

"I'm on it, Miss St. James!" Peony squeaked, tripping over suitcases as she scurried toward the food court.

"Can you beat that, a mongrel in search of dogs?" Brenda muttered as she turned to assist the next passenger.

"So what is there to do at Brownmoor? Chasing the dogs on foxhunts? Having tea with the Queen? Ooh, maybe playing polo with Prince Harry?" Sophie quizzed, watching the scenery race by as the car bore them into deepest Flemshire.

"My area of cultural expertise is Peru, but I know those English stereotypes aren't accurate, sweetie. The English have become what they've most disliked – American. Or, at least, Americanized."

Terrence, the driver, raised his eyebrows but refrained from comment. The reverse American invasion of McDonald's and *The Simpsons* didn't constitute a triumph comparable to that of Lord Horatio Nelson.

"Do you think there'll be any kids my age there?"

"I don't see why not. I'm sure Laddie's sister has children and grandchildren."

"What's she like?"

"I don't remember much. She was some sort of wildlife expert. She was made a dame by Queen Elizabeth II sometime in the seventies, I think."

"That's correct, Mrs. Bloom, in 1972, to be precise," Terrence stated. "And descendants of Dame Glasscock are indeed at Brownmoor, as well."

"Is that it up ahead?" Sophie asked.

"This is it," he said as the car turned onto a private drive. An understated metal sign engraved with the title "Brownmoor" on the adjacent wall was all that indicated they had arrived. They drove through an iron archway and continued on the road which wound through wooded landscape. Just when it seemed the road would wind forever through the trees, the car made a final turn and the main house loomed.

"Wow," Sophie whispered.

Mina didn't speak, overwhelmed by her memories of Brownmoor. They say places and people seem bigger than life in childhood memories (or was it only Olivia deHaviland who said it in *Hush ... Hush, Sweet Charlotte*), but to her adult eyes the house seemed much larger now.

Brownmoor was a massive structure, and something of an oddity. The original house had been a Norman castle built in the 11th century, but the whims of the Fotheringays and Bottomlys long buried that simple fortress with every conceivable architectural fashion. The ornate façade, a Gothic Revival fantasy of gigantic proportions, was the architectural wet dream of Laddie's great-great-great-grandfather, Lord Percival Fotheringay. The building was a maniacal rhapsody of the stone-cutter's art with details peeking up and forward in a frenzied climb to an asymmetric roof-line marred by a broken tower. That tower and its entire wing were sealed off and remained unrestored for the sake of economy following the fire.

The car stopped in front of the broad stone steps, leading to the immense front doors which swung open. Pet emerged and rushed forward, flinging herself into Mina's embrace.

"It's good to see you, in spite of the circumstances," Mina gushed. "And here she is, here's Sophie."

"Is it okay if I call you Pet?" she asked, looking from mother to cousin.

"Yes, I'd like that," Pet agreed.

Sophie examined her cousin: major height, olive complexion, wild curls, blue eyes. Pet was the love child of Janice Dickinson and Paul Bunyan.

"Is that your Aunt Gwyda?" she asked, noticing the elderly woman standing inside the doorway at the terrace landing.

"Yes. Don't worry, Sophie, she's formidable, but only when it's necessary. Which is most of the time," chuckled Pet.

They were ushered into the foyer of the grand hall. From the vaulted room rose an enormous walnut staircase, the steps of which were unusually short, making for a lengthy walk to the second floor landing. (The strange staircase had been designed more than 150 years ago by Lord Merrick Bottomly for his bride, Dorcas, who had been born with exceptionally short shins.) Tapestries emblazoned with family crests, archaic medieval weaponry, and portraits in hand-carved frames covered available wall space. The overall effect was smothering and vacant at the same time.

Pet made the introductions, and Gwyda said, "Mina, Sophie, welcome to Brownmoor. Please let me know if there's anything I can do to make your visit more comfortable. Mrs. Dutton will be happy to show you to your suite."

"I'll take care of them, Aunt Gwyda," Pet offered.

"That's fine. You can relax after your long trip. Shall I have some tea sent up? We dine at eight in the formal dining room. See you then." With that, Gwyda left with the housekeeper for the kitchen, as Pet led Mina and Sophie to the second floor and their assigned suite.

"Don't hesitate to ask if there's anything you need," Pet assured as she ushered them to the suite, modern and inviting in contrast to the house's imposing architecture.

"Thank God this room isn't stuffed with glaring portraits and unhappy gargoyles," Mina remarked.

"The grand hall is a bit much, but Aunt Gwyda would cringe if anyone suggested lightening it up. Tradition and all that."

"Can I ask a question?" Sophie ventured.

"Oh, sweetie, I forgot to give you a heads up. And you knew not to ask in front of her," Mina slapped her hand to her forehead.

"You forgot to tell Sophie about Aunt Gwyda's one arm?"

"It's been a long time since I last saw her," Mina winced.

"You weren't kidding about her being intimidating. There's no way I'd have asked," Sophie widened her eyes.

"In 1960, she was studying an almost extinct breed of bear, the *Royal Ursaline*, when she was confronted by the last one in a remote area. He nearly killed her, but managed to only tear off her arm," Pet related.

"Oh, God," Sophie breathed.

"It did little to faze her, though. There's a famous photo she took of herself, standing over the dead bear, her clothes covered in blood."

"How did she manage to do that?" Sophie gasped.

"Adrenaline can turn an ordinary human into the Incredible Hulk. She was determined to finish her task of documenting wildlife, even if she had to cheat death to do it. Then she managed to walk miles to a highway, where a traveling mime troupe found her. She became quite famous, bringing more attention to her work. Which, I guess to Aunt Gwyda, the end justified the means."

"That's kind of nuts," Sophie said, shaking her head.

"I warned you about Aunt Gara, but I should have extended that warning to British eccentrics, too."

Pet laughed. "There are a few others, whom you'll meet at dinner. Let's see if I can get you up to snuff."

Pet was thorough in her dossiers on the Bottomlys, the Fotheringays, and the Glasscocks. Gwyda held court at the head of the table, with Nolan at the foot. At Gwyda's side were her son Archie and Pet. At Nolan's side was his son Albert. At various points along the table were Archie's son Willis and daughter Carolyn, and their spouses, Louise and Cliff. Beside them were Willis and Louise's sons, Henry and Miles. In the middle of the table were Mina and Sophie.

Nolan bore a striking resemblance to a young Laddie, with a large head, a pronounced nose, and a shock of greenish-silver hair. (The unusual birthmark was famously commented on by Mrs. Patrick Campbell, who said, "Leave it to the Bottomlys to be born with corroded silver spoons in their *hair*!") Both he and Pet shared their father's pale blue eyes.

Albert bore little resemblance to Nolan; his dark, handsome features came from his mother, Mirabelle Peña, who had been a Spanish singer.

Gwyda's son Archie took after the Glasscocks, for his appearance bore little trace of Bottomly influence; he resembled the blandly handsome third-string actors who played lawyers, accountants, and policemen in '40s films.

Unfortunately for Willis and Carolyn, the Bottomly traits returned full force in their generation. Willis could sort of get away with looking like a brutish mobster in a film noir (if one squinted, he looked a bit like Dan Duryea), but Carolyn (resembling a young Nancy Walker with an excellent figure) had a harder time pulling the look off.

The attractive Louise Edmonds (a lesser Kay Kendall) brought pretty genes to the bloodline, as Henry and Miles were handsome young teens. And in a not unusual twist, Carolyn's husband Cliff was a Fotheringay, thus bringing distant intermarriage into modern times. Carolyn and Cliff (a slightly handsomer version of Gary Merrill) had no children, but doted on their cockapoo, Chester.

"Did you hear from your mother today?" Gwyda asked Pet as the staff served dinner.

"No, I thought she'd arrive today. That was the plan, according to her assistant. I expect she'll arrive tomorrow."

"Why does she travel with an assistant? Has she become infirm?" sneered Nolan.

"No, she's fine. But she relies on Peony for everything," Pet said, biting her tongue from saying more.

"Hollywood people are so needy, always relying on others," Louise observed, waving aside the maid's offer of potatoes.

"That has little to do with it. There's a lot of needy behavior on display in this very house," Pet said slyly.

"You would know," Nolan added.

"We mustn't give our guests the wrong idea about the Brits. They'll think we're horrible snobs," Gwyda admonished.

"But we *are* snobs," joked Henry. Sophie gave him a sidelong glance; he responded with a wink.

"That's enough, Henry," Willis barked.

"That's *quite* enough," Gwyda said in a voice that let all know she would brook no further shenanigans. "We can expect Gara to arrive tomorrow, and will proceed with the funeral the day after that. Laddie can be laid to rest ... and I'll add anyone to the interment who doesn't behave with the proper respect."

Something told Mina that Gwyda may have issued a warning to the family to mind their P's and Q's, but the unspoken recipient of that statement was the dreaded Gara.

STRANGE INTERLUDE 2

She's just like in the movies, only bigger and older!

From *Leopold Maltby's Movie & Video Guide*
　　　The Janitor and the Jailbait (Essemtoo Studios, 1945) Directed by Frank Winsocky. Starring Kane Richmond, Baby Gara, Veda Ann Borg, Tim Ryan, Wanda McKay, Anthony Warde, Ralph Lewis, Willie Best. Low-budget programmer of forbidden romance between a school janitor and an underage temptress. Bizarre story falls flat, particularly with the miscasting of Baby Gara (rather past the "Baby" stage) as the junior high Lolita. Gara seems both younger and older at the same time; naïve confusion coupled with a mature face and unflattering figure is an unappealing combo. A competent supporting cast tries to put some realism into the proceedings, but it adds up to very little. This is bottom of the barrel, even lower than poverty-row Monogram films of the same period.

Excerpt from Gara St. James's credits at *www.imdb.com*
65. *Two of My Favorite Things* (1945) .... Patient (uncredited)
64. *When the Redbuds Are in Bloom* (1946) .... Chorus Girl #6 (uncredited)
63. *The Gauche Gaucho* (1946) .... Señorita #4 (uncredited)
62. *High School Hercules* (1946) .... Girl in Glasses (uncredited)
61. *Pauline on Patrol* (1947) .... Plain W.A.C. (uncredited)
60. *Honeymoon in Bogota* (1947) .... Sausage Peddler (uncredited)
59. *Drill Me With Kindness* (1948) .... Girl Riveter (uncredited)
58. *Murder Under the Big Top* (1949) .... Sideshow Geek (uncredited)

Business Card
　　　Have Baby Gara live at your party!
　　　She'll sing, dance, and tell jokes!
　　　She's just like in the movies, only bigger and older!
　　　Call CR3-5432

Manager, Dena Schmerkin

Los Angeles Daily News photo caption, February 19, 1946

A mature Baby Gara cuts the ribbon at the opening of the newest Oinky's Supermarket in Greater Tulare. Dressed in an old movie costume which no longer fit, Baby Gara entertained shoppers, many of whom did not appear to remember her.

Lord resigns amid scandal, by Michael Worth, *The Times of London*, 16 June 1947

Lord Lindale Fotheringay Bottomly resigned yesterday from the House of Lords amid rumors of personal scandal. "Laddie" issued no statement and left at once for an unscheduled trip to Paris.

His wife, the former Alice Asquith, filed for divorce three days ago after his longtime affair with Winnie Potter, an unemployed chorus girl, came to light. Miss Potter had been receiving a monthly stipend to remain quiet about details of their affair, which included the birth of a daughter, Evie, in 1939. (The child died in 1941 during the blitz.)

Miss Potter stated, "I wasn't bleeding 'im dry, I was only gettin' what was comin' me. 'E didn't want wha' I know ta come out." She would not elaborate further.

Laddie's father, Lord Percival Bottomly, was an influential legislator before his death in 1942, at which time, Laddie assumed his father's seat. Laddie did not embrace the same authoritative role as his father, preferring to remain on the periphery of the political sphere and devote most of his time to social commitments.

Fellow members of the House had no comments on the scandal. Members of London's social scene were more forthcoming in discussing the matter. Geraldine Bennett, the socialite and actress, stated that Laddie's reputation as a lothario was well-known, and well-deserved. "He's very charming and has always had a weakness for ladies who perform onstage. I'm not surprised this Winnie Potter person appealed to him. A well-turned ankle and a prominent bosom have enriched more than one lady's coffers, and I daresay there'll be others."

Lady Bottomly remained in seclusion at the family estate, Brownmoor, in Flemshire. Her sister-in-law, Gwyda Glasscock, the noted expert in matters of animal husbandry, issued a curt, "No comment," and requested the press respect Lady Bottomly's privacy during this trying time.

Hedda Hopper's column, July 2, 1948

Good morning, film fans! Let's get right to today's items, including a "whatever happened to" update on a forgotten star and info on two beautiful new starlets who are sure to be among tomorrow's leading players!

I was at RKO Studios yesterday and observed the filming of a charming wartime comedy, *Drill Me With Kindness*, starring Diana Lynn and Robert Ryan. One of the extras in the factory scene looked oddly familiar, but I couldn't place her. When the director told them it would be another half-hour, that girl emitted a familiar, "Harrumph!"

"Gara? Baby Gara!" I yelped. The girl turned with a friendly scowl toward me. "Gara, that *is* you, isn't it?"

Gara loped over to me with the grace of a Clydesdale. "Sssh!" she cautioned, obviously wanting to avoid a crowd of autograph-seekers and the like.

"Whatever are you doing working as an extra, a big one-time star like you?" I wondered aloud.

"Just learning every aspect of movie-making. How can a star appreciate their stardom without understanding what it's like for the peons?"

What a brave front Gara's put on. A huge former child star, now an awkward and plump teenager, reduced to bottom-of-the-barrel extra work. Many former stars retire gracefully from the screen when their stardom ends. Think of Norma Talmadge, who, when recognized long after her silent heyday, told a fan, "Go away, dear, I don't need you anymore." Think of Gloria Swanson, who appeared in a few mediocre sound films and is now enjoying her permanent retirement from the screen.

Will Gara fade into obscurity, or will she make a comeback one day? Time will tell.

Yesterday afternoon, I attended a tea sponsored by the Prudence Hills Playhouse, designed to introduce unsigned talent to the major studios. I was entranced by two teenaged starlets who will surely attain screen stardom in the near future. Gloria Prescott is a Latin lovely from Mexico City. She hails from the aristocratic Perez family and started as a dancer, taught by her talented mother, not unlike her countrywoman Rita Hayworth. "*Mamacita* taught me her special technique of whipping her skirts higher and higher. The spectators love it," enthused the beautiful brunette. Sounds like quite a show!

Also catching my eye was the stunning blonde Barbara Lamont, who hails from Kansas City. You know she's a good girl, since she was accompanied by her mother! Barbara zeroed in on one of the guests, lovely Carole Landis, and was getting advice on making it in Hollywood.

Carole got advice in return from Mrs. Lamont. I noticed she gave Carole something, and when I asked about it, Barbara's mother said, "The poor dear's not sleeping well, so I gave her some special nighty-time pills I got on a trip to Agua Caliente. It's sure to knock her out for a long time." Such charming generosity. That's the way to get ahead in Hollywood!

New theme restaurant opens by Susan Lancaster, *Los Angeles Daily News*, November 9, 1948

Doubles, a new diner on Santa Monica Boulevard, opened last week with an appealing menu of tasty treats. But the real draw isn't the food, it's the wait staff, who are all movie star lookalikes. You can order soup from "Clara Bow" or a sandwich from "Gary Cooper." It's a hit with patrons, who enjoy friendly service and impromptu entertainment performed by the "stars."

We enjoyed our appetizers of shrimp cocktails, and were pleased with the beef stew and the meatloaf, both of which were cooked to perfection.

One criticism, however, is the less-than-favorable performances of some staff members. We enjoyed a slice of chocolate cake and a song from "Ginger Rogers," but diners at an adjacent table didn't care for their waitress, "Baby Gara." The look-alike was too old for the part, and there was none of the doll-like charm of the original star. When the diners asked for more enthusiasm, "Baby Gara" harrumphed, "I'll give you enthusiasm." Shockingly, she then "cut the cheese!"

As long as the restaurant's owners recast a couple of the "stars" on staff, it looks like they've got a winner!

Excerpt from *Hollywood Babylon II* by Kenneth Anger

As a child star, Gara St. James emulated Shirley Temple and later took publicity hints from Elizabeth Taylor. After Taylor published the charming *Nibbles and Me* about her pet chipmunk in 1946, "Baby Gara" published *Seventh Heaven with Seven Guinea Hens*, about her supposed pet fowls. The truth is that Baby Gara's career was in serious decline and the hens paid for their keep by providing her with eggs to sell at the Farmer's Market. The photo at right depicts the corpse of one hen after she served them to guests at a 1950 dinner party during a Los Angeles catering strike.

Dancers arrested in Oakland by Mike Markowski, *Police Gazette*, April 7, 1949

Six female dancers were arrested last week when police raided the Oakland nightclub Tzitzit. The police were acting on tips they received that "indecent performances" were taking place at the nightclub, billed as a "Jewish men's club." Instead of dancing behind ostrich feather fans like Sally Rand, these barely dressed young ladies, billed as "Seder Dancers," danced suggestively behind large engraved Passover platters. It is suspected some of the dancers were underage. They may also have given fictitious identities when they were arrested and later released. The women identified themselves as Mary Smith, Jane Jones, Alice Johnson, Jean Williams, Glara Schmerkel and Marie Dressler.

CHAPTER 3

Ugh, realism. That's never been my forte.

Sitting in the library, Pet couldn't concentrate on the newspaper. Gara had yet to arrive at Brownmoor, and the funeral was set for tomorrow. It wasn't unusual that her mother was late, but this situation was different. And with expensive airline tickets involved, Gara would have operated with greater gravitas. Pet knew her mother counted every cent and shilling.

"You've been reading that same page for the last ten minutes," Mina observed from the opposite couch.

"Thank you, and yes, I'm worried about Momsy. She doesn't answer her cell, and neither does her assistant. They probably had to make some flight changes. They should arrive today ... shouldn't they?"

Their ears perked up at the sound of tires crunching on gravel. "That must be them now," Mina said as they made their way through the great hall.

"Has your mother finally graced us with her presence?" Gwyda asked as she joined them at the door.

"I – I'm not sure now," Pet admitted as they observed two cars come to a stop outside.

The drivers emerged and as if on cue, opened the back doors. Shrill voices emitted from both vehicles.

"It was your responsibility," Binky whined.

"How am I responsible for the entire airline industry?" Babs asked.

"Now, it's no one's fault, everything will get resolved," Gloria advised.

"That's easy for you to say, it's not your mother," Barbara lamented.

"Do you know who these people are?" Mina whispered.

"Not a clue," Pet replied.

"Hello!" Barbara waved to the confused greeting party.

"I thought we'd never get here. Who knew the English countryside was so rugged? It could be Culver City. *Hola*! It's lovely to be here!" Gloria trilled as they mounted the steps.

"Yes, but who the hell are you?" Gwyda demanded.

"I thought the English were supposed to be unfailingly polite," Didums observed.

"Now look here, Mrs. Danvers, we've had a terrible time. We landed outside of London because of a mechanical problem, then we had to hire cars to get here," Barbara complained.

"And on top of that, the airline lost some of our baggage," Gloria added.

"My mother is hardly baggage!" Barbara flared.

"That's your opinion," Gloria said under her breath.

"What does all of this have to do with us?" Gwyda interrupted.

"These people are acting as if they don't know us. They showed our movies in England. I'm certain I've been warmly received by the Brits before," Barbara huffed.

"Yes, but we're not talking about your social life. Besides, Mrs. Danvers looks like she last saw movies directed by Edison himself," Gloria observed.

"Will you stop referring to me as 'Mrs. Danvers.' I am Dame Gwyda Glasscock. Now who are you before I call the local constabulary to have the lot of you arrested?"

"This is Barbara Lamont, and this is Gloria Prescott. Surely you've seen their movies, or at least their publicity photos," Babs interjected, as Binky and Didums giggled like tipsy schoolgirls over the surname "Glasscock."

"Barbara Lamont? Didn't she die in Madrid?"

"No, I didn't. Honestly, one little time running with the bulls in Pamplona, and the story gets blown out of proportion."

"And you've blown it out of proportion yourself. You weren't running with *el toro*. You were gored, in a manner of speaking, by one of those dishy matadors in Seville," Gloria reminded.

"How could I forget that? I couldn't walk for a week."

"I'm sure we don't care whether you're able to walk *now*. Miss Lamont, am I to understand your being here has something to do with your mother, Myrtle Dempster?" Gwyda demanded.

"Yes, that's right. If only she were here with us," Barbara wailed.

"Has she passed away as well?"

"No, the airline lost her! She could be on a plane bound for Timbuktu for all they know!" Binky complained with a sniff.

"And so the lot of you have descended on us for the funeral. And the reading of the will," Gwyda said stonily.

"Didums, didn't you advise them we were coming?" Gloria asked.

Didums rolled his eyes. "Mother ..."

"Very well, we'll sort all of this out later. Please, come in. Welcome to Brownmoor. If you'll relax in the parlor, I'll see about getting some rooms ready. Mrs. Dutton?"

"Yes, Madam?" The housekeeper appeared at her elbow.

"As big as this place is, I'm sure you can throw together some suites for us. Now, I take jasmine essence for my bath, and instead of a mint on my pillow, a gin and tonic will suffice," Barbara instructed.

Gwyda ignored the request. "Mrs. Dutton, please have Emma and Mel prepare rooms for our additional guests."

"Emma and Mel? Do you mean old Spice Girls don't die, they become maids in dreary English castles?" Binky wondered aloud. Mina and Pet exchanged glances. Gara still hadn't arrived, and already uncontrollable insanity had descended on them from that place called Hollywood.

"Yes, I understand. Thank you, Warren. I'll see you tomorrow at the funeral," Gwyda concluded her conversation and hung up the phone.

"What did he say?" demanded Nolan.

"You know he can't reveal any details from the will. He said there's no reason Myrtle Dempster shouldn't be here."

"I can't believe that old crone wormed her way into Father's will," Nolan fumed.

"We don't know any of the particulars. Perhaps he willed her some piece of sh– That is to say, an *objet d'art* – for the sake of sentiment. Or guilt."

"*Sentiment*? That marriage was bloody hell."

"None of your father's marriages were successful. It can't be blamed on the women, especially your own mother."

Nolan didn't respond.

"We'll be kept in the dark regarding the will for now. Meanwhile, we've additional guests to deal with. Suppose you introduce yourself to those *actresses*. I do believe you share that trait with your father, don't you? That weakness for female entertainers?" Gwyda insinuated.

Nolan didn't respond, but his raised eyebrows did.

"Is one of these men Laddie?" Babs asked, peering at the portraits in the grand hall.

"I doubt it. They all seem to have worked for King Arthur," Didums observed, noting the period costumes.

"How come no one smiled in the old days? I know they didn't have toilet paper back then, but gee, wasn't there anything to feel happy about?" Babs said, peering at one particularly forbidding specimen with an imposing Cro-Magnon brow and scowling, thin lips.

"And why were men so unattractive in the old days? Where were the Brad Pitts, the Jude Laws, the Ashton Kutchers?" Binky lamented.

"They were there, sweetie, they were just busy with Guinevere and Michelangelo," Barbara stated as she emerged from the solarium. "Babs, can you call the airline and find out what they did with your grandmother? Maybe they discovered her in the cargo hold of a plane bound for Saskatchewan."

As Babs went to attend to her mother's request, Barbara herded the boys into the solarium where Gloria sat, trying to give herself a manicure.

"Didums, *mi cielo*, help *Mamacita* with her cuticles," Gloria beseeched, holding out an emery board.

"What a shame that horrible Gara's not already here. She'd have a full set of hand equipment. She always had that manicure fetish," Barbara said as Didums inspected Gloria's nails.

"Don't remind me. What was with that bizarre phobia of hers? Who's frightened of hangnails?" Gloria scoffed.

"The stories we could tell," Barbara clucked.

"Ixnay, dearie," Gloria cautioned as Pet entered the room.

"That's quite all right. No one knows better than I what a character my mother is," Pet said. "And of course I remember you both, Miss Lamont, Miss Prescott."

"Little Petal, such a dear child. I can still picture you and Gara in matching pinafores for that May Day party at Gordon and Sheila MacRae's," Barbara reminisced.

"Oh, and those beautiful outfits we had on, those marvelous sequined bouffant skirts," Gloria reminded.

"Even as a tot, Didums was a dream with a needle and thread. The compliments Little Babs got on her beaded Brownie uniform!"

"I remember, you made dresses for my Barbies," Pet reminisced. "Are you still designing?"

"He is, he is," Gloria interjected before Didums could speak. "He does all my clothes. And he did work a brief time with Bob Mackie on those Barbies he does, but Bobby's such a strict task mistress with the beading, even worse than Edith Head on a good day."

"Don't say a bad word about my beloved Mackie," Barbara warned. "He's done all the outfits for my specials and Vegas shows. It's in every contract I sign."

"Well, anyway, Didums makes divine dresses for a little shop in

West Hollywood," Gloria said proudly. "He's a natural talent. Why he isn't as well-known as Stella McCartney, I'll never understand. After all, they both have famous parents."

"Mother ..." Didums pursed his mouth as he inspected the progress he was making on his mother's manicure.

"He doesn't like me bragging. Barbara, why don't you brag about my godchildren."

"Oh, Binky's a multi-talent, like his mother. He's put those dance lessons and years as an 'anatomically-correct fitness model' to good use as the lead singer of the band Dietrich Seeking Garbo. Surely you've heard of them."

"I'm not sure," Pet hedged. "What sort of music do they perform?"

"It's dance with a mix of symphonic trance and Cajun swamp rock with Maori war chants thrown in for good measure," Barbara chanted like a press agent. "Very cutting edge. Kind of 'Scissor Sisters meets The McGuire Sisters.' They're big in Europe, *huge* in Luxembourg."

"Sounds ... fascinating. Oh, and Babs, how's she?"

"Babs, well, she –"

"– mostly gets married and divorced to D-List celebrities, when she's not trying out for reality shows and thinking about writing that book," Gloria added.

"Now, I've quite nipped that tell-all in the bud. Don't forget, it spilled some of your secrets, too. And that abominable title, *Mother's on Location: My Life as the Daughter of a Minor Star*. That must have been the idea of that terrible Carrie Fisher. How dare she suggest writing as occupational therapy for Babs. First she rips Debbie a new one with her books, then decides to set my little Babs against me. An ungrateful child is a terrible thing."

"And what is it you do, Pet?" Gloria asked.

"I'm a photographer, in San Francisco."

"Taking pictures of stars? Perhaps I need some new headshots. Is your stuff like Hurrell?"

"No, I'm afraid I don't do celebrities. I'm more of a photojournalist; realism, you know."

"Ugh, realism. That's never been my forte. I preferred the soundstages to all that outdoor work," Barbara shuddered.

"It's a good thing you're so freakishly tall, you can aim your camera over everyone else's heads to catch all the realism," Gloria gave Pet a compliment of sorts.

"Well, I've learned a little realism from the airlines," Babs said as she rejoined the others. "Myrtle ended up on a flight to Tokyo, but the

Japanese authorities stopped her from entering the country as an enemy combatant because of that old scheme to wreak havoc on their economy. But it's been ironed out, and they're routing her back to London."

"Thank God. Did they let you know when she'd arrive?" Barbara breathed a sigh of relief.

"They couldn't give me a definite timeframe. I don't know that she'll make it back in time for the funeral tomorrow."

"If she's lucky," Gloria muttered, as Barbara responded with an irritated nudge.

"I'm not looking forward to a funeral, either, but really, Gloria. No offense, Pet, dear," Barbara added.

Pet acknowledged the limp apology with a nod. She wouldn't admit it out loud, but tomorrow wasn't something anyone was looking forward to, and that included both the funeral and her mother's arrival.

STRANGE INTERLUDE 3

Next to the fake princes in this town, a genuine lord is a welcome change of pace.

In Society column by Eliza Von Crouse, *Los Angeles Daily News*, October 7, 1949

New to Hollywood's British community is Lord Lindale Bottomly, a former member of that famous House of Lords. He's been making the nightclub scene and turning the heads of stunning starlets and famous actresses alike. He danced with Adele Jergens at the Mocambo and Constance Bennett was heard to say, "Next to the fake princes in this town, a genuine lord is a welcome change of pace."

There's been a whisper of scandal in this lord's past, a quarrelsome divorce and accusations of alienation of affection concerning a burlesque dancer, but that matters not a whit where this gentleman is concerned. The ladies in town have sat up and taken notice of "Laddie," as he's called by intimates back in England and new friends here in the movie colony.

Even British royalty can get bitten by the Hollywood bug. We hear the lord has signed a contract with Columbia Pictures and will start work on a film with Janet Blair next month. That Anglo touch of class is sure to shine onscreen!

Sheilah Graham's column, January 19, 1950

Don the Beachcomber's was the site last night for the *Moviegoer* Awards, given out by that magazine for recent notable film performances. One winner who was celebrating enough for ten starlets was Gloria Prescott, who was named "Most Startling New Screen Presence" for her performance in the recent *Escalator to Happiness*. Miss Prescott performed a Mexican hat dance on the bar, crushing a cabbage rose on Hedda Hopper's chapeau in her enthusiasm. Hedda wasn't too upset, though, and laughed off the damage. "I predicted this girl was going to be a star years ago!" crowed the columnist.

"Not that many *años* ago," Gloria pouted, ever mindful that flaming youth rules in Tinseltown!

Also celebrating was Gloria's best friend, Barbara Lamont, herself recently appearing in the musical-comedy *Lunch Counter Serenade*. "I knew we'd make it big in this town," boasted the beautiful blonde. "Being in the right place at the right time counts for a lot. Why, I'd never have gotten that contract with Zanuck if I hadn't caught –"

"– caught the acting bug," interjected Myrtle Lamont Dempster, the star's attendant mother. "Excuse me, dear, I think I see Linda Darnell across the room." And off Mrs. Dempster went, no doubt to secure her daughter a part in that star's next film.

As an aside, I heard via the studio grapevine that poor Linda's recently received some threatening fan letters. The things some poor stars have to go through!

Also at the party last night was Gara Schmerkin. Surely you remember the former Baby Gara, that old child star. Miss Schmerkin suffered a few lean years after star parts dried up.

But now she's passed those awkward years, and has blossomed into a handsome young lady, ready for adult film roles. Surely her figure has blossomed, and then some! She has a small role in the forthcoming Claudette Colbert feature, *The Secret Fury*, and hopes to regain her former stardom. "You can lose a lot of things in this town, and believe me, you can lose it multiple times. But determination and true star quality always win out in my end," Gara crowed with the confidence befitting a real star!

Excerpt from *Movie Musicals of the Fifties* by Cheryl Hughes

Sun Valley Soufflé (Columbia, 1950) Directed by Claude Binyon; with Adele Jergens, Lindale Bottomly, Kathleen Ryan, Robert Warwick, Howard Wendell, Phyllis Coates, Ralph Moody, Chick Chandler. Disappointing musical fails to deliver in this latter day Sonja Henie castoff. Jergens an ice-skating café singer stranded in rundown hotel, and thinks classy Bottomly is her ticket to the good life, little realizing that he's as much of a fraud as she is. All turns out well in the end, however, and that decrepit inn is turned into a showplace featuring Jergens's skills both on and off the ice, as well as Bottomly's character turnaround. Mildly promising premise peters out in this hybrid of *Holiday Inn* and *Thin Ice*, due to miscasting of novelty star Bottomly, who displays little screen charisma or acting ability. And that's not mentioning his dubious musical talents (his singing is dubbed by Ben Gage, then better known as Mr. Esther Williams; his klutzy dancing, unfortunately, is not).

Hedda Hopper's column, September 12, 1950

Today I've got quite the scoop, dear readers. Lord "Laddie" Bottomly, the distinguished British nobleman and actor, and Myrtle Dempster, the manager/mother of actress Barbara Lamont, eloped yesterday to Las Vegas.

As previously reported, Lord Bottomly was recuperating in the hospital after a freak accident in which he was almost decapitated by the collapsing lid of a grand piano while shooting publicity stills. He met Mrs. Dempster in Cedars-Sinai Hospital, where she was recovering from a gunshot, believed to have occurred during a botched kidnapping attempt (under investigation by the L.A.P.D.). Myrtle was so taken with Laddie that as soon as they were both discharged from the hospital yesterday, they raced across the California desert for Vegas.

I talked to Barbara Lamont late yesterday, and got the exclusive word that her mother sent her a mere two-character cablegram, "#5," earlier that same day. It's no wonder her mother's a whiz as her agent, since she's an expert at numbers!

Speaking of numbers, Linda Darnell was absent from the set of *The 13th Letter* for several days. (Linda had to be sedated by her doctor for nervous stress, perhaps because of those threatening letters we've heard about.) The director, Otto Preminger, wasn't pleased with this turn of events, and made the set a difficult place for the remaining players. Coincidentally, Barbara Lamont has a supporting part in this thriller as a nurse.

"Why are nurse uniforms so drab and unflattering?" Barbara asked. "They could do just as good work in an elegant cocktail dress that would show my figure to its best advantage."

Well, a birdie told me that Barbara made overtures to Preminger to step into Darnell's part in the star's absence! When I asked Barbara to confirm this rumor, she blurted, "I don't see what this has to do with my mother. She wasn't anywhere near Linda Darnell's house that night." Apparently the poor dear confused the two stories!

Barbara ended the call before I could find out about her movie or her mother's new marriage, but rest assured, I'll get those stories in the near future!

Excerpt from *The Production's on Me: The Life of Super-Producer Jory Plummer* by Jory Plummer with Julius Petard

My greatest success was the selling of Gara St. James. Gara had been a child star years before, but had suffered a lean period of living on the fringes of Hollywood, surviving just above poverty.

Gara had everything Toby Wing had, and plenty more. She was beyond voluptuous; that tendency to plumpness needed to be tamed. And one had to photograph Gara carefully. With the wrong cinematographer, she could look like a creature from a Universal horror feature. (Gara was once described by Clive Barnes as a cross between Ginger Rogers and Bela Lugosi.)

When I first met her in 1951, she had done a few supporting roles, but wasn't having luck rising above newer actresses. I can still see her striding into my office that day. (Actually, she wasn't much of a strider, more of a galumpher.) But I knew the raw material was there, and if I succeeded in pulling this one off, it would be a miracle on the scale of man's first step on the moon (which came later, so in a way, I was ahead of my time).

I told her I thought we might be able to work together. First we had to change that name. "After all, you can't go by 'Baby Gara' anymore. And 'Gara Schmerkin' is not a marquee name."

Gara stared dumbly at me as she tried to think of a new moniker. I threw out a few possibilities. "We should keep the name Gara, it'll remind people that you were once a star. Gara Smart? No, that doesn't fit ya. Hmm, Gara Small, Smear. Gara Sin? Gara Sanmark. Saints –" Suddenly it came to me.

"Gara St. James!" I yelled, as she responded with a startled expression, followed by a small burp.

"Gara St. James?" she bellowed. "Oh no, you don't! You're not gonna turn a good Jewish girl like me into an agent of Catholicism!"

CHAPTER 4

I guess what's good for the goose is good for Gara.

Thud. The sound of a dirt clod striking the bronze coffin with titanium-reinforced hardware shook Pet from a brief reverie. She adjusted the already-perfect collar of her jacket and returned her gaze to the satin-draped bier. Despite her father's advanced age and the inevitability of death, she was less prepared than she had expected.

However, the distraction of the Hollywood contingent made for a useful diversion. As both a photographer with good credentials and the daughter of a former film star, Pet had known her share of egotistical celebrities. But the delusions of the Lamonts and Prescotts were a special case indeed. Pet and Mina had shared enough glances and eye-rolls that one might think they were attending a Julia Roberts play.

June weather notwithstanding, Gloria huddled in a fur scarf and muff, alternately shivering and patting a fine sheen of sweat from her brow. Barbara, angling for the best possible light, shook her head now and then, stage-whispering, "Poor stepfather. I knew him, Horatio." Binky kept pulling out a tiny compact to examine his left eye for a floating lash. Didums applied melon-flavored lip balm every three minutes. And Babs scribbled copious notes in her pocket diary, her minute observations destined for the pages of a future tell-all.

Truth be told, family members behaved much the same. Gwyda, attended by her son Archie, possessed eyes in the back of her head: those beady stares of silent disapproval threatened misbehavers. Nolan threw resentful looks at Pet, which she tried to ignore. (Nolan's son Albert, on the other hand, gave both Pet and Mina reassuring glances.) Willis inspected his watch, as if willing the ceremony to its finale; Louise examined her glassine manicure for imagined imperfections. Henry and Miles, bored teenagers, fidgeted (Sophie, too, despite her best efforts). Carolyn and Cliff pouted, as Gwyda had forbidden them from bringing their cockapoo, Chester.

The funeral, held in the local parish church, was dignified, as befitted a service to the glory of God and the comfort of family, ex-politicos, and minor aristocracy. The family followed the hearse to a private cemetery on the grounds of Brownmoor. The tiny graveyard contained a crumbling mausoleum and moldering crypts, reaching back many centuries. Now Laddie would join his forbearers for an eternal rest.

The vicar concluded his blessings over the bier, closed his prayer book, and approached the bereaved with formal high-church condolences. The vicar clasped Gwyda's withered hand as the coffin descended into the open crypt. As he moved on to Pet, the first noise was heard. Mina, acutely auditory, turned.

The bluster of a car motor in need of a tune-up grew louder as all revolved to locate the source. Suddenly, a large sedan rounded the bend. Rather than following the primitive road that led to the graveyard's outskirts, the car veered across the grass and headed for the narrow gate.

"Who is that? Surely they don't mean to drive right in," Nolan muttered. Even the funeral hearse stopped outside the formal grounds, and the coffin was borne into the cemetery by the pallbearers (able-bodied men and not ancient contemporaries of the deceased).

The sedan continued on its disastrous course, as the sides of the gate scraped metal. Hitting a couple of outlying headstones, the car then struck a deep rut in the ground and jumped across a line of graves, like an Evel Knievel stunt or a bizarre scene from *The Dukes Of Hazzard*. Everyone scurried out of the car's path (Gwyda was surprisingly agile for her advanced age) as it struck the bier, the front tires plunging into the freshly dug grave. Appalled faces registered disbelief as it came to rest atop Laddie's coffin.

They tried to regain composure, even as raucous voices spilled from the sedan. With varying reactions – consternation, amusement, outrage – they witnessed the long-awaited Gara behind the wheel.

"You horrific cow!" screamed Gwyda. "You nearly killed us all!"

"Did you think they could pile us all into the open grave?" Willis demanded.

"My fox! Make sure *Mamacita*'s fur is okay!" wailed a supine Gloria, extending a hand to Didums.

"Mother, is your hair on fire? Did it get too close to the tailpipe?" Binky yelped, snatching off Barbara's smoking wiglet.

"I told you we'd make it okay," Gara grumbled to the car's occupants as she opened the door after a short struggle.

"My dear, I am not used to behavior like this!" the timid male passenger wailed as he exited.

"Wait, Miss St. James, wait, let me put these vinyl slipcovers over your shoes so they don't get muddy!" Peony admonished.

"Momsy, what do you think you're doing?" Pet gasped.

"Petal! My darling little Pet!" Gara blubbered, throwing open her arms and pulling her daughter close to her more than ample bosom. "I got here as soon as I could!"

"I must ask you to stop doing that! I'm the only one allowed to write it all down!" the strange little man sniffed, trying to snatch the pencil from Babs's hand.

"Who do you think you are?" she demanded.

"I'm Cadmus Polk, official biographer to the stars, engaged by Gara St. James to tell the world her life story," he sang out in a disdainful fairy tenor.

"Now, now, Caddy, time for that later," Gara said, waving him off.

"But right now you're going to explain this," demanded Nolan. "What the bollocks do you mean by racing in here, almost killing us, and crashing into my father's coffin? This is the most inexcusable thing you've ever done!"

"What about Miss St. James? She could have been injured!" squeaked Peony, holding her arm at an awkward angle.

"Are you okay?" Pet asked.

"Don't worry about me, I'll pop my arm back into its socket later. It's Gara whose perfection mustn't be marred!" Peony insisted.

"I think she might be suffering from shock," Mina observed.

"No, that's normal for her," Pet answered drily.

"Stop it! Everyone stop this instant!" Gwyda boomed. "We're going back to the house right now, and just to let you know, some of you *really* may end up stacked in an open grave!"

Peony snapped to attention as she stood on guard duty outside Gara's room. "Excuse me, Miss St. James can't be disturbed now," she beseeched Cliff and Carolyn as they walked down the second floor gallery toward the staircase.

"I'm sure we don't care," Cliff snapped. Chester snarled in Peony's direction as Carolyn whispered calming words.

"Miss St. James will gladly sign autographs later, $3.00 each, $5.00 for an added 8x10 glossy," Peony called after them. "Oh, wait, we're in England, aren't we? I'll figure out the exchange rate for pounds. Or is it Euros now?"

"I can't wait until this madness is resolved, so we can return to the sanity of Impswich. Isn't that right, Chester?" Carolyn trilled as they descended the stairs.

They entered the solarium where the family was gathered. Chester yipped at the general din of the room.

"Carolyn, quiet that beast now," Gwyda demanded.

"Why can't you be nice to him? Wasn't it your life's work to understand creatures in the wild?" Carolyn sulked.

"In the wild, dear, not in my living room."

"What about the problem in the cemetery?" Cliff asked, eager to change the subject.

"The car is being towed away. And the vicar will ensure the burial is completed," Archie explained.

"They've had to tear down the fence just to get that truck in to pull out that crone's broomstick," complained Gwyda.

Warren patted her shoulder. "It will all be taken care of," the attorney assured her with authority.

"Warren, how soon can the will be read? I will not have that creature in this house longer than necessary."

"I can have everything in order tomorrow afternoon."

"Perhaps we should take a break from this commotion. It's been a very stressful day," Albert counseled.

"Yes," Gwyda sighed. "And Cook's preparing a lovely dinner tonight. Everyone must eat, alas."

In the dining room, Barbara examined the tablecloth. "So this is good Irish linen? The wardrobe department at Metro could do better than the convent girls who made this."

"I guess the nuns don't beat them enough. Ooh, quick, come look!" Gloria beckoned from the window.

In her haste, Barbara bumped into Gara's luggage standing near the doorway. One of the brass initials, *G.A.S.*, on the trunk snagged her hose.

"Oh, see what that bitch did now! Cheap letters practically coming off her dime store luggage. Look, even her initials are full of hot air."

"Worry about that later, dear. Quick, look at the latest car she totaled," Gloria urged.

The women watched as the tow truck, carrying the damaged sedan, chugged past the house. "That woman's a bigger danger than Halle Berry in a crosswalk," Barbara mused.

"I suppose it's lucky the only victim this time was already dead. Remember back in '56?"

"How they kept that out of the awful tabloid media, I'll never know. Poor Montgomery Clift, he never saw Gara barreling around that curve in

Benedict Canyon. So he swerves, hits a telephone pole and loses his looks, while she drives on without a scratch."

"I don't know why the L.A.P.D never investigated. She couldn't have been that valuable to the studio. She complained it was Monty's own fault because she was busy driving and reading a book at the same time," Gloria explained in an incredulous tone.

"As if Gara ever read a book."

"I know, since it was studio policy for stars to read only scripts and fan mail."

"I never saw her even touch a book. Do you remember in the early days when we were rooming at that cute little complex, the Venus De Milo Arms?"

"Of course I do. *Gracias a Dios*, we were able to room together, although we all had to share a bathroom with Gara, that was scary enough. Poor Bahamia got stuck rooming with her. Even growing up in the Caribbean didn't prepare her for that breed of jackass," Gloria clucked. The dancer Bahamia, a fellow relic from the old days, lived in semi-retirement in the Carribean with her husband, a shoe designer.

"All it took was one of her nuclear farts and Bahamia threatened to tap dance on her face."

"It did inspire her to create 'The Dance of the Noisy Guernsey' for that *New Faces* Broadway revue, and Arthur Siegel wrote 'What Cow, My Love?' just for her. Out of tragedy, great art is often born."

"I wonder if this little trip to England is going to work out as well for Gara when the will is read," Barbara snickered. Gloria's laugh echoed round the chilly, ancient walls.

Henry and Miles eavesdropped across the hall. At 14 and 12 respectively, the boys didn't grasp the references, but they understood the mysterious Gara must be a real piece of work.

Henry, noticing Sophie descending the staircase, whistled softly to get her attention.

"Have you recovered from the monster truck show this morning?" Henry asked. (Unrealistic expectations of foreigners weren't unique to the U.S.; citizens of other nations often expect Americans to behave like out-of-control hillbillies drunk on moonshine slushies and candied possum.)

"Just about. What are you guys up to?" Sophie asked. Although she thought Henry was cute and Miles was nice, Sophie felt at a disadvantage on their home turf, and so kept her defenses up.

"Trying to find out about this Gara. She's your great-aunt, is that right? What's she like?" Miles asked.

"I haven't been around her much myself. I know more from stuff I've read on the Internet."

"Why didn't we think of that?" Miles asked.

"Quiet," an annoyed Henry shushed. "So what kind of stuff did you find out? Is she as crazy as they say she is?"

"Just old gossip, saying and doing whatever she wants, even if she comes across as a goofball sometimes." She didn't think she should have to defend Gara, since she *was* something of a nutcase. But part of Sophie knew that family counted for something, and Great-Aunt Gara was *their* crazy family member.

"So you're not going to give up the dirt? Maybe it runs in the family," Henry teased.

"Geez, Henry, don't be such a dickhead," Miles said as a hurt Sophie turned to leave.

Realizing his mistake, Henry retracted his showboating. "I'm sorry, I didn't mean it. My big mouth works before my brain sometimes. I was just joking, really."

"I know. It's just ... Look, I don't know her at all. She's just as big a mystery to me."

"Everybody else knows her, but they're not talking, at least in front of us," Miles said.

"When your first exposure to someone happens when they jump tombstones in a car aimed at you, it makes an impression," Henry joked, hoping Sophie had really forgiven him.

It appeared she had. "You're right. And we'll have a chance to see what she's like up close soon enough."

"This isn't the same suite I had when I lived here before, is it?" Gara asked.

"No, that was in the wing that burned down long ago," Pet explained.

"I knew it wasn't the same. My old room had eight-legged Chippendale chairs and a special foot tub for my bad toenails. No, don't write that down, Caddy," she admonished with a wag of her finger.

Hoping to keep her mother somewhat on track, Pet asked, "Did anything happen to keep you from getting here sooner?"

"That airline stranded us in Chicago for God knows how long, and then we had to make a side trip to Manchester to pick up Caddy before coming here."

"Allow me to formally introduce myself. I am Cadmus Polk, former president of Miss St. James's now-defunct fan club, U.K. edition, and now biographer to the stars, author of the life stories of Samantha Eggar and Francesca Annis, soon to be the author of the Gara St. James story," he said brightly, extending a hand to Pet, which she ignored.

"I can write off the entire trip as a tax thing now, since it's business-related. That's what Peony thinks. And at this time of bereavement, I need people who have nothing but love for Gara! I'm broken up over Laddie's death. He was your father! And he was the only decent one of my three husbands."

"Marriage number one, June 4, 1954, to athlete and jockey Frederic 'Pancho' Rosenbloom, lasted until November 7, 1955. Marriage number two, June 7, 1957, to Roderigo Hujeapenosa, 'the Hot Sauce King,' lasted until August 19, 1959. Marriage number three, October 11, 1961, to Lord Lindale Fotheringay Bottomly, lasted until September 20, 1968. Marriage number four, February 14, 1970, to Bill Merman, né Zimmermann, dancer and cousin of Ethel, lasted to August 18, 1970," Caddy rattled off from rote memory.

"*Three* marriages, Caddy, that last one was annulled, so it never happened," Gara corrected. "That Bill was no cakewalk. I think Ethel set us up to get back at me for setting her up with Ernest Borgnine on that blind date. Geez, could she hold a grudge, worse than Joanie Crawford! You didn't see Ernie treating me like crap afterwards."

Pet, feeling a bit like Bette Davis in *Now, Voyager* (before the rejuvenating ocean cruise), tried placating her mother. "I'm just glad you're here now. No matter how old Daddy was, I wasn't as prepared for his passing as I thought I'd be."

"You were always so attached to people. I guess I did something right when I raised you. Myself, I've been prepared for Laddie's passing for ages now." Gara enveloped her daughter in a bone-cracking hug. "It's hard to lose a parent, I know. When I lost your Grandpa Ben and then *Bubee* Dena, not to mention your Uncle Ronnie ... It's a lonely feeling to be the last one."

Gara's voice broke on the last word, but she forced the humanity back to its dark, secret place. "I hate to think how sad you'll be when I pass on to my reward. It'll be hard on you, and my millions of fans. I wish I could be there to see it."

She released Pet from the hug and held her at arm's length. "Baby doll, if you only knew the mess I went through to have you. You're my only child, my only girl, my only Petal!"

"Technically, that's incorrect. The twins, Kimmy and Primmy, you adopted while married to the Hot Sauce King," Caddy interjected.

"Again, Caddy, that was annulled. I mean, I sent them back to the orphanage. How was I to know they'd turn into foul-mouthed and not-so-attractive toddlers? I don't know why Joan didn't think of it herself, she'd have saved herself a lot of bother later on."

Anxious to be rid of the Charlotte Vale-esque feeling, Pet suggested, "Why don't you settle in. I'm going to rest awhile."

"Good idea, a little nappy will get those worry lines off your forehead. I'll see you later at the dinner being thrown in my honor. Isn't it swell of my old in-laws welcoming me so warmly?"

Warmth was the last thing on the family's minds as they assembled for dinner in the grand dining room, but there were attempts to greet the event with pleasantries. "I can't remember the last time the table was this full," Archie offered gamely as they settled into their chairs.

"Rather like the old days, when we had weekend hunting parties and holiday gatherings," Gwyda agreed.

"Yeah, I remember at one hunt, I aimed for that fox and accidentally shot Peter Finch in the tuckus," Gara guffawed.

"A charming memory," Gwyda said through gritted teeth as Henry, Miles, and Sophie struggled to retain their giggles.

"My, this goose is delicious," Didums said, making an attempt to be a model guest.

"It's one of Cook's specialties," Louise added.

"She's improved since I used to live here. She used to make the most God-awful rabbit stew. Or is it some new girl named Cook?" Gara said as she made an inappropriate gesture to one of the maids in an attempt to get more gravy.

"We lived off the land a lot then. Those hunting weekends sometimes netted geese, wild turkey, deer," Archie said.

"And to think I only thought of shotguns as something to protect me from family inside the house. I could have been hunting in the woods of Bel Air," Barbara marveled.

"Laddie loved hunting. He'd bag more quail than anyone else," Gwyda recalled.

"In the fields *and* in the pubs," Albert joked.

"That's uncalled for," Nolan said stiffly.

"Dad, I meant no disrespect. It's good to remember the funny things, too. Grandfather had a rep for liking the ladies a lot. These days, they'd call him a player."

"Really," an unamused Carolyn chided.

"Don't be so formal. Albert already explained he meant no harm.

It's good to share stories. I for one would welcome funny memories of Daddy," Pet stated.

There was a moment of discomfort, and then Gloria cleared her throat. "I recall one evening at Don the Beachcomber's, Laddie showed up with Arlene Dahl, but spent time talking to Charlotte Greenwood and her husband. And Arlene was just steaming mad with jealousy for whatever reason.

"So she picked a fight with Charlotte, who aimed her patented highkick for Arlene's face and ended up kicking Laddie in the back of his head! The first time I saw anyone fall flat on his puss at Don's and it not be because of a Mai Tai!"

There was scattered, uncomfortable laughter after the story. "I guess you had to be there," Gloria pouted.

"Laddie was quite the gentleman, even when he was passed out," Barbara suggested.

"That he was," Gara piped up. "Oh sure, he let me down when we got divorced, but he promised me his will would take good care of me."

"What do you mean, his will would take good care of you?" demanded Nolan.

"Just what I said, Bub. I'm getting it all," Gara replied with a matter-of-fact air.

"Like hell you will! There's no way he did that. For starters, he didn't own everything," Gwyda spit out.

"Well, whatever he had is mine, simple as that."

"That can't be. My mother always claimed he left *her* something in his will," Barbara exclaimed.

"What is it with you Hollywood trash, coming in here and trying to destroy what's ours?" Archie boomed. "None of you will get one red cent, I'll see to that!"

Loud arguing commenced around the table with almost everyone joining in. The kids kept quiet but enjoyed the out-of-control scene.

"Shut up! All of you, shut up!" Gwyda shrieked. For emphasis, she abandoned decorum, picked up a roll from the bread basket and, really putting her shoulder in it, hauled off and hit Gara in the face.

"Oh! Why, you ancient, old biddy!" Gara picked up the mashed potatoes and flung them across the table. They didn't reach Gwyda, but landed on Willis.

Once it started, there was no stopping them. The few rational dinner guests and the servants tried to halt the fracas to no avail. The kids couldn't resist participating in the food fight; both Henry and Miles were excellent pitchers and made more than one target of their overbearing father.

"No, no, this is Balenciaga! Vintage!" Barbara screamed as gravy spilled down her dress.

"Mother, a weapon, the salad tongs!" advised Binky.

"That's my baby!" she replied and grabbed the tongs to hurl clumps of spinach.

"No, stop that at once!" Caddy demanded, hunkered under the table as he scribbled in his notepad. With his free hand, he tried to throw a roll at Babs's furious writing. She blocked the roll with her pocket diary and flung a dish of pâté at her rival scribe, hitting him in the noggin and splattering both his jacket and notepad with the sticky hors d'oeuvres.

The fight hadn't left Gwyda yet, and she grabbed the goose from the table and drew aim for Gara. Even with one arm, she made a perfect pitch. The bird sailed across the table just as Gara yelled, "Oy! You crazy foreigners!"

The force of the strike threw Gara back into her chair with an audible crack. The damaged chair teetered, but didn't fall.

The shock of this latest attack stopped the food fight cold. Everyone stared at Gara, her mouth wide open and stuffed with the parson's nose end of the goose.

Overwhelmed, Mina blurted out, "I guess what's good for the goose is good for Gara."

Gwyda scraped food from her dress into the kitchen sink. "I cannot believe that creature has driven me and my family to a common food fight," she complained as Mrs. Dutton attempted to help her.

"She's gotten worse over the years, which I thought couldn't possibly happen," the housekeeper remarked.

One of the maids approached. "Mrs. Dutton, there's a delivery at the kitchen door," Sandra said.

"A delivery at this time of night? Oh, dear," Mrs. Dutton said as she went to deal with the problem.

"You can sign for this?" the delivery man asked.

"That depends. What exactly is 'this?'" she asked, eyeing the strange object behind the man.

"Delivery from British Airways. Item rerouted from Japan to Heathrow," he replied.

"Must belong to one of those Hollywood people," she said, signing the form.

"It's for a ... Barbara Lamont," he read off the form.

"Sandra, please get Miss Lamont from the dining room," Mrs.

Dutton instructed.

"What's going on? Do I have to wash dishes as my punishment?" Barbara asked as she entered.

"A delivery from the airline, for you," Mrs. Dutton pointed out.

Barbara took one look at the huge metal object and screamed. "Binky! Babs! Everyone!"

Barbara spun around as her bedraggled Tinseltown cohorts appeared. "It's Myrtle, still with her hyperbaric chamber! Quick, help me wheel her in!"

"A perfect ending to a perfect day," Gwyda hissed through clenched teeth as she picked spinach from her hair. "Tomorrow's going to be just lovely jubbly!"

STRANGE INTERLUDE 4

She ignored my acting advice, and look what happened to her.

Excerpt from *Acting Techniques and the Major Studios During Hollywood's Golden Age* by Antonia Hamill

The training of contract players and major stars at MGM overlapped with more frequency than one might suspect. One person who wielded considerable power was Lillian Burns, a drama teacher at the studio. She'd been an actress in silents, but a more important credit was her marriage to the director George Sidney, who helmed the MGM successes *Bathing Beauty*, *Annie Get Your Gun*, and *Show Boat*, among others.

Burns honed the tenuous skills of starlets in need of acting technique, but also exerted her influence on major actresses important to the studio. Esther Williams discussed her disagreements with Lillian in her autobiography, *Million Dollar Mermaid*. She felt Lillian's approach consisted of a "one size fits all" method which relied on gestures such as lifted chins, quick turns, and cutesy mannerisms.

Others felt her coaching was beneficial. Gara St. James cites Burns's assistance in shaping her performance in the 1952 MGM film *The Ungrateful*. "Boy, did Miss Burns help a girl out. I mean, what's a Jewish girl from Chicago know about playing a Protestant bacon heiress from Boston?"

After childhood stardom as a minor league threat to Shirley Temple, Gara spent a decade struggling to regain her former status. Eventually Gara won the coveted role of Abigail Preston-Smythe, the selfish heiress in the Gothic drama. *The Ungrateful* became a hit and Gara was again in demand for film roles.

"I didn't know how to approach the role, because I'm as far from selfish as you can get. But Miss Burns taught me how to raise my chin, how to turn so my hair flows beautifully, flare my nostrils, that sort of thing. People still talk about the scene where I danced the can-can while my mother, played by Gladys Cooper, died on the gallows. Jory Plummer, my agent, talked me up at MGM, and all the good will I put out helped me get a two-picture deal at the studio, and returned me to worldwide superstardom, just where I belong."

Excerpted entries from *Leading With Your Chin to Acting Success: The Lillian Burns Story* by Peter Vanderblume, *Chapter 8: Words of Wisdom*

"Ladies, fur on the shoulders when descending a staircase; trailing by the non-rail-holding hand when ascending. Watch Lana. WATCH! *PurrrrRRRRfection.*"

"Gara, it's been reported that you harrumphed after my instructions regarding acceptable screen kisses. Harrumphing is very unladylike."

"Gara, a lady doesn't wobble like a gelatin dessert as she dances the cha-cha, she glides gracefully and shakes her shoulders demurely."

"Gara, a lady doesn't plop down in a chair, she slides into the seat as delicately as a whisper."

"Barbara, a lady never fidgets with her hands. No, no, it's not appropriate suggesting warming them in a man's pockets."

"Gara, there's no reason to continually roll your eyes and harrumph over Bahamia's scene."

"Bahamia, we do not pull knives on fellow students in this class, even if Gara was somewhat condescending."

"Gara, pretend in this scene that you are waiting by the phone for a luncheon invitation that will never come. No, no, not uncontrollable rage, sadness and ennui!"

"Barbara, it's not necessary to carry a flaming torch for this scene. After all, Gara isn't really the Frankenstein monster."

"Gloria, I seriously doubt that a novice would writhe so passionately, alone in her bed and dreaming of sainthood."

"No, Gara, you may not leave class early today. I'm not sure I buy this story of an invalid friend you must care for. Perhaps if you were more attentive in class, you'd be more convincing."

"Bahamia, that may be acceptable in Paraguay, but American audiences would be offended by an overly suggestive shimmy."

"Gloria, we know you were 'too well brought up,' but a lady doesn't stick *that* out and shake it to get a man's attention, she gives a small wave with her hand."

"Barbara, your aspirations of wearing beautiful clothes in nightclub scenes is admirable, but you must shoot higher. Look to the example of your classmate Timima Bossi. She won't rest until she plays a corpse for Hitchcock."

"Gara, it's unprofessional to criticize another performer's screen test. Margaret Elliot is, after all, a former Oscar winner."

"Gloria, a good foundation garment is the most important ingredient in giving an Oscar-worthy performance. Yes, that's good, write that one down."

"Girls, never forget the lessons I've taught you. Think of that unappreciative Frances Farmer. She ignored my acting advice, and look what happened to her."

Louella Parsons's column, August 18, 1952

Hollywood has always celebrated glamorous marriages between actresses and royalty. In the good old days of silents, Gloria Swanson, Mae Murray and Pola Negri wed princes and marquises. Things slowed down a bit after the war, but we take glamour where we can get it.

It was two years ago when Myrtle Dempster, the manager and mother of actress Barbara Lamont, eloped to Las Vegas with Lord Laddie Bottomly. But wedded bliss didn't last in the case of this union, and as of yesterday, they are officially divorced.

I never expected this marriage to last. They seemed quite ill-suited to each other, from the age difference (the lord is 19 years the senior of Myrtle) to the contrast in their temperaments. Laddie was charming and docile, while Myrtle had the disposition of a fire-breathing dragon with a corn on her foot. (But don't get me wrong, I like the former Lady Bottomly, I really like her!)

Although they seemed an odd match, they shared a great passion for each other. Unfortunately, they often saw fit to put it on public display, bordering the limits of good taste. That old story about a certain actress and a noted director under the table at Ciro's pales in comparison to the public stunts the Bottomlys staged. The parking attendants at Chasen's won't soon forget finding Myrtle and Laddie creating a passionate scene on the hood of Gregory Peck's car!

Myrtle claimed "deliberate cruelty" in her official complaint and though Laddie at first denied the charges, he allowed the claims to go unchallenged. An insider told me he had intended to bring suit first, but was prevented from doing so when Myrtle had him tranquilized, and bricked over his bedroom door! (Two construction workers, who were doing some foundation work for Barbara Lamont at the time, managed to extract the lord from his temporary prison.)

Myrtle had no comments for the press regarding the divorce. Barbara stated, "Laddie was a deer, literally. Mother is a crack shot. Beyond that I won't comment." Whatever do you think she means by that?

Speaking of royalty mingling with the common people, I hear Gloria

Prescott, star of the recent tropical potboiler *Snake Queen of Volcano Island* (meant to be a comeback vehicle for Maria Montez, who couldn't handle that slimming hot tub cure and died before filming could begin), has been on a European goodwill tour for the studio. That snake-charmer Gloria mingles with her betters and in Monaco, she just happened to run into that country's reigning monarch, the dashing Prince Rainier.

Gloria was in one of the festive casinos and had used her last chip on a losing game of baccarat. Spying a stray chip on the floor under a slot machine, she tried to retrieve it in order to rebuild her winnings, and in the process managed to trip the prince.

"*Ay Dios mio*! Don't throw me out again, *Señor*, I wasn't doing anything wrong this time!" she protested, tangled on the floor with the prince mistaken for a concierge.

Gloria realized her mistake, and discarded the chip for the potential of a far bigger jackpot. The prince was charmed by the Mexican actress and they were swept away to the casino's dance floor. Reportedly the two have enjoyed intimate dinners and the prince has extended his country's every courtesy to Miss Prescott. Might one day she be changing her title from Miss Fire Hose, Miss Ratchet & Lube, and Miss Bundt Cake (previous contests Miss Prescott has won in her climb to stardom) to Princess Gloria? Time will tell!

American Movie Classics Schedule, May 4, 1997
A Birthday Tribute to Gara St. James
12:00 P.M. EST - *Clip Joint* (First National, 1952) Directed by Edwin L. Marin. Starring Randolph Scott, Gara St. James, George Brent, Broderick Crawford, Bahamia, Stephanie Bachelor, Lloyd Nolan, Flora Robson. Woman determined to aid in Korean War effort gets job at what she believes to be a beauty parlor; learns too late that a clip joint isn't a manicure palace, it's a seedy nightclub designed to part losers from their money via beautiful "hostesses." Shocked St. James gets everyone on the side of right when she stages a fund-raiser for the armed forces, and even the gangsters give their cut to the boys in uniform. (Role somewhat of a precursor to Gara's later real-life position as an amateur conservative pundit.) St. James almost sells her number "I'm True To the Navy, Or Is It the Marines?" A better moment is the sexy Bahamia in the naughty song, "Anything It Takes For the Boys."
1:30 P.M. EST - *The Broken Chair* (MGM, 1953) Directed by Otto Preminger. Starring Ralph Meeker, Gara St. James, Ed Begley, Tina Mara, Frank Latimore, Martha Scott, Ron Randell, George Tobias. Gara clicks in mystery of murdered secretary found naked in magician's trunk; only clues

are broken chair, partially-eaten chicken dinner and cowboy hat. Preminger's attempt to recreate suspense of *Laura* doesn't live up to that film's classic status, but has its own merits. Meeker a standout as detective suspicious of Gara's colleagues who offer contradictory stories about the victim, ranging from hard-boiled career woman to innocent lamb to Circe-like seductress. Surprise twist ending (how does Meeker figure that Gara would never have left the chicken skin uneaten?) results in satisfying conclusion. Footage of St. James reapplying lipstick after hiding beneath boss Begley's desk was cut from initial production, but restored in 1992 video release.

3:00 P.M. EST - *A Fool I Am* (Warner Bros. 1953) Directed by David Butler. Starring Gara St. James, Robert Cummings, Philip Carey, Martha Hyer, Keith Andes, Robert Arthur, Ann Doran, Hal March. No-nonsense advice expert St. James gets reputation as fool after series of public embarrassments; in effort to regain her reputation, she discovers flair for theatrical comedy, leading to new career success. Gara adept at the goofy comedy routines; one might suspect she's not even aware that she's supposed to be funny. The sight of St. James in a tight lamé sheath continually slipping through dancing partner Andes's arms still produces chuckles. Shockingly, the censors didn't eliminate close-ups of Gara jiggling in her too tight gown (they were too busy making sure Russell and Monroe didn't do the same in *Gentlemen Prefer Blondes*).

Hedda Hopper's column, June 5, 1954

I'm pleased to share with you a wedding scoop. Actress Gara St. James, now appearing in the Alamo epic *Fire over San Antonio* with Jeff Chandler, married that divine jockey Frederic "Pancho" Rosenbloom in a ceremony attended by Hollywood's elite. It was an enormous wedding party, with 27 bridesmaids! Not even in the days of Vilma Banky and Norma Talmadge did we see such opulence. And I saw it all up close as the exclusive press presence.

The bridesmaids glowed in lemon organdy and big picture hats trimmed in daffodils. "Sure, *you* look great in yellow," Gloria Prescott was overheard telling Barbara Lamont and Bahamia. "I look as sallow as a canary swimming in tapioca."

"Nonsense, you look as lovely as a crocus tree," Dena St. James, the bride's mother, cooed to the girls with a guttural trill. "And don't worry, girls, you'll find a man yourselves one of these days.

"I'm so happy that my baby's found happiness with such a nice Jewish boy with a job. Oy, it's a dream come true for a *schviger*," Dena gushed, using a charming Yiddish term for "mother-in-law."

"I wish my Benny was still here to walk her down the aisle, but my Ronnie will do his brotherly duty and escort our Gara down the path of happiness." Ron Schmerkin is quite handsome, and should be in movies himself.

Gara was a vision in a white gown with puffed sleeves, an enormous hoop skirt, and a 35-foot train, all encrusted with seed pearls and translucent sequins. She designed the gown herself. "It's sort of a *Gone With the Wind* meets *The Prisoner of Zenda* thing," she confided.

In a break with tradition, the groom came down the aisle after the bride. Gara glowed when Pancho, attired in a black satin racing-inspired tuxedo, rode down the aisle of the synagogue astride Mr. Euripides, whom the jockey rode to victory in last year's races at Santa Anita.

Agent and producer Jory Plummer, who spearheaded Gara's film comeback a few years ago, described the ceremony like "something right out of a Shakespearean play, but not one of the ones where everybody dies."

At the reception, the plan was supposedly to screen one of Gara's favorite romantic films, *The Enchanted Cottage*. There was a mix-up, and instead the attendees viewed a hygiene film short called *The Enchanted Cottage Cheese*, which extolled the virtues of milk and dairy products for growing children. (Gara had a small role in the 1949 filmstrip as a school nurse.)

Gara showed off her exquisite ring. "Jewish tradition states the wedding ring should be simple, but there's a time and a place for tradition, and my finger ain't the place for it," she crowed.

Gara also broke with tradition when she stomped on the glass placed on the floor right after Pancho had performed the same ritual. This supposedly signifies the last time the groom will get to put his foot down! Gara laughed, "I just wanted to make sure he knew my foot overrules his from the start!"

The happy couple is bound for New York, where they'll visit Manhattan, Saratoga, and Niagara Falls. The falls may never be the same after a visit from "The Midwestern Matzo Ball" (one of Gara's charming nicknames from her fans)!

I also attended a party at Ciro's, where they were celebrated the annual custom of choosing "Miss Ciro's," the lovely Barbara Lamont. Lucky Barbara, to get two mentions in today's column!

"They don't give this title out for reading books!" she bragged. So sorry, Emily Dickinson, but Barbara's right!

Darling Nancy Davis was a bit perturbed at Barbara's win. "I don't know what she's upset about. Because Peter Lawford was on the judging committee, she thought he owed her some favor. Something about having once fixed his transmission or some car-related thing," Barbara shrugged.

"Barbara won it fair and square," insisted her mother, Myrtle Dempster, the former Lady Bottomly. "It has nothing to do with that 'bachelors only' dinner my daughter hosted with that Gloria Prescott. You know, some of the tricks one learns in Kansas can also be learned in Mexico!"

Anything for international relations!

Excerpt from *Biblical Films in Hollywood of the '50s* by Nicholas Baldry
An unusual 1954 entry is the Paramount film *Land of Confusion*, which hangs its plot onto the story of the Tower of Babel from the eleventh chapter of Genesis. The plot is barely related to the Bible's version, but that was par for the course in most Hollywood films. Directed by John Cromwell, the film stars Dana Andrews, Gara St. James, David Farrar, Cleo Moore, Tommy Sands, Bahamia, and Cantinflas.

Farrar and Moore are villainous court members scheming to unseat the king, played with dignity by Andrews. Bahamia performs a scintillating Eastern dance in her role as a temple priestess in love with Sands, who plays the king's son. The young lovers provide the few touches of genuine emotion.

On the other hand, St. James is no model of restraint onscreen in her role as Andrews's queen. She refused to be upstaged by her costars; her crown is larger than Dana's, her wigs are bigger than Cleo's, etc. She even performs a dance after Bahamia's more authentic number; her attempt at a "dance of the seven veils" is more "dance of the damask slipcovers."

One is thankful when the city's evil inhabitants are finally rendered confused by dueling dialects. A benevolent God allows the young lovers to escape, but no salvation is granted to the other stars, including St. James, who falls into an underground pit of boiling tar.

Behind-the-scenes stories intimate that Gara was arguing with the entire cast. The unattractive costumes indicate that designer Edith Head feuded with her, as well. Apparently director John Cromwell wasn't pleased with Gara's unprofessional behavior. On-camera angles are unflattering to Gara, and one might guess that Cromwell deliberately chose her worst takes.

Devotees of Hollywood urban legends still wonder if Gara's muttered comment, "Oy! This is ridiculous!" as she sinks beneath the tar was scripted or if it was an intentional slight on the star's part to ruin the take, and if the director left it in as a comment on the star's scenery-chewing performance. If so, Cromwell took that secret to his grave, refusing to ever discuss it any interview before his passing in 1979.

St. James has likewise ignored questions about it. The one time Barbara Walters broached the subject, Gara only said, "I got paid, didn't I?"

Cover blurbs from *Confidential*, February, 1955

UNNATURAL DINNER GAMES BETWEEN JORY AND GARA? "I WAS APPALLED," SAY BROWN DERBY DINER!

JUNE ALLYSON'S SEXY SECRET: THOSE PETER PAN COLLARS HIDE HICKIES FROM HOT-BLOODED LOVER!

LORD LADDIE ESCAPES WRATH OF SOUTH AMERICAN PRIME MINISTER AFTER AFFAIR WITH HIS WIFE!

THE REAL STORY: WHAT HAPPENED THE NIGHT BAHAMIA TURNED DOWN SINATRA!

MYRTLE LAMONT: HOLLYWOOD'S MOST POWERFUL MOTHER? WHY BARBARA REPLACED JEANNE CRAIN IN NEFERTITI FILM!

MARIA CALLAS: WHY SHE REALLY HATES RIVALS TEBALDI, HUGHSENSKAYA AND LA STAGGÉE!

THE MECHANIC WHO HELPED COOL DOWN GLORIA PRESCOTT'S OVER-HEATING CAR (AND THE OVER-HEATED STAR)!

Radie Harris's column, March 7, 1955

New York is known for its nightlife and Broadway shows. We tend not to get too starstruck here in Manhattan, being used to stars treading the boards in an attempt to get accolades on the legitimate stage, be it musical-comedy or classic drama.

But yesterday I had a late lunch with one traveler from Hollywood who might soon make an intriguing splash on Broadway. Gara St. James, star of such films as *Underwire Heiress* and *How Green Was My Valet*, has relocated to the East coast. Ostensibly, it's to accompany her husband, the jockey Pancho Rosenbloom, as he readies for races at Saratoga. But there's been a hint of dark clouds on the horizon for that marital paradise, and whispers from Hollywood tell me that the studios have been less than happy with Gara's recent faltering box office, not to mention star temperament.

"Not true at all," Gara insisted to me at 21. Our luncheon did not get off on the right foot, as I was running a bit late. (The pedestrian words are in-jokes, as you'll soon see.) When I hopped in with breathless apologies, Gara sniffed, "I've been sitting here hungry for fifteen minutes!"

"But, Gara," I stated, "surely you know it takes me a bit more time to get around, with my leg trouble." [*A horseriding accident resulted in the amputation of her right leg as a child, and Radie learned to walk with a wooden prosthetic.*]

"That's no excuse," she retorted. "Ronnie Reagan had both legs cut off, but he managed to get Ann Sheridan in the end, and was still on time for every meeting when he was president of the Screen Actors Guild!"

Who knew Gara was such a card? That amusing outlook on life was in great evidence throughout our luncheon. When I asked if the rumors were true that she had come east to consider a play, she replied coyly, "Perhaps, perhaps. That Funt and Lontanne better watch out!"

She expressed an interest in the classics, like *Hedda Gabbler*. "That's one I'd like to try, but only as long as they lighten up all the depressing stuff. Why does she have to shoot herself in the end? The audience would care more if she sat down on a whoopie cushion and bust out laughing. That would show what a swell dame she is."

She laughed heartily when asked if she considers herself a "real actress" or a "movie star."

"What planet are you from? I'm the biggest thing in pictures today. I go way beyond acting or starring. Of course, I owe all my success to my fans. That's what my dear friend Joan Crawford says, and she's right! But the real marks of stardom are my influences and the ways I've influenced others."

When asked to elaborate, Gara named silent great Clara Bow as the inspiration for the famous St. James pucker. "Clara's lips were bee-stung, but mine are practically swollen. And they've all copied from me, those thin-lipped actresses named Gloria, like Grahame, DeHaven and Prescott."

When asked about her husband, Gara became rather shy. "Our marriage is sacred and he should stay in the background. He's a jockey, so he's a lot shorter than me. Usually I can make sure he stays in the background just by standing up!"

As lunch drew to a close, Gara expressed hopes of catching some shows and getting ideas about what it might be like to be onstage. "I might look into *Witness for the Prosecution*. I'd make a good witness, I pay close attention to everything. Maybe not as much as that Barbara Lamont. I swear, she's got vision like those fish with the eyes on the side of their fins!

"Or maybe I'll check out *Silk Stockings*. My legs are freshly shaved. I always did like nice clothes *and* Don Ameche! Or what about this one, *Fanny*. That doesn't mean I'd have to fall flat on my fanny every night, does it?"

Oh Gara, with that sparkling wit, you won't be falling any time soon!

CHAPTER 5

Should I start inventorying the house while you're with the lawyer?

"What do you think I should wear? Is that what you're wearing?" Barbara asked Gloria as she primped in the mirror.

"Yes. This is perfect for a will reading. The charcoal houndstooth says, 'I'm sad,' but the mink collar and skirt trim say, 'Even sad people should enjoy a little luxury.'"

"Hmm, I see your point. Okay, I won't wear the pink Gucci, I'll go with the navy Westwood."

"Are the children attending to Mother Lamont?"

"Yes, they've been reviving her since five this morning. Binky and Babs can get her ready for the reading. All they have to do is show her their matching handguns and she'll behave, at least as long as it takes the lawyer to hand out the money."

Gloria reminisced about will readings past. "I wore something similar for Burgess Meredith's will reading."

"I can't believe he left you that thing in his will."

"Men always want to leave me things. Burgie wasn't handsome, but that wasn't important in the *horizontal* position! And I was *muy bonita* in that sexy costume when I appeared on his comic book show. You remember those publicity photos. I've signed more than a few photos of me as 'The Golden Swallow' at those conventions," Gloria swooned, picturing herself in the lamé bathing suit accentuated with gilded wings, metallic heels, and golden lipstick.

"And for all that, he left you one of the umbrellas he used as 'The Penguin' on that *Batboy* show?"

"*Amiga*, I auctioned it off on eBay and made a mint!"

"What do you think these chairs are worth? I'm always looking for nice chairs. Your *Bubee* Dena always said I was hard on furniture. That's how Peggy Ann Garner stole the role of the young Jane in that version of *Jane*

Eyore, because in my audition I broke the stool I was standing on. But I did get to work with Orson Welles later, when we did that TV production of *The Icebox Cometh*. He sure liked playing jokes on me. I had saved my seat at rehearsal with a plate of snacks, but then he took my seat *and* my bridge mix! Do you think they'll serve us something at the will reading?"

"I don't imagine they will," Pet replied as Gara changed channels with her mental remote control like an overzealous Betty Hutton.

"Aren't they supposed to give us tea and crumpets? Maybe they can move it up a bit. I can't go without nutrition for long. I need to remind them that I'm hyper-gly-semen."

"Hypoglycemic, and you never did show me the medical papers for confirmation," Caddy admonished with a wave of his pen. "You know I insist on backup for everything I write, except for what's made up."

"There's time for that later, Caddy. I have to make sure I look right for this will reading. I'm the widow, after all," Gara trilled, checking her Cossack hat for effect in the mirror.

"Momsy, you shouldn't call yourself that in front of everyone. They won't like that."

"Oh, who cares what they think? They're just gonna be mad when Laddie's will gives it all to me."

"Should I start inventorying the house while you're with the lawyer?" Peony asked. "Or should I be at the reading so I can write down everything he left you?"

"I can do that, my pen is always at the ready!" Caddy offered.

"No, I'll be there, and I'll remember everything myself," Pet insisted, hoping to avert any potential scenes.

"That's a good idea. Those English people won't be writing anything down. If they had their way, I'd be on a plane bound for home right now without all the money that's coming to me."

"Now remember, I don't want any scenes during the will reading. Once it's over, we push that cow out of the door with her hangers-on pronto," Gwyda told Nolan in sotto voice.

"Maybe we should have the gardener bring the wheelbarrow around and dump her out with the weeds," Nolan snorted.

"Wouldn't that be appropriate, if it were that easy. Last night's dinner fiasco notwithstanding, we have to be somewhat civil to her, if only for Pet."

"The sooner she's gone as well, the better."

"You should have outgrown this rivalry long ago. My word, you were already an adult when Pet was born! It's quite foolish to feel such jealousy of your sister some forty years now."

"She's no sister of mine. I had one sister, Hannah."

"Clearly Pet is your sister, too. You both have the same eyes as your father."

"She could have gotten that from some caveman on her mother's side, or whoever her real father is. Where does that dark complexion come from?"

"This conversation is going round and round, and I'm getting seasick. Let's concentrate on the issue at hand. We'll know the will's contents soon enough, even if *you* weren't able to get any info out of those flibbertigibbet actresses," Gwyda nudged.

"Don't get on my case. I tried to pump those pillocks for information, but they're too self-absorbed to know anything beyond hairspray and martinis. They make Gara seem intelligent ... only as intelligent as an Irish setter, but still."

Archie approached the two. "Mother, Warren's ready in the den as soon as everyone can assemble."

Gwyda squared her shoulder. "Very well, let's get this show on the road, and that daft bitch, as well ... preferably under a lorry."

"They'll be in the den for awhile, so what should we do?" Miles asked.

"Let's do something outside. It's too nice an afternoon to sit inside reading," Henry said.

Sophie looked up from her British gossip magazine. "I get the hint. I don't recognize all the celebrities, anyway. So what can we do outside? Play cricket? Polo?"

Henry hooted. "We aren't *that* upper crust, no matter what our dad and mum pretend."

They exited the foyer to the front driveway. "Let's explore the old wing," Henry suggested, quickening his pace.

"You know Mum and Dad don't like us going there, much less Great-Gran," Miles reminded as they aimed for the ruins.

"They're just afraid we'll get hurt, but we'll be careful," Henry insisted.

Little was ever done to clean up the wreckage of the northeast wing. The hall, which once connected the main house to the wing, had long been sealed, but instead of clearing out the debris, the damaged wood and charred stonework were allowed to crumble and fall into disrepair. A vestige of the tower, which local wags dubbed "Old Stumpy" remained.

Even though the family insisted it wasn't economically feasible to restore the wing, it was assumed the deaths of Laddie's middle children, Hannah and Barnaby, were too much to bear. And so nothing was done to restore the house to its former glory. Adding further sorrow to the tragedy, Hannah was to have married the Earl of Wimpleham mere weeks later. (The earl later married a former pop singer who'd had a few chart hits; over the years, when society pictures turned up in the press, someone always commented on the sad-eyed nobleman with the smiling blonde, and theorized he had never gotten over Hannah's death. That made for good copy, but truthfully, the earl's basset hound eyes were inherited from his mother, who resembled the cartoon dog Droopy.)

And so a fog of odd foreboding continued to hang over the destroyed architecture. But instead of sticking out as an eyesore, it somehow fit in with the bizarre amalgamation of structural styles displayed by the mansion's edifice.

"So this is where the fire started a long time ago?" Sophie asked.

"Yeah, then it spread to the old barn and the groundsman's cottage," Henry pointed to the north. "They were destroyed before it could be stopped by the local fire brigade."

"And your cousins were trapped in the house when the fire spread?"

"Mm-hmm. Your Gara was in that wing, too, during the fire, but she escaped." Miles chuckled. "I've heard Great-Gran say 'Why that Medusa escaped the fire and the children didn't, I'll never know.'"

"Hey guys, up here!" They turned to see Henry had scaled a chunk of the remaining wall and was peering over the barricade.

"Get down from there! You know Dad will get mad if one of us gets hurt!" Miles chided.

"Who's hurt? I'm fine. It's interesting up here."

"Maybe so, but I'd feel better if you came down," Sophie urged.

Henry turned and picked his way back down. "Now luv, that's all you had to say," he teased.

"Geez," Miles mocked and moved further along the wall. "I don't think we've ever looked this far back. I wonder if there's a spot we could get inside and see what's there."

"Good afternoon, ladies and gentlemen. I'm glad you could be here to attend the reading of the last will and testament of Lord Lindale Fotheringay Bottomly," Warren Campbell, the family barrister, stated to the group gathered in the den.

The air bristled with hostility among the room's various factions. Gwyda, Nolan, and Archie shot withering glances at the American interlopers. Gwyda's grandchildren and their spouses didn't spend much time glaring at rivals, but one could see their mental calculators adding up the expected windfall from Uncle Laddie's estate. A group of longtime retainers sat respectfully at the rear, and seemed to be the ones most genuinely saddened by the somber event in progress.

Pet tempered her sadness with worry of her mother's incorrigible behavior and fear of what the others might do if Gara was indeed declared the will's sole beneficiary. Luckily, Mina and Albert functioned as Cromwell to her Fairfax in the recreation of the Battle of Naseby going on in the den.

Gara's low cries as she dabbed her eyes with a lace handkerchief were the only subtle thing about her. Her suit was black, but most mourning clothes weren't adorned with multiple net ruffles festooned with fluffy black pompoms. A heavy veil attached to a big picture hat completed the picture of "the loony widow."

Barbara and Gloria sat at attention, studio training in evidence with perfectly crossed ankles and ramrod-straight backs. Babs, Binky, and Didums sat behind them and attended to Mother Lamont. If Gara appeared a bit loony, this group tipped the scales in the direction of the asylum. Myrtle wore a paisley caftan and turban, accessorized with a gem-encrusted oxygen mask and matching tank. She tapped one finger against her knee, a clanking of jeweled rings with each tap.

Babs was the most discreet in a dark suit, even if the skirt was cut rather high. Forbidden from scribbling during the reading, she instead fiddled with her jacket, the interior pocket of which contained a tape recorder (equipped, unfortunately, with malfunctioning batteries). Try as she might to appear nonchalant, the hunching of her shoulders and apparent slapping at her breasts did not leave this impression.

Binky and Didums were quiet, but their attire did the loudest talking in the room. Binky wore a green Dolce & Gabbana jacket and kilt, which showed off his legs to their best advantage. He eschewed traditional footwear for platform ankle boots. A miniature top hat in green velvet, held in place with a grosgrain ribbon, completed the overly striking look.

Didums wore a tailored suit, but most men's suits weren't constructed from cranberry moiré satin. Sharkskin pointy-toed loafers didn't look out of place, but the purple hair and big glasses with mauve lenses were definitely left of center.

Warren shuffled papers and cleared his throat. "Let's begin."

"Can you see anything?" Sophie asked as Henry peered into the small break in the retaining wall.

"No, maybe there's a better spot a little further down, or on the wing's other side."

"I suppose antique furniture or famous paintings must have been lost," Sophie speculated as they made their way along the wing's shell.

"I guess. Dad was just a kid, but he can rattle off a list of lost Van Goghs and the like," Henry derided.

They rounded Old Stumpy and continued down what remained of the wing's opposite side. "Hey, that looks like a possibility," Henry pointed.

"I don't know," Sophie hesitated as they examined the opening between broken stone slabs.

"Let's check it out, we won't go far," Miles enthused, warming to the idea.

"We might find a shred of that famous Van Gogh in the dirt," Henry said as he plunged headlong into the darkness.

"More likely a shred of something we don't want to come across, like rats or snakes or –" Sophie cautioned as she followed.

"Those are all in the den reading the will," Henry quipped in the abyss.

Warren had arranged more profitable business mergers, had saved more aristocrats from prison terms, and had overseen more wills of the obscenely wealthy than he could remember in a legal career spanning 43 years. But keeping control of this afternoon's proceedings might be the most difficult assignment of his career.

The beginning of the reading proceeded in a reverent manner. The last will had been prepared almost 2 years ago, and at that time Laddie's estate was valued at £93 million, and with shrewd investments and excellent business acumen, the estimated value had risen to £102 million. Warren could almost hear the collective drool hit the floor.

There was a quick overview of bequests which did not concern the family, such as gifts bestowed on professional organizations and humanitarian causes (including the Asquith-Bottomly Health Care Coalition, the pet progject of Laddie's first wife, Alice). It could be said these bequests *did* concern the family, as some members were visibly annoyed at any amount that didn't remain in their pockets.

Laddie had provided loyal servants and other retainers with comfortable bequests (not enough to tell the family to take this job and shove it, but enough to breathe a sigh of relief that the retirement years would not be spent scavenging for bits of steak and kidney pie in restaurant back alley trash bins). And then things began to get interesting.

The will provided substantial sums to his sister Gwyda and her descendants. Gwyda and Archie betrayed not a single emotion (impeccable and aristocratic breeding counted for something), but the grandchildren and their spouses could not stifle looks of disappointment and sneers of disapproval at what they considered an affront. (For those family members, equally flawless upbringings could not offset being raised in the ego-stroking of the '70s and the mercenary greed of the '80s.) Despite the generous bequests, they felt Laddie should have put out more.

The reading moved to Laddie's immediate family, with a significant bequest to Albert and the bulk of remaining assets to be divided between Nolan and Pet. Nolan glared at his sister, who appeared to have not heard, lost in memories of her father as fresh waves of grief washed over her.

The Hollywood brigade seemed on the brink of an indignant mutiny at their apparent slight until Warren cleared his throat and bravely continued. "There are a couple of other items here, things Laddie insisted on bequeathing last."

"Finally," Gara grumbled, lifting her veils so she could appreciate the expected windfall Laddie had provided.

"Better be worth the wait," Myrtle croaked right before clearing her throat and hocking a noogie into the handkerchief automatically proffered by Binky without a glance.

Warren glanced at the den's exit, computing the time it would take to escape once the reading was completed. With a quick prayer heavenward, he plunged forward.

"The best thing about my second wife, Myrtle Lamont Dempster, was the short period of our marriage, so that hell only lasted two years," Warren read aloud with apprehension. "However, I admit we generated a lot of heat together. Even dead, I'll not soon forget that weekend in Santa Barbara. I'm not sure how we knocked down those ceiling tiles, but we had fun doing it!"

"Really," a disapproving Carolyn clucked.

"And so, in remembrance of the love we briefly shared and other unmentionables, I bequeath to Myrtle the sum of five million pounds."

"Hallelujah!" Binky exclaimed.

"Damn straight," Myrtle muttered.

"Bless you, Jesus, Mary, and Joseph!" Barbara twinkled.

"Five million pounds! Five million pounds!" Babs muttered into her jacket.

"As a proviso, Myrtle is aware this is contingent upon her continuing silence regarding certain issues."

"Issues? What issues?" Nolan interrupted.

"What's that about, Warren?" Gwyda demanded.

"Even if I knew what Laddie was referring to, I wouldn't be able to say anything," Warren explained.

"Five million to that old bag," Willis lamented as Louise patted his knee.

"If I may continue," Warren sighed, and plunged ahead. "My third marriage, to Gara St. James, provided me with my beautiful daughter Pet. For that, I remain grateful to Gara, although she has done a lot to degrade that gratitude. As with my bequest to Myrtle, this gift to Gara is contingent on maintaining her silence on a particular matter, and I remind her that I took certain of her secrets to my grave."

Confused, Pet glanced at her mother, whose look of dull insouciance (she was once famously described by critic Bosley Crowther as "a face unclouded by thought") remained.

"Gara shall receive the oversize portrait of herself currently residing in one of the storerooms. Sorry I once felt the urge to stab it a dozen times, but I'm certain it can be repaired, the bill of which will be paid by the estate. I also leave her the sum of seven million pounds," Warren concluded.

"How did that bitch get two million more than me?" Myrtle gasped, clutching her oxygen mask for a blast of fresh air.

"Fiddled out of twelve million pounds, I will not stand for that!" Nolan erupted.

"Nolan, please, this is not the time –" Pet started.

"You! You were in on it, making sure your bitch of a mother and that Hollywood hag ruined us," he accused.

"You shouldn't be complaining, you got quite a haul yourself just a few minutes ago," Barbara threw at Nolan.

"Sure, compared to the pittance we got," Willis spit out.

"Stop that, it's unseemly to fight in front of outsiders over money," Gwyda hissed.

"But they're the ones taking our money," Carolyn sniffed.

"I earned that money," Gara exclaimed. "I should have gotten everything. I may have my attorney contest the will."

"Like hell you will. If anything, we'll have Warren contest it ourselves," Archie declared.

Warren rubbed his forehead. "The will was vetted by a team of barristers. It's ironclad and will hold up in any court."

"We'll see about that!" Nolan shouted, throwing open the doors and storming out. The arguing continued into the great hall as the servants beat a hasty retreat to the kitchen.

"Wouldn't you rather lie down for a bit?" Mina asked Pet.

"No, I'm fine. I'm his daughter and I'm not going anywhere," Pet insisted.

"How could you let this happen? What kind of bloody attorney are you? Not to mention a longtime friend! Some friend, like the Plantaganets swallowing up the whole of England!" Gwyda accused Warren.

"That's unfair. You know I couldn't divulge the contents of his will, even if he was your brother," he defended.

"But you helped created this deplorable situation. How do you propose we clean up this mess?" Nolan sneered.

The front door crept open. "They must still be in the den. Quick, before we get caught," Henry said as the kids started to sneak in.

"What in the world have you been doing?" Willis demanded to the startled teens. All three were covered in dirt. Miles's jeans were torn and there was dried blood on Sophie's forehead.

"What happened?" Mina asked, rushing forward to examine Sophie's injury.

"Just a scratch, I'm okay."

"We were just exploring around outside," Henry hemmed.

"And I know where you were exploring, the old wing, wasn't it? After all the times I've told you not to poke around there!" Willis boomed.

"It's dangerous, you could have gotten hurt," Louise added, pulling out a handkerchief to clean up Miles's face.

"What's that you have?" Mina asked Sophie, who looked down at the object in her hand.

"I don't know, we found it there," she explained, handing the object to her mother.

Mina wiped the dirt away and held it up. It was a charred cherrywood tube, embossed with patches of black lacquer and decorated with the faint images of painted silver blossoms.

"My favorite cigarette holder! Where did you find it?" Gara blurted, taking the item from her niece. "Lucille Ball gave me this a long time ago. She said if anyone should die smoking in bed with this in their hand, it was me."

"And you *should* have died back then, back when the house was burning down," an angry Nolan growled.

"Nolan!" a shocked Pet cried.

"That fire was no accident!" Gwyda shrieked. "You did it! You left a cigarette burning in that confounded holder and killed your own stepchildren!" She pointed an accusing finger at Gara, who appeared confused by the entire scenario.

"What? What did she do?" Myrtle (who refused to wear a hearing aid despite a partial impairment, insisting it would make her look old and undesirable) asked Barbara.

"Well, Mother, it looks like Gara may be known for burning sensations on *both* sides of the Atlantic!"

STRANGE INTERLUDE 5

Honey, if you've ever read a tabloid, you know what bitch I'm talking about.

Excerpt from *The Production's on Me: The Life of Super-Producer Jory Plummer*
by Jory Plummer with Julius Petard

My work on Gara's behalf knew no limits in the early fifties. I
engineered her film comeback at MGM, I produced her hit Broadway
musical *The Branded Cowgirl* (which introduced the signature tune "There's a
Surprise Under My Hat") and I got her name in the columns with the
frequency of Elizabeth Taylor and Ava Gardner. I thought I might make
Gara "Mrs. Plummer" (six women eventually bore that name; what can I
say? Hefner had his Bunnies, but I had to work at it!), but it was not to be.

We had a tumultuous relationship from the start, but that made it
exciting. I always did like a woman I could argue (and make up) with, and a
woman who could practically suck the meat off a platter of barbecued ribs!

During one of our "off again" periods, she met and married Pancho
Rosenbloom, the famous jockey. I bowed out gracefully, though we
maintained our professional relationship, which continued to bring us both
fame and success.

But things spiraled out of control on the set of our 1955 film
Crestfallen in Chinchilla. The rapport we'd shared in the past seemed to have
soured, and Gara was hell-bent on opposing me each step of the way. She
fought with the director, Norman Taurog, she feuded with the cast
(including her leading man, Robert Ryan, and her onscreen rival, Corinne
Calvet), and nixed every dress design Michael Woulfe offered.

I imagine her unhappiness and unprofessional behavior was due to
her faltering marriage. She refused to confide in me. I tried to reach her, but
she told me, "You *kaker punum* (a Yiddish expression for 'shit face'), what
have you ever done for me?" A long memory was never Gara's strong suit.

Her moodiness and hostility were apparent to the audience, and the
film was not a success. When news of her marital woes hit the columns, I
understood. Our relationship improved and we later collaborated on more
projects; I produced her 1970 record album and helped her out of a tight

scrape or two, even proudly agreed to be her daughter Pet's godfather. But our intimate time together was at its natural conclusion. I couldn't create miracles for Gara anymore, and she could no longer give me good make-up sex nor the thrill of seeing her devour an entire luau pig. When the magic's gone, no appetite can't bring it back.

From *Leopold Maltby's Movie & Video Guide*

Suffering in Sable (R.K.O., 1956) Directed by: Norman Taurog. Starring: Jeff Chandler, Bahamia, Ralph Meeker, Timima Bossi, Raymond Burr, Fred Clark, Tige Andrews, Nancy Kulp. By-now familiar tale that money doesn't buy happiness is enlivened by good performances. Poor girl Bahamia marries rich Chandler, but is appalled by what goes on behind closed mansion doors. Pool party scene where guests take turns singing lines from "Two Debs in De Shade of a Golf Tee" is a treat (Nancy Kulp doing the limbo must be seen to be believed!). If one looks at this as a modern update of the *Dancing Daughters* films (which made Joan Crawford a star at MGM), one can enjoy this light entertainment for what it is. This third installment of producer Jory Plummer's "Forlorn in Fur" series is not quite as good as *Miserable in Mink* (the first, which starred Barbara Lamont), but a vast improvement over the middle offering, *Crestfallen in Chinchilla* (a failure for star Gara St. James).

Excerpt from *The Columnists of Hollywood's Golden Age: How and Why the Real Stories Were Never Reported* by Stéphane Lambert

Stars like Rock Hudson and Montgomery Clift benefited from the columnists reporting on made-up heterosexual romances with leading ladies and studio secretaries, and turning a blind eye to close friendships with male studio personnel and poolside orgies in San Francisco. But one star who benefited from columnists ignoring bad behavior had nothing to do with scandalous sexcapades: Gara St. James.

Once a minor child star, Gara endured rough years until her comeback in the 1952 MGM film *The Ungrateful*. She later made films at all of the major studios. Without the muscle of a long-term studio affiliation, her ability to skirt scandal in the press is remarkable. The reason for it is two-fold.

Most of the columnists liked Gara; her Midwestern roots enhanced her image as a regular gal whose open manner was refreshing in Tinseltown. She was one of the rare stars beloved by both Louella Parsons and Hedda Hopper, who gave her good mentions in their columns on a regular basis.

Gloria Prescott, a frequent target for derisive comments in Parsons's column, maintains that St. James came about her preferential treatment by accident. "We all knew Louella adored Gara because she rescued her poodle from drowning once," Gloria revealed. "Little did Louella know it was Gara who kicked the poor thing in the pool to start with because the poor dog got between her and a plate of burgers. And she only rescued it from the pool because she mistook it for a mink stole!"

A second reason for the apparent whitewashing of Gara's behavior in the press is the sheer oddity of the scrapes in which she managed to become entangled. For example, 1956's *What's That You Said?* was a bizarre comedy of marital mix-ups and the McCarthy hearings in which Gara plays a housewife who breaks out into a flop sweat whenever she hears Joe McCarthy's voice on television and, through a series of farcical mishaps, mistakes her husband for a Communist. (Possibly her costars, Joel McCrea, Ronald Reagan, and Yvonne DeCarlo, influenced her interest in the Republican Party and conservative politics.)

A comical scene in which Joel, as Gara's husband, attends an ice show to meet a business investor created a potential real-life press scandal. In the film, Gara tails McCrea to the arena and ends up in a skating chorus line supporting Belita (once a minor league Sonja Henie, she made films for Monogram in the '40s) in the show.

During each take, Belita performed the stunts with perfection, to Gara's irritation. She believed Belita was trying to upstage her and during the fourth take, Gara pulled a handgun from her pocket and tried to shoot the skates off Belita's feet! (Yvonne DeCarlo, herself a firearms aficionado, may have shared gun tips as well as political opinions.) The bullet missed the skates but caused a rupture in the ice, sending fourteen cast members into the tank's freezing water.

The story never made it into any column, in part because the studio didn't want the negative publicity. And Parsons, Hopper, Graham, et. al., knew the incident to be true, but correctly deduced that no one would believe such a bizarre thing had ever happened.

Sidney Skolsky's column, March 24, 1956

I had the privilege of interviewing stars last night at the premiere of the new Warner Bros. drama *Serenade*, starring Mario Lanza and Joan Fontaine. It's sure to be boffo at the box office and provides thrills for the ladies in the audience.

In attendance were William Holden and his wife Ardis, Gregory Peck and his wife Veronique, Tab Hunter and Barbara Lamont, and Anthony

Perkins and Gara St. James.

Gara has kept a low profile since her divorce from jockey Frederic "Pancho" Rosenbloom in November. She's kept busy with film projects and spending time with her family.

Gara's mother Dena was also there, accompanied by her handsome son Ron. Gara's brother, who bears a resemblance to Robert Mitchum, should be in films himself, but don't expect to find him there. "Being a movie actor doesn't interest me in the least," he told me after several female fans inquired what movies he had been in. Sorry, girls, but he's happy in the insurance game!

Gara was pleased to pose with Tony Perkins for the photographers, even with her recent sorrow. "Making the decision to end a marriage is not a decision I made lightly," Gara confided. "But when it became obvious that he'd rather spend time with his horse than me, what else could I do? A horse is a horse, of course, even one that helped him earn a million dollars last year. But he'd rather spend money on getting that horse new shoes than buying me some, and he knows I'm hard on my shoes! Shouldn't I be treated better than something that's gonna end up at the glue factory one day?

"I'm free and a single girl again," she crowed, enveloping Tony Perkins in a bear-hugging squeeze.

"Gara, please," he croaked, struggling to free himself from her strong grip.

"Get used to it, Tony, there's more where that came from!" she guffawed and squeezed Tony once more before allowing his good friend Tab Hunter to extricate him from the situation.

"Dear, one shouldn't scare the man away like a grizzly," her friend Barbara Lamont urged. "Look at me and Tabbie. I act like a pussycat and we get along fine!"

Good advice, Barbara! With knowledge like that, they're bound to both purr their way to continued success in the movies *and* on the arms of handsome male stars!

Fox Movie Channel Schedule, December 15, 2002
Spotlight on Films from 1957

1:00 P.M. EST - *In the Shadow of Sainthood* (Universal, 1957) Directed by Vincente Minnelli. Starring Michael Redgrave, Gloria Prescott, Ralph Bellamy, Karl Malden, Lee Patrick, Tom Tully, Tina Mara, Suzy Parker. Bio-pic of the Spanish Saint Rosalita of Andalucia. Direction by Minnelli is somewhat tepid; film almost worth it for the devout performance by Prescott. Scenes depicting the miracles associated with St. Rosalita are faithfully recreated, including the notorious healing of the lisping eunuch. Lee Patrick, as the salty Mother Superior, has one of filmdom's great lines as she counsels the sainthood-bound novice, "My child, the Lord works in mysterious ways ... and you are one of his greatest mysteries." Mara good as the nun jealous of Prescott, and Parker rather too lovely as another bride of Christ. The starlets play guitar and sing a charming lullaby, "Call Me Sister," to a group of the cutest kids this side of the Von Trapps. One curious matter: would a real nun wear such a tailored habit (lined in sequins, no less!) and heavy mascara?

3:00 P.M. EST - *This Schoolhouse is Condemned* (Warner Brothers, 1957) Directed by Rudolph Maté. Starring Richard Widmark, Barbara Lamont, William Demarest, Joanne Dru, Grant Williams, Mike Mazurky, Josephine Hutchinson, Tommy Rettig. Small town scandal and asbestos contamination cause a schoolhouse to be condemned with the faculty inside. The allegorical tale confused audiences at the time (and appears to have confused some of the film's stars, as well), but ensuing years have enhanced the film's status. Lamont has a memorable freakout scene when she tries to storm the barricaded doors, only to be held back by Mazurky, who appears to cop a feel when one hand gets too close to Barbara's chest! Film noted at the time for use of the then-forbidden word "crap."

5:00 P.M. EST - *Her Stony Gaze* (United Artists, 1957) Directed by Gerd Oswald. Starring Gara St. James, Gig Young, Dina Merrill, Phil Carey, Timima Bossi, Otto Kruger, Gene Nelson, Margot LeMora. Archeologist's niece uncovers ancient text turning her into a modern-day Medusa. Anyone sparking anger or jealousy in her is turned into stone; sorority reunion with former rivals spells trouble. St. James dives into her role with enthusiastic relish; one suspects she wishes she really had the power to turn Merrill, Bossi, and LeMora into museum specimens. The climax has noteworthy special effects as Gara is tricked into gazing in a mirror; the scream on her lips as she turns herself into stone causes her to shatter into 1,000 pieces. Do we see Bossi happily grinding her heel into shards of St. James's face in the concluding scene?

Michael Musto hosts classic film screening by Mark Pilchard, *The New York Blade*, April 1, 1998

Michael Musto, columnist and gay culture enthusiast, will preside as host for a screening of the 1957 Universal classic, *Imitation of Nice*, at Lincoln Center for the Ragland Film Society. Many of the film's stars are expected to attend, including Gara St. James, John Saxon, John Bromfield, Julie Adams, Bahamia, Peter Lupus and Donna Loren. (Not expected are

Gilbert Roland, Grant Williams, Judy Canova and Mari Blanchard, as they have passed away.)

The film, revered by American gay camp enthusiasts and a legion of fans in Norway, was not a hit on its initial release. However, it gained a cult following upon its TV arrival in the late '60s. The plot concerns the rag-to-riches Hollywood tale of Mindsey Peters, a beloved actress with a reputation as "the nicest gal who ever appeared in Cinemascope." The truth is far uglier, as behind the scenes reveal that she is a raging egomaniac despised by family and friends. The character has been a staple of Halloween costumes on Christopher Street since the '70s, especially in the pink and green sequined gown she wears in the scene where she crashes a party at the Coconut Grove.

A question and answer session will follow the sold-out screening. "It will be an interesting evening," opines Mr. Musto. "Some of the stars haven't seen each other in ages, and would probably like to keep it that way."

Bahamia, the still sexy "Caribbean Bombshell," speaking with reporters in New York after an appearance in her recent show "Oh, the Peaches I've Sold!" at the Rainbow Room, said she was looking forward to the event. "Just don't sit me next to that one wench. I might pull the chair out from under her."

When pressed to identify the woman, Bahamia replied, "Honey, if you've ever read a tabloid, you know what bitch I'm talking about. Let's just say, this movie was one big slice of cinema verité."

Excerpt from *They Said What? The Unpublished Quotes Celebrities Said Off-The-Record (Until Now!) Over the Years to Life Magazine* by Angela Theroux and Sage Mallick

Gloria Prescott: I shouldn't have bothered with Eddie Fisher, he wasn't worth the trick – I mean, the treats, you know, the tea cakes and coffee at the Beverly Hills Hotel. I was the one who ended up having to pay the waitress *and* the concierge! There was once a time when men in this town were gentlemen. Now you could put the lot under a bathhouse and they wouldn't muss a hair.

Gara St. James: Each time I tried to get in to see Zanuck at Fox, that old piece of gym equipment, Gloria Prescott, was under him every time. For seven weeks straight! And one afternoon she called me, high as a kite – you do know she used to have a problem with "the weed," right? – gushing that Darryl had given her a pearl necklace. Thinking back, it's funny she never did show it to me.

Barbara Lamont: Gloria Prescott is my best friend, and we've always leaned on each other for support. But there are times professional help is what's needed. I can still hear Gloria screaming, imagining everyone was trying to upstage her. She even pulled a curling iron on Martha Hyer once! And Mary Benny told me she and Jack used to wonder about those screams from Gloria's hacienda next door. I shouldn't talk, I've had my own stays at those places. I even got to room with Gene Tierney once, so it's nice to know that a nervous breakdown doesn't diminish one's star status.

Jory Plummer: Being the greatest producer in Hollywood had its perks, not the least were the women willing to do *anything* to get into the movies. Gara St. James was dying for a comeback; I had a feeling I could pull it off, but not without some payback, and not just financial. And Gara was willing to do whatever it took. She said, "That's something you won't find many Jewish girls doing, even after she's married! But you have no idea what I've had to do the last few years just to make it in this city, so giving a blowhard ain't a problem."

Rosemary Clooney: That Gara St. James was always warning me against ending up on watch lists by signing petitions or filling out cards. I told her she was full of gefilte, but she insisted that true patriots didn't sign petitions against our elected officials. "You don't want to end up like Lee Grant, do you?" she'd sneer. I think Charlton Heston's to blame. If they hadn't done that Biblical film together, *One Touch of Jehovah*, she'd never have been exposed to those conservative killjoys.

Arlene Dahl: I loved to learn about acting and enhancing my technique, but some of those Method types just went too far. I'd be following the script to the letter like Miss Burns taught me, and without warning, John Garfield would fling a beer can at my head! It was a relief in the '80s to appear on stuff like *The Love Boat* as the high school sweetheart of Howard Duff, fighting to keep him from the clutches of some blonde gold digger played by a Landers sister.

Lillian Burns: Valedictorians in my acting class were few and far between. Gloria Prescott was always saying she was a skilled orator and gave marvelous diction, but I think she must have confused that with something else. She did have lovely manners, which some of her colleagues could have used. I think Bahamia must have been raised in a chicken coop! And Gara St. James was always provoking arguments. Once she was acting out a scene with Gloria, and there was a little tiff, because suddenly Gara whipped out her elbow and slammed Gloria in the chest. One of her boobs actually popped out of her gown!

Bahamia: John Ford? Yeah, I knew he was gay. Mean bastard really put me through my paces on the set of *She Wore a Golden Turban*. I noticed how his eye kept tracing the outline of Nick Adams's trousers. Who did he think he was fooling with all that gruffness? Bitch just wanted some hardwood, which I guess I shouldn't blame him for.

Lord Lindale Bottomly: In retrospect, I shouldn't have made those movies, as they sullied the family name. But the thought of being in a film was appealing, and I always did have a weakness for actresses. With so many pretty birds about, I surprised people when I married Myrtle Dempster, who was no beauty. In fact, she resembled the comedian George Formby, albeit a bit more masculine. But her looks were no indication of her sex appeal. The things we did in the hospital – the beds go up and down for purposes other than medical!

Myrtle Dempster: The moguls used to make stars ... in more ways than one. My daughter has absolutely no talent. *None*. Case closed. And that friend of hers, that Mexican girl, don't get me started. Still, they both looked pretty in a reclining position, and that used to be enough in this town.

CHAPTER 6

Even the threat of the cattle prod doesn't always deter her.

"What do we think about this accusation against Gara?" Barbara asked as she poured drinks in the library.

"I wouldn't put it past her, but it would have involved more smarts than she ever shown, onscreen or otherwise," Gloria replied, accepting the proffered gimlet.

"I thought that old Mrs. Danvers was going to slug Gara right across the face with her one fist," Barbara clucked as she sat down on the opposite settee.

"Hmm."

"What's wrong? You usually like it when Gara comes off like a big fool. Remember that time she was supposed to sing 'The Star Spangled Banner' at that Bicentennial celebration, but she forgot the words and started singing 'Have You Never Been Mellow?'"

"Ha, that was a good one," Gloria chuckled. "Oh, nothing's wrong. It's just that was the first will reading I've attended that I didn't get something."

"I wasn't expecting anything myself, and I was at least his stepdaughter for the blink of an eye. Why did you think he might leave you something?"

"I knew him back in Hollywood, too. The least he could have done was leave me a nice emerald clip or a diamond bracelet," Gloria pouted.

"There, there, dear, no one suffers quite like you," Barbara said drily. "I guess it's lucky he went when he did. Mother could have gone herself anytime before getting those millions."

"She was practically buried back in 1978, remember, when she couldn't be revived for four days? You had Mackie working on the designs for your mourning dress and had picked out the orange crate for Mother Lamont's final rest."

"Mother always said, 'Don't blow that cash on the stiff, they can't spend it in hell.'"

"But was she referring to herself when she mentioned the 'stiff?' And speaking of referring to things, did she ever tell you what it was she had on Laddie to get that big payoff?"

"No, she'd just say, 'Don't worry, what I know is enough to make that old bastard toe the line.' I once thought it was better to stay in the dark about Mother's little schemes. But over the years, I've realized I need to keep up with my lovable old battle-ax if I don't want to end up in jail myself."

"Didn't you just have some problem with her? Something about trying to kill Angela Lansbury?"

"You wouldn't think a group of elderly ladies could get so worked up over a game of canasta. Patty Andrews hightailed it out of there as soon as the trouble started, but Marsha Hunt tried to break them up, to her own detriment. Poor thing, she almost ended up with a separated shoulder when Mother did one of her Oriental 'chop-chop' movements and Marsha got in the way."

You'd think those girls would know better. Didn't Zanuck once say, 'I'd rather follow your mother *into* a bar fight than have her behind me?'"

"Too true. I only broke up the fight by threatening them with one my smaller pistols. Anyway, I suspect this will all be settled out of court. Mother said she has some negatives Angela would prefer to remain unseen. That's Mother for you!"

"Where is she, by the way?"

"The children returned her to the hyperbaric chamber. I'm afraid the excitement at the reading was too much for her. Once she's perked up a bit, we can take her out again. I used to complain about the expense of that thing, even though I saved a bundle by buying one at Michael Jackson's charity garage sale years ago. But it has practical uses, like keeping her out of mischief."

"Rather like keeping pets off the carpet, isn't it?" Gloria speculated as she glanced at her empty cocktail glass. "I'm ready for another round, how about you? Plus another round of bad-mouthing our dear Gara."

"Do you really believe Gara started the fire that killed Barnaby and Hannah?" Albert said.

"I do. Two less people to get Laddie's fortune. She was thinking about the money as far back as then," Gwyda nodded.

"Why is that Gorgon still in this house?" Nolan huffed.

"You know the old saying, keep one's friends close and one's enemies closer," Gwyda sniffed. "I won't allow that bitch to rape our family's coffers, much less get away with murder."

"It could have been an accident. We don't even know the fire was started by Gara's cigarette," Albert counseled.

"Why are you defending that witch? Have you forgotten which family you're a member of?" Nolan boomed.

"Dad, I'm just reminding everyone that we shouldn't let anger about the will morph into accusations of murder."

"And that's another thing, how did she con Laddie into giving her our money?" Archie questioned.

"And that bit about keeping his secrets all these years, what about that?" Willis asked no one in particular.

"That bloody Warren, I can't believe he was privy to it all and didn't breathe a word," Gwyda groused.

"He couldn't, even if he wanted to. It was a confidential matter between him and Laddie," Albert reminded.

Gwyda breathed in deeply and released in an exasperated manner. "Albert, I do adore you, but right now you're getting me a bit hacked off."

"I'm going to talk to the law firm and see if I can get more information," Nolan volunteered. He gestured to Albert that he should leave the room as well. Albert shrugged his shoulders and followed his father, leaving the room to the complainers licking their financial wounds.

"They're down there trashing me, I know they are," Gara wailed as she lay across the bed like Camille near the end.

"Don't worry about those people, Miss St. James. They don't know how to treat a real star of your girth and magnitude," Peony chirped soothingly.

"Momsy, it's to be expected. They had no idea Daddy was going to leave you a sizable amount of money."

"That little pittance, when he was supposed to leave me a great big chunk. But what's important is that he made sure our precious flower, our little Petal, was taken care of so well."

Mention of her apparent financial windfall made Pet nervous and a bit worried the family would think her avaricious. "I miss Daddy more than any money could replace."

"Good, good, you keep saying that and maybe those vultures downstairs won't pick your bones dry when the check clears the bank," Gara advised.

There was a soft knock at the door and Mina entered with a tray. "I thought some tea might be a good idea."

"What, no cookies?" Gara complained.

"You got seven million pounds, and how much did Pet get?" Caddy asked, busy scribbling.

"Perhaps now isn't the time," Mina suggested.

"And what's this about you keeping his secrets, and secrets of your own?" he persisted.

"Oh, that," Gara waved aside with a too loud laugh. "Who knows what he was talking about. Senility runs in these crazy British families from all that marrying each other. Look at his nutty sister, claiming I started a fire to kill his kids. She's one step away from Howie Hughes territory."

Noticing the change in Gara's demeanor, Pet asked, "Are you sure that's all there is to it?"

"What do you mean, pumpkin? Of course that's all there is. What kind of secrets could I have?"

"Well, there's that fling with Laurence Harvey," Caddy offered as he scanned his notes. "And there's the time you –"

"That's quite enough, Caddy. Besides, those aren't secrets, those are just private matters."

A knock interrupted Pet from pursuing the matter further. Peony opened the door to two butlers bearing a large package wrapped in brown paper.

"It's the portrait of Miss St. James, from the attic," one man explained as they brought the bulky item into the room.

"I haven't seen this in decades," Gara crowed, jumping from the bed like a child on Christmas morning as Peony removed the wrapping from the portrait.

"He wasn't kidding about the stabbed canvas," Mina commented.

"At least he didn't stab the face," Caddy offered.

Everyone lapsed into silence as they regarded the unusual artwork. Painted in 1963 by the renowned British portraitist Sir Ralph Musgrove, the over-sized painting depicted Gara as a cross between Empress Sissy and Etta Candy. Her pale auburn hair was arranged in cascading ringlets and complimented by a diamond and garnet diadem. (The tiara, once owned by Laddie's great-great-great-great-grandmother, the Countess Elspeth of Buxley, disappeared from Brownmoor sometime around Gara's departure from the estate at the end of the marriage. Despite accusations from Gwyda, the diadem's true fate was never determined.) She wore a frothy pink ball gown with deep décolletage, voluminous skirt held aloft by petticoats, and puffed sleeves trimmed in ermine. Instead of holding a scepter or jeweled globe, Gara was depicted holding a bag of potato chips.

"Ralphie kept yelling at me to put down that bag of chips and threatened to paint it in if I didn't stop eating during the sittings," Gara chuckled. "He named it *Lady of the Tayto Crisps*!'"

"So that's the famous portrait," Albert said from the hall.

"What do you think? Is it repairable?" Pet asked.

Albert examined the canvas. "Yes, most of the tears are clean. I can recommend an excellent restorer in London. I've worked with him in the past for my own gallery."

"I didn't know you owned a gallery," Mina interjected.

"I guess we haven't had much time for small talk, have we. Yes, The Bottomly Gallery, what else can I do with a degree in art history from Oxford. My interest in art never manifested in actual painting talent, so I pursued the business side of it."

"And he's done quite well on that side," Pet bragged about her handsome cousin. "He has a knack for spotting up-and-coming talent. He even helped mount my first photo exhibition."

"You must visit the gallery in London while you're here," he urged.

"I'd like that."

"I'd like nothing more than to kick that fat wanker out of here," Archie groused.

"So would I, but after Nolan's discussion with the lawyers, we'll have to see her a bit longer," Gwyda sighed.

One of the firm's lawyers who had assisted with the will reiterated that the bequests to the ex-wives were within Laddie's right. And in the event they wanted to challenge the will in court, the potential benefit of keeping a few millions from gold-digging Americans was outweighed by negative publicity and digging around by tabloid journalists to unearth the secrets to which the will alluded. The lawyer's final verdict: "I suggest keeping a stiff upper lip and be glad Laddie didn't give those women more money."

"So what do we do now? Do we let them all waltz out of here without doing something?" Nolan asked.

"Over my dead body. There must be something we can do. Why didn't Laddie warn me?" Gwyda complained. "He hated Gara to his dying day. Even in his final days, if her name came up, he'd grunt and struggle to give her the finger."

"If we knew what it was she had on him," Archie suggested.

"And how do you propose we find out what that was?"

"Maybe there's something left behind in his bedroom. Or perhaps he left a clue within the text of the will."

"Or maybe we can weasel the information from those stupid

Hollywood people."

"As if they'll give away their trump card that easily."

"We'll soon see. I've got Willis, Carolyn, and the others working on those oddities as we speak, those poofters and their strange sister," Archie stated with confidence.

"Good, good. The odd talking to the odd," Gwyda responded drily.

"I thought we'd never get your grandmother settled down," Didums complained, settling into the couch and thumping his feet onto the coffee table in the salon.

"Sometimes the old girl puts up quite a fight," Binky agreed. "Even the threat of the cattle prod doesn't always deter her."

"That's when we have to get as mean as she can be. Give her back some of her 'take no prisoners' approach and she'll have to acquiesce," Babs explained.

"Listen to her, with the ten dollar words," Didums teased.

"You know, Mother regrets sending you to that writing camp when we were kids, the same summer I went to drama camp. Who knew we'd both get into so much trouble?"

"Trouble? I only wrote an exposé about the unsanitary conditions of the camp cafeteria. You were the one juggling three bunkmates *and* a camp counselor!"

"They almost shut down 'Camp Happy Pants.' That one TV star told Mother I'd corrupted her little angel. Honey, he didn't need corrupting, let me tell you," Binky recalled fondly.

"Nothing that fun was happening in my cabin," Didums complained.

"You were too busy turning the mosquito netting into togas for the camp production of *Antony and Cleopatra*. And those popsicle sticks you turned into golden headdresses and breastplates! At least your mother had bragging rights. I can still hear ours saying, 'When I sent you to drama camp to develop your talents, you were supposed to become another Bobby Darin, not another Pamela Des Barres!'"

"Are you talking about Lady Pamela D'arbanet?" Louise said as she entered with Willis, Carolyn, and Cliff.

"I think we're talking about two different people," Babs hesitated.

"Oh no, sis, they had it right," Binky said impishly. "Yes, Lady Pamela, isn't she the party gal. I can still see her at my last show in Birmingham, straddling the speaker and shaking her knockers at David Beckham."

Carolyn's eyes widened in shock. "That can't be Lady Pamela. She's eighty-one years old!"

"Yeah, that's her. The Stones wrote 'Honky Tonk Woman' about her. That chick can tear it up!"

Realizing that Binky was stringing them along but mindful that Archie had entrusted them to learn what they could, Louise laughed tightly. "Very amusing. You're a rock and roll singer, correct? That must be interesting."

"It can be, especially on the road. We were once booked into a country and western bar in Fort Worth. I was fit to be tied until it turned out that joint was full of cowboys light in their boots! Ooh, they *do* make 'em bigger in Texas!"

"How nice that things worked out so well," Willis choked.

Carolyn asked Babs, "And you write things, don't you? Might I have read something you've written?"

"Only if you're perusing the obituaries," Didums teased.

"They don't write themselves. Those alimony checks from Vince Van Patten and Bronson Pinchot don't pay for things until I've sold my novel, or that Hollywood tell-all."

"Oh, a tell-all, you must know everything," Louise praised, steering the conversation in the desired direction.

"You must know all of your grandmother's stories. Do tell us some," Carolyn enthused.

"Hmm, let's see. Should we start with Grandmother's connection to Jimmy Hoffa's disappearance, or how she knows the real story about the Black Dahlia?" Binky offered.

"Or what about Mother, and how she was driving the car that forced Jayne Mansfield to crash into that truck?"

"Mother also supplied Lana Turner's daughter with the knife that killed that gangster boyfriend."

"And I hear your grandmother was really 'Deep Throat,'" Didums supplied.

"Which one, the one who started Watergate or the one who made those 'art films?'" giggled Babs.

"Both!" screamed Binky, and the three collapsed in convulsions of laughter.

"You have all been so rude," an offended Louise sniffed.

"We only came to talk as a common courtesy," Willis added.

"Maybe common, but nothing courteous about it," Babs threw back.

"It wasn't worth our trouble, being polite to people who know nothing about decency or manners," Carolyn huffed.

"Polite? You came in here to weasel us into blurting out our grandmother's secrets so you can steal her inheritance."

"We don't have to stand for this," Cliff said.

"You Brits can't out-play us. We've been taught by the best high-class grifters who know all about getting ahead in Hollywood," Didums said proudly.

"And that outranks anything you cheap limey assholes could ever dream up," Binky said with a curtsy. In a final slam, he spun around, flipped up his kilt, and mooned them.

The offended quartet stormed out of the room as Babs quipped, "I guess it's true what they say about the English. Once in a blue moon is all they can handle!"

In turn, the kids had gotten all they could handle from their parents. Henry and Miles had endured a strict tongue-lashing from their father, but Louise had softened due to their bedraggled appearances and rueful expressions. "That's enough, Willis," she said and, taking charge, ordered the children to clean up and stay in their room until dinner.

As Willis lorded it over the boys like the patriarch of *The Barretts of Wimpole Street*, Mina gave Sophie the Irene Dunne treatment from *I Remember Mama*, consisting of a short and thoughtful lecture, ending in a promise from Sophie to be more careful.

And Sophie managed to be careful, sneaking down to check with the boys before scooting back to her own room without being detected. Mere minutes had passed after her successful subterfuge when Mina and Pet entered the suite.

"Did you already sneak out and check to see how the boys fared with their parents?" a knowing Mina asked.

Sophie gulped, her face already registering the truth. But Mina laughed. "I knew you'd do that. I'd have done it myself. In fact, I'm sure I did, back during those summer vacations when Pet and I would get into trouble."

"Don't remind me. Momsy would act like I'd given her latest movie a bad review. Once she even asked if we had spiked her cheese fondue with tobasco! I don't know where she came up with that one," Pet recalled.

"But your dad always soothed things over. The sun rose and set on you for him."

The thought reminded them of Laddie's passing and the day's events. "Yes, I was a daddy's girl," Pet said softly.

"A daddy's girl, I have a costume for that," Barbara trilled as she and Gloria joined them in the hallway.

"Yes, but I have a feeling they're not talking about playtime activities," Gloria suggested.

"There you are, Mother," Binky called as his group rounded the corner. "We just put those nosy Brits in their place. They were trying to worm information out of us."

"They're all against us. Which ones?"

"Not the older ones, the prissy ones around our age with prematurely dry and aging skin."

"I'm sure Archie put them up to it. They wouldn't have the wherewithal to think that up themselves," Pet snorted.

"It must run in the family. One of those other men tried pumping us for information a few days ago," Gloria said.

"Now which one was it, that son of the old Dame, or was it Pet's brother with the anger issues?" Barbara wondered aloud. "I can't tell any of the men here apart. It'd be so much easier if they were better looking."

"And what a cheap trick, anyway. Did he think we hadn't learned anything after all those years sidestepping Hedda and Louella?" a shrewd Gloria sniffed.

Sophie remained, hoping the adults would ignore her so she could continue enjoying the bizarre conversation.

"It's good that we've run into each other," Pet said, steering the conversation from Hollywood frivolity. "I was told the will is going to be filed with the court. They consulted the lawyers and don't plan to contest it."

"Marvy, simply marvy!" Barbara clapped her hands in glee.

"Does this mean the press might start trying to get interviews with us?" Gloria asked (realizing she had no opportunity to cash in on the will but always thinking ahead).

"I suppose it's possible," Pet conceded.

"The press likes a story with English titles, big money, Hollywood stars," Mina goaded with barely contained laughter.

"Don't encourage them," Pet whispered, pinching Mina's arm.

"That awful tabloid media gets worse every day. This never would have happened in the old days," Barbara lamented. "Why, *People* magazine had the nerve to ask me last year if my bones are brittle!"

"Today's starlet can get away with falling down drunk and flashing her hoo-ha as she steps out of limos, and no one cares," Gloria agreed. "Girls of our generation have to comport ourselves with dignity. One never knows when the press is lurking about, hoping to snap a photo of June Blair with her finger in her nose, or Felicia Farr adjusting her underwear from riding up, or *me* buying bladder control panties!"

This comment was one too many, and Sophie couldn't contain her laughter. This set off Mina and Pet, who collapsed against the door in gasps and coughs of giddy hysteria.

Gloria, in complete seriousness, replied, "I know, it's crazy, isn't it? The things we stars have to deal with. The general public never knows about this."

"Let's worry about the press when that situation arises," Barbara cautioned. "I think we'll tell Mother about the will. That might give her the energy to kick up her heels and do the Black Bottom like she did in the old days."

Myrtle sat on the side of the bed, bracing herself with one arm against the headboard. She clutched her oxygen mask and took gasping breaths as Barbara opened the bedroom door.

"Mother! You're supposed to be getting rest!" an alarmed Barbara shrieked. She snapped her fingers at Binky and Babs, who jumped into service to assist Mother Lamont.

"I was getting rest just fine," Myrtle croaked. She hit Binky over the head for grabbing her arm just a mite roughly.

"Sorry, Gram," he replied.

She hit once again. "You know better than to call me that! Men might think I'm too old to get picked up in bars!"

"Sorry, Myrtle."

"How did you manage to get out of the hyperbaric chamber by yourself?" Barbara persisted.

"I didn't have any choice, not after someone unplugged the damn box," Myrtle snapped.

"Unplugged?" Gloria gasped. They turned to see that the chamber indeed had been disconnected from the power source.

"How did that happen?" Pet asked.

"I don't know," Myrtle gasped between breaths. "I was awakened by the sound of the generator cutting out. I was groggy, and when I turned my head, I barely made out someone leaving and shutting the door."

"Someone deliberately unplugged you?" Barbara wailed, clutching her bosom (a gesture long out of theatrical fashion but which Barbara recalled from appearing in the David Edwards play *A New Word for Happiness*).

"What do you make of this?" Mina whispered to Pet.

Pet shook her head. "I may have underestimated their decision against challenging the will in court. Maybe someone decided to challenge it by getting rid of the competition permanently."

STRANGE INTERLUDE 6

Trust me, I had her number, but she's never completely had mine.

Surprise wedding for Gara St. James by Ruth Ellis, *Los Angeles Daily News*, June 8, 1957

Actress Gara St. James and Roderigo Hujeapenosa (better known to Mr. & Mrs. America as "The Hot Sauce King") married in a surprise ceremony yesterday afternoon in San Luis Obispo. The wedding took film insiders by surprise.

"I know this comes as a shock, but it was a whirlwind romance and we decided to get married practically overnight," Gara gushed to reporters just before the happy couple left en route to the airport for a honeymoon in Mexico City.

The wedding, conducted by the mayor of San Luis Obispo, was attended by only a handful of well-wishers, including the bride's mother, sister-in-law, and brother, who gave his sister away at the ceremony. "I wish my Gara would have gotten married in temple to a nice Jewish boy, like the last time," Mrs. St. James lamented. "But that one didn't work out good, so maybe a ceremony at City Hall to a nice Catholic boy – Oy! – will bring her happiness."

"We can only hope," the maid of honor, fellow actress Bahamia, added. The dancing sensation, who performs a memorable mad mambo in the upcoming film *Crime in the Cabana* which costars St. James and Steve Cochran, said she didn't expect to be a witness to a wedding. "I thought we were going to the studio to loop some dialogue. I should have known better than to let Gara pick me up in her Chevy Bel Air, everyone knows what a lousy driver she is. So I have to play a cameo role in another of Gara's weddings! How long am I going to have to pay for being stuck as her roommate all those years ago?"

Despite Bahamia's comic monologue, Mrs. St. James had praise for the ceremony. "Those Catholics know how to put on the dog, even in an office. That Roderigo filled the room with my baby's favorite flowers, gladiolas. She used to call them 'garaolas' as a little girl! And that mayor guy showed proper respect for a real star in his courtroom. He was much nicer than that judge when Gara was in court the last time, all because the Sinatras were mad about the smoke damage drifting over the fence from the kosher barbecue for our celebration of the Jewish feast Sukkot."

Fox Movie Channel Schedule, July 23, 2005
Spotlight on films featuring 'Great Houses'

6:00 P.M. EST - *The House of the Seven Grables* (Twentieth Century Fox, 1957) Directed by Edmund Goulding. Starring Gara St. James, Pat Boone, Gary Crosby, Timima Bossi, Pat Hingle, Barrie Chase, Tom Pittman, Franklyn Farnum. Parody of gothic drama mixed with musical mayhem fails to ignite due to odd script and lethargic direction. Cast brings brief moments of enjoyment in tale of theater troupe using a house, once owned by Betty Grable, as a summer retreat. Boone and Bossi perform a charming song and dance to "Can You Spell Poughkeepsie?", and Chase performs a mild striptease to "It's a Hot Night in the Klondike." St. James, as the troupe's diva, tries to out-Grable the iconic star by recreating her hula from *Song of the Islands*, but the grass skirt doesn't undulate as much as cause gale-force winds. Betty made a cameo at the film's end as a favor to Twentieth Century Fox, although she said (according to Earl Wilson's *Show Business Laid Bare*), "Some way to end a movie career, appearing opposite that old cow with the $1.99 legs."

8:00 P.M. EST - *The Strange Knockings at Fallen Oaks* (a.k.a. *How Dark Was My Dilbeck*) (Columbia, 1958) Directed by John Frankenheimer. Starring Burt Lancaster, Barbara Lamont, James Darren, Ed Wynn, Barbara Lang, Robert Burton, Peg Hillias, Gary Cockrell. A suburban murder involving robbery, adultery, and Green Stamps. The murder actually takes place two doors down (in a home designed by renowned architect Charles Dilbeck, providing a publicity tie-in) from the manor Fallen Oaks, where Lamont cuckolds husband Lancaster. The murder is tied to goings-on at Fallen Oaks, where strange knockings at the windows precede visits by Lamont to the estate's gatehouse. Don't miss Anita O'Day singing in a low dive populated by old-timey bar trash where Lamont meets a surprising blackmailer, providing a satisfying conclusion to the mystery.

10:00 P.M. EST - *Murder at the Ilona Massey Theatre* (Republic, 1958) Directed by Irving Lerner. Starring Ralph Bellamy, Gloria Prescott, Lyle Talbot, Brandon De Wilde, Millie Perkins, Hume Cronyn, "Snub" Pollard, Madame Sul-Te-Wan. Murder occurs during a musical revue at the Ilona Massey Theatre, and it's up to the cast to determine who killed Prescott as "The Mexican De Milo" (a novelty act where the famous statue sprouts arms and checks out "modern times"), singing "Fill My Arms With Love" in the opening number. Flashbacks help flesh out the case as Bellamy, playing the house detective, tries to finger the killer. Massey makes an amusing appearance (sweeping by, she comments, "I'll not attend a performance at my own establishment again, at least until I install a pinball machine in the lobby!"), and Mamie Van Doren appears in an uncredited cameo as the orchestra's maestro (as a favor to pal Prescott). Strangest must-see musical vignette: Madame Sul-Te-Wan performing "The Laziest Gal in Ouagadougou!"

Cover blurbs from *Confidential*, October, 1957

TIMIMA BOSSI'S ASSAULT ON SALESLADY AT RODEO DRIVE BOUTIQUE: "SHE WASN'T HELPFUL ENOUGH," CLAIMS STAR!

MOTHER REPORTED GARA ST. JAMES KIDNAPPED WHILE STAR WAS DANCING AT MOCAMBO!

INGRID'S PENDING DIVORCE FROM ROSSELLINI: IS ROBERTO LEAVING BERGMAN FOR BAHAMIA?

LORD LADDIE FLEES JEALOUS SEÑORITAS IN MADRID RIGHT INTO TRIANGLE WITH JEALOUS MADAMOISELLES IN ALGIERS!

TROUBLE FOR ROCK AND PHYLLIS: WHAT THAT BELLBOY REALLY WAS DELIVERING TO ROOM 305!

ZSA ZSA CONSIDERS WEDDING NUMBER 4 TO GARA'S DISCARDED JOCKEY!

GLORIA PRESCOTT IGNORES HER MEXICAN FAMILY IN POVERTY! "I SEND THEM A NEW COW EVERY YEAR," STAR DEFENDS!

Excerpt from *Being Bahamia: Stardom Looks Good on Me!* by Bahamia with Lajuana Pagewell

Barbara Lamont and Gloria Prescott are my dear friends, and have been since our early days barely making ends meet and sharing an apartment as we pursued our careers in Hollywood. Though we don't get to see each other as often as we'd like, I know our friendship endures.

I can't say the same for another old acquaintance (and I do mean "old"). While Gloria and Barbara shared one room of the boarding house apartment, I was stuck sharing with Gara St. James. I've never seen such a slob. She'd leave her things all over the place. She'd make a huge mess in the kitchen, making these weird noodle pudding and matzo cracker sandwiches. And I don't even want to think about her lousy grooming habits, including her bizarre obsession with her fingernails. I had a real problem with her clipping her nails in the bedroom. Sometimes those shards would hit me!

Her overbearing and clueless nature turned me off to getting to know her better. That didn't stop her from finagling me into standing up for her at each of her four weddings! (And I did not return the favor to her for my own two marriages.)

I could have dealt with her pushy nature, if that's all there was to it. After all, you don't get ahead in Hollywood by being a shrinking violet. However, Gara's general stupidity strained my ability to deal with her. Anyone who knows me knows one of my rules for living is, "That ain't my problem." In Gara's case, *her* being a nimrod shouldn't become *my* problem.

But oh, did she push me. For one thing, she always mispronounced my name. As any fan knows, it's pronounced "Baa-Haa-Mee-Ah." Gara would usually call me "Ba-Ham-Eee-Ah," with an emphasis on the "Ham," trying to make some kind of joke at my expense. But then, Jews who kept kosher weren't supposed to get around ham, so maybe she should have taken that as a hint!

And then there was her response to the scandal that temporarily halted my career. As a child, I had seen American and Mexican films and knew that I was destined for stardom, never thinking my background would prevent me from attaining the heights. Apparently the Cuban and French portions of my heritage were just fine, but the African side was the *bête noir* of Hollywood stardom!

And so I blithely went toward my destiny among the cinema firmament. Unaware, the studio played up my exotic background without specifics and dubbed me "The Caribbean Bombshell."

However, as the '50s turned into the '60s with an interest in cultural origins, I proudly discussed my background with *Ebony*. I was not prepared for the repercussions, which affected my career adversely. (Although Ross Hunter told me once at a party if he had known before filming started, he might have cast me as Sarah Jane instead of Susan Kohner in *Imitation of Life*.) Lead roles, even small supporting parts, dried up. Luckily I decamped to Broadway and European cabaret to great acclaim, and film roles later returned with enlightened times of renewed interest in diversity and the civil rights movement.

Those cultural revolutions must have bypassed Gara. Once she watched me rehearse and had the nerve to say that I danced like a white girl! When I confronted her about it, she laughed and said, "I wasn't making fun of your foot-kicking there. I was saying you danced like Cyd Charisse. Don't be so *meshugena*!" Trust me, I had her number, but she's never completely had mine.

Hedda Hopper's column, February 5, 1958

I've got joyous news for our country, as well as good news for one star and her husband. First off, I'm sure the Supreme Court is going to do the right thing and rule the blacklist didn't violate anyone's rights by denying employment to suspected Communists. Although some "liberal" press folks and bohemians cry about "violations" of people's first amendment rights, real Americans know the "Reds" are still a threat to freedom and should be exposed for the cowards they are.

A star I know who agrees with me wholeheartedly is the always righteous Gara St. James. "Better a blockhead than Red," she's fond of saying. She's living the all-American life with her new handsome husband. And now they're enhancing that life with the next logical addition, children!

No, Gara isn't expecting a "blessed event," but she and her husband, Roderigo Hujeapenosa, the president of that famous hot sauce company, have adopted darling twin girls.

As readers may remember, Gara and Roderigo wed in a surprise ceremony last year (and yes, I've forgiven that naughty girl for forgetting to call me with the scoop). And now they've added children to help make their lives complete.

"I want to squash those rumors that something's wrong with me or Roddy," Gara told me. "We're both completely normal and perfect as God intended. We'll have real children of our own one day, but we saw these little babies at a charity function hosted by Jane Russell." (Gara is referring to the World Adoption International Fund, which Jane founded and has helped thousands of poor and displaced orphans find happy homes.)

Gara continued, "I misunderstood and thought W.A.I.F. was W.A.I.T., a new group to help stars find maids and wait staff! I may not have gotten new maids out of them yet, but we couldn't resist these cute little girls!"

Nannies brought out the tykes for an appearance. Kimmy and Primmy have fluffy auburn curls and rosy cheeks. "Aren't they adorable?" Gara cooed. "Central casting couldn't have done better!"

Gara has big plans for these lovelies. "Joan Crawford sent over some layettes and clothes from when Cathy and Cindy were little. And we're planning a christening as soon as my pal Bahamia agrees to be a godmother."

She reflected fondly on their days sharing a room at a Hollywood boarding house. "Gloria Prescott and Barbara Lamont shared the other room. We had a common sitting room, kitchen, and bathroom. Thank God I shared with Bahamia. I don't want to make disparaging comments about my good friends Bar and Glo, but they have rather free attitudes when it comes to one's moral fiber. But Bahamia's the sister I never had. Did you know she insisted on being my maid of honor when Roddy and I got married, and was ready to step in and give me away if my brother Ron didn't make it in time?"

That's friendship in Hollywood for you!

Turner Classic Movies Schedule, February 6, 1999
Part of the month's theme: A Salute to '50s Style

12:00 P.M. EST - *Pickup on Ballerina Lane* (Paramount, 1958) Directed by Martin Ritt. Starring Stewart Granger, Gloria Prescott, Howard Duff, Jan Sterling, Henry Daniell, Carl Benton Reid, Thelma Ritter, Harp McGuire. Girl from wrong side of the Louisiana sticks hitchhikes her way to fame and fortune. Most notable pickup occurs when she gets a ride to the state capital in teamster "Pap" Boulez's limousine. Edith Head lets her imagination roam with sumptuous gowns as Prescott rises from the backwoods to the penthouse. Wally Westmore's makeup and Nellie Manley's hairstyles make a real difference in the opposing images of the white trash beauty and the grand cosmopolitan lady. Gloria gets a rare chance to really act in this film. Her breakdown scene at a fundraisers pancake breakfast is a shocker; one might suspect she isn't acting, so good is her portrayal of mental collapse.

2:00 P.M. EST - *Meet Me in St. Petersburg* (MGM, 1955) Directed by Mark Robson. Starring Maurice Chevalier, Barbara Lamont, Jacques Bergerac, Keenan Wynn, Leon Ames, Betty Field, Frankie Darro, Gigi Perreau. Charming period musical of Russian family makes pre-Revolution days seem idyllic. Splendid costumes by Helen Rose and elaborate wigs by Sydney Guilaroff are the film's real showcase, but the stars give it all they've got. Lamont exquisite as the beautiful daughter who turns the head of the young Duke (Bergerac) next door; their romantic duet in Red Square a winner. Perreau a delight as the youngest who nails Rasputin in a snowball fight. Most famous scene is Lamont's song and dance to "You Can't Catch a Bolshevik with a Hun." She steps out of a Fabergé egg and performs an amazing 65 uninterrupted highkicks in a sable gown and 15-lb. tiara!

4:00 P.M. EST - *Fashion Riffraff* (Universal, 1959) Directed by Charles F. Haas. Starring Gara St. James, Jeff Chandler, Richard Denning, Bahamia, Charles Coburn, Mary Astor, Sam Levene, Nestor Paiva. Designer becomes toast of Paris, but hides secret of her dirt-poor Alabama past. Fashion world is at first aghast, but of course comes around. One must hear Midwesterner Gara attempt a "Su-thun" accent! Jean Louis provides stunning gowns for the female stars. Style-watchers love this film for Gara's ever-changing hairdos. Hairstylist Hibiscus outdoes himself, transforming her in a different look for each scene (from poodle cut to short gamine locks to enormous falls). In a pageboy, Gara serenades a café audience with "Orange Colored Sky;" magically, her hair turns into a bouffant during the scene! Bahamia, delightful as a sexy model, also manages a saucy song and dance number, "The Crawdad's a Lobster's Cousin."

Excerpt from *Growing Up Hollywood: Adoption and the Movie Stars* by Glendolyn Rouselle

Sometimes stars discovered the heavenly existence of perfect tykes was but a pipe dream. Much has been written about Joan Crawford's less than idyllic life with Christina and Christopher. Although the younger children, twins Cathy and Cindy, have refuted those charges, it's believed that Christina's accusations have some basis in fact.

While that situation more or less permanently sullied Crawford's reputation, another star's disastrous experience with adoption remained secret, until now: Gara St. James and her adoption of twins, Kimmy and Primmy, in 1958.

Then wed to condiment tycoon Roderigo Hujeapenosa, Gara adopted the tykes with the help of W.A.I.F., the organization founded by Jane Russell. Photos of a beaming Gara clutching her twins made the fan magazines, and the star capitalized on her new maternal role by starring in the hit comedy vehicle *The Petrified Mother*. But what initially seemed delightful soon turned less attractive.

Gara was unprepared for the sometimes rambunctious behavior of toddlers. At first, the children did nothing too out of the ordinary; coloring on the nursery walls, breaking items left within their reach, spitting up on her gowns. Even with a revolving door of nannies at her disposal, Gara couldn't get the children to behave as she thought they should.

A cigarette lighter carelessly left out in the open was used to set fire to a baby doll on the nursery floor; Gara nearly had a stroke when she thought one twin had set the other afire. (It's been suggested that novelist Doris Hume used insider gossip to craft a similar scene for the novel *The Sin of Susan Slade*, on which the Connie Stevens melodramatic soaper *Susan Slade* was based).

The final straw occurred when the toddlers dumped three bottles of Hujeapenosa Hot Sauce into a bowl of gourmet dip at a fancy party thrown by Gara. Dozens of sick partygoers later, Gara had enough and returned the children to W.A.I.F.

Jane Russell recently told this writer, "I should have known Gara wouldn't make a good adoptive parent when she asked if getting those children came with some kind of reward or cash prize! Luckily, we placed those girls with a good family in Pomona. I've often wondered what hell that daughter Gara later had went through growing up." (Kimberly Morgan Griffith and Primrose Morgan Sellers both refused to be interviewed for this book.)

Louella Parsons's column, March 2, 1959

I've got two huge scoops today. Let's start with news of a happy sort. Barbara Lamont, appearing onscreen in the romance *The Bridle Path* with Tony Curtis, strolled down her own "bridal" path yesterday in Las Vegas. She married Cyril Lamont, a member of the famous Kempinski family of jewelers dating back many generations. (Legend goes that the Kempinskis provided the diamond necklace purchased by Marie Antoinette which instigated the French Revolution. I say, *C'est la guerre, c'est l'amour, c'est la vie!*)

Barbara wore an ivory wedding suit of silk shantung made by Irene, and was accompanied by her mother, Myrtle Dempster (the former Lady Bottomly). Barbara's sister Athole and her friend Gloria Prescott served as attendants in dresses of lilac organza, also designed by Irene.

From their roots in vaudeville, I supposed one could say that Barbara and Athole are something of a lesser Gypsy Rose Lee and June Havoc. That's not a slam at their talent, oh my, no! I'm sure Mrs. Dempster is quite proud of her girls's accomplishments.

I asked Barbara how she managed to marry a gentleman with the same last name. "Just luck, I guess. When I had those towels engraved 'B.L.' – you know, Zanuck always calls me B.L. – I figured I'd better marry a man whose last name began with L. Who knew I'd manage to get one with all the other letters right, too?"

The couple left for a honeymoon in the Poconos. "One of my girls, finally someone else's to take care of," mused Mrs. Dempster. "Maybe we can get you married off next, Athole."

"There's always hope," trilled Gloria, the lucky recipient of the bridal bouquet. Athole seemed to have misunderstood Gloria's comment, for she grabbed the flowers and struck Gloria over the head with them!

Girls, these tests of temper are what happen when you aren't married as nature intended! Perhaps Mrs. Dempster and *Señora* Prescott need to find those willful girls some husbands who will keep them in line.

Well, as one marriage begins, another ends. I must break the sad news that less than two years after they wed, Gara St. James began divorce proceedings yesterday against Roderigo Hujeapenosa, "The Hot Sauce King."

Their wedding surprised everyone (even me, since I did not receive the scoop about the ceremony) and their divorce seems designed to surprise, as well. The couple had appeared happy at both premieres and condiment conventions.

Gara confided, "We were too different. I'm Jewish, he's Catholic. I'm focused on my career, he took no pride in my movies. Plus he was too interested in round-the-clock weather reports! He claimed he needed to know because of all the tomato farms and pepper gardens for his hot sauce. What kind of fast one was he trying to pull on me? Hot sauce comes in bottles!"

Gara claimed Roderigo didn't understand fundamental realities about her career. "He expected me to become a little housewife and cook and clean. If that's what he wanted, he should have married Margot LeMora! I tried, though. He wanted me to learn to cook those Mexican dishes, so I conned – I mean, I asked my pal Gloria Prescott to teach me about burritos and tacos and cucarachas, but I couldn't understand how that stuff goes together. Plus, I don't think any of that meat was kosher!

"So I tried convincing her to cook everything and I would take the credit, but she wouldn't go for it. Some kind of friend! I'm sure I saw Lucy and Ethel do that on TV. You'd think Gloria wouldn't mind being my Ethel."

Even the addition of adopted infants last year didn't help the marriage. "He never lifted a finger to help. Whenever those kids cried, it was *me* who had to yell for the nannies to get off their duffs and do the job they'd been hired to do."

Perhaps prophetically, the Hujeapenosas are no longer raising the twins. "The real mother wanted her children back, and we did the noble thing and returned them. Oy! Those kids were a real piece of – Well, they were such a joy, and I'll miss them like you don't know."

Gara looks to the future and remains hopeful. "I won't rule out getting married again, but no time soon. My mother's getting a little tired of attending ceremonies. She told me, 'Why can't you be more like your brother Ron? He's happily married to Margaret. They haven't given me grandkids yet, but *you* bought me grandkids, and then gave them back!' I can't do anything right lately, except onscreen.

"Which reminds me, be sure to see my new movie, *Lumberjack Girl*, with Audie Murphy and Jack Palance. Whacking off a tree gets all the aggression out, especially when you pretend that tree is a witchy costar or a soon-to-be ex-husband."

Consider it done, Gara dearest!

CHAPTER 7

I may be a bit older now, but my boobs are still perkier than Clara Bow's!

"How did you sleep?" Gloria asked Barbara as they sat down to breakfast. "I slept divinely, like Sunny Von Bulow!"

"Not well, I didn't get more than seven hours from worrying about Mother," Barbara sighed as she accepted poached eggs from the maid.

"Did you move her into your room?"

"No, the kids agreed to watch over her, as long as the alarm was set on the unit. Binky's never forgotten that time we were vacationing in Cairo and Mother tried to have him entombed! She said she wanted him to have the full Egyptian experience."

"I applaud her interest in making the travel experience fulfilling, but that was a bit much. And wherever did she find that roll of gauze?"

"Who knows. Mother adores the children, but anytime she's on a new medication or had too many Mai Tais, she turns into darling Betsy Palmer from that *Friday Part 13* movie. You see why the kids had firearm training and judo lessons early on."

"Is that some Hollywood-style exercise program?" Nolan asked as he entered the dining room with Archie and Albert.

"This sneering attitude toward all things Hollywood isn't becoming. Besides, I recall a murder attempt last night that took place here in merry old England," Barbara snapped.

"That vivid imagination is quite useful in your business, but it's rather ill-placed at Brownmoor," Archie countered. "No one tried to kill your mother. She probably forgot to plug in her space age coffin."

"Easy for you to say. You can't imagine how many people have tried to kill Mother Lamont in the past, or wanted to," Gloria stated as she smeared marmalade onto toast. "Sam Goldwyn, Zanuck, even Lela Rogers. Why, Barbara's own sister has tried more than once."

"And that's why Athole's in that prison – I mean, hospital in Oregon now. I can only handle so many homicidal threats in my own home!" Barbara exclaimed.

"If someone here wanted to off the old dear, I'm sure they'd have done so long *before* the reading of the will," Nolan pointed out, accepting fresh coffee from the maid.

"That's why someone wants to kill her now, to keep her from those million she so richly deserves," Barbara added.

"No one tried to kill your mother," Gwyda stated with authority as she entered. "Each member of the staff had a full accounting of their whereabouts at the time. No one was near her room."

"Of course your staff denied it, no one wants to get fired. Besides, the butler didn't do it, it was one of your crazy family members."

"I refuse to have this foolishness continue. If you believe Brownmoor is dangerous, you're free to move into a hotel," Gwyda declared.

Ever mindful of expenses, Barbara demurred, "I suppose there's no need to leave just yet. Perhaps it's best if we stay a bit longer, just to sort things out."

"The only thing to be sorted out is finding who pulled my plug," Myrtle wheezed as she loped into the room.

"Mother! I said I would have them send up breakfast on a tray. Why did the children let you come downstairs alone?"

"They're no match for me, even with bum lungs and arthritic knees. Too much time on those cold, concrete floors in Kansas City years ago. The things I did for you and your sister's early careers! I may be a bit older now, but my boobs are still perkier than Clara Bow's!"

"Mother Lamont, have you had your morning pillies yet?" Gloria asked.

"Yes, I have, Glory. I'm as sharp as that tack I put on Vera-Ellen's chair so Barbara could step in and do that number for her. But Vera's ass was so skinny, she missed it entirely! And I'm sharp enough to remember that someone unplugged my sleeping box yesterday!"

"She hasn't said that many words in a row since the time she threatened to run Mike Todd out of town on a rail after he ditched me for Liz," Barbara marveled.

"If only we all were so lucky," Gwyda pronounced drily.

"Are you sure you know where the cool stores are?" Sophie asked Pet, craning her neck to take in the city sights.

After the stress of yesterday's will reading and wild accusations, Mina had suggested a shopping trip into London with Pet and Sophie, to which they readily agreed. A respite from those grasping relatives and the eccentric Hollywoodites would refresh them like the English matrons in *Enchanted April*, but with more stylish clothes.

"We can find everything in Oxford Street," Pet glanced in the rearview mirror. "The big stores, Harrods, H&M, little shops, too, with all the latest fashion trends."

"The latest fashion trends *within reason*," Mina cautioned. "I'm going to be checking skirt length and waistband height, not to mention the amount of exposed skin."

"Maybe we should just go straight to Nuns-R-Us," Sophie responded with an eye roll.

"I'm sure we can find a happy medium."

And they did, with an enjoyable morning in the department stores and a typical English lunch (Sophie's interest in bangers and mash disappeared as soon as she learned what it entailed, but she was satisfied with the substitute, fish and chips).

They continued their fashionable pursuits in the smaller boutiques of the side streets in the afternoon. Sophie's enthusiasm infected her mother and cousin, and they also selected attractive items for themselves.

Pet indicated an empire-waisted blouse. "Twiggy could have worn that back in the sixties."

Mention of the '60s reminded Mina of the tragedy many summers ago at Brownmoor. With trepidation, she asked, "Do you remember much about the fire all those years ago?"

Surprised, Pet looked up. "Why? You're not buying the idea that Momsy started that fire, or that someone tried to kill Myrtle last night?"

"All of the craziness just made me think about the fire itself. I only remember vague generalities."

"We were just kids. I'm two years younger than you, and I don't remember it at all."

"I keep feeling like I do remember something, but I can't put my finger on it." Mina pretended to examine the stitching on a pair of jeans. "What do you remember about Hannah and Barnaby?"

These memories were pleasant and Pet relaxed. "They were already in their twenties, and glamorous, like movie stars. Barnaby was so handsome, with black hair and blue eyes and those pretty eyelashes," she almost swooned, conjuring images of Leonard Whiting in Zeffirelli's *Romeo and Juliet*.

"He was quite handsome," Mina agreed. "And Hannah was beautiful."

Pet brightened further, remembering her sister as a saucier Sharon Tate. "Yes, with that silvery-blonde hair like Nolan had, before it took on that greenish tinge like Dad's. She'd let me sit at her dressing table while she made-up, and sometimes she'd put a little lipstick on me. Momsy would let me watch while she made-up, too, she loved an audience, but she didn't let me play with her makeup. But we did sneak into her makeup and jewelry sometimes, remember?"

"Yes! I loved playing with the jewelry," Mina enthused at the memory. "I'm surprised we didn't get caught more often than the few times we did."

"I don't remember Momsy catching us."

"Didn't she? I could swear I remember that," Mina mused. She reached out and touched her cousin's hand. "Look, your mom might be a real firecracker, but I don't think she started the fire. It could have started any number of ways. Your relatives are angry about the money. Next they'll decide that Myrtle hired an arsonist."

"They might even say we did it, juvenile firestarters at seven and five. I'm glad you suggested we get out and enjoy the day. If we have to deal with the crazies much longer, we'll have to plan trips into London more often."

"That suits me!" Sophie chirped, her arms loaded with jeans and other selections, which luckily were more Disney tween star and less attention-seeking red carpet starlet.

"It may not suit my pocketbook, but compared to what's happening at Brownmoor, the price may be worth it," Mina agreed with a wink at Pet.

Barbara and Gloria sat before rows of bottles filled with lavender liquid and jars of scented creams, like faithful pilgrims lighting candles before an altar to Elizabeth Arden. A wide range of beauty products lay at their disposal, all designed to reduce lines and increase firmness.

"How nice to have the time to enjoy our beauty treatment," Gloria gushed. "Unlike that time I was at Madame Jimmie's salon. I almost had to kick that little Vietnamese foot massager for rushing my bunion treatment to start on Tori Spelling's feet. We didn't have to rely on Daddy to be a star! We relied on the ability to do a highkick in a vertical or horizontal position! Oh, and talent," Gloria added.

"Of course. To think of the opportunities we both missed, just because of jealous costars or directors without vision," Barbara lamented as she examined the selection of eye serums.

"I know. Remember how I nailed that audition for John Ford for that part in *Seven Women*?"

"I thought it was John Ford who nailed *you*."

"Well, that too, merely insurance on top of the brilliance of my audition. I can still hear him saying, 'Yes, yes, oh God, yes, Gloria, it's yours, yes!' And then he turns around and gives my part to Patricia Neal! And when she suffered those ill-timed strokes, did Pat bother to say, 'Oh, John, give that part to Gloria Prescott, she really deserved it?' No, not a word! So he turns around and gives the part to Anne Bancroft! Stabbed in the back from competitive actresses *and* a double-crossing director!"

"And they think the only terrorists are in the Middle East," Barbara sympathized.

Then the door opened and Gara stuck her head in. "Here you are," she sang and bounded into the room.

"Speaking of terrorists," Gloria muttered under her breath.

"We haven't had a chance to play catch-up, have we?" Gara trilled, plopping down on the settee next to Barbara. "Didums told me you girls were doing spa treatments in here, and I thought I'd make myself at home with my old roomies."

"Aren't we lucky."

"Yes, aren't you. I've got my special manicure set. I've always done my own nails, ever since that awful experience at the Max Factor salon with that dreadful girl Ann Miller recommended to me. She left my hands in the paraffin bath too long. I had waxy blocks for hands an entire week! I never used to get hangnails before that happened. And then Ann steals the part I wanted in *The Opposite Sex* at MGM!"

"Annie was a piece of work," Gloria clucked. "Remind me to tell you about the time she tried tripping me down the stairs with the train of her gown when we did that number in *Stepping Out on My Baby*."

Gara ignored Gloria's offer of anecdote-sharing. "There's nothing more frightening than bad hands. I'd love to help you girls out with those ragged nail beds," Gara said, grabbing Barbara's palm for a critical look.

Barbara jerked her hand back. "I assure you, my hands are in perfect shape."

"They should be, Barbara's known in Hollywood for her hand jobs," Gloria joked. "One of her first paying jobs – in films, that is – was doubling for Judy Garland's chapped charwoman paws in close-ups of her reading love letters in *In the Good Old Summertime*."

Gara opened her carrying case and removed tubes of cuticle cream. "No one has time to write letters anymore. I guess everyone's writing their own life story these days, like I'm doing."

"How is that coming along with your oddball writer, Crappy Pork, is it?" Barbara barely contained the sneer.

"It's Caddy Polk, and it's coming along fine. What about that hatchet-job – I mean, that memoir your daughter's been working on? I'm sure there's a market for it. I mean, if someone can publish the biography of Bella Darvi, then someone in the world must be interested in the Barbara Lamont story."

Not fond of Gara but disliking heated scenes, Gloria said, "*Por favor*, let's concentrate on our manicures and facials instead of sniping at each other. Anger causes character lines. Besides, it's nicer to be silent if you have nothing nice to say. You know me, too well brought up."

"As you're fond of reminding us all the time," an exasperated Barbara sighed.

'Yeah, you've been spewing that line since we first met. I think you'd come up with something new by now," Gara agreed.

"Fine, sue me for being too well – I mean, being positive," a hurt Gloria pouted.

"Stop being so sensitive, you've been my best friend for over fifty – I mean, for some time now," Barbara soothed. "This all started because *she* crashed our facials."

"I was only trying to help," Gara insisted, starting to gather her beauty implements. "I've always been nice to you girls, but you've never been nice to me in return."

"Nice? You've never been nice a day in your life. According to recent tales going around here, you were less than nice to your own stepchildren!"

"Now you stop right there, that's a complete lie! We've known each other for a long time. How can you think I could kill anyone? If I had it in me to kill anybody, I would have offed *you* years ago," Gara barked, temper flaring.

"There's that murderous rage I've always suspected was in you!" Barbara declared, jumping to her feet. In doing so, her bowl of moisturizer was catapulted onto Gara's more-than-ample chest.

"Oh! You did that on purpose!"

"It was an accident, I didn't mean to do it. Your boobs are so big, they couldn't help but get in the way."

"Yeah, well, *this* is no accident, I promise you," Gara grabbing a handful of mud mask goop and flinging it at Barbara.

"*Basta*! Enough!" Gloria admonished, moving to place herself between Gara and Barbara. Unfortunately, she did this right as Gara lobbed a container of makeup powder and Barbara squirted an oversized tube of clarifying gel.

Drenched, Gloria spit the concoction from her mouth and wiped her eyes. "Being too well brought up isn't what it's cracked up to be!"

"The longer we stay here, the more I think we're in a real life version of the game Clue," Didums mused aloud as Babs chalked the tip of a cue stick. "The lounge, the study, now the billiard room."

"And with strange things going on, I expect we'll find Dame Glasscock in the ballroom with a candlestick," Binky added, unable to contain his persistent giggle over the family name. "You know, I was never good at billiards."

"And here I thought you gravitated to anything involving precision with balls," Babs commented drily.

"That was beneath you, too easy. I expect better."

"Sometimes one can only reach the lowest common denominator." She aimed the stick and led the break. "This business over Myrtle has me distracted."

"It *is* cause for concern. Although the Brits are convinced it wasn't plugged in correctly," Didums reminded.

Binky followed the break with his own shot. "I know it was plugged in correctly, *I'm* the one who did it. We know Gram's capable of her own schemes, but she's always been on the money when someone was trying to pull a trick. Remember her intuition regarding Jane Wyman?"

"Oh, that *Night of 100 Stars* debacle. Somehow Myrtle knew Janie was going to try and upstage our moms in that all-star kickline," Babs agreed.

"And they were prepared, and pushed Janie behind them when she tried stepping forward with that highkick. She should have known better than try that with experienced dancers. She must not have heard that tale about Mother and Angie Dickinson," Didums recalled.

In the days before Hollywood stardom, Gloria had been half of the dance duo "Chico and Perez" in Mexico. They would dance a torrid paso doble, then Chico would shoot at her feet while she tapped out a furious fandango. "That came in handy when they were filming *Loves of a Bolivian Puma* in '66. Angie tried pulling rank, but Mother wasn't having it. So Angie retaliated by pulling a gun on her, not realizing she had training dodging bullets. Oh, Angie was furious; she railed about how she still had connections with the Kennedys and could have her taken care of 'like that!'" Didums laughed with a snap of his fingers. "Bacharach had to drag her to her dressing room to cool down."

"If we could only get Myrtle to cool down so easily. But at least that ice and formaldehyde bath she's having is helping."

"We should keep an eye out for trouble. If Gram's a target, shouldn't Gara be looking over her shoulder right about now?" Binky asked, sinking his targeted ball in the right corner pocket.

"If she can move her fat neck to look fast enough. She's never been quick with her feet or mind. Lucky she's got that entourage to watch out for her, including Pet and Mina. Yes!" Babs cheered as she struck her next target.

"With the looks they've been exchanging, I wonder if they don't think it might be easier if someone *did* take care of Gara," Didums speculated.

"Gara might be an old cunt, but you don't cut off what might be fixed with a little KY," Babs aphorized.

Binky choked as he scratched. "No fair! I applaud the return of that brilliant wit, but not at the expense of my game."

Didums was distracted by the sound of muffled laughter beyond the room's door. "It appears to be a game right up these guys's alley," he said with humor as he caught Henry and Miles in the corridor.

"We didn't mean any trouble, we just like hearing you talk," Miles insisted.

"So you can report back to your parents what we're saying?" Babs asked.

Henry scoffed, "It'd be more fun to make up stuff so they think you're far worse than they already do."

"They told us we should stay away from you because you're morally indecent," Miles admitted, "but that made us more interested in listening in."

"Ha! So there's hope for new generations of Bottomlys and Glasscocks," Binky laughed.

"We don't mind you hanging out with us, as long as you don't get into trouble with Louise and Willis," Didums decided. "How good are you boys at billiards?"

"We can play a little," Henry said. He took the cue stick offered by Babs and sank a shot with ease.

"Play a little, he says. I think these two might even be able to navigate the mean jungles of Hollywood," Babs teased.

"Wow, Hollywood. Do you know Selena Gomez?" Miles asked.

"Is she on one of those MTV reality shows?" Binky wondered aloud, unfamiliar with the popular Disney star.

"You guys are pretty sharp. So what's your opinion? Do you think someone unplugged our grandmother's sleeping machine?" Babs asked.

Henry and Miles exchanged glances, deciding they should trust the outsiders their mother had deemed "American WAG filth not fit to clean our toilets."

"I wouldn't put it past some of them," Miles admitted. "But I don't think Mum and Dad would have the nerve."

"And Aunt Carolyn and Uncle Cliff aren't the sharpest knives in the drawer," Henry theorized. "But any of them might do something if Great Gram put them up to it. And Gramps and Uncle Nolan are capable of pretty much anything."

"The will's got them angry enough to do almost anything," Miles added.

"I can understand that part," Binky agreed. "Our mothers hate to part with a cent that doesn't return an investment threefold."

"They've never liked paying unanticipated expenses, like having to pick up the tab at Spago or pay blackmail to the paparazzi. But as Virginia Mayo was fond of saying, 'If they're willing to blackmail you, at least you've still got your star status!'" Didums quoted.

"But nothing's happened to Gara yet," Miles pointed out.

"Nothing that could be pinned on her in a court of law," Babs quipped. She gave an affectionate tap on Miles's shoulder. "Let's keep our eyes and ears open. You guys might know what's going on before anyone else."

"Hold still, Miss St. James," Peony squeaked as Gara struggled against her assistant's cleaning attempt.

"My chest is very ticklish," she complained. "Roderigo always took advantage of that when we were married. He'd threaten to squirt my bosom with hot sauce to get me to behave! And then I would threaten to squirt him in the balls!"

"This stuff is like cement," Peony commented as she scraped off the dried facial mud from the spa debacle.

"No surprise, I'd expect Bar and Glo to use inferior products. No wonder their pores are the size of the Grand Canyon!"

"'... pores are the size of the Grand Canyon,'" Caddy repeated as he transcribed the conversation in his notebook.

"And the nerve of them, inferring that I had something to do with that fire," she complained. "Well, I shouldn't put it past them. They were always scheming behind my back to steal a part or a date from me. I'm still convinced they're the reason Miss Burns kicked me out of her acting class. That excuse Burns used, that I'd frightened Dore Schary when I snuck into his office by hiding on the bottom of that commissary cart. I was trying to get him to cast me in *The Next Voice You Hear...* as the voice of God. How was I to know a booming voice coming from under the tablecloth would give him a panic attack? But it's a good thing I kept that trick in my repertoire. It always worked with Jory!" Gara recalled fondly.

"We must talk more of you and Jory. How come he never asked you to marry him?" Caddy asked.

"Maybe he asked once when my attention was on something else. He loved to watch me eat. Barbecued ribs, frankfurters, corn on the cob, anything long and thick. Now what do you suppose that was about?" she guffawed, slapping her thigh.

"You were close for a long time, but then there was a falling out," Caddy prompted.

"Well, I had a momentary career setback or two. Plus my latest marriage wasn't doing so well. Ah well, Marlene only did so many films with Sternberg before the magic was gone. Still, Jory was my friend until his passing, *Yiskor*, God bless his soul. If people knew what he did to help me in my lowest moment," Gara whispered, tears rising in her voice.

"What? What?" a breathless Caddy urged.

"Yeah, what?" Peony, mesmerized by the story, added.

Realizing sentiment had lowered her resolve, she erected the walls again. "Oh, the usual low stuff stars go through: a bad review, losing a People's Choice Award, having to wear an ugly dress to the Golden Globes. I think I'm gonna take a bubble bath and get the rest of this goop off me."

A knock at the door interrupted her escape. Peony opened the door to an imperious Gwyda.

"Just checking to see if you need anything to which I can alert the staff. Extra towels, fresh linens, glass of cyanide."

"I think we're fine on those things," Peony squeaked.

"I want to be able to alert the staff to when you'll be vacating the premises," Gwyda pressed.

"I'm staying put as long as Pet stays. She needs me," Gara stated, her protective instincts rising.

"Brownmoor's hospitality isn't open-ended. Besides, Pet doesn't seem to need you as much as you think. She went into London to spend the day with Mina and Sophie," Gwyda said with a raised eyebrow and a hint of a malicious smirk.

"Which I'm sure has done her a world of good. Getting out of this House of Usher for a bit will probably help ease her sorrow over her father's passing," Gara responded, channeling her role as the steely matriarch in the short-lived '80s primetime soap *Unfresh Secrets*.

"Pet is always welcome at Brownmoor, as long as she wishes to stay."

"And I suppose that's a veiled remark to remind me that *I'm* overstaying my welcome? I see your attitude toward me hasn't changed in all these years. You and those descendants of yours have to accept that Laddie left me that money in his will," she spat, her iron will continuing to rise.

Gwyda's face turned several shades of granite. "That money will win you no favors. Just as it won't provide succor to the beastly wife that preceded you."

"And what am I to infer from that statement? Watch out, lest my sleeping chamber also be invaded by vengeful Englishmen trying to unplug me?"

"You can take it to mean whatever you wish. Until I have the pleasure of ridding you from my house, may I bid you, ta-ta," Gwyda spit, turning to leave.

"And may I wish you a swift ride into the arms of Morpheus yourself, your dameship," Gara pronounced, descending into a deep bow befitting a Ruritarian film epic.

"That was masterful!" Caddy gushed from the thrill of witnessing a star scene.

"That's telling her, Miss St. James! Joan Crawford couldn't have done better to the board of PepsiCo!" Peony approved, shutting the door.

Gara released a deep breath as she returned to her usual disposition. "I don't take kindly to threats to me or my daughter. That withered old vine better watch out. I wouldn't have any problem pulling up that little Miss Stinkweed by her barren roots!"

"I'd say today was a great success," Pet said with pleasure as they carried shopping bags into the house.

"Yeah, my friends are going to be so jealous of all the cool labels!" Sophie enthused.

"No one's jealous of the credit card bills," Mina said as Sophie rolled her eyes.

"I saved you money in the long run. These would have cost more back home," Sophie reasoned.

"Or I could have saved money and not spent anything," she teased in return.

"Spending your ill-gotten windfall so soon?" They turned as the somber presence of Nolan entered the great hall.

"Why don't you and Sophie bring your things upstairs, and I'll join you later," Pet suggested. A silent message, "Don't worry about me, I can handle it," passed from Pet to Mina, who understood and corralled both daughter and packages toward the immense staircase.

"Getting an early start on racing through my father's fortune?" he continued in the insulting vein.

"He was *my* father as well. And I don't need to spend his money. I have a successful career and can buy whatever I like."

"You keep thinking that. You're cut from the same cloth as your money-grubbing mother. You were never a true Bottomly."

"I *am* a Bottomly. Your sister. I never did anything to you. Hannah and Barnaby loved me. Why couldn't you?" she asked.

His face darkened and his somber mood became downright demonic. "Don't you dare mention Hannah and Barnaby to me. I've done everything to keep their good memories alive in ways you can't imagine. They were my brother and sister, and you have no claim on them, nor on me, nor my father," he thundered.

Despite the momentary shock of his outburst, Pet would not back down. "Hannah and Barnaby were my family, too, and they loved me like you never could."

"They didn't care about you. You never knew them, *really* knew the truth about them the way I did. Your mother filled your head with all kinds of fiction, like the name of your father."

"This is useless. It's clear he was my father, too. I'd even agree to a DNA test if I thought that would satisfy you. But you can't be satisfied. You've spent your whole life being miserable; you can't stand to see anyone else enjoy whatever it is you've missed."

"I haven't missed anything. The only thing that'll make me happy is to see you and Gara out of here, the sooner the better."

He turned to leave, and his attempt to have the last word infuriated Pet past the point of decorum. "If that's what it'll take, then you can bet I'm going to stay here as long as I like, and so is my mother. So just get used to it, you wretched, motherfucking wanker!" she shrieked, the Brit in her rising to the surface.

The words echoed in the great hall, and the faces on the portrait collection of Bottomlys and Fotheringays seemed to blanch in response to the heated language. Then Mrs. Dutton poked her head out from the archway to the dining room where she has been polishing silver.

"I daresay, Miss Pet, your ancestors might be flabbergasted by such language," she said gently.

"I'm sorry, Mrs. Dutton, I didn't mean to offend you," a chastened Pet responded.

Mrs. Dutton shook her head and tut-tutted. "I'm not offended, dear. But if I may say so myself, I'm just wondering what took you so long to tell the old wanker off!"

Dinner was a chilly affair that night, with few words exchanged between the warring factions. Barbara and Gloria glowered at Gara, who shot angry glances at Gwyda. Pet and Nolan refused to look at each other, both filled with ire over the argument. Archie's children and their spouses directed disapproving stares at Binky, Babs, and Didums. On the positive side, the teens exchanged conspiratorial smiles with the bigger Hollywood kids. Albert gave an impish wink to Mina.

After dinner, they dispersed to their various claques and lairs. Some adjourned to their private suites, but a few lingered downstairs.

Gara settled down in the lounge, Peony and Caddy at the ready for anything she might require. The fight with Nolan had rattled Pet enough that joining her mother for companionship seemed a sensible idea. Mina and Albert joined her as additional support, not unlike faithful Thelma Ritter to any number of screen employers.

"Did you enjoy your shopping today?" Gara inquired. "I haven't shopped in London in ages. Actually, I haven't shopped for clothes in forever. I tend to run between sizes, you know."

"Smack dab between an eighteen and a thirty," Barbara declared as she and Gloria entered and left in the blink of an eye.

"What's that she said? I still look thirty? How sweet. I guess they feel guilty over starting that fight earlier," Gara beamed, hearing what she wanted to hear. "Now what was I saying? Oh yes, shopping. That reminds me, Bertie, what about my portrait? Did you have it taken care of yet?"

"I had it delivered today to my restorer. You understand it will take some time to repair the canvas," Albert indulged.

"Everything takes longer these days," she nodded. "Back in the old days, we got it done lickety-split. I'd be working on two films at the same time back. We worked ten hours or more a day, six days a week. You name it, Ma had me doing it.

"But she didn't force me to do anything I didn't want to do," Gara defended. "Sure, she pushed me to be the best, but that's what I wanted, too. From the time I was a tot, I wanted to be a star. And I became one! Can you imagine what it's like to have millions of little girls dressed just like you with the same hairstyle?"

"How tragic that you've kept that same dreadful hairdo all these years," Gwyda said as she appeared at the door.

"I'm not in the mood for you," Gara spat.

"I'm checking that the doors and windows are secured. It's my nightly ritual," Gwyda sniffed.

"Is that before or after your other ritual, the one where you rise from your coffin to steal the blood of the living?" Gara guffawed.

Gwyda turned and opened her mouth, readying a scathing retort. But she closed her lips, allowing an amused smirk to spread. "If you stay here long enough, perhaps you'll find out for yourself." She turned and stalked out.

Gwyda's cryptic threat had cast a pall on the room, which remained quiet for a few uncomfortable moments. "Perhaps it's time to turn in," Albert spoke, breaking the uneasy silence.

The others followed suit and they traipsed up the grand staircase, separating on the landing to their various domains.

"That woman was just awful to be so mean to you," Peony sympathized as they made their way down the hall.

"She doesn't scare me. She's a million years old and she's only got one arm. How much trouble could she cause?" Gara reasoned.

Peony rushed forward to open the suite's door in preparation for her boss's entrance. One of Gara's fluffy marabou-trimmed mules skidded on the carpet as she dragged her feet, a habit from years of stubborn galumphs instead of graceful strides (as prescribed by Miss Burns).

"Peony, my shoe!" she bellowed as she caught herself, with Caddy's assistance, from falling. Peony's hand left the doorknob as she rushed to her boss's aid. The door swung open as they helped steady Gara.

A creaking noise caught their attention. An ax swung from the top of the doorframe, slicing through the air and imbedding itself in the heavy oak door.

"What the hell?" Gara bellowed.

"What just happened?" a frightened Peony cried.

Despite the shock, Caddy was not at a loss for words. "I thought the only battle-ax we had to worry about was that old dame!"

STRANGE INTERLUDE 7

That's not a waiter, that's a lord.

Army Archerd's column, February 7, 1960

Tales of childbirth and romance (not necessarily in that order!) abound in today's column. Barbara Lamont, now onscreen in the noir thriller *Touch of the Brute* with Jack Palance, gave birth to a girl yesterday in Los Angeles. Married almost a year to jewelry magnate Cyril Lamont, Barbara bubbled about the birth to me via phone.

"Barbara Jr. started making her presence known before midnight, but didn't appear until 6:30. That's a movie star baby for you, announce the arrival and then keep 'em waiting!"

As for naming the child after herself, she said, "Cyril and I had decided if it was a boy, we would name him Cyril Jr., so I said if it was a girl, she should be Barbara Jr. After all, Alice Faye and Nancy Sinatra named daughters after themselves. It's a star tradition. We'll call her Babs."

Flowers and gifts from fans and friends have filled her room since morning. "Bahamia sent a lovely arrangement of lilies and roses, Gara sent a supply of diapers, and Gloria sewed and embroidered a christening gown! Isn't that darling?"

Barbara's friends also figure in today's column. Bahamia is appearing at the Mocambo in a musical extravaganza, dancing and singing calypso in a tribute to her Caribbean birthplace. It's unfortunate that movie offers dried up after her interview in the Negro press last year. What does it matter that her heritage encompasses Africa as well as Latin America? If you're in Los Angeles, do yourself a favor and rush down to the Mocambo to see a star in action!

Gloria Prescott is in New York, applauding the latest play by her new beau, the eccentric Irish playwright Tristan Musgrave. Known for avant garde theatrics like *Adam's Apple* and *The Sensuous Inquisition*, Musgrave's newest effort, *Sweet Nectar of Adonis*, premiered at an off-Broadway venue three nights ago to enthusiastic audiences of a certain persuasion. The tale of a swishy Greek shepherd who seeks immortality by partaking of the aforementioned Olympian refreshment wouldn't appeal to a broad audience of normal sensibilities, but the lavender community loved it.

Gloria has been seen with Musgrave at the smartest Manhattan nightspots. "Tristy is a brilliant writer, with all that symbolism and metaphors. I don't get it all, but it looks lovely, and *that* I understand," Gloria enthused. "Plus, those boys in the audience love me and my movies, too!"

Gloria hinted that marriage may be around the corner. "Marriage must take place between equals, both in romance and in the creative fields. Tristy just adores me. He even helps select my attire for dining and theater-going. Now, I ask you, if that isn't devotion, what is?"

Which brings us to Barbara's third friend, Gara St. James, who's in the thick of romance herself. It was a month ago that she met Lord Lindale Bottomly, known to intimates as "Laddie," and already they've become inseparable. A former member of England's House of Lords before scandal forced him to resign, Laddie was once married to Myrtle Dempster, Barbara Lamont's mother and manager. (See how neatly this story folds in on itself?)

And we also make a return of sorts to Bahamia's Caribbean, specifically to Barbados. Claudette Colbert was hosting a holiday gathering at her vacation home with the crème of Hollywood and international society.

Cary Grant and wife Betsy Drake laughed at a joke told by Irene Dunne's husband while Peter O'Toole shared a drink at the bar with Alan Bates and Richard Harris. The men contemplated the feminine wiles of a trio of sirens (the luscious Italian Virna Lisi, the British beauty Joan Collins, and the exotic Algerian fashion model Ysabel Fanon) across the room, while the ladies were more interested in comparing makeup tips.

Elsa Maxwell was also in attendance and witnessed the event which brought about Gara and Laddie's meeting. "Gara saw Laddie across a crowded room and mistook him for a waiter," tittered Elsa. "She shouted, 'Oh, waiter!' to which Claudette replied, 'That's not a waiter, that's a lord.'

"'Jesus Christ!' Gara shrieked. 'You gentiles kill me. To whom do you have to pray to get a drink around here?'"

Elsa instigated a proper introduction, and the much older lord and the actress spent the rest of the evening together. "They were quite taken with each other. I wouldn't have thought of it myself, but I didn't understand his attraction to Myrtle, either. Ah well, they say love is blind, and isn't that what really matters?"

American Movie Classics Schedule, October 31, 1994
Spotlight on Halloween Horror

6:00 P.M. EST - *They Came to Eat Us* (American International Pictures, 1959) Directed by Roger Corman. Starring James Darren, Gloria Prescott, Dave Willock, Luana Anders, Michael Carr, Sam Jaffe, Carolyn Hughes, Dick York. Space travelers make contact with distant planet, whose inhabitants are receptive to overtures of intergalactic friendship. They unwittingly lead the aliens back to Earth where the truth is revealed; their human visages are disguises for their horrifying true forms which feast on human flesh. Darren makes an appealing hero and Gloria screams prettily, for what it's worth. Director and producer Corman indulged his taste for garish special effects. Most famous scene, the banquet where the invaders feast on human hors d'ouevres and starlet tartare while the terrified prisoners watch, is sure to cause terror and nausea!

7:45 P.M. EST - *Of Inhuman Frondage* (Hammer Films, 1960) Directed by Terence Fisher. Starring Peter Cushing, Barbara Lamont, Paul Massie, Martita Hunt, Francis De Woolf, Percy Cartwright, David Oxley, Mona Washbourne. Loose retelling of Maugham's classic tale spiced with a gothic horror atmosphere almost works. Lamont not bad as the slattern barmaid who enslaves Massie's weak-willed scientist, whose family harbors a dreadful secret. Just when Barbara thinks she's snared a financial jackpot by marrying Paul, she learns the horrifying truth: the family's men are infected with a generation-skipping genetic mutation, causing them to turn into vicious, man-eating vegetation during the biannual solstices. Before becoming dinner for Cushing disguised as an overgrown weed, Barbara grabs a fast-acting herbicide which kills a visibly mortified Cushing. Camp classic scene: Washbourne exclaims, "I say, that's the largest dandelion I've ever seen!" just before becoming plant food!

9:30 P.M. EST - *Bride of the Golem* (Kibbutz Films, 1960) Directed by Myron Elanbaum. Starring Zero Mostel, Gara St. James, Larry Blyden, Shelley Berman, Molly Picon, Andrew Sachs, Alfie Bass, Robert Clary. Kibbutz Films, an attempt by Jewish filmmakers to utilize their own cultural talent, made only eight films in its short time. *Bride of the Golem*, although the most profitable for the company, is perhaps its nadir in terms of quality. The sinister quality which made the previous year's *The Golem* a horror classic is absent from this sequel, and perhaps it was a mistake to utilize so many comic actors (which may account for its boffo box office). Despite this, the major problem appears to be St. James in the title role. The bride's first appearance is silly rather than chilling when Gara trips on her garment of muslin wrappings and blurts, "Oy! That *faigelah* dressmaker screwed up!"

Excerpt from *Hollywood's Love Affair With Love : Th e Great Romances of the*

Movie Stars by Cecelia Parkington

As the studio system crumbled in the '50s, the studios's power to force actors into factory-sanctioned romances weakened, as well as their ability to put the kibosh on players being seen in public with inappropriate companions.

But romance remained an important component of the publicity relationship between the factories and the media. As we'll examine later in this chapter, the biggest and most scandalous romance in film history, Elizabeth Taylor and Richard Burton, could only have flourished in the freer environment and *la dolce vita* of the '60s.

Actress Gloria Prescott tied the knot with playwright Tristan Musgrave in May of 1960, and she milked every ounce of publicity from the odd pairing. It was believed but unspoken that Musgrave was gay, so Gloria was considered a fool in many quarters. It seems obvious in hindsight that Prescott must have known of Musgrave's proclivities, considering some of her comments to the columnists. Winchell quoted Gloria as saying, "I wish we had time for a real honeymoon, but with Tristy starting a new play and me starting a new movie soon, there's only time for a quick weekend on Fire Island. I hear those private parties can be really gay!"

Romances between royalty and lesser personages, then as now, were worthy of press attention. Gara St. James became involved with Lord Lindale Bottomly, and the press ate up coverage of the older British aristocrat and the abrasive Jewish actress. During a visit to Gara's hometown, Chicago, the couple's every move was reported (and in some cases, misinterpreted) by the media. Gara's offhand remark that she was showing Laddie her old haunts somehow resulted in a column announcement that she would begin rehearsals for a revival of the Ibsen play *Ghosts*.

When asked about the rumor, the confused actress replied, "Ibsen? Never dated him. You must have mistaken my escort for some other guy. *This* is the famous Lord Bottomly of the House of 'em over in England. I'm flattered this Ibstern guy thinks I'm beautiful, but I'm a one-Lord woman now. Oy, that doesn't make me a *shiksa*, does it? Ha!"

Sheilah Graham's column, October 12, 1961

This column is via London, where I attended the wedding of actress Gara St. James and Lord Lindale Fotheringay Bottomly, which took place on the grounds of Brownmoor, the family estate in Flemshire. The autumn day was sunny and cool, perfect for the day's events.

Brownmoor was festooned with ribbons and flowers in shades of heliotrope and rust. The bridesmaids wore Empire-waisted gowns with bodices of bronze satin and floral chiffon skirts in sienna and orchid. "I think she intentionally picks colors each time that make me look horrible," Gloria Prescott commented to Barbara Lamont and Bahamia.

After her little joke, Gloria told me about the recent birth of her son, Didley Montenegro Musgrave. "He was too young to travel with us, but he's safe with his *abuelita* taking care of him and my dear goddaughter, Barbara's little Babs."

When asked why her mother (and the English groom's previous wife), Myrtle Dempster, wasn't watching Babs, Barbara replied, "Mother has too many business endeavors to keep up with a tiny tot. Besides, there's a good chance I'd come home to find Babs on a burlesque stage doing a Lily St. Cyr routine!" (an amusing reference to Barbara's vaudeville beginnings).

Gara's handsome brother Ron made quite an impression. It's been mentioned that Ron resembles Bob Mitchum, and in a tux, that resemblance might cause one to swoon! But this beefcake has his own cheesecake, his lovely wife, Margaret, who resembles an even prettier Deborah Kerr, if that's possible.

Attendees in Flemshire included many of Gara's Hollywood colleagues, including Charlton Heston and his wife Lydia, Ronald and Nancy Reagan, Dick Powell and June Allyson, among others. Members of Britain's acting community (represented by Laurence Harvey, Peter Finch, Rex Harrison, Margaret Leighton, Stewart Granger, and Rachel Roberts) were in attendance, as well as aristocracy and politicians, such as the Countess of Hornsbie, the Earl of Wimpleham, and Lord Barrington Mayfair.

The groom's sister, Gwyda Glasscock, was a gracious hostess, in spite of her infirmity, the loss of an arm after an altercation last year with a bear in pursuit of her zoological studies. A celebrated photo, which gained worldwide attention, left no doubt as to the victor in the showdown between animal and woman. I imagine Gwyda would do just fine swinging through the jungles of Hollywood!

The ceremony began and Gara finally appeared, wearing a reproduction of a gown once worn by a Bottomly ancestor, the Countess Elspeth of Buxley. The dress was made of heavy ivory satin and swathed in cinnamon chiffon velvet fleurchons and jewels in a tri-petal floral pattern. The huge skirt took up the entire width of the aisle. (Her brother Ron had to walk behind her as he gave her away.) An over-sized ruff of pleated net and linen encircled Gara's neck, and the veil was attached to an ornate tiara of diamonds and garnets once owned by the countess.

"Finally my little girl is a real lady," Mrs. St. James sobbed into her handkerchief. "I always trained her to behave as one, even if she had to elbow Jane Withers out of a two-shot or steal Ty Powers's key light. But now everyone's going to know what a hell of a lady my Gara is!"

The newlyweds left for a honeymoon on the Continent, where they'll tour Paris, Lucerne, Venice, and Athens. May I add a hearty *"Mazel Tov!"* to the happy couple!

Excerpt from *They Said What? The Unpublished Quotes Celebrities Said Off-The-Record (Until Now!) Over the Years to Life Magazine* by Angela Theroux and Sage Mallick

Dena St. James: Those jealous ex-roommates said marrying a lord couldn't make my Gara a lady. Like they had room to talk. I don't want to rehash old rumors, but we all know Barbara and Gloria calling their early careers "night modeling" is a bunch of hooey. And that Bahamas girl, trying to pass herself off as white. I always had my suspicions about her, 'cause she'd always eat the watermelon first when I served fruit salad at parties.

Gloria Prescott: People say I must have known Tristan [Musgrave] was gay, or bi or whatever. He wasn't gay with me. He'd be near the top if I ranked my lovers, right between Aldo Ray and Rosey Grier. He first introduced me to the idea of wearing costumes to spice up nighttime play. Sailor costume, cop uniform, Indian headdress, leather chaps, I wore 'em all.

Mitzi Gaynor: People think I had some kind of running feud with Barbara Lamont. Nothing could be further from the truth. I hardly know her. After all, I'm an enormous musical-comedy star, and she's not. I guess she can almost carry a tune and do a step or two, but she was no competition for me. And while I can still perform a complicated Cincinnati time-step, she can barely put one foot in front of the other. I suspect she's got brittle bone disease.

Ron Schmerkin: My sister [Gara St. James] has her faults. And those flaws became worse in Hollywood. They'll look the other way if a monster ran amok, as long as he made them money. I was even offered a screen test to become a second Robert Mitchum, but that was a sacrifice I couldn't make. I'd already allowed them to turn my sister into a horrific creature attacking a small Japanese city.

Zsa Zsa Gabor: Dahlinks, I didn't understand these girls who sacrificed everyzhing for a good-looking man. The vurthless bastards! If he can't get you diamonds and fur coats, he isn't vurth the trouble. I vas always telling Gloria Prescott, "Dahlink, zhat man can't provide you vith jewelry and minks, I don't care how good he looks in a Speedo! A bulging svimsuit von't get you squat at Cartier!"

Bahamia: You'd be shocked if I told you the names of stars who shunned me after that magazine interview. And you may ask, that bitch who loves to call me her "best friend," what did she have to say? She told me she didn't quite understand these racial stories about me because I didn't *sound* black!

Doña Sobrina De Assis: Gara got me fired from an episode of *Gunsmoke* we were both doing just because my costume was prettier! You do know she forced me and my husband out of our new house because she wanted it for herself, don't you? What some people will do for a Malibu address! And the story about that fist fight Gara had with Karen Black in the powder room of the Trocadero? Poor Karen's eye was never the same afterward.

Dorothy Kilgallen: Many celebrities took physical defects and turned them into a positive. Frank Sinatra called me a "chinless wonder", but did I wear veils and high collars to hide it? No, I stuck it out, such as it is, and kept going forward. Look at Gara St. James with those zaftig hips. She got bigger dresses and had bigger sets made so she'd look petite. And Gloria Prescott practically kept the waxers in business with that moustache and other hairy regions. My heavens, it was like Mighty Joe Young in a backless dress!

Myrtle Dempster: Of my two girls, Athole was the one with more natural star quality. "Dainty Athole and Her Little Sailors" was a huge draw in vaudeville, but that girl developed like you wouldn't believe. I had to put her in a cast iron bra and girdle when she was eight! By the time she hit thirteen, we couldn't get away with calling her "Dainty" anymore, and Barbara had developed far too well herself. Burlesque and a stripping sister act was the ticket. And none of that fake Gypsy Rose Lee shit. I told 'em, "God gave you that cooter and those tits for a reason, so throw 'em out there and get some bucks in return."

Excerpt from *They Put That on TV? The Weirdest Programming That Ever Showed Up on Television* by Paul Stevens and Richard Anthony

My Favorite Divorce (1962-63, NBC, 11 episodes). Cast: Barbara Lamont (Barbara Sawyer), David Bruce (Mark Davis), Jimmy Lydon (Tom Finn), Jeff York (Jeff Truman), Sue Ann Langdon (Tina Barnum), Bea Benaderet (Cousin Abigail), Jerry Colonna (Uncle Boniface).

Lamont juggles ex-husbands Bruce and York, steady beau Lydon, and wacky business partner Langdon as she tries to scale the heights of Manhattan society as a party planner. With sharp scripts, the unusual concept might have worked, but this show came from the hit-or-mostly-miss writing team of Mickey Stepp and Eddie Fetschik, which had previously produced the leaden comedy *Mrs. Kringle & the Graven Image* and the failed variety show *Kelloggs Presents the Magda Gabor Hour*.

Barbara has chemistry with her male costars and isn't afraid to embrace the slapstick plots. Her clueless reactions reveal a genuine comic skill. Benaderet a plus as starchy Cousin Abigail, as is Jerry Colonna as swingin' Uncle Boniface. Legend has it that in the infamous Christmas episode, a drunken Colonna, dressed as Santa, exposed Lamont to "The North Pole" just out of camera range! Barbara's stunned adlib, "It's uncut!" is said to have made the air on its initial airing after Lamont insisted she said, "It's Uncle!" However, that particular scene has always been trimmed (pun intended) in rare syndication, so it's never been determined if the urban legend is true.

Fox Movie Channel Schedule, February 27, 2001
Spotlight on British Films

1:00 P.M. EST - *The Harlot Bride* (Pinewood Studios, 1960) Directed by Hugo Fregonese. Starring Robert Wagner, Barbara Lamont, Gloria Prescott, Anthony Steel, Bryan Forbes, Horst Buchholz, Malcolm Pembrooke, Peter Illing. Henry VIII, Catherine of Aragon, and Anne Boleyn do not enthrall in this tepid film. Wagner an odd choice for the king, having none of the bombastic spirit required by the role. He's overshadowed by his female costars competing for who can chew the most scenery. Prescott's role is less showy than Lamont's, but she manages to turn lighting candles and praying to the saints an excuse for *sturm und drang*. Lamont insisted on "authenticity" by asking costume designers to sew an extra breastform into her gowns, requesting makeup artists glue an extra finger on each hand, and asking for a scene where she gets to cast spells around a cauldron (despite historians's dismissal of such bizarre allegations against Boleyn).

3:00 P.M. EST - *Tally Ho, Lord and Lady Kettle!* (British Lion Films, 1961) Directed by Roy Boulting. Starring Hope Emerson, Charles Lane, Ian Carmichael, Cecil Parker, Joan Hickson, Liz Fraser, David Lodge, La Staggée. A late entry in the *Ma and Pa Kettle* series; indeed, some filmographies don't consider it part of the official series, since neither Marjorie Main nor Percy Kilbride, who played Pa Kettle for most of the film series (Parker Fennelly played Pa in the penultimate film *The Kettles on Old MacDonald's Farm*), agreed to appear in the new film (Charles Lane, known for playing humorless skinflints in dozens of screwball comedies, took over as Pa; Hope Emerson, a tall, large-framed actress known as a screen heavy, had her final screen role as Ma). But this film is better than its reputation suggests. The premise, that Pa Kettle has inherited a Lordship upon the death of a distant

English relative, offers some funny "fish out of water" situations that were hallmarks of the series, especially at a *de rigueur* royal ball sequence. Bahamia's fans were pleased by her specialty dance in a party sequence in her first film after being blackballed by Hollywood a few years prior. Funniest sequence: Emerson making a spectacle of herself, fumbling with binoculars at the opera, where classical diva La Staggée makes a rare film appearance; the displeased look on her face when Emerson yelps, "I thought people spoke English here, too!" is priceless.

5:00 P.M. EST - *Nightshade* (MGM-British Studios, 1961) Directed by Alfred Hitchcock. Starring Richard Harris, Gara St. James, Leo G. Carroll, Timima Bossi, John Williams, Ian Hunter, Stringer Davis, Francesca Annis. One of Hitchcock's lesser efforts and a bit of a disappointment, coming between *Psycho* and *The Birds*. Harris good as the man caught in the wrong place at the wrong time, embroiled in a plot to kill a high-ranking member of the House of Lords to ensure a complicated financial scheme. St. James a poor substitute for Hitch's usual icy blondes. (Was it a bad bleach job or poor lighting that resulted in hair the color of Listerine?) Her attempt at a classy British accent falls somewhere between Claire Bloom and Lainie Kazan. Hitchcock said, "I wanted a beautiful blank slate for the part, but I didn't think I'd end up with someone who erased the chalkboard herself!" Bossi has a memorable turn as a sexy florist murdered in an unusual manner (stabbed in the heart with a rare spiny cactus coated with the title poison).

Earl Wilson's column, November 19, 1962

I'm pleased to report that Gara St. James and Lord Lindale Bottomly welcomed a baby girl two days ago. The couple has enjoyed a year-long honeymoon around Europe and Northern Africa, finally settling in a little French village after announcing their impending parenthood.

The happy couple had previously made appearances in the society press, but became incognito when they opted for the bohemian lifestyle. They remained in the chateau during the final months of Gara's pregnancy, with only a Negro housekeeper for company. The desire for privacy was somewhat unusual for Gara, who never met a publicity angle she didn't like.

It was a home birth with only her husband and the housekeeper to assist the delivery, which went smoothly. (I guess that housekeeper did windows *and* midwifery!) Laddie is pleased as punch to be a father again. (He has three adult children from his first marriage.)

They've named the girl Petal Denima. ("Petal" comes from a design element in Gara's wedding gown; she says the three petals are symbols of her, Laddie, and their precious baby. "Denima" is a combination of the names of the baby's grandmothers, Dena for Gara's mother and Jemima for Laddie's.)

We wish happiness for the new family and look forward to the first pictures of the bundle of joy.

Speaking of pictures, everyone's been raving over *Paris Match* photos of a stunning Bahamia in Yves Saint Laurent fashions. She's been the toast of Paris, appearing at Chez Régine in a singing and dancing showcase, following in the footsteps of other American Negro performers like Eartha Kitt and Josephine Premice.

Her fashion success came about when Yves attended her show. With Saint Laurent's favorite model, the exotic Ysabel Fanon, a no-show at recent events, he invited the American star to pose in his garments, which resulted in ooh-la-la!

I'm happy that Bahamia has garnered acclaim in Europe, but nothing would make me happier than a triumphant return to the United States. Any producers in need of an exotic and talented actress, singer, and dancer, give this lady a call!

A star who'll have to pass on any calls is Barbara Lamont. She recently made the leap to television by starring in a comedy series, the wacky *My Favorite Divorce*. "Other glamorous stars have been successful on TV, like Lucille Ball, Loretta Young, and Ann Sothern. The screen is smaller, but the glamour can be just as big as in Cinemascope!" Barbara declared.

The show is now on hiatus with the announcement that Barbara is expecting another bundle of joy. "They thought it wouldn't look right since my character, though twice divorced and with a steady boyfriend, was unmarried. Personally, I thought it might reach a whole new audience!"

She already has a girl and is hoping for a boy. "A little brother would be perfect for Babs, and he'd be an adorable playmate for my godson." Barbara's referring to Didley Musgrave, the son of her best friend, fellow actress Gloria Prescott. "I never can wrap my mouth around 'Didley.' My Babs calls him Didums. Perhaps a little undignified, but rather sweet, don't you think? Anyway, who cares about dignity when you're getting press coverage?"

Truer words were never spoken!

CHAPTER 8

We're all aware you're a big queen, but take off that crown!

"So that's where the ax came from," Mina said, examining the empty space on the great hall's wall, otherwise covered with ancient weapons.

"I don't think Aunt Gwyda can dismiss that as easily as she dismissed the unplugging of Mrs. Dempster," Pet observed. The empty space was within easy reach from the staircase, so anyone could have removed the ax.

"I can't dismiss it, either. I'm concerned about safety, especially for the kids."

"But, Mom, this is the coolest thing to happen yet!" Sophie protested, resisting the thought of leaving the scene of so much action.

"Cool or not, your safety is the most important thing to me," Mina insisted.

"I wish Momsy were as concerned as you. She believes it's just a ploy to scare her off from Brownmoor and the inheritance. She doesn't think that ax could have done her any damage. She said, 'Big deal, that door's made of oak. *I'm* indestructible!'"

"That may well be, but this has got me worried, too," Albert said as he joined them on the landing. "Aunt Gwyda thinks Gara staged it herself to get sympathy, but I'm not buying that."

"Neither am I. This is making me uncomfortable."

"Not that this will really make you feel better, but I don't think anyone else is in danger here. After all, Myrtle and Gara are the targets of the animosity," Albert surmised.

Remembering her argument with Nolan, Pet mused, "I'm not the most popular person around here myself."

"Dad can be as charming as Boris Karloff in a mad scientist's lab, but I don't think you have to worry about a tire iron to the head anytime soon," Albert tried humor to diffuse the situation. "Everyone's too focused on Laddie's ex-wives. They're interlopers in the eye of whoever's doing these things."

"See, Mom, no one's going to do anything to me," Sophie said confidently.

"Don't speak so fast, it might be *me* doing something to you," Mina threatened lightly with a touch of *Mommie Dearest*.

"And think about this: The entire thing had to be planned out. Unplugging Mrs. Dempster may have been a spur of the moment choice, but whoever set up that ax had to plan it, then escape by the balcony to the room next door," Albert said.

"I hadn't thought about that," Pet gasped. "How am I going to convince Momsy her life might be in danger?" Gara might well be one of the two surviving ex-Mrs. Laddie Bottomlys, but Pet didn't have experience keeping her mother from becoming one of *The Two Mrs. Carrolls*.

At that moment, Henry and Miles rounded the corner of the landing. They blurted greetings, then asked, "Um, Sophie, you doing anything this morning?"

Mina sighed and chuckled at her daughter's expectant face. "Go ahead, and try not to get into any trouble. Remember, just the act of opening a door has become dangerous."

"Don't be silly, no one's in any danger," Gwyda insisted to the others in the study.

"Grandmum, someone rigged an ax to fall on that Gara's neck. It didn't jump up there on its own," Willis snapped.

"Don't be rude to your grandmother," Archie scolded. "However, Willis has a point. *Someone* set that ax in place –"

"And I'm certain that someone is Gara herself, no doubt for sympathy or publicity," Gwyda reasoned.

"That seems rather beyond the mental capabilities of that stupid bint," Nolan remarked.

"If not her, than one of those fools who work for her, that bubble-headed pipsqueak or that dunce waving his pen about," Gwyda said.

"Maybe even that daughter of hers," Nolan added.

"I hardly think Pet would do something like that," Archie interjected. "But after that unplugging incident with Myrtle Dempster and now this, I'm beginning to wonder just what's going on in this house."

""And what's to stop something else from happening? Another weapon might fall on my baby Chester," Carolyn whined.

"Don't give me any ideas, Carolyn," Gwyda disdained.

"Did the servants see anything?"

"No, nothing. Mrs. Dutton was with me when I questioned the staff, weren't you, Mrs. Dutton?" Gwyda asked as the housekeeper set down a tray in front of her employer.

"Indeed, madam. No one saw or heard anything strange." She hesitated before continuing. "If I'm not being too forward, I don't believe Miss St. James was responsible. Emma was in the hallway when Miss St. James left her room with her companions to come downstairs for dinner, and she didn't return upstairs until the incident occurred with the ax."

"That hardly seems conclusive," Archie commented.

"Still, it does seem likely someone else planted that weapon," Willis mused aloud.

"I'm not convinced she's blameless," Gwyda replied. "However, I suggest everyone keep their eyes open and be aware of what's going on around them. Mrs. Dutton, please alert the staff to be on guard for any suspicious behavior."

"With some of the characters staying at Brownmoor, 'suspicious behavior' might be a tad difficult to qualify," Nolan snorted.

"Are you sure this is the correct position?" Gloria asked.

"Yes, I'm sure. I've been in this position hundreds of times," Barbara replied.

"I know, but we're talking about actual exercise this time, not the bedroom variety," Gloria panted as she tried to maintain her stance.

"I can do Joey's workout with my eyes closed. Anyway, I wasn't sure if British DVD players would recognize American discs so I didn't bring it. You know, I never was able to see those 'art films' Binky made in Amsterdam because of that European coding."

"As if we need your eyebrows racing up that high. You'd end up looking like Priscilla Presley." Gloria wobbled awkwardly. "I think I'm having problems keeping steady because of my long, model-like legs."

"More likely you're having a problem being steady because of those vodka tonics last night." Barbara broke position and placed her hands on Gloria's hips. "Here, keep your hips forward with your legs slightly bent."

"I know it's hard to find a man in your golden years, but that shouldn't be an excuse to go lezzie on us!" Gara bellowed from the doorway.

Barbara dropped her hands. "As if anyone would believe that. I could tell you stories of the many, *many* men I've known in the Biblical sense."

"And that's not mentioning the made-up stories she sold to the press herself for publicity," Gloria huffed as she broke rank and stretched her legs.

"We all need a little extra cash now and then," Barbara defended. "Those residuals from my old sitcom don't roll in like they do for Marlo Thomas or Patty Duke."

"And marrying rich doesn't always work either, lest I end up with another scandal in my own *casa*," Gloria remarked.

"Dear, it's a wonder you're still able to tend to your bougainvillea. One would think you'd be terrified of gardening implements after those deaths in your greenhouse."

"We all have to rise above tragedy. It got me the covers of more tabloids than I'd like to remember, not to mention a starring role in that mini-series. So I win, and so do millions of TV viewers."

"We should all have such problems," Barbara praised.

"A better problem to have than excessive cellulite on your thighs," Gara noted.

"That's not cellulite, I was sitting in a wicker chair. Anyway, stop looking at my legs, and take a look at your ass," Barbara protested. "If anyone needs exercise, it's you."

"Yes, stop picking arguments and start exercising. Get that heart rate up and moving," Gloria agreed.

"I'd say she's already got it up. Imagine, narrowly missing death by a falling ax."

"Aw, one of those fools must have left their crap lying around and didn't pick it up," Gara said as she fell in line.

"You can't believe that. Who accidentally leaves an ax balanced on the casing to fall when the door opens?"

"How am I supposed to know? I lived here years ago, but I can't be expected to remember all those weird British customs," Gara huffed as she attempted to stretch.

"Even you can't be that naïve. Someone was trying to send you a message," Gloria urged.

"Some message, even e-mail doesn't slice off your head," Barbara observed. "To quote Whoopi Goldberg in *Ghost*, 'You in danger, girl!'"

"I'm not in any danger. What about your mother? Didn't someone unplug her life support?"

"Big deal, that couldn't kill her. Believe me, I've wondered about that," Barbara added as an aside. "Besides, they've forgotten about her, and are after you now. And an ax aimed at your head is a little hard to ignore."

"I'm not going to let these British jerks scare me out of my inheritance. I played a circus performer years ago in *Murder Under The Big Top* and dodged an actual tomahawk from the knife thrower in my big scene.

Mervyn LeRoy insisted on realism, you know. I can face down anything they try."

"Well, Gara, I've always said, you have the stout-hearted will of a water buffalo."

"Now, that's one of the nicer things you've said to me over the years!"

"Just how many attics does this place have?" Sophie asked as she picked her way around a mahogany bedframe and a giant floor lamp.

"More than one person can go through in a day, but not enough to store all the skeletons," Miles quipped as he looked through the contents of an open box.

"So why are doing this again?"

"With everyone worried about the ax, this is a good opportunity for us to snoop," Henry admitted. "The only time we ever find out anything is when they're not paying attention. Who knows what we might find?"

Sophie surveyed the room, dusty and stuffed to the gills with boxes, discarded paintings in peeling frames, strange glassware, and musical instruments out of tune. It looked like the *Antiques Roadshow* reject room. She leaned against a dilapidated spinet and ran her fingers across the broken strings of an oversized harp. "If we can find anything in here. Don't you Brits ever throw anything away?"

"Probably not. Anyway, the good stuff is bound to be in one of the boxes."

"What are you kids up to?" a voice came from the doorway.

"Geez, now we'll get it," Miles muttered, closing the open box.

"Relax, it's just us," Babs said as she pushed open the door, with Binky and Didums bringing up the rear. "We saw you guys on a mission and thought we'd get in on the fun."

The kids explained they were just taking advantage of the family's distraction to snoop in the attics. "You never know what we might find."

"Like that cigarette holder, which set off a round of accusations. Who knows, we might find out what's going on with the unpluggings and boobytraps going on around here," Babs surmised.

"You and that writer's imagination," Binky scoffed.

"You don't think it's odd that someone rigged an ax to try and off Gara?" Didums asked.

"Well, sure that's odd. But admit it, who hasn't met Gara and wanted to off her?"

"Not funny," Sophie protested.

"No, that wasn't funny." Babs gave her brother a piercing look and put her arm around Sophie's shoulder. "He didn't mean anything by that."

"I know she rubs people the wrong way, but I don't like the idea of anyone trying to hurt her."

"Why don't we look through some of these boxes. Maybe we'll find something interesting," Henry said, hoping to dispel the mood.

"Don't mind me, Soph, sometimes I speak before I think," Binky apologized.

"Not his first time being premature," Didums snarked.

"Oh, like you would know," Binky rolled his eyes.

"What's in this box?"

Babs looked over Miles's shoulder as he reopened the box at his side. "Looks like ... old farm records, charity papers, legal documents," Babs catalogued aloud.

"Nothing interesting. More of the same in these," Henry added.

"Ooh, now *this* is my kind of box!" Binky exclaimed.

They turned to see Binky wearing a jeweled crown and preening in front of an enormous tarnished mirror. "Leave it to you to find something sparkly and shiny amid all the dust," Babs observed. "Where did you find that?"

"In that box, behind this fabulous mirror. Do you think we can get a couple of those hunky footmen around here to bring it down to my room?"

"I recognize that crown!" Miles blurted. "The Countess of Buxley's diamond and garnet tiara!"

"The one Gara wore when she married Laddie. And everyone thought she took it with her," Henry said.

"Grant-Gran always fumed about that. 'Imagine, a tiara that graced the head of royalty now glued to the head of a graceless rhino.'"

"I wonder how it ended up in this box."

"Got packed away accidentally?" Didums theorized.

"Anything else in there related to Gara?"

"Maybe. Magazines, *Harper's Bazaar*, *Marie Claire*. Some publicity photos, some other pictures ... Is this how Brownmoor looked before the fire?" Sophie asked, displaying a photograph.

Henry looked over her shoulder. "I guess. Yeah, that must be the old wing and the tower."

"Interesting. These other pictures don't look familiar."

"Did you look at these papers?" Didums asked, glancing at the pages. "I think this is some kind of official report about the fire."

They decided to take the box downstairs before examining its contents further. "Umm, Binky?" Babs asked with a sing-song lilt.

"Yes?"

"We're all aware you're a big queen, but take off that crown!"

"Back where it finally belongs," Gwyda pronounced as she held the crown, turning it to let the light hit the jewels.

"Back? It never left, isn't that correct?" Caddy interjected as he scribbled in his notebook and, with his other hand, tried to steady his camera phone to snap a photo of the fabled diadem.

Gwyda scowled at the little man, sending a shiver down his spine. "The maids accidentally packed it away, no doubt, when they cleaned out that cow's room when she left Brownmoor."

"Moo!" Gara bellowed in defiance of the insult. "I told you I didn't take that crown when I left, but you didn't believe me."

An exasperated Gwyda sighed with the force of a leaf blower. "It was perfectly reasonable of me to think you'd taken it. You wore it on your wedding day and posed with it in that putrid portrait. You seemed rather attached to it."

"It looked fabulous on me, like my head had been made for it," Gara recalled with pride.

"The countess didn't lose her head to the guillotine, but in your case, we could make an exception," Nolan sneered.

"That's the heartless attitude I'd expect from you awful foreigners. I told you people I didn't take it. Did you have to have Scotland Yard accost me at Heathrow when I was flying back to New York all those years ago? It gave me bad publicity to be seen in handcuffs with those Bonnies."

"Bobbies, British constabulary are referred to as Bobbies," Caddy corrected.

"Ooh, are those British cops as dishy as the boys in blue back in the States?" Barbara wondered aloud. "I've never understood why they didn't make the uniforms snugger, especially the pants."

"Only in MGM musicals," Gloria added.

"In any case," Gwyda stated, her voice rising, "the crown has been found and can be returned to the vault, to be brought out on special occasions."

"I suppose we ought to be miffed at you kids for snooping in the attics, but –" Willis began.

"But no one's angry at you for finding something so important and valuable," Louise shot her husband a withering look for even suggesting the children were in trouble.

"In any case, it's time to get this back into the safe," Gwyda concluded. "A crown that once graced the heads of royalty shouldn't be a plaything for silly woofters prancing about."

"Don't hate just because I'm good at giving head in more ways than one," Binky pouted.

"Not in front of the little ones!" Carolyn bleated, clapping her hands over Miles's ears. He struggled to free himself from her censorship.

"Geez, I've heard worse!" he protested, struggling to get out of her grasp.

Gwyda stood and gestured. "Archie, Nolan, come with me. Let's return this to the vault."

Pet turned to Mina, who looked at the box remaining on the table. "So, one mystery solved, even if it's not the one we're worried about."

"Baby doll, there's nothing to worry about," Gara insisted. "That crown never left the house, just like I said. See, I'm never wrong! So nobody's trying to do anything to me."

"For once, she's right," insisted Cliff. "Nobody cares enough to do anything to her."

"Whatever the truth is about that, we might at least be able to use what's in this box to find out the truth about the fire all those years ago," Mina said.

"What does that have to do with what's going on here?" Louise asked.

"It may not, but this box also has papers about the police investigation. It might tell us what happened back in 1967, so people can stop placing blame."

"I object to that insinuation," Willis huffed.

"What's wrong with checking out these papers?" Albert reasoned with his cousin. "It might answer questions we've all wondered about. Where's the harm?"

Willis didn't answer, and Louise stepped forward and took his arm. Miles and Henry exchanged a quizzical glance. The gathered faces exposed looks of troubled concern and sudden curiosity. Mina and Albert looked at each other, then returned their attention to the box, which had taken on the properties of that one opened by Pandora millennia ago.

Gwyda carefully placed the tiara in a velvet bag and closed the drawstring. She placed it in the vault and stepped aside, allowing Nolan to close its door and spin the dial.

"Safe at last," Gwyda murmured.

"Back where it belongs. Now if we can only get Gara back where she belongs, out of our lives," Archie complained.

"In due time." She paused and glanced from son to nephew. "While we're alone, I will say this just once. I'm all for ridding Brownmoor of the interlopers, but I won't stand for these dangerous games going on. Someone could get seriously hurt."

"I thought you were convinced Father's ex-witches were the ones playing games on us," Nolan reminded.

"I'm not ruling out that possibility, but I also know how this family acts and thinks. If either of you know anything about unplugging that chamber or planting that ax, I just want to make sure these dangerous stunts aren't going to continue."

"So you think one of us is trying to kill those women?" an incredulous Archie asked.

Gwyda drew a breath and gave the men her most intimidating gaze (which had been known to cause university students to quake in fear, and had even given the Queen pause when she accidentally punctured Gwyda while in the process of pinning the decorations to commemorate her Dameship back in 1972). "I know well what kind of men you both are. Neither of you is above behaving like a pillaging Viking. I should know, since I'm a Bottomly as well."

"So are you admitting you should be considered just as suspect as us?" Nolan questioned, his eyes narrowing.

"Don't tempt me to prove just how vicious I can be," she expelled, as if belching fire. "You've been a bloody bastard your whole life, even as a child. And you," she turned, spewing venom on her own son, "you were almost as bad. If either of you is staging these murder attempts, or if either of you put your children up to to it, I'm telling you to stop it all now. I will not have further scandal ruining our names."

"I resent this," Archie fumed. "I might be an arsehole in the boardroom, but I won't stand for being called a murderer. And there's no way I would put Carolyn or Willis or anyone else up to doing my dirty work."

"*Your* dirty work? Slip of the tongue, cousin? Sure you don't know something about what's going on?" Nolan insinuated.

"Naff off, you prat," Archie responded, moving forward with a raised fist.

"Stop it, both of you right now!" Gwyda thundered. "I will not bandy this about any further. If anyone here knows anything about these recent incidents, then stop them now. End of discussion."

With that, Gwyda stomped out of the room, leaving Nolan and Archie glaring at each other. The traces of distrust hung in the air, and suspicions were clearly starting to form. And only the lack of strange incidents (or the next bizarre murder attempt) would tell if Gwyda's threats were effective.

The day passed without event as the various factions regrouped to lick wounds, revel in vindication, or forget the recent outlandish incidents. Gwyda was in the study when Mrs. Dutton appeared at the door.

"Madam? There's a call, a Mr. Scarborough with the Royal Flemshire Children's Hospital regarding a charity event next week."

"I don't recall anything about that. Is that listed in the diary? I must think about hiring a new secretary. That last one could hardly spell without counting on her fingers," she shuddered as she picked up the phone.

"This is Dame Gwyda Glasscock," she announced formally to the caller. She listened silently, but her expression changed from perfunctory interest to consternation to barely concealed outrage. "Yes, I see. I seem to have misplaced the details on this. Could you courier over a packet of information so I can refamiliarize myself with the event? Thank you so much. I'm sure this will be an unforgettable evening." She replaced the phone in its cradle and then pounded her fist on the desk.

"Madam?" Mrs. Dutton voiced concern.

"Oh, that insufferable woman and her schemes! I may change my mind about disapproving any attempts on her life after all!"

The noise roused others from adjacent rooms. "What's wrong, Mother?" Archie asked as he entered.

"That bitch! She's arranged a charity screening of one of her film horrors and promised the family's attendance."

"What's the problem? We simply won't go," Carolyn reasoned.

"It's not that simple. It's benefiting the Royal Flemshire Children's Hospital as well as the Asquith-Bottomly Health Care Coalition, and members of the royal family are expected to attend. I don't see how we can say no to that."

"How could she do that to us?" Willis fumed.

"A whole evening of pretending to like that fishwife? I won't do it," Nolan insisted.

"How did she arrange that so quickly?"

"With my whipper-snapper of a staff and the grace of the good Lord!" Gara exclaimed as she plodded in, her praised retainers in tow.

"How the hell could you do this?" Gwyda demanded.

"This is a good thing, it'll benefit people ... plus it gets me publicity!" Gara protested.

"It's all about you, that's what this has been all along! Plunder our family's estate, get publicity! Kiss sick kids, get publicity!" thundered Gwyda.

"Am I going to have to kiss those kids?" Gara, with a distasteful look, questioned Peony and Caddy.

"This is ridiculous! If you think we're going to spend an evening making nice with you, you're crazy!" Nolan persisted.

"You also get to see a marvelous film classic starring Gara," Caddy added by way of enticement.

"Yeah, either *Swoosie Todd, the Beautician of Buffalo*, or maybe *The Wurst of Everything*. They're trying to find prints of both," Gara waved her hand, as if dismissing her talent with false modesty.

"They can show *Gara Meets an East End Gorilla*, for all I care," Archie fumed.

"I thought I knew your entire filmography," Caddy piped up, flipping through his notepad. "When did you make that one?"

"They can show a movie that hasn't been made yet!" Willis shouted. "I refuse to be a party to this travesty!"

He loped out of the room, followed by his wife and sister. Gwyda glared at Gara.

Before either spoke, Peony piped up, "So I should tell the charity people, 'That's one less for the dinner?'"

STRANGE INTERLUDE 8

A life without beautiful things is unbearable.

Dorothy Kilgallen's column, June 16, 1963

Beautiful things are a joy to behold, and that includes glamorous stars of stage and screen. Among the loveliest are Barbara Lamont, Gara St. James, and Gloria Prescott. Gloria appears in the upcoming murder mystery *So Well Brought Up*, in which she convincingly portrays a high society murderess (said to be inspired in part by the real-life scandal of Ann Woodward, who accidentally killed her husband, heir to a banking and equestrian fortune) and wears some stunning Orry-Kelly gowns.

Barbara last appeared onscreen in February in the domestic thriller *His Golden Appendage*, wherein she portrayed a war bride unprepared for her husband's return from a veteran's hospital and his physical changes. The film was a hit, in no small part due to the adult subject matter and allusions to the title appendage, and a denouncement by the Catholic Legion of Decency (although they insisted it was because of the film's unattractive depiction of everyday housewifery).

Barbara's absence from movie theaters is due to a happy event, as she has given birth to her second child. Barbara and her husband, jeweler Cyril Lamont, welcomed a son, Cyril Bingham Lamont III. "He's perfect, just like his adoring big sister," the new mother bubbled at a hospital press conference in Los Angeles.

"Babs tried pronouncing 'Bingham' and came out with 'Binky.' Isn't that the cutest?" Apparently still feeling woozy from the anesthesia, she continued, "Parenthood is a breeze, easier than raising cane. Ha! That's what I once told Marilyn and she said Jack used to say the same thing!"

Barbara was returned to her room, bringing the press event to a close. When pressed on the identity of "Jack," Cyril stated he believed Barbara had referred to Jack Lemmon, with whom both she and the late Marilyn Monroe had worked.

While Barbara has happy news, her friend, Gloria Prescott, has sad news on her agenda. She and her husband, the playwright Tristan

Musgrave, are separating and divorce is imminent. The couple, married three years, have a son, Didley.

"I did everything I could to make Tristy happy," Gloria confided. "Trust me, you don't want to know the lengths I went to please him. You'd gain three inches in your chin if I told you!" Oh, that Gloria, such a comedienne, even in the wake of a failed marriage.

Gloria will relocate to the west coast. "We were quite the bi-coastal couple, and although Manhattan is divine, I always miss Los Angeles. If I have to be both mother and father to my Didums, I can do that. Marlene always said that I wore the pants in my marriage!"

Musgrave, busy in rehearsal for his new play, *Spring of My Greek Sailor*, was unavailable for comment.

Someone who always has lots of comments is Gara St. James. The star lives in England with her husband and their daughter Pet, an enchanting child with black curls and a naturally tanned complexion (there must be "Black Irish" somewhere in Pet or Laddie's heritage). But distance and an ocean haven't stopped her from sharing her mind with President John Kennedy!

Recently in New York to pitch some ideas for television projects to the networks, she confirmed the reports of her writing letters of advice to the President.

"I may be living the English lifestyle, but I'm still a good American," Gara stated, an unusual British accent coloring her strong Midwestern U.S. inflections. "I don't agree with having the Catholics in charge of the White House, but I think it's my duty to respect his position as President and make my opinions known so he has all the angles, rather than just the one he's been told to have."

Gara claims to have advised President Kennedy to rethink his position on the nuclear weapons ban and on Communist activities in Southeast Asia. "These crazy people need to be confronted with force, and what's more forceful than a bomb?" she reasoned. "A little threat works wonders, be it on a stingy boyfriend or an uppity foreign nation."

Gara balanced her criticism with praise for Kennedy's devotion to civil rights issues. "He's got the right notion on equality. I admit, I only ever used to think about the coloreds when they did a bad job housekeeping or didn't get dinner on the table on time. But then my friend Bahamia admitted she was one, which surprised me. You know, she could have played that part in *Show Boat*, because she passed real good, unlike Lena Horne, who you can tell is colored even though she has pretty 'white girl' features. So I'm with the President on this issue. *Now*, some of my best friends are black!"

Excerpt from *They Put That on TV? The Weirdest Programming That Ever Showed Up on Television* by Paul Stevens and Richard Anthony

It's Gara's Show! (1964, CBS, 14 episodes). Variety show starring Gara St. James. Then married to a lord and living primarily in England, the performer met with U.S. network executives in New York and pitched show ideas (one was a sci-fi series called *Watch Out, That's My Asteroid!*; we can only imagine what that might have turned into), and Gara heard rumblings that CBS wasn't happy with *The Judy Garland Show*, which was regularly beaten in the ratings by NBC's *Bonanza*. She suggested scuttling the struggling variety series and replacing it with one starring Gara. It's believed that her overtures to the network may have hastened the demise of Garland's show.

It's Gara's Show! wasn't scheduled opposite *Bonanza*, but a better timeslot on Wednesdays as a summer replacement. This didn't help Gara in the ratings, however. After a promising debut, ratings for subsequent outings continued dropping until it was canceled after fourteen airings.

What was passable as movie entertainment seemed strangely magnified in the intimacy of home viewing. Gara's personality was at odds with her attempts at comedy sketches and dramatic monologues, which garnered confusion from the audience. (Oddly, some sketches prefigure the bizarre humor which made *Rowan & Martin's Laugh-In* a success.)

That memorable debut episode featured her old roommates from their early days in Hollywood: Barbara Lamont, Gloria Prescott, and Bahamia joined Gara onstage and they performed a medley of well-known standards, including neat Chordettes-style harmonizing on songs from Gara's kiddie features. Barbara and Gloria also duetted on "Scarlet Ribbons." Dancer Bahamia made her first appearance on U.S. television since being blackballed in the late '50s after extolling her African-American heritage in the press, and performed a much-admired dance tour de force. This moment garnered positive reviews and signaled a resurgence in entertainment opportunities for the maligned star.

Despite this bright spot, the show never offered a real reason for viewers to tune in, and the star's sometimes off-putting persona was no draw. She sprinkled odd political jokes skewering liberals and seemed to resent the presence of guest stars stealing her limelight. And was Gara aiming at "truth in advertising" for her theme song, a rousing brass band version of the bossa nova standard "How Insensitive (*Insensatez*)"?

Turner Classic Movies Schedule, February 28, 1999

Spotlight on films about writers

1:00 P.M. EST - *The Big Book* (1961, Columbia) Directed by Alfred E. Green. Starring Barbara Lamont, Barry Sullivan, Geoffrey Horne, Polly Bergen, Rex Thompson, Harry Morgan, Jim Hutton, Larry Keating. The career of a beautiful language expert translating an ancient text is almost ruined when the book's secrets are revealed in this film based on the scandalous play by G. Madison Delacy. Subject matter is dealt with discreetly when star realizes the book she's translating is a "marriage manual!" Film has a modern take on relationships and gender roles, which accounts for its resurgence in cult popularity. Barbara torn between upstanding Barry Sullivan and naughty Geoffrey Horne; guess with whom she ends up (you might be surprised)? A musical number is worked into a scene at a campus soda shop where Lamont and chorus kids perform "The Phoenicians Had a Word for It (Did They Ever)!"

2:30 P.M. EST - *The Writer's Blockhead* (Warner Bros., 1962) Directed by Frank Tuttle. Starring Gara St. James, James Garner, William Demarest, Susan Kohner, George Tobias, Ed Wynn, Jim Backus, Virginia Wiedler. Authoress St. James attends a champagne reception for her latest tome, but finds herself arrested for petty larceny after confused bookstore employees mistake her for "Glad Hands Glenda," a pickpocket wanted by local police. Lame attempt at screwball comedy falls flat despite strong cast. Kohner a delight as the acidic publishing agent who gets off a few zingers on the confused cops played by Wynn and Backus. Margaret Hamilton is funny in a cameo as Glenda. In the most bizarre scene, Gara serenades her fellow inmates (including the unbilled Zsa Zsa Gabor and Hedy Lamarr, in a foreshadowing of their future arrests) with a dance and song, "I've Been a Bad Girl, But This Time I'm Innocent!"

4:00 P.M. EST - *Defining Darla* (Allied Artists, 1964) Directed by Hugo Haas. Starring Gloria Prescott, John Agar, Lance Fuller, Richard Crenna, Phyllis Thaxter, Robert Cassidy, Jack Albertson, Frank Faylen. A prim dictionary expert seeks to revise an out-of-date reference volume with assistance from those who've had "real life" experience, which leads her to a handsome bum on the lam from gangland criminals. This mélange of *My Man Godfrey* and *Ball of Fire* doesn't come close to attaining those heights. For a low-budget programmer, though, the film has a moment or two. (Prescott, smarting from a costly divorce, made the feature for quick cash.) A musical sequence is squeezed into a tiny room that's supposedly the main floor of the Library of Congress! If the censors were still in charge, they might have challenged the obvious inferences of Gloria's energetic hipswaying and pouting lips as she tells us in song, "Mr. Dewey Makes Me Dewy!"

Movie star manages to lose it all by Barbara Bennett, *Redbook*, October 1964

Gloria Prescott had it all; a successful film career, a handsome husband (the playwright Tristan Musgrave), and a precious baby. She thought it was never going to end. But in one fell swoop, it vanished overnight.

"I had no reason to think Tristan was unhappy with the marriage," Gloria revealed to me as we sat over tea in the gracious drawing room of her Beverly Hills home. "True, I was often here working in TV and film, and he was often in New York working on theater projects. But I believed in that old adage, 'distance makes the heart grow fonder.' He *acted* liked he did, too, dressing me up in the newest fashions, encouraging me to think about new hairstyles, sharing the latest theater gossip."

But shared interests weren't enough. "I was floored when he requested a divorce. I suspected another woman but found no evidence. He appeared to be spending most of his time with his latest find, that male dancer he was grooming for stardom. I understand the amount of time that's spent creating a new star, but it shouldn't come at the expense of one's happy marriage!"

Nothing could have prepared her for the next sting; she was going to be left almost penniless. "I didn't understand all that financial stuff, and like a good little *esposa*, I signed whatever Tristan gave me to sign. I thought we were partners. If this is how he treats his partners ..."

"He didn't even care about our son's well-being. How would I be able to raise our baby in the style he was accustomed to? Didums could already tell the difference between an authentic French silk crepe de chine and a cheap, man-made synthetic!"

The shock caused Gloria to suffer a complete breakdown. "I was helping Barbara [Lamont] pick out new layettes for her baby, my new godson, at I. Magnin. I realized I wouldn't be able to buy my baby, or myself, extravagant gifts anymore. A life without beautiful things is unbearable. It must be that way for everyone, even native tribes in the hinterlands."

Gloria began screaming before dissolving into a catatonic state. "I thought she was giving me her opinion of the blouse I held up!" Barbara exclaimed. "I said, 'Darling, it's a Galliano, what's wrong with it?' By that time she had collapsed on the floor and pulled a rack of parkas on top of herself."

Gloria spent three months convalescing at a private hospital. "I had so much support. Gene and Vivien sent me the dearest cards, as did the fans. It made me feel better to know so many people cared."

Now she's focusing on her career and raising her son. "I'm prepared to let people know that Gloria Prescott is back and better than ever! My baby thinks I'm *numero uno,* and everyone's going to remember I'm *their* number one, too!"

Charity leader Bottomly passes away by Evelyn Markham, *The Daily Mirror,* 8 January, 1965

Charity organizer Alice Asquith Bottomly passed away yesterday in her Sutton home, reported a representative for the Asquith-Bottomly Health Care Coalition for Children and the Poor. Mrs. Bottomly was a leader in the attempt to organize better health care for London's children and less-affluent residents in the years after WW II.

Alice, the daughter of tin magnate Humbreth Asquith, was born in Shropshire in 1919 and was one of England's leading debutantes. She married Lord Lindale Bottomly in 1938 and they were a fashionable symbol of London before and during the war years. They had three children, Nolan, Barnaby, and Hannah. The marriage ended in scandal and divorce, when details of the lord's affair with a showgirl were made public.

Instead of retiring from public life, Alice took an interest in social services, and formed the coalition to remedy health care services. She remained on friendly terms with her ex-husband, so much so that he was a major financial backer of her charity. He limited his public participation so as not to take away from her accomplishments, although his current wife, the actress Gara St. James, has been criticized for her attempt to gain publicity from the work of others. (She hosted a poorly organized benefit for the group where accusations of financial improprieties were raised.)

Nolan, Barnaby, and Hannah have assumed the stylish public mantle their parents once did. Nolan has confined his press to the financial arena, although his wedding several years ago to the Catalan chanteuse Mirabelle Peña made news in the society and fashion pages. Barnaby and Hannah have both been in the columns for their glamorous images and party-going.

Funeral services have not been formally announced. Her children have asked that anyone interested in remembering their mother may make charitable donations in Mrs. Bottomly's name to her namesake charity.

Excerpt from *Reel and Real Hollywood Fashion in the Sixties* by Abigail Monterey

A brash new brand of designer began making an impact onscreen in the '60s. Theadora Van Runkle, Danilo Donati, and Donald Brooks were among those who emerged and created exciting costumes that helped shape fashion, both onscreen and off. Van Runkle's stunning costumes for *Bonnie & Clyde* and *The Thomas Crown Affair* engineered fashion trends and solidified star Faye Dunaway's image as a fashion leader.

At the start of the decade and on the opposite end of the budget spectrum, Barbara Lamont appeared in the minor romantic comedy *The Diplomat Wore Tights*. In the pivotal scene, she shocks the international community by attending an official function in a spangled halter, a bolero jacket, and the afore-mentioned tights. However, her eloquent speech turns the room to her favor, and she seals the deal by brokering an important agreement between the U.S. and the tiny nation of Catadorra, winning the heart of the Crown Prince Casimiro (played by George Chakiris).

Tights became de rigueur attire for female beatniks and teens, and remained a fashion staple for much of the '60s. Everyone from Gidget to Barbie sported the look, which managed to be both casual and elegant with the correct accessories.

The film's designer, Arturo Villareal, explained that Barbara wanted the costumes to show her figure off to its best advantage. "It didn't matter if she couldn't sit in them, but they had to still allow her to execute one of her highkicks. The recent invention of elastane [more commonly known as spandex] allowed me to create tights that showed off Barbara's famous fanny to its best advantage."

In contrast, a fashion institution that fell out of favor was the wearing of hats. In the '50s, it was still considered bad form for ladies to appear in public without hats and gloves. But as the decade ended, casual styles blossomed and women felt those accessories belonged to an earlier era.

One star who loved hats was Gara St. James. She started a brief trend in the '50s for the stylized cowboy hat she wore in the Broadway show *The Branded Cowgirl,* and had even had a hat named after her, the "Gara" (a capotain with a narrow brim and complemented with a dunce-style crown), from her days as a child star.

She believed her star quality could revive the trend. Recalling tales that Garbo had designed the peaked skullcap from *Ninotchka,* Gara designed a hat that might be described as a combination yarmulke/Cossack hat. Small, it sat on the back of the crown and stood almost a foot high. (It stayed in place with a discreet comb attachment.)

She wore them for a time in London (they appeared as incongruous with Carnaby Street fashions as Garbo's "Empress Eugenie" hat from *Romance* had looked with 1930's American daywear) and even wore one in her film *Lady in a Cave*, but wasn't able to spark another fashion trend.

Fox Movie Channel Schedule, October 1, 2002
Spotlight on films about "ladies"

12:00 P.M. EST - *Ladies From Hades* (1958, Paramount) Directed by Allen Reisner. Starring David Niven, Bahamia, Timima Bossi, Gloria Prescott, Robert Sterling, John Sutton, Paul Douglas, Ed Begley. A trio of Salem witches tries to avenge their wrongful deaths by destroying the corporation which ultimately made millions by exploiting their innocent homeopathic medical remedy. A Broadway show investment scheme designed to ransack the company's coffers turns into a big hit with the glamorous ladies onstage. This mélange of *I Married a Witch* and *Down to Earth* came late in the musical-comedy cycle and wasn't a big success in its initial release. But the dialogue's snappy and and the plot's romantic contrivances are pleasing, so what's not to like? Bahamia performs a scintillating dance number and song ("Take My Temperature") which raises eyebrows, even today.

1:45 P.M. EST - *Sadie Was a Lady* (1962, MGM) Directed by Robert Wise. Starring Jack Lemmon, Barbara Lamont, Karl Malden, Ray Danton, Betty Field, Andrew Keir, Henry Daniell, Sela Hughesenskaya. Bio-pic of the theatrical great Sadie Barrows, from humble beginnings in Ohio to stardom onstage in dramatic roles. Unfortunately, Lamont doesn't show what made Barrows a legend. More appropriate casting (such as Anne Bancroft or Patricia Neal) would have made the difference. During the recreation of Barrows's triumph in Shaw's *Caesar and Cleopatra*, Lamont seems more concerned with the lines of her gold lamé gown than the lines she's declaiming onstage. Best scene is the recreation of the real-life restaurant brawl between Lamont and opera diva Hughesenskaya (as theatrical rival Nazimova) over who is really the first lady of the American theatre.

4:00 P.M. EST - *Lady in a Cave* (1965, United Artists) Directed by George Roy Hill. Starring Gara St. James, Rod Taylor, Trevor Howard, Timima Bossi, Dennis Price, Pamela Franklin, Mark Stevens, Margot LeMora. Construction of a new suburb upsets geological formations, awakening a frozen cavewoman in an underground grotto. Neanderthal is brought into stylish suburban living when found by new neighbors, mistaking her for a realtor who fell into a muddy building zone. Confusion reigns when the coffee clatch crowd transforms the bedraggled St. James into a cul-de-sac cutie, catching the eye of Taylor as the construction company exec. Bizarre concept works as a screwball comedy and a subtle diatribe against suburban conformity. Gara reveals comedic skills worthy of Jerry

Lewis; her grunting harrumphs and clumsy galumphing in a designer dress is a sight to see. Scene at a country club cotillion where St. James inadvertently starts a new dance craze ("The Caveman Twist") is sure to inspire chuckles.

Army Archerd's column, February 7, 1966

The Mocambo was the place to be last night where a joint birthday party was thrown for Zsa Zsa Gabor and Bahamia by their friends. The eternally young and beautiful stars were pleased by the surprise. "Dahlink, it's always lovely to get expensive gifts on ze occasion of my birth, as long as vun doesn't vurry about ze actual year," Zsa Zsa giggled.

"I should have known something was up when Gara wanted to take me to dinner to discuss a play she wanted us to do, as if she's ever been literate," Bahamia joked.

I'm pleased that Bahamia's career is in top form again after some slim years. "It's great to be back in Hollywood with so many projects in the works," the star agreed.

"I was glad to do what I could to get people to see my good pal is talented and deserved to work," Gara broke in. "I insisted they hire Bahamia for my TV variety show. I said, 'I know a girl who dances like a Mexican jumping bean, only she's black, and she'll be glad to work for peanuts 'cause no one'll hire her.' I sure did say that, and it helped my best girlfriend get noticed in this town again."

"Words can't express my gratitude," Bahamia agreed, but instead of telling me those words, she went across the room to greet pals Barbara Lamont and Gloria Prescott.

Since Gara had me politely trapped, she bent my ear about her marriage. "Laddie and I are so happy together," she said, waving to her husband across the room as he chatted with Rita Moreno and Diahann Carroll. (He didn't notice until Gara yelled, "Hey, you! Quit chatting up the skirts for two minutes and wave hi to your wife!" She turned back to me and said, "He loves it when I tease him like that.")

She gushed about their daughter Petal, who turned three last year. Mother and child posed for a recent *Family Circle* fashion layout, and the pretty girl with blue eyes and dusky skin is sure to become a beautiful woman one day, just like "Momsy Womsy," as Gara likes to be called.

"We call her Pet, like our friend Petula Clark. Isn't that adorable? My Pet's such a well-behaved girl. I don't allow her to watch television or see Momsy's pictures," she continued, the lilt of British cadence entering and leaving her voice like a seesaw, which is probably also forbidden for her child.

"I follow my friend Joan Crawford's example. Cathy and Cindy were the best behaved girls in this town. They were almost like statues. Joan says discipline is key, and I agree. I don't want my children ending up like those brats of Barbara Lamont, or a dandy like that Prescott boy. Is Gloria grooming him to be a studio hairdresser?"

Gara is also strict about Pet's chores. "At her age, I was already working sixteen hours a day in the movies, so keeping one's room clean and being an obedient child should be a cakewalk," she reasoned. "She never misbehaves like Bar and Glo's kids. I've seen those little hellions behave like a marauding pack of hyenas, but Pet knows better. Only once did I have the nanny tell her if she behaves like those rotten demons, she'd have to go out to the garden and pick out a switch that is the same thickness as her wrist. And she's never misbehaved or left her room a mess. Her room is neater than Cindy and Cathy's ever was and that is saying something. I have to think Joan is the teeniest bit jealous. Well, she has an Oscar, so I have to one-up her the best way I can."

When asked if she used this same technique on the twins she adopted while married to Roderigo Hujeapenosa in the '50s, Gara denied they had even existed. When I pointed out that I had once interviewed her with them in the room, she conceded, "They were adorable at first, but eventually it was like living with evil, little poodles! They were happier at the orphanage, anyway. I'm a Jewish girl, so I don't know anything from the Catholics, except what Loretta Young tells me, but I hear the nuns are real harpies with the discipline!"

Under that threat, I think I better wind this up for today!

CHAPTER 9

Plus, we've both played detectives onscreen, so we've had training!

Upon inspection, the mysterious box unearthed few clues. The official police paper was a preliminary document concerning the fire investigation and only related the already known facts in the matter, probably given to the family as a courtesy. There hadn't yet been an official cause listed for the fire.

Magazines and assorted photographs added to the impression that the box had been packed and stored away after Gara's departure. Each magazine included an article on the actress, and the photos were mostly publicity stills of Gara. (One needed to keep up with one's publicity, even in its then diminished state, although how these bits missed inclusion in the sixty-plus scrapbook volumes of her career, lovingly compiled by Peony, is anyone's guess.) The remaining photos, taken in the '50s, were of Brownmoor in its former state of glory.

Rather than answer questions, the contents of the box seemed to inspire more uncertainty. The less intellectually curious Bottomlys and Glasscocks dismissed the box's contents as unimportant relics, but the others weren't convinced. As a photographer, Pet was taken with the pictures of the castle. She thought more inspection might reveal something a less qualified individual would overlook, though she hoped it wouldn't evolve into the plot from *Blow-Up*.

Mina and Albert also felt the box's contents held onto remaining secrets, especially regarding the long-ago fire. He suggested they might find additional info in the local library's newspaper archives, and so the pair, like Nick and Nora Charles, quit Brownmoor for their own investigation as Pet continued inspecting the historical photographs of Brownmoor.

Though they didn't dare voice questions as the family remained within earshot, they each wondered: Would they be able to learn more about the fire investigation? Had the family, always influential in Flemshire, used its influence to keep the police from fully pursuing the matter? And was someone within the family intent on keeping it that way?

145

Gloria twisted and turned in the mirror, catching her image from every angle. Barbara entered the room after a quick knock. Gloria didn't miss a beat as she continued posing.

"What are you doing?"

"Trying to decide which gown to wear to that charity film screening," Gloria replied.

"Who said we were invited?"

"No one has to *say* it. Don't you think there'll be a panel discussion after the film is shown? They'll want us there to offer tidbits about Gara's performance, insider tips about her career, information on *our* careers," she reasoned.

"Yes, but that means we'll have to watch the movie, and I don't know that I'm up for that," Barbara moaned.

"Maybe they'll decide to show one of the ones we did together. *You* got a big inheritance in the form of your mother, I need to get something out of this trip, even if it's only a bit of publicity. What do you think of this gown? I have to wear gold lamé, it's my onscreen trademark. That, and the way I smooth the fabric down my torso. I've done that in every film since *Her Past Was Off Limits.*"

"And no one did it better than you, dear, although that move seemed a bit suspect when you did it in *In the Shadow of Sainthood.*"

Gloria, far too absorbed in self-adoration, didn't hear the teasing comment. "Of course, you're going to wear something in your signature color, flesh? You always look so good in that. Remember that dress Didums designed for you when you got your star on the Hollywood Walk of Fame?"

"True, it's been my signature color, even though Kim Novak tried to steal it from me."

"Now, now, that disaster was averted when you suggested she try lavender, and didn't that work out for both of you?"

"I suppose so." It occurred to Barbara that their usual entourage was absent. "Where are the children? I haven't seen them for some time."

"They were handling your mother's morning routine, so she should be out for a few hours at least."

"The best side effect from those designer colonic treatment bags. What won't Donna Karan slap her name on?"

"Then I think they were going to do more 'investigating' with the younger children."

"I'm sure this interest in investigating is right up Babs's alley. You know, I had to destroy all the journals I once kept after she found them when she was just six. It was pure luck she didn't know half those words at such a young age!"

A strange look crossed Gloria's face, which meant she had stopped thinking about herself and was contemplating something far deeper (a rare occurrence). "Are we missing out on something by ignoring the investigating? Perhaps we should get involved, too."

"I believe Pet, Mina, and Albert were already looking at the items in that box. How did that terrible brother of Pet's end up with such a good-looking son?"

"His mother was Mirabelle Peña, the singer, remember? We saw her during one of our trips to London in the sixties."

"Oh yes, you two got along famously, didn't you? All that conversing in Spanish."

"We didn't mean to exclude you, *chica*."

"That's okay, I just assumed you two were saying terrible things about me right under my nose."

"Darling, as if. I'm sure we said horrible things about Gara. Remember, Gara was then married to her husband's father."

"That's right, she knew her, too. I think you're right, we should get involved in this investigating. We should make ourselves look useful. That old Dame might try to make us earn our keep by serving tea and beating laundry against rocks," Barbara said, tapping her cheekbone with a worried finger.

"Playing Nancy Drew is preferable to dusting porcelain figurines and polishing silverware. Not as glamorous as posing for publicity stills after-hours embracing Hugh O'Brian, but then, what is?"

Pet had pored over the pictures to the point of blurred vision. The different views of the manor house, the pre-fire wing and tower, the also-destroyed barn, the stables, the gardens. A clue seemed to be under the surface, but she couldn't put her finger on it. She turned away and rubbed her eyes.

"Are those photos so interesting?" she turned to see her aunt in the library's doorway.

"From a purely historical standpoint, they are, since they preserve Brownmoor's appearance from the fifties," Pet offered.

"I must say, I don't quite understand this interest in the past," Gwyda replied.

Sixth sense told her that Aunt Gwyda's indirect probing might reveal more than she planned to. "You must admit, it was quite a discovery for the kids, finding this box with the missing crown and all these papers. And so coincidental, considering the recent accusations that my mother may have had something to do with that fire so long ago."

"I was only letting off steam at the will reading. I didn't want Laddie giving away a fortune to her out of some sense of duty, and I let my anger get the better of me. The fire was an accident. The police determined it was so."

"Do you know anything about this police document?"

"It was given to your father. We had decamped to Impswich temporarily, where the Glasscocks and Fotheringays still have property. The Bottomlys were quite powerful in Flemshire ... I suppose we still are. The police wanted to keep the family informed."

"Did you or my father ask the police to halt the investigation?" Pet asked suddenly with the precision of Charles Laughton in *Witness for the Prosecution*.

Gwyda refused to bend. "Of course not. Why in the world would we have asked them to do that? In fact, when your father received the official results of the investigation from the police, he didn't even read the documents. He burned them rather than have to endure reading the details. Is that the act of anyone with something to hide?"

"I didn't say there was anything to hide. We were just interested in knowing the full story." Pet kept her voice even and casual with some effort.

Gwyda, realizing the discussion would continue in its circular vein with neither of them getting what they wanted, sat down on the opposite side of the desk. "Nothing I say is going to keep you from looking into this, will it?"

Pet chuckled and clasped her aunt's hand. "Probably not."

"That inquisitive journalist's mind is always on." She paused, and then used the only weapon left in her arsenal. "Do what you must, but please remember: poking around in the past can hurt people today. The fire was a great tragedy. Your father never recovered from the loss of Barnaby and Hannah. I don't want anyone still here to feel hurt again."

"We're only interested in the truth."

Gwyda shook her head. "Sometimes the truth is the last thing people want. Please don't get involved in cockamamie theories that may do more harm than good."

"What's this about Mamie and some cocks?" Barbara asked as she entered the library.

"Van Doren strikes again! Is she in the *Daily Mirror*? That girl is always on top of things, usually a hunky lifeguard or tennis instructor," Gloria clucked with approval.

"And I'll stay on top of things by keeping my mouth shut and taking my leave," Gwyda declared with a sniff as she rose and departed.

"I'm quite impressed by how quickly that old Dame gets around, without both arms to balance her," Barbara observed.

"I know, it's amazing! Joan Fontaine can barely walk a straight line, and she has perfectly good arms and legs. Gwyda must have studied yoga after that accident when she danced with that bear," Gloria noted.

"Danced with a bear?" Pet asked.

"Isn't that what happened? She used to be a circus performer and that dancing bear ate her arm instead of dipping her during a tango?"

"You never get the story right. That bear attacked her when she was harvesting honey from a bee farm. Haven't you heard of Dame's Finest Honey?" Barbara corrected.

"Is there anything I can do to help you ladies?" Pet diverted attention from the wildly off-target tales.

"We're here to help *you*, darling! We thought we should get in on this detective work, too."

"You want to help?"

"Of course! The children have been ferreting out clues like that Scooby Doo gang, except they don't have a dog. Well, there's that dog of Carolyn's, but he hasn't proven to be helpful so far," Barbara reasoned.

"Plus, we've both played detectives onscreen, so we've had training!" Gloria offered.

"What should we do first? Dust for fingerprints? Look at doorknobs through a magnifying glass? Flirt with handsome male suspects?"

"We haven't gotten that far yet. Er, why don't you look through this box and see if anything seems unusual," Pet said, resigning herself to Barbara and Gloria's help and consoling herself that at least her mother hadn't also joined to make the investigation more difficult.

Barbara and Gloria applied themselves diligently to the box's contents for several minutes, but their short attention spans tired of the unglamorous task at hand. Bored, Gloria pushed past the contents of the box and found the more interesting magazines at the bottom. "Ooh, *Marie Claire*, *Harper's Bazaar*, *Tatler*! These need examining."

Barbara grabbed one of the titles from Gloria's hands and they both began flipping through the periodicals. A running commentary ensued. "Look, here's Hannah Bottomly, the one who died. What a gorgeous wedding gown. Gloves are so quaint, why don't those come back in style? Some of our colleagues could use them; have you seen Faye Dunaway's gnarled hooves? Oh, look at Dovima. Is that the pic of her and the elephants? You know, I have my own iconic animal fashion shot, the one with me in the

Jacques Fath gown posing with the platypus. Ha, here's an article about Gara and her perfect life. Listen to this gem of wisdom: 'Children are the second most important things in a family, after money.' Well, I'll give her that one, I suppose."

Pet felt rather like the sensible Florence Nash as the frivolous Roz Russell and Phyllis Povah gossiped in *The Women*. She avoided the bruising associated with excessive eye rolling and tried to keep her attention on the photos.

Gloria picked up *The Lady*. "Another article about Gara's domesticity. Oh dear, a recipe for spiced salmon knishes. Ugh, was that one of the dreadful snacks she used to make in our kitchen at the old apartments?"

Barbara noticed the glossy photos beneath the remaining magazines. "More fashion layouts. Look at Ysabel Fanon in this gorgeous YSL suit. Oh dear, here's Gara in the same suit. Not the same effect, is it? Well, you can't put a pit bull in a designer gown and expect it to look like a poodle."

Gloria laughed and started to toss her magazine aside when a photograph fell out of the back pages. She picked it up and absently opened it. "Pet, darling, a snapshot of you as a baby," she said.

Surprised, Pet took the small photo. It must have been shot the day she was born. A smiling Gara (always a movie star, far more glamorous than any average woman who had just given birth) and Laddie proudly held their new bundle of joy. How odd to suddenly become part of the box's ephemera.

"How adorable you are," Barbara praised. "You were born at home, right? In a French chateau? Gara cleaned up rather well, considering she had just given birth. She remembered at least a bit of our studio training; I'm sure Miss Burns advised us on that. I should have followed that advice, I must have looked a sight at that press conference after I had Binky. Well, 'Publicity at any costs' had been drilled into me at an early age by Mother."

Pet turned the picture over, then narrowed her eyes and looked closer. "Strange. The date here is November 12, but it should say November 16."

"That's doesn't look like Gara's handwriting. Probably the maid wrote it down wrong. The French are lazy and don't listen. Whenever I'm in a French restaurant, those waiters never get the order right, and they sneer when I speak to them in their own language!" Gloria huffed.

Barbara gave out an excited, "Whoopee!" They turned as she examined another official-looking document. "A deed, property in London belonging to Laddie! But someone scratched his name out and wrote

Mother's name in red ink. This must be worth a fortune now!"

"It's worth enough, although it used to be worth more," Myrtle said as she loped into the library.

"Mother! How did you get away from the children? I mean, what are you doing?"

"It was no problem escaping from those three. The girl snuck off to do God-knows-what, probably scribbling in that tablet of hers. And those boys are on the phone, all a-twitter with whoever called."

Making a mental note to send the children for a refresher course in nurse's aide training, Barbara turned her attention to the matter at hand. "What do you know about this property?"

"That deed's out of date. It's been in my name since the fifties," Myrtle answered.

"What do you mean by saying it used to be worth more? Is it in a bad section of London, one of the parts that haven't been gentrified yet?"

Myrtle cleared her throat and snatched the document from Barbara, who took it back. "I'm sure it's in a fine part of London. I just meant ... It was a wedding gift from Laddie, so it was worth so much more at the time. Give that back to me."

"Don't you want me to check on its worth? I mean its current worth, not its worth in sentiment."

Myrtle grabbed the paper back and stuffed it down her dress and into her bra. "Don't worry about stuff that doesn't concern you. I haven't ended up in a grave yet, although you've tried to put me into the ground on more than one occasion."

"Mother, that wasn't my fault! The coroner had already declared you dead!" Barbara protested.

"Grandmother! I mean, Myrtle!" Binky squealed as he sped into the room on his limited edition Christian Louboutin "Wheelies," spinning and trying to avoid her outstretched fist at calling attention to her age.

"You boys have been falling down on the job!" Gloria accused as Didums, attempting to catch up, accidentally rushed into Myrtle's punch.

"Ow! It's not my fault! I thought she was still having that colonic," Didums protested.

"Besides, we've got good news!" Binky trilled as he danced about the room, still managing to avoid Myrtle's continued attempts at striking him.

"I wish we could say the same," Albert stated as he headed a new contingent, consisting of Mina, Babs, Sophie, Henry, and Miles, into the library. "What's going on?"

"I wish I knew," Pet groaned, feeling as ready for the rubber room as Olivia DeHaviland in *The Snake Pit.*

"Darling, I thought you were investigating these pictures. Should we take over and be in charge?" Gloria questioned.

Albert, Mina, and Pet shared a series of quizzical glances and understanding nods.

"It turns out Babs and the kids had the same idea we did. They were already at the library when we arrived. And with all of us checking, it took less time," Mina explained.

"It was the kids who thought of it, I was just elected team leader to shepherd everyone over," Babs admitted as the kids grinned at the acknowledgement of their ingenuity.

They had uncovered several archived news items about the fire and an announcement that the police were launching an investigation. But there was little follow-up, except for an article or two on the fire's first anniversary. A suspicion remained that there may have been a cover-up.

Gloria, not wishing to be left out of the limelight for long, mentioned the discovery of Pet's baby picture, as well as the deed owned by Myrtle.

"No one's heard my good news!" Binky crowed. "My agent called. He got me booked for a club appearance in London!"

"But your bandmates are in the states. How's that going to work out?" Barbara asked.

"Not a problem. I've got the music tracks on CD, and with a couple of backing vocalists, it'll be just fine."

"And where are you going to find vocalists now?"

"Right here, Babs and Didums can carry a tune well enough to back me up!" he replied.

"Us?" Babs protested. "I don't know about that. Just when has this appearance been scheduled?"

"Next week, Thursday night."

"But that's the night of the charity film screening!" Barbara demurred. "We'll need you there!"

"Who said you were invited to *my* movie screening?" Gara demanded as she entered the room. "I don't think I put your names on the guest list."

"Your name's already on one of *my* lists," Gloria fumed.

The room descended into quarrels and warring conversations. Albert leaned in to commiserate with an exasperated Pet. "Do you think there's still a chance we might find out anything amidst all this?"

Pet managed a wan smile. "An insanity defense rarely works for individuals, but it's always believable when applied to friends and family!"

The news of the various discoveries made the rounds of the house that afternoon. There were suspicious grumblings from the Glasscocks about the deed belonging to Myrtle, and the lack of decades-old media attention to the fire convinced them of the silliness of anyone looking into the matter any further.

Pet, Mina, and Albert weren't so sure. Pet admitted there was something about the photos that bothered her, but she couldn't put her finger on it. And while the library trip resulted in less information than desired, there were still options. "I've got an idea," Albert said.

Before he could elaborate, there was a scream down the hall from Myrtle's room. They almost collided with Babs as she raced out.

Barbara was overseeing Binky and Didums as they attended to a wildly gesturing Myrtle. "What happened?" Mina asked.

"Mother needs her oxygen, but her tanks have been emptied! She can't have sucked out that much so fast, despite the stories Harry Cohn used to tell of her skill in that area!"

"Air ... shortage," Myrtle gasped, repeatedly poking Binky in the ribcage.

Babs raced back into the room, holding a small portable tank. "I got the spare!" she said. Within moments, Myrtle's grating rasp evolved to a softer wheeze.

"Thank heavens for the spare," Barbara praised her daughter's resourcefulness.

"I know one tank was full, and the other was still two-thirds full. So how did they end up empty?" Binky questioned.

"Maybe whoever did it realized pulling the plug on the hyperbaric chamber didn't work, so emptying the tanks was the next option," Didums theorized.

"Do you think it's another attempt on Mother's life?" Barbara almost swooned.

Babs thought it was a possibility. "Everyone must have heard about the deed to that property. Someone might feel like it's another piece of the estate Myrtle wheedled from Laddie."

Before anyone else could comment further, Gloria burst into the room. Oblivious to the apparent emergency situation, she struck a dramatic pose by grasping the edge of the door. "Hold the presses! I figured it all out!"

"You know who tried to kill Grandmother?" Binky cried.

"Someone tried to kill Mother Lamont? Again?" Gloria asked

incredulously.

"Yes! But what are you going on about? What did you figure out?"

"The box! I know all about the box!"

"Dear, if this is about you learning new words for your hoo-ha –"

"Listen, I've heard studio pitchmen talk all about thinking outside the box, but this is one time thinking inside it worked!" Gloria paused and drew breath. "I don't think Gara or the maids packed that box everyone's been investigating. I think Laddie did it!"

STRANGE INTERLUDE 9

Ugh, if I have to make one more casserole, I think I'll scream!

American Movie Classics Schedule, May 17, 1994
Foreign film festival
    7:00 P.M. EST - *To Serbia With Love* (1966, British Lion) Directed by Lewis Gilbert. Starring Alan Bates, Barbara Lamont, Nicol Williamson, David McCallum, Otto Kruger, Anna Sten, Danielle Kusnal, Bernard Cribbens. Tale of bittersweet love between a theater usherette and a Yugoslavian soldier, separated by war and tragedy. The sincerity of the stars count for a lot, despite their unbelievabilty. (The film's success was owed in part to moviegoers curious about tabloid gossip of Lamont's romantic escapades in Europe.) Sten good as the stern but loving mother of Lamont and Kusnal (who has showy moments as the bad sister; her eventual denouement as a sodden prostitute in Ye Olde Timey Bar where chanteuse Genevieve sings "The Streets of Kraljevo" is heartbreaking). The scene of Lamont refusing to have her spirit broken by insensitive postal employees is a standout. How can a girl be expected to know the correct postage for a love letter to be mailed to the front?
    9:00 P.M. EST - *Tristezza da Linguini Sensa Marinara* (a.k.a. *The Sadness of Linguini Without Marinara*) (Risata No Più, 1967) Directed by Umberto Felluci. Starring Gian Maria Volonté, Gloria Prescott, James Fox, Elsa Martinelli, Gabriele Ferzetti, Isa Miranda, Jean Bouise, Tiberio Mitri. A handsome ne'er-do-well becomes enamored with a Spanish refugee, but all is not as it appears. A neorealist throwback with some bizarre Jerry Lewis-styled *commedia all'italiana* touches, this film signaled a decline in the quality of Felluci's oeuvre. (Gloria had appeared to divine effect in Felluci's earlier *The Missing Bedroom*.) Volonté and Prescott are beautiful to look at, but scenes of dramatic tenderness are undercut by bizarre shtick in the background. Why does Gloria begin screaming into a phone, "You've blinded me!" while Elsa is flirting with a club-footed Pedrolino?
    11:00 P.M. EST - *Les Pantalons de Phillipe* (a.k.a. *Phillip's Trousers*) (Madeleine Films France, 1967) Directed by Jacques Demy. Starring Dirk

Bogarde, Gara St. James, Laurent Terzieff, James Coburn, Jean-Louis Barrault, Jean-Pierre Cassel, Giovanna Ralli, Gabriel Jabbour. Whimsical romance of mistaken identities somehow works despite the miscasting of St. James as the shopgirl torn between Bogarde and Terzieff. Gara looks pretty, although she's a bit past the age to be dressing in the style of yé-yé girls like Françoise Hardy and France Gall, with day-glo makeup and white lipstick. She giggles with a weird harrumph and speaks French with an odd accent, but she has chemistry with the male leads. Watch for the scene where Gara, instead of skipping down the Champs-Élysées and warbling a pop tune, galumphs down the street and wobbles on the concrete (fans swear you can make out the actress skidding on a dog's "calling card")!

Excerpt from *They Put That on TV? The Weirdest Programming That Ever Showed Up on Television* by Paul Stevens and Richard Anthony

Arse of Nick in Old Lace (1966-67, BBC, 12 episodes). Cast: Gara St. James (Emmaline Bartleby), Jeremy Burnham (Nicholas Bartleby), Harry Littlewood (Lyndon Jaffe), Clifford Rose (Mel Peacock), Beatrix Lehmann (Katie Atkins), Len Jones (Tommy Keith).

Amusing Britcom starring American actress Gara St. James as the prim wife of a prime minister, who has a compulsion to dress in ladies clothing; each episode centers on Gara's slapstick efforts to keep it from the press. As a result, the prime minister retains an impeccable reputation while his wife is considered an oddball. The brainchild of writer Milton Mannheim (who also created the sitcoms *My Radgie Rellies* and *Fanny Adams & Flaming Nora*), the show was well-received by viewers. Gara's divorce from a British lord and her subsequent return to the U.S. ended the series.

Wacky hijinks coupled with risqué humor made for entertaining TV. One classic episode depicted Nick's upcoming appearance at a royal event, at which he wants to wear lace undies beneath his tux. Eventually even this isn't enough, and he determines to wear a red satin ball gown. Emmaline tries to keep this from happening, and it's an embarrassed Emmaline in ruffled granny panties who's exposed to the Queen!

Brownmoor fire claims lives of Bottomly heirs by Vincent Gartside, *The Daily Mirror*, 26 July, 1967

A fire at Brownmoor in Flemshire, just east of London proper, claimed the lives of Barnaby and Hannah Bottomly. They are survived by their father, Lord "Laddie," brother Nolan, and half-sister Petal.

The brother and sister were often seen in the social press and in the city's fashionable nightclubs. Barnaby was named one of London's most eligible bachelors by several magazines. His sleek, jet-black hair and flashing eyes recalled images of matinee idols such as Ivor Novello and Tyrone Power.

"More than one woman lost their heart to him," confided the teary pop singer Arlene Arden, who had been dating the heir. "He was quite handsome, although I admit there was always something unsettling about him. And he had a swift temper. Once we were at a nightclub and some young rogue was bothering Hannah, and Barnaby leapt to her defense. He almost beat that silly teddy boy to a pulp."

Hannah was a fashion press fixture. With a silver-blonde mane and blue eyes, her weakness for the latest Carnaby Street fashions was widely emulated. The fiancée of Richard Canfield, the Earl of Wimpleham, Hannah had been featured in a recent bridal fashion layout in *Harper's Bazaar*. Tragically, the wedding ceremony had been scheduled for 6 August.

Avant garde designer Georgie O'Toole, who had designed Hannah's gown and trousseau as well as the bridesmaid dresses, said, "This was to be the wedding of the season, and now no one will see my beautiful dresses."

The family has repaired to Impswich, site of Garland's End, the ancestral estate of the Fotheringays, shared forebears of the Bottomlys. Relatives of Gara St. James, the actress wife of Laddie, had been visiting for the summer and are returning to the United States.

Richard Canfield's sister, Lady Virginia Dickens, issued a statement asking that the press respect the family's privacy in the wake of the tragedy.

A wing of the castle and outlying buildings were added casualties of the fire. Its origin is unknown at this time and is under investigation by the local constabulary.

Excerpt from *Tinseltown a Go-Go: Hollywood and the Terrific, Turbulent, & Trippy Times of the Sixties* by Oliver Littleton

Bored celebrities on the lookout for thrills helped the drug scene flourish in 1960's Hollywood. Many stars were eager to prove how "with it" they were and didn't hide their drug-fueled adventures.

No less a star than Cary Grant discussed his experimentation with LSD in mainstream magazines such as *Good Housekeeping*, *Look*, and *Ladies Home Journal*. Psychotherapy involving the use of lysergic acid diethylamide was the latest fad to relieve inhibitions and reveal the secret to happiness. (Considered a legitimate prescription medication, LSD wasn't yet classified as illegal.) Esther Williams, Gloria Prescott, and Grant's wife Betsy Drake also sought treatment to relieve anxiety and depression.

A nervous breakdown after a marital breakup in 1964 left Gloria Prescott eager to try LSD. Unlike her colleagues, she didn't find answers to life's questions. She revealed in an interview some years later, "All my visions under treatment revolved around a hulking Amazon destroying the countryside and trampling the villagers, begging for love, affection, and wealth from everyone she encounters. Isn't that crazy? What meaningless dreams it gave me!"

Despite Gloria's familiarity with LSD, she blamed an accidental ingestion of the drug later in 1968 for sensational tabloid headlines. A pool party hosted by Jackie Gleason was hijacked when a prankster spiked the punch bowl. The last thing Gloria remembered is sipping a cup of Kool-Aid; 48 hours later, she found herself in Las Vegas, married to Don Knotts, a fellow partygoer. (The marriage was quickly annulled and ranks with Hollywood's shortest unions.)

The drug scene also fueled onscreen romps like *Skiddoo*, *Candy*, and *Wild in the Streets*. Leading ladies who had once found themselves in glamorous situations and surroundings now tried to maintain star status with less enchanting scenarios. Lana Turner was driven to the brink of madness after being poisoned with LSD-spiked sugar cubes by her money-grubbing relatives in *The Big Cube*. Jennifer Jones played a former porn star seduced by an evil rock group which destroyed her wealthy family with drugs, kinky sex, and devil worship in *Angel, Angel, Down We Go*. Gara St. James ditched her square lifestyle to run wild with the flower children in Central Park and dove into a pig sty full of shit in *Rainbow Powderkeg*. (Would Garbo have been forced into such depressing movies if she hadn't retired?)

Turner Classic Movies Schedule, March 29, 2002
The month's theme: Hippies, Drugs & '60s Style
9:00 9.M. EST - *Lollygagger* (MGM, 1968) Directed by Fred Coe. Starring Christopher Jones, Barbara Lamont, James Farentino, Pamela Franklin, Robert Morley, Malcolm McDowell, Robert Fields, Teresa Graves. Jaded housewife embarks on a journey of self-discovery and sexual identity after a series of disturbing personal incidents: her husband is having an affair with his secretary, her daughter is drugging with lowlifes, an obscene phone caller won't stop calling. It isn't quite the sensation of *Belle de Jour* or *I Am Curious (Yellow)*, but it has its moments. In a famous sequence, Barbara applies heavy makeup and dolls herself up in a belted trench coat and leather boots, and she sucks a lollipop seductively before heading out to

explore her sexual fantasies.

11:00 P.M. EST - *Daisy Chain* (United Artists, 1969) Directed by George Marshall. Starring Gloria Prescott, Richard Egan, Barbara Parkins, Richard Crenna, Sylvia Miles, Peter Van Eyck, James Franciscus, Nyree Dawn Porter. A famous review described this as "Dorothy misses Oz and lands in *Peyton Place* on acid." It's a parody of Douglas Sirk glossy '50s soaps crossed with a tongue-in-cheek view of '60s counterculture films. (It could also be considered a big budget forerunner of future John Waters films.) Prescott flees the banality of suburbia by experimenting with group marriage, domination and submission, and better living through pharmaceuticals. She rolls her eyes and spits out the camp line, "Ugh, if I have to make one more casserole, I think I'll scream!" A well-publicized protest from the Catholic League of Boston helped make the film a success.

1:00 A.M. EST - *Rainbow Powderkeg* (Paramount, 1970) Directed by Joseph McGrath. Starring Charlton Heston, Gara St. James, Michael Parks, Roddy McDowell, Pamela Tiffin, Myrna Loy, Lee J. Cobb, Bob Balaban. Infamous flop about the hippie/flower children scene. McDowell shimmies in Central Park and leads a parade of nudists, Heston and Tiffin smoke a joint and marvel at the "colors," Loy and St. James share an uncomfortable lesbian kissing scene. St. James doesn't realize the film is trying to make a "statement" (her acting makes another statement entirely). In a movie full of embarrassments, she walks off with the prize when she dives into a filthy pig sty at an out-of-control orgy! Revolutionary hair design and wigs by Hibiscus (certain styles pre-figure the Farrah Fawcett, Dorothy Hamill, and Sinéad O'Connor hair crazes) are the best reasons to watch.

Excerpt from *Hollywood's Love Affair With Love: The Great Romances of the Movie Stars* by Cecelia Parkington

The instability of the late '60s affected relationships across the country, and Hollywood wasn't immune to these outside forces. Marriages which had once seemed steadfast were vulnerable just like that of Joe and Betty Suburbia.

One nasty divorce was between Barbara Lamont and Cyril Lamont, with wild accusations flying from both sides. Cyril inferred that he owed Barbara nothing in the way of support, because their marriage wasn't even legal! His investigators stated Barbara had secretly married a chorus boy in the '40s, and he alleged the marriage was never dissolved.

She refuted the claim, stating that she and Bruce Gayle never lived together as husband and wife, and the marriage was annulled at the insistence of her mother and manager, Myrtle Dempster.

"It seemed like a good idea at the time. Besides, the marriage was never legal, because I was under the age of consent." Barbara wouldn't confirm her actual age at the time (various sources reported her age then as 9, 11, or 14). "I was always advanced for my age and photographed mature. I already had a healthy bosom at nine years old!"

Barbara confronted the conflict with Cyril with aplomb and wit. "I refuse to let my soon-to-be ex-husband drag my name through the mud. I can do that well enough on my own! It's not like I didn't put up with things, too. Did you ever hear me complain about his recurrent problem with lumbago, even if it ruined our physical happiness?

"And our children are traumatized! Binky has been acting out, dressing up in my peignoirs and striking poses in the mirror. He thinks if he becomes a star, too, Daddy will come home. And Babs has been scribbling non-stop in her tablets. She's lost herself in schoolwork, I'm afraid, trying to be my perfect little girl.

"Anyway, Mother's in *my* corner, and Zanuck, Cohn, and Dore Schary have all feared the wrath of Myrtle Dempster at various times!" Barbara concluded. (The terms of the divorce were hammered out behind closed doors thereafter, so perhaps the threat of Mrs. Dempster was put to good use.)

A divorce involving class and titled nobility came under special press scrutiny. Rumors of marital discord between Gara St. James and Lord Lindale Bottomly began making the rounds after the fire which destroyed part of Brownmoor, his ancestral castle in England, and more tragically, resulted in the deaths of two of his adult children from his first marriage.

When the couple married in 1961, they were inseparable. Indeed, they took an extended honeymoon and were seldom apart, especially after the birth of their daughter Pet. But Gara returned to occasional acting roles and "Laddie" returned to the international party scene.

When rumors of problems in the marriage first surfaced, Gara was quick to deny them. "That's a dirty lie, whoever said it is insane!" she told Sheilah Graham. "I can't even describe the heavenly happiness Laddie and I enjoy. If Romeo and Judy had been half as happy as us, they wouldn't have resorted to drinking bathtub gin or whatever it was that killed 'em."

But there was gossip of Laddie romancing other women (including Daliah Lavi, Countess Vivi Dublitsky, and Luciana Paluzzi), and the couple began spending time apart. Gara became disinterested in her career and focused her attention on their child. The inevitable announcement of separation and divorce were met with resignation and empathy in some quarters, glee and schadenfreude in others.

Gara after divorce: "I'll be okay" by Martin Barris, *Parade*, February 9, 1969

From kiddie stardom in features such as *Breadline Baby* and *If You Knew Susie* to adult fame in movies like *Automat Affair* and *Nightgown of the Phantom*, Gara St. James has weathered the ups and downs of a Hollywood career. Her third marriage to a British Lord was out of a fairy tale, but as readers know, a happy ending isn't always in the cards.

Gara and the lord divorced last year ("Make sure your readers know I didn't leave *The* Lord – I may be a good Jewish girl from Chicago, but I think The Lord's a swell character, too!") and returned to Hollywood to reenergize her career. But with newer (and younger) actresses making waves, will it be easy for Gara to recapture the stardom she feels is her birthright?

"If my old pals Bahamia, Barbara Lamont, and Gloria Prescott can still have careers, then I won't have any worries," quipped the humorous star. "Bahamia's still kicking those legs up, even if she might be getting a little arthritis in those knees. As for Bar and Glo, they've always known what side their stardom is buttered on. I guess you can teach an old dog new tricks, so if they can keep turning tricks, I can do one better!

"Besides, I have to take care of my little Pet," Gara said softly as her daughter played nearby. The child, raised in rainy England, has acclimated to the sunny Los Angeles weather, for she's already brown as a berry.

Rumors continue to swirl about what caused the split between Gara and Lord Bottomly. Gossip columns seemed to take particular glee in recounting stories of Laddie's wandering eye. "I know what a 'wandering Jew' is, but what's a 'wandering eye?'" the actress guffawed. She wouldn't comment further, waving asides questions that one rag even went so far as to say she had threatened to list "fraud" as the reason for the divorce filing. (An allegation of fraud in a Hollywood union hasn't been used since the ill-fated coupling of actress Margot LeMora and chorus boy Percy Federline.)

Is it possible she's carrying a torch for Jory Plummer, the producer who guided her career back to adult stardom? They never wed, but remained friends, and he produced her upcoming record album ("I did some extra songs that didn't go on the album, like a killer swing version of 'Dreidel, Dreidel' with Jack Jones. Maybe I should do a holiday LP.").

Now that she's single again, she won't rule out dating. "My pal Ethel Merman keeps telling me I need to go out with her cousin, who's supposed to be a dreamboat. Well, I don't know, I've had a few dreamboats that turned into Titanics right before your eyes!"

Her focus is on raising her child and resuming her rightful career. "It's like I've been someone else these last few years. I can hear Bahamia joking, 'What's wrong with that?' But now I'm hiring a staff to help manage 'Gara's World.' How could I handle things when I didn't have an assistant? I just interviewed this girl named Penny Lipstick or something like that. I might end up hiring her if no one better applies."

Despite the heartache, St. James looks ahead. "This time it'll be about the acting, not about the sideshow. And if acting doesn't work out, there's money in the sideshow, too. Ha!"

Excerpt from *Weird Celebrity Recordings* by Sunny P. Kaye

Sunshine on My Mink, Gara St. James (Columbia Records LP, CL-2467, 1970). A strange "sunshine pop" entry is this LP from actress Gara St. James. This was an attempt to cash in on the success of groups like The Mamas & The Papas and The Beach Boys.

The album was produced by Jory Plummer (the movie executive also had legitimate music credentials via work with singers such as Joanie Sommers and The Four King Cousins) and boasts top-notch musicians (one of whom was future star and Eagles member Glenn Frey). Columbia Records spared no expense in the recording studio.

But St. James insisted on penning the tunes herself. Instead of joyful inspiration from colorful sunsets or brotherly love, Gara sings of pleasure derived from selfish pursuits. With song titles such as "I've Looked at Life From One Side Now," "Don't Move In Closer, Baby (You'll Ruin My Tan)," and "I'll Make My Own Kind of Music," it's obvious that Gara's impression is miles away from sunshine pop's intent. Her strident vocals overpower the warm instrumentals, and listeners will probably tire of these tunes quickly.

The two singles, "Dream a Great Big Dream of Me" and "A Whole Lotta Me (A Lot Less of You)," were flops at radio. The LP was forgotten until its rediscovery in the '90s by vinyl enthusiasts who appreciated the camp appeal of the cover, which depicts Gara swathed in mink and a big picture hat dripping with daffodils, reclining on a beach with apparent disdain for the sand at her feet.

Excerpt from *Politics and Hollywood Celebrities: The Conservative Connection* by Franklin Butterworth

The media exposure of the Vietnam War didn't pass unnoticed by the stars, who mostly spouted liberal rhetoric. Surprisingly in Hollywood, there were also conservative voices who stressed reason and faith in the government's decisions.

One star who spoke out was Gara St. James. The actress found herself back in Hollywood after her 1968 divorce, facing the difficulty of getting her career back on track. To make matters worse, she found herself at odds with liberal coworkers and overly-tolerant producers.

Rather than remaining quiet for fear of not being considered for jobs or offending those in power, Gara defended the conservative viewpoint. She made a splash hosting a barbecue fundraiser for Richard Nixon's presidential bid. In a witty touch, she had the meat on the spit arranged to resemble Nixon's rival Hubert Humphrey, and enjoyed asking each guest, "Hey, want a piece of Humphrey's ass?"

She also campaigned vigorously for Ronald Reagan in his re-election bid for Governor of California. "Ronnie said he was going to get rid of the welfare bums, and he did. He said he was going to clean up that mess at Berkeley, and he shut those kids up real good. Plus, Nancy made the ultimate sacrifice, you know, giving up stardom for her husband's career. I guess I'm not as conservative as her, but I've got something to look forward to when I get older, like Nancy."

These political successes galvanized St. James, and she grew more outspoken. She spoke out against Vietnam protesters and hippies ("Those unwashed kids who go barefoot and won't cut their hair, and I'm sure they'd stop that foolishness if they'd realize they're embarrassing their parents").

When Jane Fonda put herself in the center of controversy with her appalling behavior posing on an anti-craft gun battery and giving pro-Communist propaganda radio speeches in 1972, Gara was the first to speak out. "Jane should be ashamed of herself. How could someone as American as Henry Fonda have a daughter who's a pinko Commie? The Academy ought to revoke that Oscar they gave her! I didn't even get nominated for *A Woman Called Methuselah*. And I only did that movie when I was up for the lead daughter in *Fiddler on the Roof*, but Norman Jewison nixed me. All I did was ask why a Canadian was making a movie about Jews, even if his *name* is Jewison. It's all a conspiracy!

"Anyway, 'Hanoi Jane,' what a name. That's almost as bad as 'Belgrade Barbara' [a nickname for actress pal Barbara Lamont, referring to tabloid gossip about her romantic escapades filming *To Serbia With Love* (1966)]!"

Lord's bride drowns in Irish Sea by Jonathan Womack, *The Times of London*, 19 April, 1970

The body of Jenny Menzies Bottomly, the fourth wife of Lord Laddie Bottomly, was discovered yesterday evening on the shore of the Irish

Sea in Merseyside, the apparent victim of drowning. Jenny, 28, was a magician's assistant in a London nightclub act when she first encountered Laddie, who was smarting from a divorce from American actress Gara St. James and the death of his children in a fire the previous year.

Laddie married Jenny on 7 September, 1969, and the marriage appeared to have been in trouble from the start, according to speculation in various gossip columns. The couple visited Merseyside as a belated honeymoon.

Gara St. James, herself having recently embarked on a new marriage to dancer Bill Merman, of the family which includes the famous musical star Ethel, was asked for comment. "Although the two of us weren't successful at marriage, I don't envy Laddie's obvious worse luck in the area."

CHAPTER 10

She's not even here and she's still the elephant in the room.

Mina admitted that Gloria's theory had merit. "Both Laddie and Gara had a connection to everything in the box. And I can see him wanting to get Gara in trouble by hiding the tiara."

""I'm certain we're overlooking the significance of the other items, though," Pet added. She picked up the photographs of Brownmoor again. "I know there's something here, but I can't put my finger on it."

"It may be as simple as not wanting to be reminded of the fire and how much everyone lost," Albert suggested. Pet conceded it was a possibility, but felt there was something more ...

"Maybe my idea will help prod us along," Albert boasted. "You may not realize it, but I've been known to inspire true genius."

"Like that blonde you once dated, the one who was surprised to learn Rodin was a sculptor and not a Japanese movie monster?" Pet teased.

He blushed, glancing to see Mina's reaction. "Hey now, you've had your share of bad dates, as well."

"Yes, I'm sorry, I couldn't resist," Pet conceded. "I've been divorced, so my track record's nothing to brag about." (She had been married briefly to a fellow photographer, dashing and rugged in a Clint Walker sort of way. But this battle of the sexes didn't foster the camaraderie of Tracy and Hepburn in *Adam's Rib,* and they split after conflicts, while not quite worthy of Liz and Dick in *Who's Afraid of Virginia Woolf?*, had left them both relieved when it was over.)

"I'm afraid Mina's the only one with the successful reputation here," Pet continued. "Mark was a great guy. You'd have liked him, Albert. Actually, you've got some of the same characteristics."

It was Mina's turn to blush, because it hadn't passed her notice. There was something both lovely and odd about being so attracted to a man again, considering the present circumstances of feuding relations and potential homicide attempts.

"Shouldn't we get a move on checking out Albert's hunch?" Mina demurred.

Pet raised an eyebrow, but decided not to needle her friends and relatives about their obvious growing interest in each other. There would be time for that, after they'd laid to rest their curiosity about a mysterious fire from decades ago and their collective worry that a facsimile of darling Betsy Palmer (from that *Friday Part 13* movie) had taken up residence in their midst.

Gloria gaily hummed a tune from one of her old films as she primped in front of the mirror. "Stepping out on my baby," she sang out, a twist that had once given Irving Berlin a start. "What he don't know, won't hurt him ..."

Barbara entered and sighed dramatically as she sat down. "Well, Mother's okay now, and that old Dame is having fresh oxygen sent over, provided by her own physician. I wonder if British oxygen is better than American oxygen. Maybe I can have it imported when we get back to Beverly Hills."

"Good idea. I think Elizabeth Taylor does the same thing."

"You're still in a good mood," Barbara noticed.

"I guess so, I just feel so smart that I figured out that box was probably packed away by Laddie."

"I'll give you that one," Barbara allowed begrudgingly, letting the spirit of competition rise to the surface. "But the next clue is on me. I have to figure that out, since whomever is doing all this tried to off Mother twice!"

"I have every faith that you'll figure it out, *mija*," Gloria soothed her friend's ego. "Where do you think we ought to investigate next?"

"Anywhere that's far away from Gara," Barbara scoffed. "Now she's wavering on allowing us to attend her charity function."

"She's trying to pull rank. Don't worry, that party'll need all the celebrity attendance it can muster. British stars aren't as interesting as Americans. Who can they get to attend her party, Rita Tushingham? Linda Thorson? They'll need *us* to provide some glamour and pizzazz."

"I'm still a bit perturbed that the children won't be there with us at the party."

"I know, but isn't it good business for Binky to make that club appearance? They can attend the party after their little performance."

"But in the meantime, we'll have to attend to Mother! And she insists on going. She says I haven't let her attend a party since she caused that scene, you know the time, when she took off half her clothes and jumped in the pool at that Clinton fundraiser I hosted back in '92?"

"Even at her advanced age, she managed a decent swan dive," Gloria admitted. "Esther said it wasn't half bad. And Bill said that if Mother Lamont were a few years younger, she'd have to watch out!"

"Yes, Hillary wasn't pleased." Barbara got an inspired look. "That's it! That's what we should be investigating next!"

"What? Whitewater? Monica-gate?"

"No, I meant we should think like politicians. They have to think like their enemies think. Let's pull the same trick those Brits tried to pull on us. We'll question them as casually as possible and find out what they know."

Gloria made a final adjustment to her false eyelashes in the mirror. "Woodstern and Bernward might have caught Nixon, but I'm sure they didn't do it as stylishly as we could! Lead on, darling. These English planks won't know what hit 'em!"

"I don't think this is a good idea," Miles said as he looked over his shoulder.

"Quiet, I know what I'm doing," Henry insisted. The boys and Sophie crept along the corridor, glancing back at the end of the hall where Babs stood as lookout. She gave a thumbs up, encouraging them forward to their task.

"We've explored the old ruins and the attics for clues. The next logical spot is Laddie's bedroom," Henry reminded his younger brother as they neared the door.

"Are you sure no one's in this part of the house?" Miles whispered in response.

"The maids have already finished with this wing. Besides, Babs will whistle if anyone's coming. What could go wrong?" Sophie asked.

They were almost at Laddie's room when the door opened and Gwyda stepped out into the hall. The startled children froze as the woman locked the door behind her and turned.

She raised an eyebrow and fixed an imperious gaze on the trio. "Have I interrupted something? Just what are you up to?"

They stammered excuses without offering a plausible explanation. A quick-thinking Babs sauntered forward from the opposite end of the hall.

"I'm fascinated by old English castles and the ghostly legends that always seem to be part of their heritage, so the kids were showing me around. Tell me, was a young woman in white murdered in this hallway? I could swear I felt the vibrations of the undead," she trilled.

Gwyda wasn't fooled by the flimsy explanation. "Surely you felt the vibration from your tape recorder, or perhaps from your personal massage device. You look like the type who would own such a thing," she snorted with a dismissive wave of her hand.

Gwyda focused her attention on the children. "Your Great-Great-Uncle Laddie's room is off limits. So if you had any ideas that you might snoop in his room for clues, I'd reconsider. There are more productive things you could be doing without causing mischief."

"We didn't mean to make you angry, Gran," Miles piped in, hoping his charm as youngest great-grandchild would help diffuse Gwyda's wrath. "Honestly, we weren't trying to snoop. We just wanted to scare Babs with ghost stories."

Gwyda was skeptical, but her affection for Miles and Henry won out. "Forgive my harsh tone. Why don't you show off some other part of the house." She fixed her eyes sharply back on Babs. "I'm only sorry there isn't a dungeon for you to tour." With that, she swept down the hall.

"Geez, I know when someone has problems with one sense, the others pick up the slack. But losing an arm shouldn't result in eyes in the back of her head," Babs commented.

"What was she doing in that room, anyway?" Sophie wondered. "Looking at Laddie's things, feeling sad?"

"Or maybe making sure certain things never left that room," a suspicious Babs theorized.

"But how are we going to know? And how are we going to be able to check out the room for ourselves?" Miles asked.

"We'll have to be patient, and think up another angle," Babs said. "That crack she made about the dungeon's given me an idea. What *is* below the ground floor? We might find a clue, if we don't find those ghosts first."

"Any more bright ideas, Philo Vance?" Pet nudged Albert as they returned to the car.

"So it didn't pan out the way I had hoped," he admitted.

"At least it gives more weight to our suspicion that things weren't adding up," Mina defended.

"Oh, so it's like that now, two against one?" Pet teased, a subtle mention of the attraction between her companions.

Albert had been convinced the police would have a complete file on the fire investigation, and with the pull of the Bottomly name on their side, it would be no problem to get a copy. And while the Bottomly name indeed still struck fear in certain parts of Flemshire, the cooperative police were able only to provide a flimsy file with notes on the preliminary investigation, not much more than the page contained in Laddie's box. The police could only say the file on the complete investigation didn't exist.

"Stop that, we have more important matters to spend time on," Albert side-stepped. "I take it we're all thinking the family used its influence to have the file destroyed."

"It did cross my mind. Now what do we do?"

"Well, we've got these few additional pages to check out. I say we return to the house and look them over before anyone else has a chance to even know what we did."

"Good idea. When we examined the box earlier, I half expected Louise and Carolyn to slip papers off the table and under their skirts!" Pet snarked.

"Carolyn would never do that, it would wrinkle her bloomers," Albert added.

Mina choked with laughter. "And I thought Brits didn't have naughty senses of humor! 'No sex, please, we're English.'"

"Ever hear of *Monty Python*? Anyway, I'm half-English, Momsy's pure American."

"I'm half-English myself. My mother was Catalan," Albert explained.

"Catalonia's such a beautiful region," Mina reminisced.

"You've been there?" Albert asked, surprised.

"Yes, Mark and I honeymooned there," she responded, surprised to feel self-conscious. "I love Spain. That's not my area of expertise, though, my graduate studies focused on South America, but the regional Spanish dynasties always fascinated me." She stopped and chuckled. "I'm sorry, I started sounding like a professor. I'm supposed to be on sabbatical and not thinking about work!"

"I'd love to talk about Spain and Catalonia some time," Albert brightened.

"I'd like that, too," Mina responded.

Pet decided to give her nephew and her cousin a break and didn't jump in with a comment on their flirtation. Mina and Albert weren't related, but their connections to her had a vintage of old English customs when families encouraged courtship between extended relations.

And family was uppermost in her mind. She held the skimpy file on her lap, hoping it would provide an answer or two. But Gwyda's caution echoed in the back of her mind, and she hoped their curiosity would reveal relief, and not regret.

Barbara and Gloria sauntered into the lounge where Nolan and Willis were engaged in discussion and Louise was reading a magazine. "Isn't this a lovely day?" Barbara asked.

"It was," Louise replied, refusing to lift her eyes in further acknowledgement.

"What are you gentlemen up to today?" Gloria vamped, perching on the corner of the desk as she'd done in countless films to entrance the likes of Guy Madison or John Saxon.

"This doesn't concern you," Willis replied with annoyance. Nolan was irked as well, but his genetic disposition for theatrical ladies weakened his resolve and he offered Gloria a somewhat interested look.

"I'm so looking forward to the film screening, and what a wonderful opportunity to raise money for charity," Barbara steered the conversation.

"And meet the Queen and other royals!" Gloria added. "I suppose that's old hat for you. With your family's many centuries of history, you must have encountered kings and queens all the way back to *David and Bathsheba!*"

"But these days we seem to be stuck with pikeys and chavs," Louise muttered from behind her magazine.

Nolan shot a glance at Louise and returned his attention to Gloria's cleavage (hoisted and still working, even at her age). "The Bottomlys and Glasscocks have been here for many centuries, it's true. But with prestige comes responsibility."

"Such as giving back, like the charity event. What a stroke of genius on Gara's part!" Gloria chirped.

"Don't oversell it," Barbara barely breathed, her voice reaching its target and vanishing without their hosts hearing (she wasn't first in Miss Burns's elocution classes for nothing).

Willis snorted at the mere mention of Gara's name. "She wouldn't know charity if it bit her on the bum."

"She knows charity, as long as it benefits her first and foremost," Louise snapped.

"Now, you mustn't worry about offending us with derogatory statements about her. After all, we've known Gara longer than your family has," Gloria goaded.

"These two didn't know her at all," Nolan said in reference to Willis and Louise. "Willis was just a child. I was already an adult, and knew she was bad news from the beginning. Why Laddie married that classless cow, I'll never understand."

"Tell us something we don't know," Barbara rolled her eyes.

"I saw things," Willis defended. "I heard Dad and Mum argue about how Laddie wasted money on her. He spent a fortune having her suites redone. She even took over part of Hannah and Barnaby's rooms so she'd have more space."

At the mention of those names, Nolan's mood changed, and Hollywood's feminine wiles had lost their power. He straightened and excused himself. Louise looked up from her periodical and glanced at her husband. In turn, they both fixed their gazes on the actresses. Gloria broke the uncomfortable silence.

"Leave it to Gara. She's not even here and she's still the elephant in the room."

Babs peered around the corner and found the light switch. "The decorators seem to have neglected the basement," she observed of the dank stone walls and dreary ambience.

"It's been a long time since we've been down here. The few doors were always locked," Henry offered.

This was still the case. The open doors revealed empty spaces and abandoned pieces of outdated furniture in disrepair. "It doesn't look like we're going to find anything here, much less a ghost," Sophie grumbled, even though the creepiness factor was not unlike Hill House in *The Haunting*.

The main corridor branched off into two side halls with more doors and dead-ends, which revealed nothing new for the detectives, not even one clammy-handed ghost.

They came finally to a side hall that was much longer than the others. This section of the cellar wasn't lighted like the main corridor, but Babs had brought along a flashlight. They were surprised to find the passageway suddenly veered to the right. The hall continued only a dozen yards further.

"That's odd, I wonder why this hall even exists," Babs wondered aloud. Henry directed the flashlight's beam along the wall.

"The stonework is different," Miles pointed out.

"This work was done more recently than the rest of the cellar," Babs surmised. "I wonder what was on the other side of this wall."

Henry moved the beam of light further around the hall. "We missed this," he pointed out, aiming the flashlight at a small recess along the opposite wall, which revealed the remnants of a stone staircase. The few remaining steps rose about two feet; the newer stonework filled in the wall to the ceiling.

"Hold on, what's that?" Miles asked as the beam of light

highlighted something glittering in the stone floor's corner. Henry steadied the flashlight as Miles reached for the tiny object. He turned it over in his hand, displaying what appeared to be a pendant on a broken bit of chain, like Maria Montez's lost "cobra jewel" from *Cobra Woman*.

"I wonder who it belongs to," Babs speculated.

"Have you guys ever seen these weird stairs?" Sophie asked.

The boys shrugged in response. "The last time we were down here, we probably *were* worried about running into a ghost," Henry grinned.

"I think we're likelier to meet that ghost than find out what everyone's been so intent on keeping secret," Babs commented with a final glance at the hall's construction. The stonework was in no danger of crumbling, but with a little more digging, she hoped the truth behind the mysterious events at Brownmoor would be revealed.

Pet, Mina, and Albert decided it would be best to examine the file upstairs than invite constant interruptions by poring over the papers in the library or lounge. Pet, donning the matchmaking skills of Dolly Levi, offered to fix a snack for the trio while the pair headed to Albert's room to begin perusing the file (or begin a little kissing; Pet would leave it up to Mina and Albert to set the romantic timetable).

Pet entered the kitchen, where she found Mrs. Dutton discussing the evening's meal plans with Cook. The housekeeper, as helpful as Juanita Moore in *Imitation of Life*, insisted on helping Pet put together sandwiches and salad.

"Did you and the others have a pleasant time in the village?" Mrs. Dutton asked in a reserved tone.

"Yes, we ran some errands," Pet responded noncommittally.

The housekeeper watched as Cook went into the pantry. "Did you report the recent ... incidents at Brownmoor to the police captain?" she asked.

Pet gave a start and asked how she knew where they had been. "I do know people," Mrs. Dutton responded vaguely.

"I see. Well, we didn't report anything that's been going on. We wanted to see the police report on the fire."

The knife in the older woman's hand wavered a moment, then finished slicing a tomato. "I know it's not my place, Miss Pet, but I don't think you should be looking into what happened so long ago. It upsets your aunt, and will cause gossip in town."

Although taken aback by the warning, Pet defended her actions. "We aren't trying to cause a problem. In fact, we're trying to bring an end to these bizarre incidents happening in the house. If we prove the fire was an accident, it'll stop whoever's been playing these games that are getting out of control. Someone could get hurt, maybe one of the children."

Mrs. Dutton glanced aside as Cook reentered the kitchen. "I'm certain no one wants that," she said softly. "But the past is best left silent. Your brother and sister died on that tragic day, and nothing good will come from disturbing their peace."

Pet felt as if she'd been slapped by the insinuation. "That's unfair. I'm not trying to dishonor their memory. How can proving the fire was an accident hurt Hannah and Barnaby?"

The housekeeper finished the sandwiches and placed the snack items on a tray. "Let's not talk about this anymore. I'm sorry for having said anything to upset you, Miss Pet. I know you have good intentions at heart." She stood up with the tray. "I'll carry this upstairs for you."

"Thank you, but I'll take care of it." Pet took the tray and carried it across the room. (Mrs. Dutton no longer shone with the glow of Juanita Moore and had taken on the dull insouciance of Agnes Moorehead in *Hush ... Hush, Sweet Charlotte*.) She glanced back and saw the sadness that crossed the woman's face. Mrs. Dutton recovered and gave Pet a tight smile before busying herself with Cook and the dinner preparations.

"She knows something," Pet thought. "But what? And – is it something I want to know, too?"

STRANGE INTERLUDE 10

Most costars regard scene-stealing as a professional challenge, not a reason to plot
pre-meditated murder.

American Movie Classics Schedule, October 31, 1992
Spotlight on Halloween Horror
      8:00 P.M. EST - *The Dark Secret of Emhouse* (Heartstrings Films, 1974)
Directed by Dan Curtis. Starring Cliff Robertson, Barbara Lamont, Bruce
Dern, Peter Donat, John Hillerman, Luana Anders, Wesley Addy, Denise
Alexander. Horror tale involving ghostly beasts, witchcraft, and murder in a
desolate Texas town. Lamont is a Dallas interior designer returning home to
attend a funeral and encounters family secrets and the supernatural. Lamont
more convincing than one might expect as former white trash passing herself
off as cultured. Shots of the desolate Texas landscape accompanied by
ominous music contribute to the creepy atmosphere. However, the film's
climax doesn't pay off. Viewers may scratch their heads over the ending,
where it's never quite explained what the house's faulty plumbing and a
ghostly herd of drunken sheep have to do with the dark secret.
      10:00 P.M. EST - *The Cawker City Murders* (Amity Films, 1974)
Directed by Milton Phlug. Starring Earl Holliman, Gara St. James, Robert
Reed, Lana Wood, John Rubinstein, Barbi Benton, Dan Barrows, Eddie Little
Sky. Murder in a small Kansas town with the unusual (and true) claim to
fame of "home to the world's largest ball of twine." This movie, however,
isn't going to win any records other than possibly "most ludicrous film
premise." Apparently that ball of twine is on a homicidal rampage as
townspeople are murdered one by one; the only clue seems to be a piece of
twine at each crime scene. Instead of checking to see who last bought twine
at the local hardware store, the police set up a roadblock around the town
square where the menacing ball of twine sits. The stupidest scene: St. James
screaming, "I'll kill you, you miserable ball of twine, for taking my Harve
away from me!" as she tries mounting the pile in a rainstorm!
      12:00 A.M. EST - *The Haunted Leprosarium* (Pulse Features, 1975)
Directed by Peter Sasdy. Starring Joseph Cotten, Gloria Prescott, Lloyd

Bochner, Misty Rowe, Scatman Crothers, Faith Domergue, Estelle Winwood, Dub Taylor. A socialite inherits a dilapidated Southern mansion once used as a leper's hospital. There are scares and chilling images in this Southern-fried gothic tale. Domergue is interesting as the local diner owner with a secret, and Winwood owns her role as a mysterious graveyard mourner. Rumors persist that the nightmarish climax, in which a terrified Prescott is pursued by leper-zombies, utilized actual sufferers of the illness (more properly called Hansen's Disease). Gloria claimed that filming this sequence was truly frightening, "but then, I just reminded myself that a leprosarium is like a rehab hospital, and I felt right at home."

Excerpt from *Operetta on Stage and on Film* by Aimee Granger

Despite a few mid-century successes [like the off-Broadway *Little Mary Sunshine* (1959), the movie spoof *Dowdy Harrietta* (1958), or *The Pleasant Peasant* in an *I Love Lucy* episode], operetta was essentially dead and buried, but it didn't stop producers from trying to revive the genre. Critic Ethan Mordden coined the term "floperetta" to describe passé musicals which had nothing to do with the recent Broadway environment. What's surprising is that interesting attempts at updating the genre appeared in the '70s.

Candide flopped on its initial 1956 run, but a newly-conceived revival in 1973 ran for several years. *The Rothschilds*, *A Little Night Music*, and *Sweeney Todd* all contained elements of operetta and met with success.

Though the Broadway revival of *The Chocolate Soldier* (1974) didn't last long, it strived for relevance by tying the story to current bohemian culture. Director Gower Champion pulled double-duty when the male lead, Howard Keel, took advantage of an option in his contract and left the troubled production.

With the out-of-town premiere in Boston approaching, the producers convinced Champion to pull double duty and take over the lead. Despite reservations, he accepted the challenge and plunged into the role with enthusiasm.

There were evident problems in Boston, but with a scheduled New York opening which couldn't be postponed, the production moved forward with few changes. Prescott took advantage of the circumstances and commenced with a great deal of scene-stealing, which audiences loved, but didn't endear her to her costars or the production staff. (On the other hand, Prescott's theatrical gestures and minstrel-style eyerolls kept the show running longer than it might have without her campy humor.)

Champion became furious with her onstage antics and at one infamous performance, he set her wig on fire! A quick-thinking Ilka Chase adlibbed, "Madame, those hippie Serbs have attacked the palace with flaming arrows!" and dumped a vase of water on Gloria's head. Prescott ate up the publicity, stating to the press, "Most costars regard scene-stealing as a professional challenge, not a reason to plot pre-meditated murder."

The following year, Norman Getz's final American operetta, *The Ballad of Kansas Pie*, premiered regionally in Wichita with a try-out period fraught with technical problems and casting missteps. Its later New York run was undistinguished, although it occasioned an opportunity for American audiences to enjoy the talents of French opera diva La Staggée. She was a bit miscast as the Midwestern heroine in this tale of lust, murder, and peanut butter/peach pie, but her worthwhile performance garnered the show's few positive reviews.

Actress Gara St. James was enchanted by the story and urged its purchase by Paramount Studios. Richard Sylbert, head of production, had a reputation of exploring features derived from literary and culturally-significant sources.

And thus *The Ballad of Kansas Pie* made it to the screen in 1976 under the direction of Jay Arruh, who had directed the Broadway production. Arruh had not directed film before, but Sylbert had been moved by St. James's enthusiastic endorsement.

The stagebound direction betrayed Arruh's theatrical background, but it's doubtful revolutionary production could have elevated the film. Gara was not an ideal heroine, despite her own Midwestern origins. She so dominated her fellow performers that the operetta's delicate balance was destroyed.

As Kansas Pie's romantic rival, Okie Puddin', the Russian opera star Sela Hughesenskaya outclassed the star. In the important confrontation duet, the jarring editing exposed Gara's repeated attempts at edging Hughesenskaya out of the frame. To her credit, the Russian diva more than held her own, but it's a shame that her hard work wasn't in a better film.

Excerpt from *Weird Celebrity Recordings* by Sunny P. Kaye

Aba Daba Honeymoon, Sly & the Family Stone with Gloria Prescott (Epic/CBS Records 45 single, E-13017, 1975). Whoever had the idea of bringing funk group Sly & the Family Stone together with Golden Age actress Gloria Prescott could be considered crazy, a genius, or both. The group recorded this single as a novelty; as for Prescott's involvement, there were tabloid tales that she was romantically involved with one of the musicians.

The song (best remembered by Debbie Reynolds and Carleton

Carpenter's frenetic pacing in the 1950 MGM musical *Two Weeks with Love*) was transformed; the BPM was slowed-down and the group's funky rock sound was flavored with dashes of island reggae and disco strings.

It's not uncommon to find listeners either intrigued and/or appalled by Sly and Gloria's unique duet. It's similar to the bizarro effect of Ethel Merman singing Broadway show tunes with a disco backbeat on 1979's *The Ethel Merman Disco Album*.

The song failed to place on any chart, but oddly enough, it had a second life in 2001. American D.J. Sin Chaise remixed the tune, turning it into a trance-heavy club stormer. It hit #1 on dance charts across Europe, Japan, and the U.S., and even reached #34 on the Billboard Hot 100. A music video was filmed featuring Gloria Prescott attired in club fetishwear and kicking up her heels in a strobe-laden discothèque (a reclusive Sly Stone couldn't be persuaded to appear).

Excerpted entries from *'70s Television Detectives: An Episode Guide* by Vance Jeffers

Cannon, "Chalet of Terror," CBS, original airdate: 1/14/76. Guest Cast: Clu Gulager (Merv Patterson), Barbara Lamont (Eva Patterson), Danielle Kusnal (Cissy Morgan), Leslie Nielsen (Count Ivan Merkel), David Hedison (Michael Sullivan), John Marley (John Wilson), Alfred Ryder (Officer Simpson), Louise Troy (Bella the Housekeeper). Cannon tries to determine who's after an American heiress in Switzerland [exteriors were filmed in Vail, Colorado; Conrad interrogating Lamont while both are supposedly on skis (in front of Alpine rear projection) is particularly hysterical]. The contrived story involves antique snuff boxes and counterfeit gold bouillon, but it leads to a satisfying conclusion. There's the bonus of seeing Lamont and Kusnal as sisters in a wintery European setting, which they had done before in *To Serbia With Love*, with Danielle even more duplicitous than she was in that film.

Police Woman, "Trick of the Night," NBC, original airdate: 10/25/77. Guest Cast: Gloria Prescott (Alexandra Hunter), Allen Case (Mark Garland), Robert Sampson (Tom McDonald), Kim Lankford (Jenny), Jonelle Allen (Loretta), Peter Ford (Derelict). Pepper and company uncover a prostitution/white slavery ring masquerading as a modeling agency. Gloria Prescott is silky and venomous as the madam, oozing insincerity and glamour as she ruins young girls's lives. The tension between Dickinson and Prescott is palpable, amping the drama quite effectively. (The discord apparently stems from professional jealousy when the two appeared together onscreen in the '60s, recounted in gossip columns at the time.)

Barnaby Jones, "Predicament in Plaid," CBS, original airdate: March 2, 1978. Guest Cast: Gara St. James (Addie McDermott), Pat Hingle (Dave Griffin), Bahamia (Monique Sellers), Glenn Corbett (Don McDermott), John McCook (Andy Reynolds), Marshall Colt (Bagpiper). A bank vault robbery leads Barnaby to a ghostly Scottish mystery in California. The story's better than it sounds, and the unusual supernatural touches are effective. Bahamia is marvelous as a sexy suspect who flirts with a visibly aroused Ebsen (keep a close eye when he turns at the end of the scene)! One must see to believe Gara in a kilt and doing a highland sword dance; watch for a quick shot of Bahamia rolling her eyes on the sidelines.

Cover blurbs from *National Enquirer*, August 22, 1977
    ELVIS'S LAST WILD WEEKEND WITH BARBARA LAMONT!
    JACKIE O. PREFERS MCDONALD'S OVER BURGER KING! "THEIR FRIES ARE TOPS!"
    DID STREISAND AND GLORIA PRESCOTT ENGAGE IN FISTICUFFS OVER HUNKY BARTENDER? "I JUST WANTED A DRINK!" BARBRA CLAIMS!
    WILL VALERIE PERRINE, TONI TENNILLE, OR BAHAMIA REPLACE FARRAH ON "CHARLIE'S ANGELS"?
    FASHION DISASTER AT JOAN CRAWFORD'S FUNERAL; TIMIMA BOSSI WORE SAME DRESS AS THE DECEASED!
    VALENTINO, BRANDO, REYNOLDS – WHY LORD LADDIE IS KING OF THE HEAP! IS HE GOING TO TELL ALL?
    MARIA CALLAS NEAR DEATH AND STILL FEUDING WITH LA STAGGÉE!
    WHICH CELEB ALREADY FEATURED ON THIS COVER MAY HAVE A BLADDER PROBLEM? EMBARRASSING WETNESS FOLLOWS!
    GARA OUTDOES LIZ AT ALL-YOU-CAN-EAT BUFFET! "IT WAS EVERY MAN FOR HIMSELF!" CRIES WOUNDED ONLOOKER!

Excerpt from *Reel and Real Hollywood Fashion in the Seventies* by Abigail Monterey
    Fashion in the decade ran the gamut from prairie dresses and granny gowns of the early '70s to the disco glam of the late '70s. Street style influenced Hollywood and fueled the changing images of '70s fashion.
    Fascination with African style was a huge influence. Black entertainers were proud to express their heritage through their clothing and hairstyles. Diana Ross, Cicely Tyson, Pam Grier, Bahamia, and Tamara

Dobson made starry splashes both on- and off-screen. *Mahogany*, *Foxy Brown*, and *Cleopatra Jones* displayed images of African-American women as stylish, strong divas. Average women took notice, and sported afros and braids to prove "black is beautiful."

The dashiki was a trend spawned by West African attire. Worn by characters on *Good Times* and *Soul Train* dancers, they were comfortable as well as an expression of black pride.

One star confused by the trend was Gara St. James. Friend and occasional costar Bahamia sported a beaded dashiki and maxi-skirt in a TV special, and Gara joked onscreen that she wanted one, too. Soon thereafter, Gara appeared in public wearing a dashiki; instead of colorful kente cloth, the blouse was made of a pink cotton print decorated with images of "smiley faces." She referred to it as a "Caucasian dashiki" and joked, "Look, even white people can get away with wearing something most people sleep in!"

Excerpt from *Being Bahamia: Stardom Looks Good on Me!* by Bahamia with Lajuana Pagewell

The '70s got off to a bad start when Gara tricked me into standing up for her again at her marriage to Bill Merman. Ethel, the other bridesmaid, was choking with laughter behind her nosegay. "I hope you have the same happiness I had when I married Ernie!" she toasted.

Gara didn't really get it, but she joked, "Yeah, and here's hoping that hit you put out on Roz [Russell] pays off one day!"

I was able to avoid her for years at a time, except for an occasional TV show or the like. She often invited me to her Malibu house called "The Plantation." "It'll feel like being back home!" she'd tastelessly cackle. But nothing prepared me for the disaster of her guest star appearance on my 1977 Emmy-winning variety special, *Ah Mia, Bahamia!*

I had a stellar group of stars lined up: Flip Wilson, Ricardo Montalban, Della Reese, Lily Tomlin, and George Jones. But the producers wanted Gara, which didn't appeal to me. But I let them wear me down and agreed. What a mistake that was!

I devised a sketch where we would trade a few jokes, and then segue into a little soft shoe and a Broadway medley. The entire segment could be shot in an afternoon after a morning rehearsal. Or so I thought!

For Gara arrived and refused to leave. She kept suggesting changes to the set, our costumes, the music, everything! She pushed her way into other numbers, and insulted my other guests. She slapped Flip on the back and said, "Where's that ghetto sister of yours, Geraldine? Damn, she's funny! Does she need a job, 'cause I'm looking for a new maid."

Then she insulted Lily. "What's up with that daughter of yours, Edith What's-her-name? She's pretty big to be behaving so loopy. Are you sure she's not retarded?"

Finally, one evening I caught her drinking and popping pills in her dressing room. She claimed it was Fresca and diet pills, but I suspected otherwise. It was then I realized that sad, old heifer was on a downward spiral that no one could help bring to a halt. Oh well, that wasn't my problem!

Excerpt from *They Said What? The Unpublished Quotes Celebrities Said Off-The-Record (Until Now!) Over the Years to Life Magazine* by Angela Theroux and Sage Mallick

Myrtle Dempster: Dena St. James? She was all right, if you like bitches. But I have to admire her, she turned that bovine of a daughter into a star. Now, if you think *my* daughter's untalented – and it's all right to think that, by the way – that Gara was less talented than Elsie the Cow.

Marlene Dietrich: Oh, that Gawa, what a tewwible pewson. So pushy, and so twashy. I was twying on dwesses at Bewgdowf Goodman once, and she bawged into my dwessing woom and accoosed me of steawing huh dwess! As if I wood be caught dead in one of huh ciwcus tents! I towd her, "You bettuh lay off the Wocky Woad, honey." I thought Gawbo was a peasant, but that was befowah I met Gawa!

Gara St. James: Jerry Lewis was a real jerk when I worked on his damn telethon. First off, he sticks me next to some of those diseased children. They might have been contagious. Then he insulted my song. I was making a joke when I sang, "All God's chillun got rhythm ... 'cept *these* kids!" So I had to set him straight and told him, "Don't you tell me off in front of these cripps! I'm a fucking lady, and don't you forget it!"

Gloria Prescott: Being too well brought up, I always make amends for the misdeeds of others, like Gara. Once we did a comedy song, "So Right in a Sarong," with Movita for a charity show. Gara had to gall to tell us, "I didn't know you were from Tahiti, I thought you girls were spics!" So I defused the situation with a musical laugh and interjected, "We didn't know you were a Protestant milkmaid from Peoria, we thought you were a Jewish girl from Shaker Heights!" But Movita sure had Gara's number, and she never invited her to any parties at Marlon's.

Barry Coe: I didn't expect to work with Katharine Hepburn, but I also didn't expect to be stuck acting opposite fiberglass mannequins. And the worst was Gloria Prescott. She makes a hat rack seem animated! It's an open secret in this town about Gloria's recurring bladder infections. It's not about being sick and more about letting too many "visitors enter the temple." Not that I know anything about it firsthand, mind you.

Dolores Hart: People ask if the sin in Hollywood is what drove me to the convent. It was more personal than that, but I will say, some things left me speechless. When I worked with Barbara Lamont on *All Night Beach Party*, you could have knocked me over with a feather when she mentioned ongoing affairs with George Hamilton, Ty Hardin, *and* Albert Finney. Then she asked if I wanted to check out her collection of her leading men's underwear! BVDs, bikinis, jockstraps; she'd been collecting for years! Is it any wonder I headed for the nunnery?

Athole Lamont: They say I'm crazy. They say I'm drunk even when I'm not. And by "they," I mean my bitch of a sister and that damn mother of ours. I can't tell you how many times they tricked me into letting myself be committed. I was the real talent. And I'm not just talking about stripping! I was the better actress, but I didn't get the breaks. I pretended to be a virgin way more times than she did! Where's *my* award?

Nancy Reagan: I even sponsored Gara's star on Hollywood's Walk of Fame, that's how close we once were. Do you know, she once had the gall to say she'd checked out her star and it was covered in footprints, and why didn't I "move my can" and clean it up! I had to worry about where to seat her during state dinners after she told the Ethiopian ambassador, "What's this great diet your people have? Every time I see Ethiopians on TV, they look as skinny as Sinatra back in '44!"

Gara St. James: People say I'll do anything for a buck, but that's not true. It's just that if I'm going to put anything out, you better pay me for it. Call me a lousy Jew, I don't care, but you're not gonna screw me over. Pork and beans don't grow on trees, you know.

Excerpt from *Rona Barrett's Hollywood*, May, 1978

Luminous, Hollywood's hottest new discothèque, just opened, and stars clamored for invites to the opening night; some big names called little old *moi*, begging to get on the list. (As if I had the power to do that, I merely had the press exclusive. I wasn't the bouncer, sillies! Although we'll learn more about him shortly!)

Stars in attendance included Burt Reynolds, Michael Landon, Jaclyn Smith, Lindsay Wagner, Bruce Jenner, Adrienne Barbeau, and Jimmy the Greek.

"This is my new favorite place," Gloria Prescott crowed as she boogied on the dance floor with a starstruck Leif Garrett.

Leif told me, "I've met so many stars tonight, and who'd have thought I'd be dancing with Gloria Swanson [mistaking the decades-younger actress for the *Sunset Blvd.* star]!"

Bette Davis held court with admirers in a red leather banquette. "Isn't this the most divine place? If only Joan had lived to see it. Ha!"

"What are you talking about? I'm still here!" Joan Collins laughed from the next booth.

Sharing drinks at the glass & neon bar were Barbara Lamont and Bahamia, who offered advice to newer stars Suzanne Somers and Pamela Sue Martin. "Girls, the time one auditions makes all the difference. A 3:00 P.M. audition will net better results than one at 10:00 A.M., if you catch my drift," Barbara confided.

"And don't let them under-pay you," Bahamia advised. "If you accept less than you're worth, you'll spend a lifetime trying to earn the difference."

"That's a good one, I'll remember that one," Suzanne nodded. The *Three's Company* producers may have to up their budget next season!

Not everyone managed to get into the party. Gara St. James, who for some reason was not on the guest list, put up a fuss when advised by the bouncer to "hit the road."

She wasn't easily swayed, poking the muscled bouncer in his chest. "You big ape, don't you know who I am?"

But he was unmoved. "Yeah, I know who you are, but you're not on the list. Why don't you go on home, Mr. Welles." The bouncer had apparently mistaken Gara for Orson Welles! (Even I admit that while Gara may have put on a dollop of weight, she's a distance from being confused with that rotund wine spokesman!)

But Gara didn't take the insult lying down. She spun him around, grabbed the waistband of his underwear, and gave him a wedgie! "In the future, dumb-ass, remember the name Gara St. James, so you can tell your grandkids, if this doesn't keep you from having 'em!" she snarled. The not-so-beautiful people behind the velvet rope broke into waves of applause at what they perceived to be an act of revenge on their behalf.

And so Gara, kept out of the party, achieved approval from those who really count, her public!

Excerpt from *Films of the Seventies: Their Themes and Knockoffs* by Cynthana Sumpter

After the financial windfall of *Saturday Night Fever* in 1977, other films tried to ape its phenomenal success. Disco films were suddenly the rage, with *Thank God It's Friday, Xanadu, Can't Stop the Music, Roller Boogie,* and *Love at First Bite* all determined to get their piece of the mirrorball pie (with various results).

One disco film achieved international success in 1979: *Diamond Dance Floor (La Pista de Baile con Diamante)*. A mild success in the U.S., it hit big in Europe and Latin America, especially in Mexico, where it was filmed. A Cinderella story set to a disco beat, it starred the inimitable Bahamia as Rosa, the scullery maid who dreams of success as a singer and dancer. Some critics felt Bahamia was a mite too old for the part, but her ageless charm and youthful energy were easy compensations, adding to the film's appeal. Legends Katy Jurado (as Rosa's mean boss) and Ninon Sevilla (as a fairy godmother in disguise as a ladies room attendant) also scored with audiences. The soundtrack spawned an international disco hit in Bahamia's showstopper, "Diamond Fame (*Fama de Diamante*)."

While disco was a specific niche in '70s moviemaking, the political thriller spanned the decade and had its roots further back in film history. The '70s produced some top-notch examples in *All the President's Men*, *The Day of the Jackal*, *Three Days of the Condor*, and *The Parallax View*. But who would think the political thriller would mate so effectively with the last gasp of blaxploitation in 1979's *White Nefertiti*?

Directed by Bobby Roth, the film dealt with a plot to infiltrate Congress and control drug trafficking into the U.S., thereby keeping African-Americans stuck in ghettos with no hope for better lives. Overseeing this nefarious plot is the mysterious crime queen known as White Nefertiti.

Gara St. James embodies the role with a ridiculous grandeur. From her first appearance in a gold headwrap and a tiger-skin fur coat, she means business. Her buffoonish traits are cause for serious under-estimation by those on the side of right, for White Nefertiti has no qualms with murdering those standing in her path (and she does it in creative ways worthy of a James Bond villain).

The entire cast, including Richard Roundtree, Rod Steiger, Chuck Connors, Paula Kelly, and Glenn Ford as the President, is quite effective and add much to the film's strength. Still, it's Gara St. James who carries the film. In a twist, it's revealed that it was White Nefertiti's plan all along to restore hope to America's inner cities by exploiting the same drug trade she ultimately hoped to break. The final shot (Gara raises a mug of beer in the luxurious splendor of the Ivory Coast and crows, "Now I'm going to sit back, put my feet up, and watch my shows. Ha-ha-ha!") is rather fulfilling.

The film's appeal widened in the '90s when Quentin Tarantino spoke highly of the movie in interviews. Gara St. James boasts that African-American fans love her for the film. "Black folks often tell me, 'Hey, White Nefertiti, I got somethin' for yo' ass!' People love me!"

CHAPTER 11

Yeah, where does she get off calling me a guttersnipe?

It didn't take them long to examine the pages, which included few additional bits of info. Chief among them was the police theory that the fire was probably caused by the faulty wiring these old homes, converted from barbarian castles to modern domiciles, frequently suffered in the early days of primitive electric circuitry.

"It's hardly conclusive, but it appears they believed it was an accident, and with no further evidence, I guess that's what we have to assume as well," Albert stated. With so little to go on, however, there was an air of anticlimactic finality to their investigation.

"At least it might resolve the others's doubt and stop those crazy tricks before someone gets hurt," Mina reminded.

Albert agreed and glanced at Pet, who remained silent and distant, her thoughts a million miles away. He gave her a tiny nudge. She apologized and gave a weak smile.

"What's up with you? There's something you're not telling us. What else is going on?" he asked.

Pet stuck her tongue out at him. "You've got to stop trying to read my mind; you'll pull a muscle you might need one day." She filled them in about the skirmish with Mrs. Dutton.

"So you think she may be hiding something? Was she here at Brownmoor back then?" Mina asked.

Albert nodded. "Yes, she's the only one of the servants who was. I wonder what she might know."

"She's a tough nut to crack."

"She fits right in, considering the mixed nuts around this place. So what's our game plan now?"

I think we should let it circulate that the police believed it was an accident, and hope that brings some peace and quiet."

"And see if that brings an end to the reign of terror from the Phantom of Brownmoor."

"How dare that bitch warn me not to cross her!" Gara huffed as she stomped into the great hall. Peony and Caddy followed, both balancing stacks of boxes and shopping bags.

"I know, Miss St. James, some people don't respect greatness anymore," Peony sympathized as they deposited the packages in the lounge where they paused to regroup.

"Imagine, her pretending she didn't recognize me!" Gara continued to complain.

Caddy pulled out his notepad. "She must live under a rock," he nodded, pencil at the ready for her next bon mot.

"Geez, I've heard of Madonna, she must have heard of me before!" Gara boomed. "I was in that boutique first, how dare she demand the store be emptied! Of all the nerve for her to tell me to get my fat ass out so she can shop without the distractions of the common people! Who's she calling common?"

"She doesn't have an ounce of your class," Peony squeaked loyally.

"And what's that's other word she called me?"

Caddy flipped his notepad back a few pages. "A guttersnipe."

"Yeah, where does she get off calling me a guttersnipe? She's from Detroit! Trying to act all hoity-toity with her fake British accent. I was perfecting my fake British accent when that little *kurveh* was still in crotchless diapers!"

Peony nodded vigorously in agreement as Caddy hurried to keep up with the speed of Gara's tongue.

Gara began pawing through her purchases. "Serves that bitch right when she fell into that rack of pedal pushers. Anyway, she didn't hurt herself, she's aerobicized her scary body into a robot, like that C3Pee-Yew!"

"Thank goodness you were able to grab that beautiful gown before she got her hands on it," Peony approved.

"I know, like she could do this dress justice," Gara agreed, unfurling the green chiffon monstrosity and holding it up in front of herself. "This will ensure I'm the center of attention at that charity event for ... who is this thing for again, besides me?"

"The poor and the sick," Caddy reminded.

"Oh yeah, them," she waved her hand in dismissal. "I guess they can share in the wealth, just as long as I'm getting the king's share of the attention, even if the Queen attends. Do we know if she's gonna show up or not?"

"Not yet," Peony admitted. "So far, only Princess Anne, Prince

Edward, and his wife, Countess Sophie, are confirmed."

"Hmm, the lesser royals. Well, they won't steal the spotlight from me," Gara trumpeted.

"We'll have already stolen it," Barbara said as she and Gloria strolled into the lounge.

"You girls aren't invited," Gara decreed with a frown.

"Yes, we are," Gloria revealed. "We already contacted those charity people, and they're dying to have *real* movie stars like us there."

'We'll see about that!" Gara retorted. Caddy gleefully transcribed the confrontation as Peony's worry level rose with the prospect of having to karate chop Barbara and Gloria if they got out of hand.

"What were you talking about in the car before we came in, Miss St. James?" Peony tried a distraction.

"About the fire," Caddy confirmed.

Gloria and Barbara exchanged a look; what luck to walk right into their investigation without having to contrive a line of questioning. "That must have been terrifying," Barbara clucked with actorish sympathy.

"Aw, it wasn't so bad," Gara pooh-poohed. "It reminded me of when I did that Joan of Arc acting scene in Miss Burns's class, and Bahamia surprised me by setting fire to my shoe. She must have taken some of those Methane acting tips from Marlon Brando when she dated him."

"Lucky girl," Gloria swooned.

"How did you escape from the fire? You were trapped in the bathroom, is that right?" Caddy inquired.

"Yeah, something must have fallen and blocked the door. I'd been relaxing in a hot bath. It always does wonders for my bad moods."

"Maybe she ought to *live* in a hot tub," Barbara said as an aside to her pal.

"So how did you get out?" Caddy persisted.

"It must have been like what happens when mothers have to lift a car to save their kids, what's that stuff they get full of? Whatever, I was full of it. (Mindful of their investigation, Barbara and Gloria admirably fought themselves from jumping at the easy bait to skewer Gara with a barbed retort.)

"I was like a bull in a Chinese restaurant," Gara spouted. "I rammed myself against that door a couple of times, and burst through as pretty as you please. It's a good thing I can be rough on furniture sometimes because when I broke out, my bedroom was flaming like the audience at a Judy Garland concert."

"So what did you do then?" Caddy asked, scribbling like an over-medicated Stephen King.

"I jumped over the flames and landed by the French doors to the balcony. I broke the windows, then climbed over the edge of the balcony and dropped down onto the bushes. Ha, it was one big bush on a pile of bushes!"

"Excuse me?" Barbara gagged.

"Well, I had just gotten out of the bathtub, so I was naked! The groundsman didn't know what to think when I landed in front of him!"

The image of a nude Gara flailing in the shrubbery was one Barbara and Gloria would rather have lived without picturing, and they couldn't hide their disgusted shudders. "Good thing the awful tabloid media wasn't hiding nearby," Barbara choked, a sour expression on her face.

"You couldn't have grabbed a dressing gown?" Gloria inquired.

"I didn't have time to think about that. I should have, I could have saved at least one negligee. I lost everything: The designer clothes, the furs, the jewels. The only thing saved was a diamond brooch that once belonged to my grandmother, and that's only because Pet and Mina had been playing in my jewelry box earlier and Mina had forgotten it pinned to her dress."

"So Laddie's older children were trapped in their rooms?" Barbara asked nonchalantly.

"Yeah, the fire must have started near his room, or hers. My suite was in the middle."

"Because Laddie had enlarged your suite by taking over part of their rooms," Gloria remarked, remembering their earlier investigation with Nolan and the others.

"Yeah, they weren't using those rooms much, they were in London or Paris half the time." Gara then frowned. "Say, how did you know that?"

"Er, I believe someone mentioned it in passing," Barbara tried covering.

But Gara's suspicions had been raised. "Say, why did you two wander in here anyway? You're paying more attention to me than you've ever paid me the whole time I've know you. You're trying to question me!"

"Why would we do that?" Gloria asked.

"I don't know, unless you're trying to get in on all the games around here, digging into the past and thinking someone's trying to kill me."

"And you don't think anyone's tried to kill you?" Caddy asked.

"Of course not," Gara snorted. "If anyone's on the chopping block, what about your mother, Barbara? How she's avoided a firing squad all these years is anyone's guess. And while we're questioning people, I should ask my own questions. Like, what was it old Myrtle held over Laddie's head that made him leave her all that money in his will?"

"If I knew, I wouldn't tell. I'm still not sure what it was Mother had on Linda Darnell when she sent those threatening letters all those years ago!" Barbara exclaimed.

"Yeah, well, maybe I ought to look into things more myself, especially if you two are snooping around. But not right now. Peony, you and Caddy get my purchases upstairs. Don't you dare let those two peek and see what I'm wearing to the benefit party. I don't want them getting any ideas on trying to upstage me!" Gara ordered.

"We could wear burkas and still upstage her," Barbara said as an aside to Gloria.

"I think I'll go ride a horse," Gara decided, once again changing gears. "Caddy, call down to the stable and tell them to saddle up one for me. That's another thing that Madonna stole from me. I was riding horses way before she thought of it. Like I always said, 'You can lead a horse to water, but you can't turn a silk purse into a pig's beer!'"

"No, no, not like that, like this," Binky corrected, performing an intricate dance step in anticipation of the upcoming club appearance.

"I don't think I'll ever get this one. Can't I just look pretty?" Didums asked.

"We can't rely on great costumes and stage presence, we need to dazzle audience with some terrific moves. You know a gay audience isn't afraid to voice its disapproval, lest anyone forget the disastrous reunion tour of Diana Ross without the real Supremes," Binky reminded.

"I can execute the great costumes with no problem, but my two left feet aren't following through," Didums admitted, tripping over his designer Mary Janes.

Carolyn entered the room. She did a double take when she realized the Hollywood gays were already there. "Excuse me," she said icily, turning to leave.

"No problem, we wouldn't want to sully your puritanical façade," Binky cracked.

Carolyn turned, a scathing retort at the ready, when she noticed the shiny, glittering costumes spread on the settee. Her eyes lighted up for a moment, then returned to their usual haughty coolness. "You two aren't worth thinking up something smart to say in return."

"Too much work for her to think of something smart," Binky offered as an aside to Didums, who had noticed her distraction by his stage fashions.

"These catch your eye?" he asked, holding up one of the sequined outfits.

"Yes, as a matter of fact, they did. I was just thinking how appropriate those would look on a blind streetwalker."

But Didums didn't mistake that flash of interest and picked up a beaded silver and black jumpsuit. "I made this for Babs. You're about the same size, aren't you? This would look killer on you." He held the outfit in front of her.

Her eyes lit up again at the prospect of wearing such a flashy ensemble. She lingered on the possibilities, but straightened her shoulders and reminded herself of her obvious higher station in life. "Don't be silly, that's something Victoria Beckham would wear, not me."

"Ooh, you're not just saying that, are you? Victoria Beckham?" Didums gushed, excited at the notion that the fashionable celebrity would deign to wear his designs.

They were distracted by screams from outside. Binky glanced out the window and blurted out, "What the hell?"

Several men were chasing after a runaway horse. Clutching the saddle was the flopping figure of Gara, trying her darnedest to hold on for dear life.

"Whoa, horse! I said, 'Whoa!'" she screamed as the horse dragged her through the garden and over the hedge.

"That doesn't make any sense. She's on Scone, one of the gentle horses," Carolyn explained as they dashed outside to better witness the fracas.

They watched the bizarre sight dashing in the opposite direction across the lawn once again. They were joined by Gwyda and Archie. "What in the bloody hell is that bint doing to one of our horses?" the dame groused.

The men were able to get the horse quiet as her wild gallop turned into a trot and finally to a full stop. Scone continued whinnying and shifting in place. The groom spoke soothing words to her and began removing the askew saddle. The groundsmen untangled the reins which were wound around Gara's legs and freed the belligerent actress.

"What the hell happened? That damn groom told me this was the nice horse! I'd hate to see the mean-tempered one!" she bellowed as the chauffeur helped her stand.

"You must have done something wrong. Scone is the gentlest of our horses," Gwyda sniffed as she approached.

"I didn't do squat. The second I plopped down on her back, she went wild," complained Gara.

"Undoubtedly she was unaccustomed to the great weight," Archie sniped.

"Madam, this seems to have been the problem," the groom stated darkly, holding a tack in his hand and displaying the two pins still embedded in the horse's back.

"Oh, my word!" a shocked Carolyn cried.

"That's horrific! Who would do such a thing?" Gwyda blustered.

"I saddled Scone myself, and I assure you, I didn't place these under the saddle. Someone else did this before Miss Gara got on," the groom stated.

"Did you see anyone around the stables who might have done this?" Gwyda asked.

"No, but there was a period of time between my saddling Scone and Miss Gara's arrival."

"It takes time to get all decked out in this finery," Gara defended, indicated her now bedraggled riding habit. (And if Barbara or Gloria had been there, one might have broken the tension by stating that jodhpurs were not Gara's friend.)

"You don't seem to be the worse for wear, but I'm perturbed that someone would hurt one of my horses." Gwyda snarled. "I will not have this foolishness any longer. The sooner you and the rest of your cohorts are gone, the sooner these shameful incidents will be over!"

She moved forward to examine the horse's injuries herself and escorted the animal back to the stable with the groom trailing behind, and the others began dispersing. Gara held her arms out toward Binky and Didums.

"Come on now, help me inside! You two have attended your mothers and Myrtle for years. One more glamorous patient isn't going to make a difference! Oy! My ass hurts like a motherfucker!"

The news of both Gara's accident and the police file on the fire investigation made the rounds of discussion within Brownmoor that afternoon. Gwyda dismissed talk of the police papers as proof that the fire had been an accident and warranted no further discussion; she was angrier about the injury to the horse and conferred with the local veterinarian to make sure Scone would recover comfortably. The others likewise seemed satisfied that the fire had been deemed an accident and were more interested in the latest apparent attempt on Gara's life.

These thoughts were in everyone's minds as they gathered at the dinner table that evening. Gwyda's glare told them she was not interested in rehashing these matters during the meal, but the Hollywoodites felt the most immune from the Dame's threatening glower and broached the matters at hand.

"You seem to have survived that boxing match with the horse,"

Barbara commented to Gara.

"Aw, I'm fine, a couple of bruises won't stop me," Gara scoffed as she tore meat off the chicken leg she held.

"I don't think we'll talk about this during dinner," Gwyda decreed.

"You know, I was almost thrown by a horse myself when I did that Western, *Hacienda Harlot*," Gloria reminisced.

"Typecasting, no doubt," Louise mocked.

"You must have gotten your orders wrong. Did you say 'Giddy-up' when you meant to say 'Whoa'?" Barbara asked.

"I didn't say anything wrong, it was those darn tacks that got under the saddle somehow. I guess I'd throw somebody off me if I was in the same position."

"Wouldn't it be better to think like Mae West and wonder where your easy rider's gone?" Gloria quipped.

"Regardless, *someone* placed those tacks under Momsy's saddle," Pet spoke up, gaining control of the conversation.

"Pet, I'm sure you feel strongly about this, but I'd prefer not to have the dinner table descend again into anarchy," Gwyda warned from her position at the head of the table; she tapped a pumpernickel roll for emphasis.

"I'm not interested in creating a problem. I only hope that since we now know the fire was an accident, whoever's playing these games will stop trying to hurt people."

"I sure didn't have anything to do with it, so explain to me why someone's tried to kill me twice," Myrtle croaked. "I wasn't even in England at the time! I was blackmailing Bob Hope into putting Barbara on the bill of his latest military tour."

"A lot of good that did, having to dodge enemy fire from the Viet Cong," Barbara complained. "How were Bob Mackie and I to know those sequins would be like a beacon to those snipers?"

"Regardless," Gwyda intoned, her voice rising, "The police record proves the fire was an accident and these odd occurrences are over, once and for all. I for one would like the conversation at the dinner table to revolve around something more interesting."

"I know something more interesting, my charity screening," Gara reminded. "I do hope everyone's looking forward to seeing one of my movies."

"We still haven't gotten complete RSVPs from everyone," Peony piped up, wagging her finger at both ends of the table.

"Which tragedy will they be showing?" Gloria asked.

"I don't think it's a tragedy," Gara mused. "I thought it would be sad enough with the sick people and the children, so I told them to pick a nice comedy or musical. It depends on what they can find at that film depository. Maybe *A Fool I Am* or *What's That You Said?* Whichever, I'm a scream in both!"

"I shall scream if we don't find something more pleasant to discuss at the table," Gwyda thundered.

Babs cleared her throat. "The children gave me a tour of the basement today. We found a walled up section and what appeared to be a closed staircase. I'm dying of curiosity to know the history behind that."

Pet noticed Mrs. Dutton enter the dining room with a silver tray in preparation for after-dinner coffee. At Babs's mention of the basement anomaly, the housekeeper stiffened for a moment, then continued with her duties.

"There used to be an outdoor entrance," Archie recollected. "There was a path to the barn, which used to be the kitchen and the smokehouse long ago, before the days of modern conveniences. And the staircase went up to the indoor kitchen. You can still see where the door was, in the pantry."

"Why did they wall it up?" Miles asked.

"Because of the fire," Nolan explained. "With the outdoor buildings burned down, and the passageway unnecessary, it was felt the best decision was to close everything off."

"We found something down there," Sophie said, fumbling in her pocket. She retrieved the pendant and its broken chain, holding it up for inspection.

There was a clatter at the sideboard where Mrs. Dutton fumbled, setting the coffee cups and the urn in place. Pet glanced at Mina and Albert, who also noted the disturbance and its potential implication.

"Do be careful with the china," Gwyda admonished. "It's not the best, but then, I wouldn't use that on *these* guests. Still, there's no reason to break the cups."

"Sorry, Madam," Mrs. Dutton replied with pursed lips.

Gwyda turned her attention back to the table. She sat forward and beckoned to Sophie. "Come here, child, let me see that thing you found."

Sophie approached and held up the pendant. She had managed to clean it well enough so that, except for its broken chain, it looked almost as good as new. The diamond flashed in its delicate, silver setting.

Gwyda sat back and her lips tightened. "Hmm, doesn't look familiar. I wonder how it got there."

Nolan turned away and paid attention to his brussel sprouts. Archie gave the jewelry a cursory glance but didn't appear interested. The women were more intrigued in the pendant than the men, although Binky and Didums were exceptions to the rule.

"A cute little diamond, although I tend to agree with Paulette Goddard that stones of less than several carats are not worth the effort one has to put out to get them," Barbara commented as she took her turn with the jewel.

No one appeared to recognize the pendant, until it reached Pet. Mina noticed the searching look in her face as Pet turned it over in her hand. Before it could be examined further, Gwyda snatched it from her hand.

"I'm sure this is a worthless piece of junk. Probably not even a real diamond," she decided, slipping it into the pocket of her dress. "Would everyone like coffee now, or shall we wait until the cake has been served?"

Gwyda swept back to her place at the head of the table, full of light conversation and pleasantries. The family didn't seem to find their matriarch's mood swing strange, but the outsiders observed the unusual change. Gwyda appeared to have recognized the pendant and thwarted Pet's further inspection.

"But why had she done so?" wondered Mina. "And did Pet recognize the pendant?"

STRANGE INTERLUDE 11

The end justifies the means, especially if it means I'm doing better.

Star's husband & gardener dead at Beverly Hills mansion by Millicent Lillas, *Los Angeles Daily News*, June 7, 1980

Police called to the home of actress Gloria Prescott yesterday afternoon discovered the bodies of her husband, furrier Donald Medcalf, and the gardener, Jorgé Guerra, in the greenhouse.

The hysterical actress was attended by her friend, celebrity hairstylist Hibiscus, and her physician, Dr. Walter Goldfein. Hibiscus soothed her wailing by combing her hair into a variety of flattering styles and cooing, "Now, isn't that pretty? Who has time for tears when one is so lovely?" (Phone records indicate that Gloria called the stylist before she called the police. In the movie industry, this may be called "getting one's priorities in order.")

According to preliminary reports, Miss Prescott was transplanting bougainvillea with the gardener when her husband confronted them. (They had been introduced in 1977 at a party given by Fernando Lamas and Esther Williams, and were married the following year after a brief courtship.)

Gloria's call to Hibiscus caught him off-guard. "All I did was say, 'Hello?' and heard a blood-curdling scream. I knew Gloria was under extreme stress. It's not the first time she's done that, but usually it was because she had been naughty and given herself a home perm without my approval."

Attired in a crisp white Lily Pulitzer sundress, the actress was sedated by her doctor. The police intend to question her further at a later date.

Prescott claims her husband caused a scene in the greenhouse, and the gardener turned the industrial leaf blower on Mr. Medcalf, which sent him sprawling. An echo caused the windows to shatter, with a shower of glass shards striking both men. Remarkably, Gloria managed to escape completely unscathed.

Neighbor Rosemary Clooney, alerted by the activity next door, spoke with sympathy as she emptied her trash. "What a terrible tragedy for Gloria. She's a strong person, she'll pull through okay. You know, Mary and Jack Benny used to own my house, and they told me they'd sometimes hear Gloria screaming at all hours of the night. But in all the time I've lived here, I've not heard a peep after midnight."

At that moment, Clooney discovered a pair of bloody gardening shears in her trash bin. In the wake of the strange incident next door, she turned the tool over to the police, who would not release additional information in the case.

Excerpted entries from *The Mini-Series and the '80s: A Match Made in TV Heaven* by Jerri Engelmund

The Perverse Garden, CBS, original airdate: February 18-20, 1981. Cast: Robert Stack, Stephanie Zimbalist, Dack Rambo, Richard Hatch, Ted Shackelford, Gloria Prescott, John Beck, Robert Reed, Cristina Raines, Ken Kercheval.

Thriller about sex and murder in San Francisco society, based upon the best-seller by Sheldon Kruntz. The seedy story dressed up in glamorous surroundings was a ratings blockbuster. The murder sequence was ingenuously filmed, with scenes of bloody violence intercut with scenes of extravagant excess.

Zimbalist had one of her best parts as the wealthy socialite mixed up in a murder plot and torn between her ruthless husband (Hatch) and her psychotic lover (Rambo). Her brittle tone combined with jaded humor plays just right, and the other players are just as wonderful.

There was tremendous sensationalism in the casting of Gloria Prescott as Zimbalist's mother, as she had just been involved in a scandal, the mysterious deaths of her husband and gardener. (The actress was never indicted, and the official ruling was that the men had killed each other.) The scene of an aghast Prescott discovering a bloody knife in the garden was cued to create ratings and controversy, and it delivered.

Beau Fauve, NBC, original airdate: May 19-20, 1983. Cast: Harry Hamlin, Morgan Brittany, Bonnie Bedelia, Bradford Dillman, Richard Thomas, Shari Belafonte-Harper, Hurd Hatfield, Gara St. James, Robert Hooks, Ellen Holly.

Based on the book by romance novelist Jillian McNulty. Sultry tales of the Old South were popular fare in the '80s mini-series game (*Beulah Land*, *Louisiana*, *North & South*, etc.). The title comes from the plantation's name (the legend claimed the whitewash intended for the house was stained with the blood of slavery, but it also refers to the salacious plots involving the

Civil War, forbidden lust and miscegenation).

The scenes of forbidden romance sizzled onscreen. The climactic sequence with St. James, in a fit of madness, setting fire to the plantation, was highly dramatic. Most of the actors eschewed attempting authentic Mississippi accents, although Gara may have based her broad performance on Aunt Pittypat by overdoing the "Glory be's!" and "Fiddle-dee-dee's!"

Actress/dancer Bahamia turned down a role (presumably the part played by Ellen Holly), telling the press, "Ain't no way I'm gonna play that bitch's 'high yella' slave!"

Target: Mount Olympus, ABC, original airdate: November 10-12, 1985. Stacy Keach, Bruce Boxleitner, Connie Selleca, Anthony Andrews, Lloyd Bochner, Barbara Lamont, Cathy Lee Crosby, Timima Bossi, David Birney, John Rubinstein.

Based on the Nathan Lipinksy best-seller, the story combines elements of Russian Cold War paranoia and classic Greek mythology in an effective fantasy/terror hybrid. The stunning visual effects were the work of Klaus Milbecht, who created music video effects for The Police and Grace Jones. In a brilliant sequence, the two diametrically-opposed realities (the Cold War of pulsating steel and cracked ice, and Greek heaven with its creamsicle marble and purple skies) meet and explode, with characters and special effects blending in an exciting climax.

The actors faced a daunting task, straddling the line between the rudiments of modern war and the broader farce of the fantasy elements. As a whole, they are up to the challenge and perform admirably. The actresses are decorative, but with Lamont and Bossi as goddesses posed in celestial tableaux, what more could one expect?

Mother of star Gara St. James passes away by Millicent Lillas, *Los Angeles Daily News*, March 4, 1983

Dena Schmerkin (sometimes identified as Dena St. James), mother of actress Gara St. James, passed away yesterday in Los Angeles. Gara stated the family was devastated by the loss and would be sitting *shiva*. (The star had been in rehearsal at the Prudence Hills Playhouse for *My Fair Radie*, a Broadway-bound musical tribute to the columnist Radie Harris, but is expected to withdraw from the production.)

Born Dena Putzkammer in Germany sometime during the teens (Dena herself insisted her birthdate was January 9, 1917), she and her family immigrated to the United States after World War I and settled in Chicago. She later met and married Ben Schmerkin, a kosher butcher and grocer.

They had two children, Ron, born in 1932, and Guneberth, born two years later. Guneberth displayed talent at singing and dancing, so they moved to Los Angeles at Mrs. Schmerkin's insistence. Baby Gara, as she was billed, became a star, and Dena was instrumental in the child's career.

She gained a reputation as "a bulldog in flowered chiffon," according to the witty Carole Lombard. Her contemporaries, Gertrude Temple (mother of Shirley) and Lela Rogers (mother of Ginger), maintained polite relations with Dena in public, but had cutting opinions of her in private. Lela, no shrinking violet herself when it came to promoting Ginger's career, once told Rosalind Russell at a party, "I wouldn't wish ill on anyone, except a Communist, but I wouldn't cry if the bubonic plague came back to claim Dena."

Gertrude Temple also hashed her behind closed doors. Myrna Loy, who appeared with Shirley in *The Bachelor & the Bobby-Soxer*, related an anecdote about an incident from the late '30s. "One day Gertrude slammed the phone down and told Shirley, 'Dena Schmerkin is nuts! She called [20th Century-Fox film executive Darryl F.] Zanuck and told him you was getting long in the tooth, and didn't it make sense to put someone younger like Baby Gara in his next picture instead!'"

Fellow star mom Myrtle Dempster, mother of Barbara Lamont, was more open about airing her dislike. "Dena was a full-blown harpy," she told Walter Winchell in a shocking 1956 interview. "She tried to intimidate me out of pushing Barbara for a part opposite Rock Hudson. Tried to intimidate *me*! She found out the hard way. All I'll say is, 'Don't let me catch you alone in the ladies room, because you'll see porcelain up close and personal!'"

Curious film fans may spot Dena in crowd scenes in a few of Gara's kiddie features, and she is featured in *The Yiddish Garden* as the maid Rivka.

Excerpt from *They Said What? The Unpublished Quotes Celebrities Said Off-The-Record (Until Now!) Over the Years to Life Magazine* by Angela Theroux and Sage Mallick

Barbara Lamont: I have to admit, there were times I wasn't happy with my children. Whenever Babs couldn't have her way, she'd threaten to write a tell-all, practically from the age of five! I should never have allowed Christina [Crawford] to babysit! And Binky, with those uncontrollable rages and substance abuse problems. I knew I had to watch out for Mother and my homicidal sister, but never in a million years would I have thought it would be Binky who tried to run me down in my own custom-made Lincoln Towncar.

Gara St. James: The worst day of my life was when my mother passed away. If Ma hadn't pushed me, I'd have ended up with the career of an Athole Lamont rather than the glorious career that was my destiny. Those jealous bitches said Dena was an evil hag out of a Disney cartoon. They just wish they'd had a "Wicked Queen" on *their* side. I always kidded Ma, calling her my "ermine ball and chain." And I wish I still had her holding on to my ankle.

Gloria Prescott: I wanted my Didums to have every happiness in the world, but I didn't count on how often his pursuit of happiness would turn my hair gray – metaphorically speaking, of course. The worst was the time he was convinced he'd been born in the wrong body and insisted I start calling him "Dittina!" Thankfully, it all turned out to be a drug-induced hallucination. *That* I could understand. Besides, if he was making clothes for himself, how I was going to get a new wardrobe each season? One diva to a household is enough!

Peony Lipschitz: When Gara St. James hired me to be her personal assistant, I felt like Dorothy in the Emerald City. I'd do anything for that woman. When you've let a star of Gara's width and magnitude use you as a human dartboard, there's nothing you won't do! It's not like she hit the target all that often, and they were minor flesh wounds. That comprehensive dental and medical plan really came through! Now, how many employers would be that considerate?

Bahamia: I dare you to find a line on this face, baby, and you won't find scars behind the ears, either. Maybe I'm an extra pale *café au lait*, but "black don't crack," honey. You won't find me wearing sunglasses all the time and only appearing at dimly-lit venues. Damn, if I have to see Sally Kellerman and Goldie Hawn with hair combed into their faces to hide the crows feet one more time, I think I'll scream.

Madonna: I'm such a strong presence, that why people haven't given me a chance to prove my acting talent. Isn't that sad? You know, I love old movies, and those actresses projected images different from their real personalities, and audiences bought it. Lots of times, smart characters were played by the dimmest bulbs. I mean, Barbara Lamont played a diplomat, a scientist, even a firefighter! And think of all the sluts who played nuns. Gloria Prescott as Saint Rosalita of Andalucia? Were audiences just dumber back then?

Dick Clark: It takes a genuine talent for stars to appeal to the game show audience. That's why Betty White and Nipsey Russell were so good on *$25,000 Pyramid*. Not all stars have that. Bette Davis might be a movie star, but she doesn't translate to the game show format. Give me a Gloria Prescott any day of the week. Just watch Gloria giving clues to "What a Woodchuck Might Say" or "Things That Are Limp." Kate Hepburn can't do that!

Nancy Reagan: Ronnie and I appreciated Gara's efforts to help us get elected Governor, and later, President. That strident personality was a great asset on the campaign trail. However, that same boisterous energy had its drawbacks. She insulted Raisa Gorbachev at a state dinner by asking, "Did you mean for your hair to look like that?" Let's not even discuss the things she said to Mikhail! Ronnie was once asked for a comment about her, and his diplomatic response was, "Certainly she's someone's favorite actress." Next thing we know, Gara's saying that Ronnie said she was his favorite star of all time!

Gara St. James: No, for the last time, I'm not related to Susan St. James! And don't even mention Jill St. John to me!

Accident averted as actress receives star on Walk of Fame by Bill Lyttle, *Variety*, May 22, 1985

Actress Barbara Lamont, known for films such as *The Enchanted Tenement*, *The Girl from Hell's Kitchen*, and *Touch of the Brute*, received a star on Hollywood's Walk of Fame. Fans and well-wishers attended the ceremony, presided by the unofficial Mayor of Hollywood, Johnny Grant.

Barbara made a splash in a sexy frock in her signature color, flesh. The garment was created by an unknown Dittina Prescott, rather than her favorite designer, Bob Mackie. Barbara's occasional costar and longtime friend, Gloria Prescott, denied a relationship to the mysterious designer, who was not at the ceremony.

In attendance were Kathryn Grayson, Shelley Winters, Connie Stevens and Jackie Cooper. "Anyone who's seen that daring can-can Barbara performs in *Meet Me in St. Petersburg* knows her place in film history is assured," Shelley said.

A late arrival was musical-comedy star Mitzi Gaynor, who said, "Barbara is such an old star from the early days of Hollywood and has deserved to be laid out on Hollywood Boulevard for a long time."

A near disaster was averted when Barbara's son Binky, driving Barbara's custom-made Lincoln Towncar, jumped the curb and almost ran down his own mother on the sidewalk. Instead his grandmother, Myrtle Dempster, was pinned between the car's bumper and a brick retaining wall before she was rescued by Victor Mature. Gloria Prescott escorted her back to her Bel Air home, saying, "It's too much excitement for the old bag – I mean, the old dear, and she should convalesce at home."

Despite evidence that Binky was drunk and/or high, his sister Babs insisted he wasn't used to driving the new car, and had mistaken the gas pedal for the brakes.

Excerpt from *They Put That on TV? The Weirdest Programming That Ever Showed Up on Television* by Paul Stevens and Richard Anthony

Unfresh Secrets (1985, NBC, 9 episodes). Cast: Lew Ayres (Martin Douchet), Stephen Collins (Carter Douchet), Gara St. James (Cristabelle Douchet), Monte Markham (Harrison Van Dyke), Lynda Day George (Helena Douchet), Andrew Stevens (Geoffrey Douchet), Duncan Regehr (Linc Van Dyke), Ruth Roman (Estelle Van Dyke), Dennis Cole (Jake Milton), Randi Brooks (Cassie Watkins), Monique Van Vooren (Germaine Tournier).

Unfresh Secrets was a bizarre 1985 effort in the prime-time soap stakes. NBC never dominated the scene like ABC and CBS, despite intriguing efforts such as *Flamingo Road* and *Berrenger's*. Instead of focusing on oil, wine, or upscale suburbia (like the successes *Dallas, Dynasty, Falcon Crest,* and *Knots Landing*), *Unfresh Secrets* focused on the power struggles and love affairs behind the scenes of a billion dollar designer feminine hygiene empire.

The odd concept is ripe for parody (like Carol Burnett's soap spoof *Fresno*), but the production appeared to play things straight without tongue in cheek. Many scenes seem to imply it wasn't meant to be taken seriously; it's debatable that the humor went over viewers's heads.

As the Douchet matriarch (surely the family name was meant as a joke?), Gara St. James huffed and puffed her way through scenes with the comedy timing of Margaret Dumont. One episode concerning a boardroom brawl over a deal to introduce designer French fragrances to their douches could have been acted out by the Marx Brothers in a surreal comedy dimension.

Thirteen episodes were filmed, although only nine ever aired. The episodic cliffhanger, in which Gara St. James and Ruth Roman, as the rival matriarchs, fought and plunged off a narrow factory walkway into a vat of experimental pink foam douche named "First Cherry," never revealed their fate.

Up-and-coming photographer has starry pedigree by Wilda Staunton, *San Francisco Chronicle*, September 9, 1987

The photographs are thought-provoking; a homeless woman smiles at a passing child, a protester marches by an angry industrialist, a politician betrays a moment of panic at an unexpected question. These pictures are even more intriguing, considering the pedigree of the photographer.

As the daughter of actress Gara St. James and Lord Lindale Bottomly, Pet Bottomly spent her formative years in London and Los

Angeles. "Maybe they should have thought twice about giving me that name," she laughs, "but people seem to remember it, so I guess it's not all bad."

A striking woman, pretty and tall with a wild mane of dark hair and an olive complexion, Pet could have pursued a career as a model or actress, like her mother. But she started using a camera given as a gift by her father. "He asked me to take pictures to show him what I was doing when I wasn't able to be with him. That way, he could see things through my eyes. This idea intrigued me so much. My mother complained she felt like she was always being followed by her personal paparazzo, although I think she secretly enjoyed it."

Pet moved to Northern California after college to pursue the field professionally. Her mother endorsed her child's creative interests. "I knew she was talented," the actress explained. "She could have used that skill to take my publicity pictures for me, but I guess taking pictures of news stuff is worthwhile, too," she added with a laugh.

The photographer's godfather, filmmaker and entertainment entrepreneur Jory Plummer, offered to help set Pet up in her own studio, but she politely refused the offer. "I admire her for wanting to reach success on her own," Plummer stated. "She's been an independent spirit from day one."

Pet's lucky break came when she was the only photographer present when state representative Hugh Bristol was involved in an automobile accident; he wasn't injured, but it interrupted a backseat encounter with a prostitute. The exclusive photo ran in statewide newspapers, resulting in the ruination of Armstrong's political career. But it launched Bottomly's career as a photojournalist, and her work began appearing in Pacific Coast magazines and newspapers. Last month, one of her photos at a political rally was printed in *U.S. News & World Report*. This is a photographer on the move.

You can catch a series of her photographs at the Soledad-Melville Gallery, 2045 Reza Street, now through October 29.

Cover blurbs from *National Enquirer*, May 26, 1987
"I WAS TIRED OF BAGELS!" WHY BAHAMIA LEFT BOYTOY, AND WHY HE'S NOW DATING CHER!

BARBARA LAMONT EMBARRASSED: ANOTHER DIVORCE FOR DAUGHTER, SON CAUGHT IN PARK RAID!

SHOCKING LIST OF WHO GAVE MONEY TO JIM & TAMMY FAYE! STREEP, BOSSI, AND DID MARILYN DONATE FROM BEYOND THE GRAVE?

GLORIA PRESCOTT NIXED FOR "FALCON CREST" ROLE? "JEALOUS JANE!" DECLARES LATIN LOVELY!

BRITISH LORD'S LOVE SECRETS! HAS LADDIE BEEN KEEPING A DIARY?

FAWN HALL: ACCOMPLISHED SECRETARY OR BOMBSHELL POLITICAL PLANT? WHAT'S HER WORD PER MINUTE?

WHATEVER BECAME OF DITTINA? NEW CLUE IN MISSING DESIGNER MYSTERY!

LATEST MINISTER SCANDAL! WHY BILLY GRAHAM IS TERRIFIED OF MYRTLE DEMPSTER!

MICHAEL JACKSON MAKES BID FOR BONES OF GARA ST. JAMES! "I'M NOT DEAD YET!" CLAIMS ACTRESS!

TBS Schedule, April 13, 2002
All-Night '80s Movie Marathon

10:00 P.M. EST - *Everybody Have Fun Tonight* (Columbia, 1987) Directed by Herbert Ross. Starring Andrew McCarthy, Helen Slater, Martha Plimpton, Julian Sands, Merritt Butrick, Joanna Going, Gloria Prescott, Gordon Jump. It's the night of the huge party and everyone is determined to do just as the title (from the Wang Chung song) indicates. Slater is an appealing gamine and McCarthy is the geeky guy who's turns out to be cool. Prescott has a small role as Bertha, the diner waitress. She's actually the catalyst for most of the resulting plots by opening characters's eyes to potential mates, exposing the bad girl's nefarious scheme to steal another girl's guy, and showing up in the nick of time with fresh party platters. Prescott steals the show, although a scene where she flirts with Julian Sands is a bit disturbing.

12:00 A.M. EST - *Deadly Ejaculation* (Orion Pictures, 1988) Directed by Roger Donaldson. Starring Willem Dafoe, Sean Young, Danny Glover, Mercedes Ruehl, J.T. Walsh, Ronny Cox, Gara St. James, Jeff Fahey. An erotic thriller combining scandalous affairs, military secrets, and murder by poisoned semen. Glossy style offsets the trashiness of the script. Dafoe and Young's steamy sex scenes heat up the screen; you're not likely to look at non-dairy creamer the same way! One is never sure who can be trusted as the film moves along to its thrilling conclusion. Gara St. James has some interesting scenes as the army psychiatrist who has a few screws loose herself.

2:00 A.M. EST - *The Stellar Scion* (Universal, 1989) Directed by Peter Hyams. Starring Dennis Quaid, Ed Harris, Theresa Russell, Ray Liotta, Dennis Farina, Arliss Howard, Bahamia, Barbara Lamont. A creature born of the stars begins devouring the universe, forcing warring planets to unite to defeat the intergalactic crisis. The film (a stew of *Star Wars* and *Dune*), attempted to be all things to sci-fi fans, and ends up pleasing few. Cast provides the movie's bright spots. Watch for Bahamia and Barbara Lamont, both unrecognizable as alien queens of antagonistic worlds; Lamont is painted blue with horns on her head, and Bahamia has glowing gold skin and six arms!

Excerpt from *Politics and Hollywood Celebrities: The Conservative Connection* by Franklin Butterworth

The eighties were the glory days of political conservatism with the patina of real Hollywood glamour. To say that Ronald Reagan exceeded GOP goals is to underestimate his greatness. His election provided irrefutable proof that U.S. was the greatest country in the world, and we would show the rest of the world what was wrong and how to fix it.

His past glory as a film star helped cinch the election for a country weary of tarnished events such as the oil crisis, an economic downswing, and the kidnapping of Americans in Iran. His charisma and previous political experience helped bring the U.S. in line for a decade full of economic growth and an expansion of American idealism around the world.

The Hollywood elite rallied to aid in his win and bask in the afterglow of success. Bob Hope, Merv Griffin, and Frank Sinatra were among the frequent guests at the White House.

One star who made her presence known was Gara St. James. She was a welcome guest at White House dinners and spoke up with vigor and humor for the hallmarks of the Reagan years, particularly family values and increased military power.

"Ronnie knows what he's talking about with this 'Star Wars' thing. People say it's gonna be too expensive. It wasn't too expensive in theaters. We all saw the same movie with that Dark Vader and Luke Skyjacker, right?" Gara deadpanned.

She also addressed complaints by radical homosexual groups which believed the Reagan administration ignored the AIDS crisis. "The White House wants to do something to contain this, but those people aren't very patient. If they were more patient, they'd have waited to have sex until they were married to women and wouldn't be dying. And they raised a fuss when somebody made the suggestion to quarantine them on an island. Sounds like a vacation to me!"

Perhaps her most outspoken moments occurred during the Iran Contra hearings in 1986 and 1987. Gara leapt to the President's defense.

"This has been blown out of proportion. Corporations do it all the time, and do you see anyone knocking their business practices? It all comes down to wiping out the threat of Communism and Russia. Isn't that worth any price?

"And does it matter if he knew or not? If he knew, that's efficient leadership. If he didn't, then that's the role of a good manager, to use proper time management and empower his lackeys. Lee Iacocca couldn't run the country better!

"Reagan's leadership is making the world better. Didn't you hear him the other day, telling that Russkie to 'tear down this wall?' His eye is always on making the rest of the world do things the American way. The end justifies the means, especially if it means *I'm* doing better. And if East Germany finally gets to see my movies, we're *all* winners!"

CHAPTER 12

With me to keep an eye on everything, what could happen?

Everyone would have preferred uneventful days leading up to Gara's big event, but this wasn't to be the case. Gara turned Brownmoor upside down with her melodramatic demands and fit-pitchings. "Don't you worry, Miss St. James, that charity party is going to come off better than a corset on Gypsy Rose Lee!" Peony squeaked with confidence.

"I know, I know, but nobody understands the stress I'm under," Gara wailed. "By the way, Caddy, did we ever decide on a title for my book? I was thinking of *Oy! It's Tough Being Great!* How will that look on bookstore shelves?"

"It certainly has possibilities," he allowed.

"And we can't forget how it'll look on movie marquees," the star continued. "They'll want to snap up rights for a bio pic. I was thinking maybe that Charlene Theron or Angelina Josie. Can they play me at four-years-old? I don't know if anyone's *that* talented!"

In between bursts of activity to ensure her continuing celebrity, she dodged two more events which appeared to be further attempts on her life. In the bathroom, she stumbled in her move from the toilet to the bidet and tried to steady herself. She turned on the bidet's nozzle and started a shower of water. Luckily she hadn't sat down because the water was scalding and soaked the bathmat.

A subsequent plumbing check revealed no problems, and Gwyda pooh-poohed talk of conspiracies.

And this morning, Gara plopped onto the settee in the lounge where Gloria and Barbara were enjoying mimosas post light breakfasts. Gara made herself a drink as well and drove her frenemies out of the room with her complaints. Gara remained on the settee and drifted into a little nap, brought on by too much self-absorption.

Waking up twenty minutes later, Gara reached for her mimosa flute and gave the beverage, which no longer fizzed with a tantalizing orange hue, a puzzled look. "Probably the cheap champagne," she thought and started to take a sip before a conscientious Peony entered the room. Faster than an Eleanor Powell tap routine, she sprinted across the room and knocked the beverage out of her boss's hand.

"Damn, Peony, I wasn't done with that! You don't have to treat me like Betty Ford," Gara protested.

Peony explained that Barbara and Gloria had mentioned the mimosas in the lounge. She went downstairs at once to ensure her boss's continued safety, and realized mimosas shouldn't be green, at least ones in champagne glasses and not Southern gardens. She sniffed it and took a tiny sip, pronouncing its too sweet taste meant it had probably been spiked with antifreeze.

The question (besides who was behind these continued attacks) was: How long could Gara's luck hold out?

After breakfast, Pet knocked on Mina's door to discuss last night's development concerning the pendant. "I knew I'd seen it before, and I was right," she said, handing over the formerly boxed copy of *Harper's Bazaar* featuring Hannah's wedding trousseau. A stunning head-and-shoulders shot of the girl showed off the same jewel nestled just below her clavicle.

"Why do you think Gwyda lied?" Mina wondered. "Was she trying to stop any talk of the past, or was it something more sinister?"

Pet shrugged her shoulders in response. "I don't think I'll be able to get anything else out of her, she's too guarded. But I might be able to get Mrs. Dutton to talk. You noticed her reaction last night, too. I thought you might be able to help me ... unless you have alternate plans this morning?" she asked, noting the extra care her cousin had taken with her outfit and physical appearance.

"Yes, Albert's taking me into London to see the gallery."

"Some time away from the house sounds like a good idea. I want you to know, I think it's jim dandy that you've taken a shine to my nephew. You have my permission to reel him in."

"Oh, now," Mina protested.

"It's okay, Mom, I really like this one," Sophie needled from the door of her room.

Mina threw up her hands in surrender. "I give up! Tell me when you've got our wedding arranged and I'll just show up on time!"

"Do you have a minute, Dad?" Albert asked Nolan from the door of the study.

"What's this about?" Nolan asked as he entered.

"Just a heads up. I'm taking Mina to see the gallery, but we'll be back in plenty of time to get ready for tonight's event."

"We shouldn't have to attend that blasted floor show at all," he said coldly.

"It's a difficult situation, I know, but it's for charity and royals will be in attendance. We must make an appearance."

"Nice words, although it doesn't reflect my feelings. But I suppose we'll have to grin and bear it," Nolan grimaced.

"As everyone has been doing since Grandfather's passing. Notwithstanding the bizarre incidents around here lately."

"The only bizarre things going on are those dreadful Americans moving in lock, stock, and barrel," Nolan complained.

"I believe everyone is planning to leave in the days after the party. Except Pet, and Mina and Sophie."

"I hope you're not getting involved with that Mina," he cautioned his son. "There's no reason to form extra ties that will ensure Pet stays here longer than necessary."

"No one's insisting you and Pet be best friends, but you need to relax about this, if only for your own sake."

"You will never understand my views on the matter, so it's best for us not to talk about it any longer." Nolan turned to leave, indicating the discussion was at an end.

But Albert stood his ground. "For someone who thinks family is so important, you've done a good job of shutting out your own sister. You've ignored me, too."

His father turned, stunned. "I've done no such thing."

"Haven't you? When Mama died, you erased her from existence. I needed her memory, and I needed you in person, but I didn't get either."

Nolan struggled to contain his anger and respect his son's feelings. "You've never been married, you wouldn't understand why I did what I did. It's not something I can explain now."

"And isn't that what the problem's always been?" Albert implored.

Nolan resisted the urge to give comfort, and retreated to the stingy coldness he'd known too long, like Uncle Ralph, the uncaring guardian out of *Nicholas Nickelby*. He walked out of the room as Albert watched him leave, feeling the too frequent sensation of parental disappointment.

"I'm not happy with any of these gowns," Gloria wailed as she sorted through the closet.

"I thought you settled on the gold lamé," Barbara noted.

"People expect it, maybe I should surprise the fans. What are you wearing?"

"I've narrowed it down to three possibilities. I'm just disappointed that it was impossible to get loaned gowns. Don't these English designers realize the importance of real stars like us appearing on the red carpet and being able to say, 'Yes, I'm wearing Vivienne Westwood?' At this rate, we'd have to say, 'I'm wearing Jaclyn Smith for Kmart.'"

"Luckily these Brits haven't seen us in our dresses, so we can get away with wearing our own castoffs," Gloria reasoned, sifting through the selections.

"Babs, you're not wearing that tonight, are you?" Barbara asked as her daughter entered.

Babs looked down at her jeans and pink rocker tee. "Well, no," she hedged, a plan having already formulated in her mind.

"Didn't Didums design you something for that club show? You need to carry along a dress to change into, so you can come to the party and help keep an eye on Myrtle. I'm still not convinced I should let her attend at all," Barbara stressed.

"Isn't it nice that the children are going to be a musical group. Maybe this will be a new career direction," Gloria encouraged. "You can rename yourselves 'Prescott Lamont.' Isn't that what those daughters of The *Mamacitas* and the Papas did?"

"You know I want to write," Babs reminded.

"Dear, haven't we quite exhausted that possibility? Please don't tell me I'm going to have to have your room swept by private detectives again," Barbara threatened lightly.

"No, I'll just wait until you're incapacitated by a stroke," Babs said under her breath. "Mother, I don't know why you can't encourage me like you do Binky."

"But darling, haven't I been supportive? I sent your writing samples to Jacqueline Susann for constructive criticism, didn't I?"

"She was already dead! Dead people don't make good contacts in the industry!"

"Tell that to Sylvia Browne," Gloria quipped.

Babs shook her head as the older women returned their short attention spans to their wardrobe. Gloria held up a pink gown with a daring slit. "Can I still get away with showing off my legs this much? To paraphrase Swanson, 'Anything I need to say, I can say with my legs.'"

"Standing or apart?" Barbara cracked.

"You would know. Making sure your highkick is one of the highest in Hollywood has kept you in minks far longer than our contemporaries," Gloria approved.

"I'm sure you're going to choose the right gowns," Babs praised, edging toward the door and making her escape. She sauntered down the hall, pleased with her ingenuity. If everything worked out as she hoped, she might have the perfect story for the writing project to end all projects.

Pet found Mrs. Dutton in her late morning location, checking off the roster of servants to their individual assignments. She gave the housekeeper her most charming smile. "Another busy day?" she sparkled.

"The usual," Mrs. Dutton replied, peering at Pet over her reading glasses with a look which indicated she was on guard against the younger woman's pleasantries. (An English housekeeper can be tougher than Paris Hilton contemplating quantum physics.)

Nevertheless, Pet pressed forward and sat down opposite the housekeeper at her desk. "I'm not going to beat around the bush, Mrs. Dutton. You recognized that pendant the children found, didn't you?"

"Yes, I did. It belonged to Miss Hannah," she responded.

Pet appreciated her honesty. "How do you think it ended up down there?"

Mrs. Dutton looked away. "Miss Pet, you haven't been here regularly since you were a child, but I always remembered you as a darling, mischievous scamp. And Miss Hannah doted on you. In memory of your sister, I think it's best to respect the good times and ignore these things you find mysterious or threatening."

"Under normal circumstances, I'd agree. But someone's tried to hurt both Mrs. Dempster and my mother. Anything out of the ordinary is worth looking into."

"I've worked for this family for more than forty years, and I don't think I'm being too forward by saying I've seen things that many people would find shocking or inappropriate. I was trained to do my job and keep my mouth shut, and in doing so, your family has been good to me over the years."

"Forgive me, but if you know something that would keep someone from coming to physical harm –"

"I never said that. I'm only saying ... that pendant doesn't mean anything. The underground passageway to the fields wasn't closed until after the fire. Anyone might have used it as a shortcut for a walk."

"Hannah obviously used the passageway before the fire. She wore the pendant in the magazine photo shoot before the wedding."

Mrs. Dutton stood up, determined to put an end to the interrogation. "I have work elsewhere in the house. There's a great deal Mrs. Glasscock needs me to do before everyone leaves for the charity event this evening." She shuffled her papers and started for the hall.

She stopped before exiting and turned back to Pet one last time. "The best thing I can do is remind you that you were a beloved child. Your father loved you, and so did your brother and sister. I remember that dear child, too." She left as Pet pondered her words.

Was there significance to the pendant being found in the old passageway? Was Mrs. Dutton just protecting forgotten family secrets ... or was she keeping those secrets safe by engaging in murderous games against Myrtle and Gara?

Art frequently confuses its viewers, and more than one person has feigned understanding some odd abstract painting covered in indiscriminate scrawls meant to signify world unrest or some such notion. The general public may not always understand art, but those who deal in the art world know this confusion is often a marketable commodity.

It's something Albert understood, and as much as he loved art, he also could appreciate it from multiple viewpoints, from a standing position where the art's meaning is fully explored, to a seated place where the financial side is worked out not on canvas but on the business landscape.

Albert was proud of his work and pleased to show off the Bottomly Gallery for an intrigued Mina. While Brownmoor clung to an ancient world of stone edifices and walnut trim, the gallery was strikingly modern in sleek brushed metal and blond wood. And while the walls of Brownmoor were covered in portraits of baroque ancestors and the milieu of the landed gentry, the gallery boasted a wide range of wares from those confusing abstracts to neoteric portraiture to huge photo blowups of urban landscapes.

"I enjoy discovering new talent," he explained. "Well, I get money out of it, too, but I enjoy what I do. And I'm lucky to have an excellent staff."

"Modest to a fault. Or is *that* your fault?" Mina flirted.

"I'm not the best judge of my flaws," he demurred with charm. "Modesty was perhaps bred from finding myself in a family full of big egos."

"That's understandable. My father was that way, having grown up with Gara. But your mother? What was she like?"

Albert's smile faded slightly. "Mama wasn't immune. She was confident in her talent as a singer."

"You called her Mama and not Mum?" Mina teased.

His eyes twinkled again. "She may have married English, but she was Spanish, through and through. Very emotional. She wasn't really egotistical, though. She worked with a vocal coach, always wanting to be better. And she was a warm and loving mother. I lost her when I was eleven. But what made it more difficult was after she died, Dad almost wiped her out of existence. Aunt Gwyda said Dad was so broken up that he couldn't bear to face constant reminders."

"Didn't he allow you any mementos?"

Criticism of one's parents is often accompanied by guilt of doing so. (Although surely when the parent is one of the current inhabitants of Brownmoor, some kvetching is understandable.) Albert was no different, as he backtracked from his initial judgment. "It was his choice, I guess. Still, I would have liked to have some things. Photos, her jewelry. She often wore a religious medal I loved, one of the native Catalan saints. She had a great deal of Spanish artwork, paintings and sculpture by Picasso, Miró, Díaz. That's one reason I studied art, to maintain a bond."

In an attempt to shift his attention to happier topics, Mina seized on the mention of Mirabelle's homeland. "It's a beautiful country. Did you ever go there?"

"Oh yes, many times. A few trips when I was a child, but many more when I grew up. I love it there. You went there on your honeymoon, didn't you?"

It was Mina's turn for her smile to fade. "Yes. I had studied Spain and its regions a lot before I focused on South American culture."

"I didn't mean to remind you of him, I mean, now that he's gone."

"It's okay. I think about him every day, especially when I look at Sophie."

"You're lucky to have her. I guess I've missed out on that, not having any children."

"You've still got time, men always do," Mina teased, feeling a bit self-conscious.

"I suppose," he allowed. "I've been too absorbed with work and family obligations to let myself get too attached to anyone for long. But now I'm thinking I've missed out on a lot."

"Like I said, it's not too late," she reminded.

"I hope not," he winked, and leaned in for a kiss.

In some quarters, Hollywood included, bitter cynicism replaces the romantic hope fostered, ironically enough, by the movies. But those cynics are often just disappointed romantics inside, and all it can take is the promise of something akin to Rhett and Scarlett to warm frozen hearts.

The afternoon passed with much activity at Brownmoor in preparation for the evening's charity event, which was being held at the conference center of the Royal Flemshire Children's Hospital. Over three hundred guests would attend an elegant dinner and the film screening with proceeds (at $1,000 a plate) to benefit the hospital and the Asquith-Bottomly foundation. The crème of London society was expected, and the guests and residents of Brownmoor were angling to put their best face forward at the evening's event.

For the Bottomlys and Glasscocks, this meant gritting their teeth, attired in finery, and remembering it was all for charity, buoyed by the thought that the Hollywood interlopers would be leaving within days.

Gwyda checked her appearance in the ornate mirror of the great hall. In a simple dress of basic black relieved only by pearls, she knew protocol and etiquette demanded a family suffering recent loss should comport themselves with dignity and quiet mourning at public appearances. Louise and Carolyn were likewise dressed in understated gowns of drab hue and little jewelry. The men, in tuxedos, resembled an infantry of soldiers in a Fred Astaire army.

Albert smiled at Mina as she and Pet descended the staircase. Mina was radiant in a gown of midnight blue with a mild vee-neckline and sheer cap sleeves, complimenting her creamy complexion and striking red hair. Simple silver jewelry completed the graceful look.

Pet was also glamorous in a gown of deep claret with long, classic lines which took advantage of her modelesque height. She accessorized with simple diamond earrings and Hannah's recovered pendant on a new chain.

"All I can say is, 'Woof!'" Albert whispered as he greeted Mina with a quick peck on the cheek.

"Where did you find that?" a shocked Gwyda asked Pet.

"It was on your desk. I didn't think you'd mind, since it's not valuable. It's pretty, though, don't you think?"

Gwyda eyed her niece warily but refused to give in. "Very nice." She turned without inviting further discussion.

A clearing of throats was heard at the second floor gallery, and they turned to spy Barbara and Gloria pausing for effect. They glided down the staircase as taught by Miss Burns, their gowns creating an ethereal billow behind them.

Barbara wore a dress of "Chippendale nude on antique satin" with a sweetheart neckline to emphasize her bosom. She accessorized with flashy diamonds and an *au naturel* stole trimmed in peach mink.

Gloria stuck to the gold lamé in a dress with long sleeves and a slightly plunging neckline with ruching down the front, ending in a slit which revealed tantalizing glimpses of gams with each step. She carried a summer fox jacket on one arm.

The actresses stepped to the bottom of the stairs and awaited applause at their grand entrance, which had been the custom at many a Tinseltown party. At this lackluster and silent reception, Gloria nudged her pal with a disappointed look and said, "*Dios*, just like those unemotional studio execs. Those bastards wouldn't know a real star is she sat down in their laps and moved around a bit."

Late applause came from the lounge as Binky and Didums entered the great hall. "Brava, ladies, an entrance worthy of Norma Shearer!" enthused Binky.

"I say," Archie blanched at the sight of the younger men in attire for their nightclub appearance. Didums wore distressed jeans embellished with chains and Swarovski crystals and a vinyl shirt in acid yellow. Red platform sneakers, alienesque silver contact lenses, and black extensions in his lavender hair completed the rocker look.

As the star, Binky was more outlandish in a red tutu-style miniskirt. The top consisted of leather straps and peek-a-boo patches. He executed steps in bondage-style footwear and topped off everything with a top hat decorated with shiny Union Jack stripes.

Having already encountered Binky's way with a skirt, the Brits averted their eyes. "Wow, that's cool!" Miles enthused as the kids bounded down the stairs.

"That is *not* cool, and you're not to get any ideas," Willis admonished.

"You kids promise not to get into any trouble while we're out?" Louise asked.

"Of course we won't," Henry replied with his most sincere obedience.

"You'd just be bored by this thing tonight," Mina assured Sophie, who responded with a nod and a warm hug.

"Well, who'm I riding with?" a voice bellowed from the gallery. Myrtle made her way downstairs with assistance from Babs. The elderly woman wore a dress with a floral print of huge pink dahlias on blue polished chintz. Her portable oxygen tank was smartly accessorized in a satin purse.

"I'm sure Willis and Louise would love to have you in their car! No? How about you, Great Dame?" Barbara tried charm to palm her mother off on another temporary caretaker.

"Why aren't you dressed?" Didums asked Babs, still in casual attire.

"I don't feel well. I hate to say it, but I don't think I should go tonight," Babs apologized, clutching her stomach. "I don't think lunch agreed with me. Maybe it's food poisoning."

"Don't give me any ideas," Gwyda sniffed.

"What am I going to do?" Binky wailed. "Didums can't handle it all by himself. Separately you're bad singers, but together there's a semblance of tone."

"Thanks a lot," Didums huffed.

"I've got the outfit here," Babs offered. "Maybe some talented drag queen at the club can help out. Or maybe ..." She held out the outfit toward Carolyn. "This would probably fit you quite well."

Carolyn's eyes lit up at the wild jumpsuit and silver heels. "That's quite out of the question," Archie interjected. "We're expected at this torture chamber tonight whether we like it or not."

"We're probably about the same size," Didums apprised Cliff's body. "I've got leather pants and a shirt that would work for you, too."

"I forbid it!" Gwyda announced. "Real Bottomlys and Glasscocks have never embarrassed themselves on a public stage!"

"I'm ready!" Gara brayed from the top of the stairs. Wearing the prized green chiffon and coordinated with heavy topaz jewelry and fluffy curls, she paused in the same manner as her fellow actresses and fixed a lofty smile on her lessers below, with Peony and Caddy bringing up the rear.

She galumphed too quickly, and gained speed down the too short staircase steps, stumbling on the last one and almost tripping. Peony raced past Gara on the broad stairs and stopped at the bottom, ready to catch her boss with her pitifully slight frame. Gara steadied herself by grabbing the banister and tried to end on a dignified high note, but not before blurting out a startled, "Bum farts!"

"As trashy as Baby Jane at an inauguration," Gloria disdained.

"I'm *tres chic*?" Gara glowed, deliberately mishearing the dig at her taste. "Pet, baby doll, you look more beautiful than the day you were born."

"Come along, the sooner this thing starts, the sooner we can get away. With any luck, the royals will make a quick appearance and leave so we can get home before *Big Brother* comes on the telly," Gwyda considered something less distasteful than an evening with Gara as she herded everyone to the foyer.

"Good luck with your show and please get to the party as soon as possible," Barbara begged the boys as Myrtle lurched behind her.

"None of this rock and roll nonsense, come on," Archie warned his youngest.

"We'll be along in a minute," Carolyn stalled, her eyes still on the glittering outfit held by Babs.

"Please behave and stay out of trouble," Louise advised, kissing her sons goodbye.

"We will," Miles promised, avoiding Sophie's eyes lest he give the game away.

"You kids will keep an eye on Chester, won't you?" Carolyn asked, fingering the flashy outfit she was dying to wear as an astonished but captivated Cliff watched her reaction.

"I'm sure they will," Babs said, winking at the children with a sidelong glance. "And I promise, they'll stay out of trouble. With me to keep an eye on everything, what could happen?"

STRANGE INTERLUDE 12

All I've had from her is twenty years of cigarette butts and chicken bones dumped on my side of the fence.

Recent losses felt in celeb circles by Amelia Tobin, *Downtown Style,* May 27, 1990

Recent celebrity passings have left the entire world wondering who's next. Deaths come in threes, they say. That number's been multiplied several times over, as the worlds of film, fashion, design, etc. have experienced significant losses. And can anyone take their places?

The world of music lost both Sammy Davis, Jr. and Sarah Vaughan. Who can forget Sammy's electrifying Vegas performances? And can anyone sing "Misty" and "Broken Hearted Melody" with the style of Sassy?

"Sammy and Sarah were originals and nobody can replace them," states jazz critic Helen Oakley-Dance.

"Sammy and Sarah influenced a generation of performers like Bobby McFerrin, Patti Austin, and Dianne Reeves," says musician Al Jarreau.

"Nobody can do it like the 'Candy Man' does. And Sarah ... That rhymes with Gara!" squeals actress Gara St. James.

Although the incandescent Greta Garbo had not made a film in decades, her image remains on movie screens and in fashion essentials, such as berets, trenchcoat, and trousers.

"There was only one Garbo, and there will never be anyone else like her," actress Timima Bossi states.

"We are more likely to see her image in the faces of supermodels like Linda Evangelista or Tatjana Patitz than actresses," exclaims style editor Carrie Donovan.

"I think there are still a few Garbos out there, like Meg Ryan or, you know, me," Gara insists.

The fashion world lost two pioneering supermodels: the stunning Dovima and the ravishing Ysabel Fanon. Dovima was immortalized by Richard Avedon in a timeless Dior gown and posed amid dancing elephants.

Ysabel was the first supermodel to transcend racial barriers, her exotic Algerian beauty standing out as the face of Prix de Beauté Cosmetics in a sea of blonde Europeans.

"Today's models can't touch the legends like Dovima and Ysabel," former Ford agent Kellie Yo sniffs.

"Naomi Campbell can trace her career back to Ysabel; black, multicultural, fierce," asserts model and beauty entrepreneur Naomi Sims.

"Look at this picture of Ysabel arching her back like a cobra. She gave a lot of people pleasure, I bet, and not just with sexy pictures like this," Gara opines.

Movie producer Jory Plummer passed away in February and accomplished more than most self-proclaimed auters can their whole lives. He oversaw the blockbuster epic *Miracle at Valley Forge*, the successful film series *Brats & Busters* (based on the comic strip), and jumpstarted Gara St. James's film comeback.

"Before Mike Todd, there was Jory Plummer. He changed the way execs envisioned film projects," George Lucas says.

"Jory inspired countless filmmakers to do it all," Sony Pictures film executive Donovan Talbot asserts.

"I'm sorry, I can't ... The loss of Jory Plummer means more than just the loss of a talented filmmaker. It's the loss of a real friend," Gara whispers.

And that's the secret: These individuals weren't just stars, they were friends, not just to other celebrities, but also to millions of fans. And they are missed.

Pension woes may be problem for studio vets by Wendy Bingley, *Daily Variety*, July 19, 1992

U.S. industries have dealt with money difficulties as pension programs have folded, and Hollywood hasn't remained immune. Essemtoo Studios, in operation from 1942 through 1951, is the latest victim. Its film catalog is owned by Warner Home Video (the archives include minor selections such as *Hangnails Over Broadway*, *The Janitor & The Jailbait*, and *The Chambermaid's Credenza*).

A recent audit at Time Warner unearthed a still functioning pension program for former Essemtoo employees. Scuttling the program will save Time Warner a relatively small sum of almost $200,000 (but in economics, every cut counts).

Survivor benefits have also stopped. Director Frank Winsocky, who started out in B-films for Essemtoo before graduating to more prestigious efforts at larger studios, passed away last year from a rare condition called monotonitis, whereby sheer lack of personality eventually saps every ounce of the individual's life force. (John Malkovich is in talks to star in a proposed biopic for MGM.)

Actress Gara St. James was asked for comment, and believed the situation was a gag. "Is this one of those *Bloopers & Practical Jokes* shows? Did that awful Gloria Prescott put you up to this? Don't mess with my money!"

Gara released a string of vulgarities, broken only when the phone was wrestled away from her by her assistant, who conceded there might be something to the news. "We can always cut something out of our budget, too. I've told her I'd be happy to eat generic brand cat food to help save money. Is that such a sacrifice for a star like the great Gara?"

Other stars who once appeared in films for Essemtoo Studios had resigned reactions to the news.

Barbara Lamont: "There was a pension program? I know that no-good accountant had a reason for always being too busy to take my calls. Well, I always thought relying on expensive gifts from attentive admirers made more sense."

La Staggée: "I never received any pension money from my five minute aria in the biblical epic *Never on a Palm Sunday*. But if a certain someone needs some extra income, I could always use a cat sitter."

Bahamia: "The loss of a tiny sum won't affect my bottom line, though it serves that one bitch right for calling me 'a white Diahann Carroll.' She tried to make it sound like a compliment, that I should be on *Dynasty*, too, but I've known her too long not to know what she really meant."

Excerpt from *Weird Celebrity Recordings* by Sunny P. Kaye

The Girl From Hell's Kitchen, Taka Boom with Barbara Lamont (Warner/Elektra Records 45 single, EKCD-8931-1, 1993). This hit might not have happened if Taylor Dayne hadn't become ill and unable to perform at 1993's Grammy Awards tribute to Little Richard. Frantic to find a replacement, the producer learned Chaka Khan's sister was on the red carpet, and he enlisted her services. Taka Boom wasn't as famous as Chaka, but she had her own soulful sound (she had minor hits on the r&b and dance charts in the '70s and '80s).

The audience sat up and took notice during her performance of "Keep A Knockin'." She signed a new record deal and a CD was released in late 1993.

The first single, the Mariah Carey-esque power ballad, "Me, Me, Me (Deal With It)," didn't perform well, and the second release, "The Girl From Hell's Kitchen," initially seemed like another flop. Taka recorded along to the original title song of the 1953 MGM drama starring Barbara Lamont (like Natalie Cole did with her father, Nat King Cole, to "Unforgettable").

The song was an ironic "white bread" pop standard in its original incarnation, considering its gritty title (both Teresa Brewer and Kay Starr had recorded cover versions for radio). But the new version came alive with modern orchestration, and Taka's strong vocals played well off Barbara's more wistful readings, adding heart and pathos to the song.

Adult contemporary radio embraced the song and made it a hit, reaching #3 on the AC charts (and #47 on the Hot 100). Taka made press rounds, including an appearance on *Live with Regis & Kathie Lee*. She expressed disappointment that Lamont hadn't lived to experience the success herself. A livid Barbara issued a statement: "I don't know who this Taco Boone person is, but she must not know anything about movie history if she doesn't know I'm alive. And what's this about a hit song on the radio? Am I getting paid for that?"

Authenticity of Gara items challenged by Tom Harlingen, *Las Vegas Sun*, June 17, 1995

A lawsuit has been filed over an exhibit of celebrity memorabilia claiming to include artifacts from Gara St. James. The exhibit in the gift shop of Chester's Fish House (billed as the "Best Fish in All of Vegas") features items including lingerie and grooming implements the actress supposedly owned.

"Miss St. James didn't own those negligees," stated the actress's spokesperson, Peony Lipschitz. "Everyone knows that a conservative Republican like Gara sleeps in a flannel nightgown buttoned to the neck.

"And Gara never used that brand of moustache wax – I mean, Miss St. James is a true lady and has never had need for items clearly made for men. Those nincompoops at Chester's should have done a little more homework."

A spokesman for the restaurant declined to comment, and the *Sun* has been unable to reach the exhibit's owner, Chicago collector Jerry B. Tithslinger. He insisted the items are authentic.

Gara and Bob Uecker, the celebrity owner of Chester's Fish House, have been friends for many years. An autographed photo depicting the pair with mouths full of fried catfish has been a fixture behind the cash register. As of today, the picture remains in place.

Lifetime Schedule, June 24, 2000

"Women in Jeopardy" Made-For-TV Movie Marathon

6:00 P.M. EST - *She Had to Kill: The Ellen Culpepper Story* (1994) Starring Lisa Hartman-Black, Jack Scalia, Timothy Gibbs, Harley Jane Kozak, Susan Flannery, Harve Presnell, Brett Cullen, Gara St. James. When police fail to stop a madman stalking a vulnerable woman, she has a mental breakdown and goes on a rampage, killing a pack of trashy teens with bad attitudes and a group of cranky senior citizens power-walking. Her actions pit the town's citizens against each other; one group blames the ineffective police force who didn't take Hartman-Black seriously while the other side demands the electric chair for Lisa's crimes. The true story opened a national dialogue about suburban crime and its effects on modern life. Gara St. James is the dying oldster lying on the sidewalk and screeching, "Oy! I knew I woulda been better off eating Wheatena and watching Willard Scott on *The Today Show!*"

8:00 P.M. EST - *A Sharp Knife Can Be Dangerous* (1991) Starring Joe Penny, Tracey Scoggins, John Wesley Shipp, Diana Scarwid, Robert Hays, Richard Belzer, Alaina Reed, Barbara Lamont. A remake of the '50s thriller starring Victor Mature and Barbara Lamont doesn't live up to the original film. Penny and Scoggins work with what they're given, which isn't much, and they're sexy and treacherous, even if they're no Mature and Lamont. Barbara Lamont appears in a small role, but why even bother having one of the original stars appear in the TV remake if all she does is appear in one scene as a receptionist to answer a phone and disappear from the rest of the film?

10:00 P.M. EST - *Mother, May I Sleep With Your Husband?* (1998) Starring Tori Spelling, David James Elliott, Lisa Banes, Anthony LaPaglia, Michael Imperioli, Trisha Leigh Fisher, Howard Spiegel, Gloria Prescott. A sequel to *Mother, May I Sleep With Danger?* The producers managed to come up with a more inane title, a stupider premise, and less thrills per minute. Tori Spelling graduates from dental school and to save money so she can start paying off those student loans (see, we said the premise was stupider), she moves in with her mother Lisa Banes and Lisa's studly new hubby David James Elliott. Despite her best efforts, Tori can't keep her hands off her stepdad's abs. Gloria Prescott is the grandmother who discovers the affair and conveniently has a massive stroke. She overacts far too much later when the deranged husband of the title determines to silence the only witness in the climax.

St. James accepts award for horror achievement by Michael De Wilk, *Scarlet Street*, September, 1997

Actress Gara St. James has endured a career that might have caused screams from Evelyn Ankers or Barbara Steele, but a recent event brought renewed appreciation. She received the annual Lifetime Achievement Award from the Horrorland Convention organization on July 27, 1997.

She first gained fame as a child actress known as Baby Gara in the 1930's and achieved adult stardom in later films. Horror fans appreciate *Bride of the Golem* and *Nightgown of the Phantom* (and its sequel *The Phantom in the See-Through Nightie*). She appeared in other horror films ('70s ventures include *The Cawker City Murders*, *The Nun Also Rises*, and *Whatever Happened to Shprintzel?*), but the earlier films are the most beloved of film fans.

"I love *Nightgown of the Phantom*," enthused fan Reggie Lemmon. "When she galumphs down the stairs of the castle wearing that little babydoll nightie, I get a sharp reaction!"

Reggie added that although he liked the sequel, it wasn't as fulfilling as the original. "The title is misleading, if you know what I mean."

The only sour note at the convention was Gara's failure to appear on time for an autograph session. She arrived an hour late, grumbling, "What's this about? What do these peons want, my hands and feet to fall off?"

Her assistant, Peony Lipschitz, stated that Gara had no animosity toward her fans, but was disappointed with failures on the part of convention organizers. "We thought an 'autograph session' meant the executives wanted a few autographed 8 x 10 glossies, not for Gara to stand for hours on end signing pictures and beer mugs for her devoted fans."

Marvin Copley, a convention official, stated the autograph session was defined in the contract, and that proper seating for Miss St. James was provided.

All disagreements were forgotten the night of the award ceremony, however, when Gara was presented her statuette by last year's recipient and close friend, Bahamia (beloved by horror fans for her films *Voodoo Vampire Virgins* and *White Witch*). "I've known Gara for years, and it's been a horror the entire time," she joked to an appreciative audience.

Gara accepted her award with boisterous good will, slapping her thigh and grabbing her side with a well-received comedy routine. "You've been a swell audience! I haven't had this much fun since I worked with Frank Winsocky," she added, referring to the late director of *Nightgown of the Phantom*.

Her joke at Winsocky's expense came as no surprise to fans who attended a Q&A session accompanied by a screening of the film the previous evening. "I made it my goal to get that jerk to smile. Once I did a funny 'Who's Under Your Skirt' routine. It was classic, right up there with 'Who's on Last.' But all that dummy said was, 'Oh yes, that's very amusing,' without cracking a smile. It was like that 1972 U.S.O. tour I did in Cambodia with Joey Heatherton. That bitch couldn't take a joke, either."

All in all, a fine time was had by one and all. The organization is already considering next year's gathering, where preliminary plans call for the award to go to Gloria Prescott (*Demon: 36-24-36, She-Wolf de Carnaval*).

Malibu landmark to be sold at auction by David Glickenspiel, *Los Angeles Times*, July 18, 1998

Papers filed with L.A. county indicate that the Malibu property known as the "Plantation *Shtetl*," owned by actress Gara St. James since the mid '70s, is being sold for unpaid back taxes. The star insists these reports are bogus.

Gara gave the property its name to reflect both its unusual Southern architecture in a climate known for hacienda culture and to respect her Jewish roots. (*Shtetls* were small communities bound together by pious Orthodox Judaism and a desire to remain socially static, not unlike the Amish.)

Malibu residents aren't sympathetic over St. James's loss, however. Neighbors have long questioned the taste of her infamous theme parties (who can forget the viewing party for TV's *Roots* where Caucasian guests were invited to dress in antebellum finery while African-American guests could attend wearing rags and burlap underpants). Others complained about boisterous activities on the lawn Gara has defended as "exercise routines; why, Jack LaLanne does the same stuff and people clap their hands!"

Neighbor Barbra Streisand, who is rumored to be first in line to offer top dollar for the property (adjacent to her own clifftop digs), stated, "Something isn't quite right with Gara. We're both Jewish, we're neighbors, she's famous, I'm famously talented, but no ... All I've had from her is twenty years of cigarette butts and chicken bones dumped on my side of the fence."

Perched above Paradise Cove, the house was built by Australian filmmaker Conweigh Polson for his wife, the actress Doña Sobrina De Assis. The property turned into a buyer's market when Polson needed quick money to fund his religious epic *My Precious Lourdes*, and St. James got the place for a song.

If St. James is unable to make good on those back taxes by month's end, expect Streisand to announce expansion plans for her beachside compound.

Gloria Prescott named ambassador of Bladder Health Organization by Nina Vance, *Hestia*, April, 1999

As an actress, Gloria Prescott has played roles such as a U.N. interpreter, a Peace Corps volunteer, even a First Lady. But her new real-life role is perhaps her most important.

The Bladder Health Organization just named Gloria its Goodwill Ambassador, and she is enthusiastic about assuming the reins. "I'm excited about doing everything I can to help raise awareness of this serious health issue," she said, reclining in the bougainvillea-filled garden of her Beverly Hills home.

Gloria recently admitted that she has suffered from a bladder condition for years. (She revealed the details in the February, 1999 issue of this magazine after fellow actress Margot LeMora made a shocking joke on *The Tonight Show* at Gloria's expense, which brought the issue to the forefront after years of "blind item" gossip.)

Gloria decided it was time to tell the truth and rid herself of her private embarrassment. "My friend June Allyson counseled me to admit it publicly like she did. It's a lot easier admitting it when you're getting a paycheck for it, but I decided to take the advice. And you know, I feel like a weight's been lifted. I don't even hate Margot for being such a cunt for making a nasty joke at my expense, when I could have said some mean-spirited and true things about her over the years."

All jokes aside, Gloria is eager to begin speaking engagements. "I'll be talking to all kinds of organizations interested in the health and well-being of slightly mature Americans. It's important that we not ignore the health of our urinary tracts. And did you know paying attention to your bladder can improve your sex life? Who knew there were exercises for that?"

Lord's photographer daughter on exhibit by Trasea Smythe, *The Times of London*, 2 August, 1999

Petal Bottomly, daughter of Lord Laddie Bottomly and the actress Gara St. James, has been a professional photojournalist for some 15 years, but she always discovers new ways of looking at things in her profession.

"Having grown up as I have, with one foot in London and on in California, I've always had to see things from multiple viewpoints. *You* try being the child of a free-spirited Englishman and a boisterous American and try keeping a sense of yourself," she laughed.

Better known by her nickname Pet, she has focused her lens on political and social matters, with her work appearing in newspapers, *U.S.*

News & World Report, and *Newsweek.*

A retrospective of her work will be on exhibit at the Bottomly Gallery, owned by her nephew, Albert. "She's always been observant, even when we were children. I could never get away with playing a trick on her; she was too quick for me! I hesitate to think how she might have been with a camera at too young an age!" he added.

The opening is tonight in 35 Routledge Street. Pet's parents are both expected at the event. This will be the first time they've seen each other in some time, so expect intense red carpet media coverage. "Laddie and I stay in contact by phone, even though we don't like each other all that much," Gara St. James quipped. "But it's important to Pet that we pretend."

Excerpt from *Politics and Hollywood Celebrities: The Conservative Connection* by Franklin Butterworth

The nineties dawned with effective leadership from George H. W. Bush and the Republican party. The successful Persian Gulf War and his smooth method of turning "no new taxes" into successful revenue increases should have kept Bush going strong, but after a decade of weak candidates, the Democrats had found a golden idol: Bill Clinton.

Next to Bush, Clinton came on as a pandering oaf and celebrity wannabe. He appeared on *The Arsenio Hall Show* playing the saxophone and on MTV, where he was asked the important political question, "Boxers or briefs?"

While vapid denizens of Hollywood embraced Clinton, Gara St. James was quick to speak up for Bush. After the Reagans departed Washington for California, she was a frequent guest of the Bushes during their years in the White House. She and Barbara Bush appeared together at events promoting literacy.

"Barbara knows what's important on this issue. If you're in America, you need to know how to read and write American. How do you expect to get jobs in the service industry if you can't read and write?" Gara asked teens at one event.

St. James didn't confine her efforts to Barbara's pet cause. She stuck up for George on many issues:

His choice of running mate: "Dan Quayle *is* qualified to be Vice President. I knew Kennedy as well as Lloyd Bentsen did, and let me tell you, having people around offering advice helped keep Jack grounded. Surround Dan with smart people like me and he'll do just fine."

The decision to become involved when Iraq invaded Kuwait: "We can't have those people thinking they can run things and take oil from other countries. That's un-American!"

The incident involving the Japanese prime minister: "No one can fault George for throwing up on that man. Have you ever tried some of that sushi? Yuck!"

Gara attended fundraisers for George, while misguided friend Barbara Lamont hosted a Tinseltown dinner for Bill, which descended into an embarrassing disaster when her mother did a naked shimmy and jumped into a pool, further making unseemly connections between Clinton and "Sodom by the Sea."

It was obvious from the start that Clinton was in deep with Hollywood when his first action as President was to force homosexuality on the military. Suddenly Americans realized they had let the fox into the henhouse. This measure was defeated, replaced with a policy that attempted to remain true to normal American ideals while keeping liberal activists at bay.

Even embarrassing whispers of Bill's adulterous activities and financial improprieties weren't enough to dim his repugnant star power, allowing "Slick Willie" to win reelection in 1996.

Clinton's supposed legendary charisma made easy prey for Hollywood denizens who should have known better. "He's dazzling in person. I go weak in the knees," Barbara Lamont squealed like a teenager, though she was much older.

"I've met Clinton, and I'll admit, he's charming and what-not, although he shouldn't be President," Gara conceded. "He'd make a helluva of a game show host! And I didn't care for Hillary. I'm sure that's because, although I've earned my own way as is my right as an American, I also believe a woman should know her place is raising children and standing behind her man. I think Hillary has her eye on the presidency herself one day, I really do! She should be spending this time raising that unfortunate-looking child of theirs."

Bill Clinton continued to ride, taking credit for a healthy economy which was due to heroic efforts by the Republican-controlled Congress. But Bill's hubris caught up with him. In 1998, the Lewinsky scandal revealed for all to see: the emperor had no clothes, he knew it, and he was reveling in his abhorrent immorality.

CHAPTER 13

I just want everyone to have a good time tonight and laugh their heads off at me!

"Welcome, thanks for coming," Gara bellowed to an esteemed guest as she stood in the receiving line. "You'll like the movie they're gonna show, *The Petrified Mother*. Boy, I'm hysterical!"

"Yes, in more ways than one," quipped Barbara.

"Why don't you head into the dining room and tie on the feedbag," Gara implored the guest.

"Don't think I'm missing those little comments you're making," she fumed at Barbara. "You're only here because I let you be here. So you two better be on your best behavior and stop embarrassing me."

"You're doing that well enough on your own," Gloria whispered.

Gara narrowed her eyes and turned to greet the next guest. Barbara nudged her pal and leaned over for an aside. "Didn't I tell you we'd outshine her? Where did she dig up that dress? She looks like The Incredible Hulk."

Gloria choked on a giggle and turned to shake the hand of the next invitee in line. "Oh Miss Prescott, what a pleasure to meet you!" the man gushed.

"Really, how sweet," Gloria flirted.

"My favorite movie is *In the Shadow of Sainthood*. You were so believable! I wish they were showing that film tonight!"

"Hey, Bub, you want Gloria Prescott, rent a DVD! Tonight it's about the kids!" Gara butted in. "Move it along. Grab some meatballs from the buffet."

The confused gentleman backed away as Gara leaned closer to Gloria. "I've got my eye on you, too. Stop trying to be sexy and stealing my thunder. You look silly behaving like Marilyn when your boobs are around your knees."

"You should talk," Gloria hissed through clenched teeth. "You could sling *your* boobs over your shoulders and cover your ass."

"I say!" They turned to see the appalled face of Princess Anne.

"*Perdón*, your royal highness!" Gloria blushed, remembering her studio training and bending into a curtsy. Gara forgot Miss Burns's tutelage and pumped the princess's hand up and down.

"It's awful swell of you to show up," Gara beamed. "I guess your mom and your other brothers were busy tonight?"

The princess was taken aback by the protocol infraction. "Er, we're pleased to be here for London's less fortunate," she managed to say, extracting her hand from Gara's grip.

"Yeah, thanks for coming! Get some chow in the dining room," she recommended to Countess Sophie and gave Prince Edward a friendly slap on the back.

"Smooth, Gara, smooth," Barbara commented.

"What'd that fool do now? And when do I get to eat?" Myrtle asked, loping up to her daughter.

"Soon, Mother. Do you want to stand here with me and greet guests?"

"I'm not getting paid for this," Myrtle growled. "Can't I get some cheese balls or a couple of Vienna sausages?"

"How dare you behave so abominably!" Gwyda accused in full "Great Dame" mode. "You offended the royals with your uncouth behavior! In the old days, they would have dragged you off to the guillotine!"

"Aw, they didn't mind. I bet they appreciated being treated like regular folks," Gara defended.

"You are an insufferable boor!"

"Did she call her a bore, like John Gavin? Or a boar, like Elsa Maxwell?" Barbara asked Gloria.

"Either way, it's accurate."

"I will be delighted when the lot of you leave and I get my house back! And you –" Gwyda turned back to Gara. "Why didn't you die in that fire forty years ago?"

Gwyda stalked off, leaving a speechless line of guests waiting to meet the celebrities. "And she said I behaved badly! That's like the pot calling the kettle corn popped!" Gara sputtered.

"Barbara!" Myrtle bellowed from the dining room. "I'm not waiting any longer! Where does the buffet line start?"

Barbara sighed and turned to Gloria. "I can't wait until Binky and Didums get here. I'm sure they're having an easier time of it than we are."

"Joan beat Olivia by winning Oscar gold first, but Livvy won two and shunned her with a curse! Davis hated Crawford with a passion unknown, so Joanie begged for more so she wouldn't be alone!

"Those were the divas! The one and true divas! Julia Who? Nicole Who? Gwyneth Who? Kick them out! Those were the divas! The one and true divas!" Binky repeated the chorus a dozen times as the song wound down. The rambunctious crowd screamed their approval, jumping and dancing in the crowded nightclub.

Didums and Carolyn finished their backup dance and struck poses at the end, waves of applause rushing over them. Didums glanced at Carolyn, pleased to see her eyes were shining.

Cliff seemed to have had as good a time as his wife. Pretending to play a synthesizer unleashed his inner rock star, and he struck an arrogant pose, feeling uber-cool in leather pants and designer sunglasses.

"Thank you, thank you! London's the best audience!" Binky cooed and blew kisses to the crowd. "Thank you!" The audience reluctantly allowed the performers to quit the stage.

"What did I tell you? You were fabulous!" Didums exclaimed, giving Carolyn a hug.

"I've never experienced such a rush!" she exclaimed. "Oh my God, I'm still trembling."

"Luv, I'm going to ignore that statement about you never having a rush before," Cliff said in a mock punk rock voice. "But if it helps matters, I'll wear this same outfit the next time we're alone."

"Oh, you!" she squealed, lunging at her husband and jumping into his arms.

"I think we were a hit," Binky crowed to Didums.

"In more ways than one!" he replied, nodding at Cliff and Carolyn.

"Congratulations, my dears! Marvy, you were simply marvy!"

They turned to see a fifty-something blonde (fighting it every step of the way) in stilettos and a low-cut dress with a sad-faced man behind her. The woman leaned in for hugs and air kisses with Binky.

"You were fabulous! How long are going to be in London? Will you be here long enough to be on my show?" she bubbled.

"Darling, you must introduce yourself," the man reminded. "Excuse my wife, she gets excited and forgets that not everyone knows who she is."

She pretended to pout. "My husband is sometimes correct, although I'm sure you know me. I'm Lady Arlene Arden-Canfield, the host of *Mid-Morning Britain Today!* And this is my husband, the Earl of Wimpleham, Richard Canfield."

Cliff and Carolyn sobered, knowing how silly they would look in front of social peers. Binky and Didums realized that standing in front of them was a former bubblegum pop singer and her husband, who happened to be Hannah Bottomly's former fiancé.

"Arlene, delightful to meet you," Binky snapped into media mode. "I've always loved your one big hit, 'Ginger Boy.'"

"I also had a hit with 'I'm Second Best But He's Still Mine,'" Arlene sulked, sticking out her bottom lip.

"And who can forget it!" Didums enthused.

Her bruised ego pacified, Arlene turned past him to the others. Her eyes widened in recognition. "Cliff and Carolyn Fotheringay! Shame on you two! When did you start moonlighting as rock stars?"

Perturbed to have been recognized, the couple stiffened and tried to laugh off the embarrassing situation. "Delightful to see you as always, Arlene, Richard," Carolyn trilled.

"Our friends here got caught in a pickle and convinced us to help them out. A one-night-only performance for us, I'm afraid," Cliff explained with an unconvincing laugh.

Arlene, however, was already processing information forward. "But of course, Bingley Lamont! Your mother's Barbara Lamont and your grandmother was married to Laddie once, bless his soul. And you're all at Brownmoor right now. Oh Richard, I should have them all on my show!"

Richard made a wry face. "Dear, I think that would all depend on what they wish to do."

"But who doesn't want to be on TV? It's all publicity, surely Barbara realizes that. I heard Gloria Prescott is here, too. And how can I forget Laddie's other wife, Gara St. James! It's a veritable Hollywood homecoming out there in Flemshire! Maybe we can do a location shoot!"

"I don't think Gwyda would be too thrilled with that," her husband reminded.

"I might think it would be a bit much for you as well, Lord Wimpleham," Didums suggested.

"Please, call me Richard," the earl insisted. "Yes, you might say that would feel a bit eerie, even after all these years."

Temporarily admonished, Arlene squeezed her husband's arm with a sympathetic look. Carolyn and Cliff knew the couple in a casual social way while Binky and Didums didn't know them at all, but it was clear to all the tragedy of Hannah's death had affected Richard, and Arlene loved him and understood the occasional sadness.

"I'm sorry, I didn't wish to awaken bad memories," Didums apologized.

"Quite all right," Richard replied, the British "stiff upper lip" at the ready.

"Don't let him fool you," Arlene insisted. "The events at

Brownmoor have always been a source of sadness, even after we found out the truth about Hannah and Barnaby."

"The truth? What do you mean?"

"Ouch! Hey, stop stepping on my shoes! Everyone's out of the house, we don't have to sneak!" Henry protested as Miles scuffed his sneaker heels.

"There's no sense in wasting time, either," Miles reasoned.

The group stopped in front of the Laddie's door and Babs examined the huge key ring pilfered from the study. "How your great-grandmother keeps track of these keys without labels is beyond me."

After several attempts, she succeeded in finding the correct key. She turned on the light and Chester dashed into the unfamiliar room. The others crept in, a bit awed by the task at hand.

"Where should we start?" Sophie wondered aloud.

"Anywhere and everywhere," Babs replied. "Why don't you check out that chest of drawers. Boys, you look through the closet, and I'll start with this desk."

There was silence for awhile as they went about their searches. Even Chester did his part, sniffing about the room. Not sure of what might constitute an actual clue, they felt a bit unclear with the investigation.

Focus seemed to weaken as the exploration expanded. The desk and chest didn't reveal anything incriminating, nor did the closet. Babs eyed the objects on the fireplace mantel and examined a figurine, then opened a cigar box. A bit chagrined at their lack of success and feeling more pressure in her role as the adult, she gave a light kick to the brass fireplace accessories stand. Her kick was harder than she anticipated, and the poker and broom crashed to the floor.

Miles moved to help with the mess. He picked up the items and noticed something in the fireplace. Reaching forward, he pulled out charred papers. Chester jumped forward, sniffing the clue.

"What's that?" Sophie asked.

"It looks like pages from a book," he replied.

Henry took one of the pages. "I've seen the handwriting before, it's Laddie's."

Babs examined the other page. There weren't many words still visible: "I never told," "she said," and "London." These random words meant nothing without any context.

"Do you think that's what Grandmum was doing in here the other day, burning letters?" Henry wondered aloud.

"There may be one way to find out," Babs said, lifting the key ring again.

Barbara swished her fork in the plate of chicken divan and rice almondine. "Why do they serve the most abominable food at these events?"

Myrtle sopped sauce up with a roll. "This isn't so bad, better than I'd get at the Motion Picture Country Home. I've seen the stuff they serve when I've visited old pals there. I'm surprised you haven't gotten any ideas when I've been there."

"Who says?" Gloria whispered to Barbara, who sighed and rolled her eyes in response, the burden of "celebrity with incorrigible parent" always present.

"Yeah, this food's pretty good," Gara agreed. "But they've got to be careful not to spend too much on the party, 'cause the money needs to go to help the needy. If you girls thought about others at all, you'd realize that."

"That's rich, coming from someone who said, 'Let them eat ramen noodles! Those things are twenty cents a package. Who can't afford that?'"

"Those reporters always take what I say out of context," Gara defended. "I was praising the Chinese people for inventing the things in the first place!" She looked down the table and gestured to Prince Edward.

"Hey, you gonna finish that cobbler?" she asked.

He blinked in surprise and picked up his plate. "Why no, you're welcome to it," he said with an amused grin.

Gara snapped her fingers at those seated between her and the prince. "Pass it along," she ordered.

Pet sighed and shared glances with Mina and Albert. Barbara and Gloria shook their heads in embarrassment, while Gwyda seethed in fury. Archie and Nolan patted her shoulder in an attempt to calm her down. Louise and Willis ignored the spectacle and concentrated on their wine glasses.

"I cannot stand this another minute," Gwyda hissed at Archie, who held onto her arm to stop her from rising.

"Don't cause a scene, Mum," he pressed.

"How in the bloody hell are we going to get through a film screening?" she asked. "I don't think I'll be able to sit through that."

"None of us will," Nolan muttered.

"We can't leave until the royals leave," Archie pointed out.

Unfortunately for the Bottomlys and Glasscocks, Prince Edward and Countess Sophie were amusing themselves by engaging Gara in conversation and were looking forward to the movie.

"I don't believe I've seen *The Petrified Mother* before," the countess mused.

"Oh, you'll love it!" Gara enthused. "I dreamed up a bunch of comedy bits that weren't in the script. I had this one gag where I was trying to diaper the baby and got so confused, I diapered the kid's head! Ha! Efram Zimbalist Jr. really thought I didn't know what I was doing and tried to take the baby from me. I said, 'Dang, how stupid do you think I am?' The director loved that ad-lib so much, he left it in."

"Sounds quite amusing," the prince offered.

"Oh yeah, I'm funny as all get-out! Why I didn't get more comedy films, I'll never understand," Gara shook her head.

"Miss St. James should be considered a comedy legend, like Lucille Ball and Mike Tyson," Peony added.

"Aw, I don't need all those accolades," Gara pretended modesty. "I just want everyone to have a good time tonight and laugh their heads off at me!"

Richard and Arlene exchanged an uneasy look. "Perhaps it's best to let sleeping dogs lie," he said.

"We don't want to make you relive unhappy times, but there's a good reason we're asking," Binky offered.

"And we're not talking about gossip, although that's interesting," Didums added. "But there have been disturbing incidents at Brownmoor. It seems someone's upset about things that happened in the past and it's essential we figure out what's going on before someone gets hurt."

The pair exchanged looks again, and turned to Carolyn and Cliff for seeming permission to talk freely.

"They're right, some odd things have been happening at the house," Carolyn admitted. "Maybe it's best if you told us anything you might know."

Richard cleared his throat. "Well, I suppose you know Hannah and I were engaged, and our wedding had been planned for a few weeks after the fire occurred. And although I hadn't said anything publicly yet, the wedding was not going to take place. I was trying to think of a way to have it called off without causing a scandal greater than the one that awaited me if I let it go forward."

The bandmates exchanged confused glances and Arlene sat forward. "You may not know I was dating Barnaby at the same time. We were all in the public eye, so photographers would often snap shots of us out on the town as a group. I'll admit, Barnaby was handsome and looked the part of the perfect escort. But he could be unpredictable, even dangerous. More than once he beat up a guy who he imagined was paying too much attention to his sister. I tried to explain it away to myself as him being an overprotective big brother, but it always stayed in the back of my mind as a red flag."

"It bothered me, too," Richard added. "It went beyond mere protection. I thought Hannah and I were a good match and once we were married, we wouldn't have to worry about Barnaby's outrageous behavior. But then I witnessed something I knew would mean disaster if we proceeded with the wedding."

"We both saw it," Arlene interrupted. She paused before continuing, as if even saying the words were distasteful. "We were out at dinner one summer night about six weeks before the wedding. Both of them seemed a bit silly that evening, but I assumed they were a little tipsy. Hannah excused herself to the ladies room, and shortly thereafter, Barnaby excused himself as well. Richard and I found ourselves commenting on their odd behavior and realized we had both found their behavior strange for some time. And when it seemed as if they were taking a rather long time coming back to the table, we became bold and decided to find them. There are times I wish we hadn't."

Richard reached out and took his wife's hand. Their audience remained silent and rapt with attention. "Indeed we found them, in an alcove near the loo where the phone boxes were. And they weren't placing a call."

"You mean ..." a horrified Carolyn couldn't complete the thought.

"Yes, they were in a phone box, doing what brothers and sisters shouldn't be doing. We were too stunned to confront them. We went back to the table in a state of shock."

"We should have left right then and there, but they came back in a few minutes, pretending as if everything were normal," Arlene said with a visible shudder.

"My word," Didums clucked.

"You must understand the situation I was in," Richard explained. "We were supposed to be married in weeks, and although I knew I couldn't go through with it, I also knew society and decorum demanded everything be dealt with in a manner better than she deserved."

"Either of them deserved," Arlene insisted.

"You can imagine the shock we had when we found out about the fire. It was a horrible tragedy, but a piece of me did think they deserved it," Richard admitted with sadness. "Their actions were so hurtful and immoral. But I had to perform as the grieving bridegroom, and only we knew the truth."

"We were there for each other," she asserted, squeezing her husband's hand. What had first been clinging to each other in the face of shared tragedy turned into a real love match, for it was obvious Richard and Arlene adored each other.

"Do you think this has anything to do with what's been going on at Brownmoor?" Didums whispered to Binky.

"Maybe someone else found out like Richard and Arlene," Carolyn replied, overhearing the quiet question.

"Enough to start a fire? And to kill others to keep it a secret now?" Cliff wondered aloud.

"Sometimes it takes less for a real flamer to set off a spark," Binky quipped darkly, "but this time, it might have been too much to extinguish. And that might be something we can only find out back in Flemshire."

Moving toward the auditorium, Gara swept past a petite brunette in a stunning Alexander McQueen gown. The woman turned at the invasion of her personal space and widened her eyes. "Gara!" she exclaimed.

Gara turned and looked blankly at the woman. "Sorry, it's a charity event, no autographs."

The woman responded with a hearty laugh. "Same darling girl," she chortled. "Dear, it's Francesca, Francesca Annis. How have you been?"

The celebrated actress, known for her award-winning acting roles in literary film classics and experimental theater, had known Gara for many years, having met on the set of Hitchcock's *Nightshade* when Francesca was just starting out in films. The British legend knew what a pain in the rear Gara could be, but her practicality and decorum ensured she would treat her disagreeable colleague with politesse.

"Oh yeah, Francie, how you doing?" Gara leaned in for air kisses. "Been a long time. I saw *Nightshade* again not that long ago. Boy, was I good. You were okay, too."

"I had a bigger role before most of it ended up on the cutting room floor. How nice of you to suggest Hitch trim my part down in the editing."

"Now, now, we didn't want to confuse the audience with all those extra scenes," Gara wagged her finger. "What have you been up to lately?"

"I just finished *Cranford* for the BBC, working with Judi Dench, Eileen Atkins, Imelda Staunton. What a treat to work with *real* actresses," Francesca sparkled, her slam at Gara sailing over her rival's head. "And *your* latest project?"

"I'm concentrating on my memoirs right now, working with this here writer. Caddy? Caddy!" she yelped, looking for the man, who was trying to hide behind Peony. Gara grabbed his hand and pulled him forward.

Francesca's eyes narrowed. "Cadmus Polk!" she spit out. "What are you doing with this shitheel?"

"Why are you insulting me?" an offended Gara gasped.

"Not you, *him*! This little scoundrel sold me on the idea of writing a book about me, claimed he was the president of my fan club!" she raged.

"Now, now, I never said it would make a potful of money. I said it was more of a 'valentine to your fans,'" Caddy defended.

"You bloody bastard, you absconded with a bunch of my money. You stole some expensive bric-a-brac from my home, you even took some of my underwear!"

"Mementos," he stammered.

"You little –" Francesca lunged forward as Caddy sidestepped her wrath.

"If you'll excuse me, I must visit the loo," he squealed. He darted behind Peony and pushed her into Francesca's grasp. In the momentary confusion, he evaded capture by the angry actress.

Francesca pushed Peony out of the way. "Where did that grotty wanker run off to?" Frustrated, she turned to Gara. "I might expect you'd have something to do with him."

"It's not my fault if no one bought his book about you," Gara insisted.

"Are you really this stupid, or are you a decent actress after all? He's just scamming money out of you, too."

"Those are necessary expenses. People worldwide are going to want to read *my* story!" the star replied with confidence.

"I know I do!" Peony piped up loyally.

Francesca rolled her eyes and shook her head. "And to think I once told Elizabeth Taylor you weren't so bad when she called you 'a big plate of moldy jelly donuts.'" With that, she turned and swept away.

"I always thought Francie was jealous of me," Gara decided. "And Liz wasn't the type to let a plate of jelly donuts get moldy! Talk about making up stories. I should have known she was that way, what with that weird name of hers. Who has a name like Francie Butt? That's worse than Vittorio Gassman. Peony, go find Caddy, we need to get into the theater so the screening can start."

"Wasn't it *bien* to see Francesca?" Gloria trilled as she approached.

"We barely had a chance to say hello, what with her racing out like that," Barbara added. "Now where do you suppose Mother has gotten herself to? She's bound to get into trouble. There are far too many temptations among the guests. She's liable to have cooked up a scheme to bilk Princess Anne out of her place in line for the throne."

"Why don't you put yourselves to good use and start herding folks into the auditorium?" Gara suggested. "I always said you girls did your best work in theaters ... in the balcony with sailors on shore leave."

"Normally I'd be pissed, but being so well brought up, I choose to hear a compliment in your ill-meant words," Gloria sniffed. She turned and, with Barbara, directed the slow throng of partygoers toward the screening room.

An assistant with the charity organization approached. "Miss St. James, don't forget you're making an introduction before the film. If you'd prefer to take the side entrance, you can get backstage right away," he offered, pointing out the unobtrusive door.

"Good, anything to avoid the masses of the unwashed," she shuddered at the guests who continued following Barbara and Gloria's direction. She turned in time to see Caddy making a break for the exit. "Peony, there's Caddy. Get his ass over here!"

With startling speed, Peony raced across the room and snatched the writer by the arms, clutching him with a martial hold. "I say, Petunia, this is most untoward!" he gasped as the loyal assistant lifted him with surprising strength and carried him back to her satisfied mistress.

"Er, Gara dearest, I don't know where Francesca got those crazy ideas," he stammered, sure that he was about to receive a pummeling at the hands of the hefty actress.

But Gara had given little credence to the exposure of his self-serving schemes. "Aw, she's always been a little off in her thinking. Like it's your fault nobody bought her book. Why, people would sooner read about Timima Bossi, and she was no day at the beach, let me tell you. Say, Caddy, why don't you help with this introduction? We can mention my upcoming book. That'll get people interested."

"The movie sure won't keep people interested," Barbara quipped to Gloria.

"C'mon, Caddy. Peony, go save us some seats in the front."

"As you command," Peony squeaked, always at attention. She released Caddy and gave him a look that said, "Don't even try it, Buster." Meekly, he followed Gara and they entered the side entrance.

"It's awful dark in here," Gara said as they made their way down the corridor. "Do you see a light switch anywhere?"

Before he could reply, a rapid movement *swooshed!* between them, and the bare amount of light from the edges of the door behind them glinted on the sound's source: A large butcher knife slicing through the air.

Caddy almost jumped out of his skin and exclaimed, "Jesus crimony!" He sprinted back down the hall to evade the assailant, who he correctly assumed was after Gara. In his haste, his precious notepad, full of pithy sayings from his benefactress, fell unnoticed to the floor.

"You won't get away this time," Gara heard from the darkness. A fist suddenly emerged and connected with her jaw, knocking her out cold. "That's one way to shut the old bint up."

"Here we go," Babs announced as she turned the key to Gwyda's room.

"It's one thing to snoop in Laddie's room, but I feel weird snooping here," Henry admitted.

"We won't stay long," Babs insisted. "I just want to check one thing." She headed for the fireplace, following the determined Chester, and examined the hearth.

The cockapoo was as good as a bloodhound; he'd picked up the scent of the papers in Laddie's room and recognized the same pages in Gwyda's lair. With care, Babs retrieved the page from the helpful dog. "I think we interrupted Gwyda the last time and she finished the job here." The page also held no clue other than a partial word which meant nothing.

"Now what?" quizzed Sophie.

"I say back to Laddie's room," Henry offered. "I think we overlooked something. You know what I'm thinking about, Miles."

Miles looked inspired and raced back to Laddie's room, with the others close behind. "What is it?" Sophie asked.

"Why didn't we think of this before?" he said, knocking on the wood panels along the fireplace. He pressed the center frieze in the woodwork and the panel popped open.

"Don't tell me the room has secret panels," Sophie marveled.

"It sure does," Henry responded, attacking the opposite side of the fireplace to find hidden drawers.

But each panel they found proved to be empty. Dejected, the boys sat down, disappointed that their flash of inspiration hadn't resulted in success. Sophie fiddled with other panels around the room.

"Forget it, Soph," Henry chided. "Those are the only panels we know about."

"Yeah, the only ones *you* know about. How often were you in

Laddie's room? Wasn't he stuck in bed the last few years? Maybe there are some panels you didn't know about."

"She has a point," Miles admitted as Henry rolled his eyes, resistant to admitting a girl might know more than him. But he joined the others as they examined the room more thoroughly.

They worked in silence until Sophie exclaimed, "Sweet!" Victorious, she showed off a hidden panel near the baseboards of the wall on the right side of the bed, with Chester already peering into the small recess.

"Is it empty?" Henry asked, leaning forward.

She gently pushed the dog aside and removed a small volume. "Looks like a book," she said, opening it.

"It's Laddie's handwriting, all right," Miles noticed.

"But the pages are different from the burned ones, these are edged in gold scrollwork," Babs pointed out.

"I don't understand the stuff I'm reading here," Sophie said, confusion tinging her words.

Babs took the book from the girl and read the open page. She widened her eyes and turned the page, reading silently.

"Well, come on, what'd he say?" Henry urged.

The woman looked at the expectant faces in front of her. She wished she could share the shocking words in the journal so the kids would feel vindication for their investigation, but knew it would be irresponsible to do so. And with Laddie gone, just one person could verify the truth behind the story held within these pages. And that person was possibly in danger right at that moment.

There was a murmur through the audience at the continuing delay of the film. "Isn't Momsy supposed to make some sort of introduction?" Pet wondered aloud, tapping Peony on the shoulder for confirmation.

"I'm sure Miss St. James is just waiting for the right moment to make a splashy entrance," the loyal assistant responded. "Maybe she's gonna use that routine she didn't get to finish on the Emmys a couple of years ago."

"Do you think I should go looking for Mother?" Barbara asked.

"She's probably sacked out on a couch in the lobby. A big meal usually prompts a little *siesta*," Gloria theorized.

"Especially if I managed to sneak some 'additives' into the dinner."

The house lights dimmed and soon the movie's title and credits began unfurling onscreen. *The Petrified Mother* had been a big moneymaker that year for its studio, due in no small part to Efram Zimbalist, Jr., Paul

Douglas, Marie Wilson, Fred Clark, and of course, Gara. The audience seemed to be appreciating the amusing plot and sharp comedy performances.

Mina noticed Pet's continuous fidgeting. "Are you still wondering about your mother?"

"Yes," she whispered back. "I can't sit here any longer. I think something's wrong." She headed for the lobby, with Mina and Albert close behind.

"You don't think it's just a ploy to milk anticipation for applause after the screening?" Albert asked.

"I just have a bad feeling. Someone was trying to hurt Momsy at Brownmoor, so what's to stop them from pulling something here?"

Mina and Albert couldn't argue with this logic, so they began making a sweep of the banquet hall, the ballroom, and the lobby. There was no sign of Gara nor was there any apparent clue to her whereabouts. "Now what?" Albert asked when their search appeared fruitless.

"I'm not sure," Pet admitted as Barbara and Gloria exited the auditorium.

"Have you seen my mother?" Barbara asked. "She seems to be missing, which could mean havoc for the British economy."

The trio exchanged glances. One disappearance seemed odd, but the disappearances of both women, apparent targets at Brownmoor, were far too coincidental. They assured the ladies that they would help in finding Myrtle.

Another sweep of the building confirmed their initial assumption. With options running out, Pet turned to the side entrance to the auditorium. "Where does that go?"

"It leads backstage. That's where Miss St. James and Mr. Polk went before the movie started," Peony responded as she exited the screening room.

Pet nodded at Mina and Albert. "Let's go," she said, leading the phalanx of searchers through the door.

They had proceeded a short distance before the darkness impeded their progress as it had Gara. Their similar attempt to find a light switch proved as ineffective. A resourceful Albert fished in his pocket and pulled out his key ring which contained a penlight. "This'll do in a pinch," he offered, sweeping the corridor with light.

"What's that?" Gloria asked as the light flashed over the floor. Peony reached over and picked up the notepad and identified it as Caddy's.

"They were here," Albert said.

"And so was someone else," Mina added, pointing to something else on the floor. Albert picked up the item, a silver medal. He flashed the beam of light and turned it over in his hand.

"It looks like a religious medal," Barbara remarked.

"That's me!" Gloria exclaimed. "I mean, it's Saint Rosalita of Andalucia."

"No, not Rosalita," Mina said softly. "It's Saint Eulàlia of Barcelona, which is in –"

"Catalonia," Albert whispered.

The group continued along the darkened corridor. They paused at the wing leading onto the stage. They could hear the film's soundtrack and the appreciate audience laughter from their vantage place. Pet motioned to Albert; he nodded and followed her lead, shading his penlight to the side to ensure the secrecy of their advance.

They moved past the onstage entrance and continued further along the wall behind the screen, where offices and dressing rooms were found. The sound from the stage was muffled now as they edged forward.

Barbara discovered an electrical switch. Before anyone could stop her, she declared, "We shall have light!" and flipped it.

Pet stifled a shriek and pointed up. On the lowest catwalk about thirty feet in the air, Nolan brandished a knife in front of Myrtle and Gara.

Shocked at the sudden exposure, he whirled to face the new witnesses. "Not now!" he snarled.

"Oh, Dad," Albert whispered. Mina grabbed his hand to provide support.

"Took you long enough," Myrtle groused.

"Mother, how was I to know a madman had kidnapped you? I thought you were stealing the crown off Princess Anne's head," Barbara protested.

"Quiet!" Nolan bellowed, waving the knife from his captives to the newcomers below.

"Dad, please come down, let's talk about this," Albert called, his voice wavering.

"Not until I've taken care of these two," he threatened, turning his attention back to Gara and Myrtle.

"Don't worry, Miss St. James, I'll save you!" Peony yelped, trying to break free of Pet's arm and save her precious boss.

"Why are you doing this?" Pet implored.

Nolan refused to answer her. "Cat got your tongue now? He's been muttering the whole time about why he's doing this," Gara snorted.

He sneered at Gara to be quiet, but the resolute star pushed aside his hand clutching the knife. "Hey Bub, I don't need cue cards, I can memorize lines like Old Yeller. I've always had a mind like a steel trap."

"Yes, but why can't it snap your mouth shut? Sorry! I couldn't help myself," Gloria protested.

"He's mad Laddie left us money in his will, and he still blames this old cow for that fire," Myrtle wheezed, nodding toward Gara.

"But the police report showed Momsy didn't start the fire," Pet protested.

"Don't you think I know that?" Nolan hissed. "I did it! I mean, *she* did it!"

Suddenly Pet realized what it was about those old photos of a pre-fire Brownmoor that had nagged her mind. The distance between the barn and the manor house ... It seemed unlikely that a fire starting in the northeast wing would have spread over the grounds to the barn so quickly without the fire destroying more of the castle first. "The fire didn't start in the house," she blurted out. "It started in the barn. You started it."

"No!" he snapped. "No, I didn't. They did. I mean –"

"He must mean Hannah and Barnaby," Binky said, bringing up the rear with his temporary bandmates.

"Oh, Binky, you're finally here!" Barbara gasped. "You can't imagine the stress your grandmother's put me through tonight!"

"Don't call me 'grandmother!' It makes people think I'm old," Myrtle reminded angrily.

"He must have discovered what was going on," Didums said.

"What was going on?" Gloria asked.

"Nothing was going on!" Nolan insisted. "Stop it!"

"Barnaby and Hannah – They were ... involved," Didums explained with delicacy.

"Oh, dear God," Gwyda gasped as she and the remaining family members joined the group. "I was wondering why everyone had disappeared, with the film unfinished and the royals still in attendance," she snapped, duty and protocol replacing shock at the revelation of unseemly family secrets. She realized her nephew was holding the American gold diggers at knifepoint and resumed her horror.

Despite the danger of the current situation, Pet was determined to get to the truth. "Is that it, Nolan? Did you find Barnaby and Hannah together?"

His resolve sputtered and he struggled to regain control, to little avail. "They laughed at me when I found them together in the barn," he recoiled with disgust. "I couldn't believe it. I was on the grounds when I saw them exiting the castle from the old underground entrance and going the barn. They seemed so conspiratorial, so giddy. I knew something wasn't quite right. Maybe I shouldn't have followed them, but I did. And I caught them in the act."

Gwyda stiffened and Archie grabbed her arm. Louise buried her face in Willis's shoulder.

Nolan continued in his strange fog, both oblivious to his audience and aware that he was telling a story he'd kept to himself for decades. "Even more shocking, they didn't care that I'd caught them. They laughed at me! When I asked if she'd forgotten that she was supposed to marry the earl in a matter of weeks, they insisted they didn't care, that her upcoming wedding wasn't going to change their love. Love! They called it love. They had even lit candles there, as if it were some romantic scene out of a movie."

There was a sudden sound of muffled laughter from the almost distant auditorium where the audience still watched *The Petrified Mother* and appreciated some brilliant comic turn. Nolan turned to its source, as if hearing Barnaby and Hannah laughing at him through time and dimension.

"I was furious. It was only a matter of time before someone else caught them and ruined the family name. I was blind with rage, and they laughed again. I couldn't stop myself. I grabbed the candles and threw them at them."

The backstage audience was rapt with attention. Carolyn squeezed Cliff's hand and tears streamed down her face, sorrow for the cousin unraveling in front of her and for long-gone cousins she knew only through photographs.

"The hay caught fire right away. I – I immediately regretted it, but part of me was glad to see them behind the flames. They look terrified and I was glad they finally had something to fear. The fire spread quicker than I expected and I had no choice but to get out of there. I ran into the woods and kept running for I don't know how long. When I returned, I realized the fire had spread to the house and the place was in a panic. Everyone was accounted for except for Hannah and Barnaby, and only later did anyone else realize they were missing."

Everyone was quiet for awhile, not sure if Nolan was going to say anything else. "Why was it assumed all these years they died in the castle?" Pet whispered.

"We ... we asked the police for a quick resolution to the investigation," Gwyda said haltingly. "Remember, I told you Laddie burned the full investigation without even reading it. It wasn't going to bring Hannah and Barnaby back. We never knew the full story. And later, he asked that the police destroy the official documents. At that time, the Bottomlys had the power to make uncomfortable matters ... disappear."

Nolan stopped staring into space and looked at Gara and Myrtle. "Forgive me, I was in the middle of something," he said, advancing toward them again with the knife.

"Nolan, don't do it, don't hurt Momsy," Pet cried out.

He turned back to the spectators. "She may well be your mother, but Laddie is not your father. This tramp fooled him, but I've never been fooled."

"That's not true," Gara blurted out. "Laddie *is* Pet's father. But – I'm not her mother."

"What are you saying?" Pet choked.

Gara bit her lip, never thinking this moment would happen, much less in what might be the last moments of her life. "It's true, Laddie is your father, but I'm not your mother. At least, I'm not your birth mother. She was Ysabel Fanon."

"The fashion model?" Barbara gasped.

"Yes, she was one of Laddie's many lady friends before I came along, and was still there after I arrived. We were on our extended honeymoon when she caught hold of us in Greece and told him she was pregnant."

"I'm amazed that didn't happen more often, with Laddie's reputation," Gloria observed.

"To his credit, Laddie told me right away. Yzzy didn't want the baby, but she wanted to tell him before she did anything. And we devised a plan. Yzzy didn't want to go along with it at first, but with enough money and Jory's help, she agreed."

"Uncle Jory?" Pet asked, tears racing down her cheeks.

"Yes. I knew a scandal could hurt Laddie as well as my career, so I called on the one man who could always be counted on to have a plan. Jory arranged it so that Yzzy would get a contract with a big French cosmetics firm after the baby was born, and that sealed the deal. She disappeared from her career and usual haunts, and we settled down in France until she had the baby and we could pass it off as ours."

Suddenly the connections between the items contained in that box began emerging. The magazines featuring Ysabel, that date discrepancy on the back of her own baby picture depicting Gara in a condition that didn't imply she'd just given birth, her own exotic coloring ... it all made sense.

But in the middle of this new clarity, Pet felt as if she had stepped into an episode of *The Twilight Zone*. Her crazed brother, the revelation of Hannah and Barnaby's twisted relationship, and now the fabric of her own existence. Only the steadying presence of Mina's arm kept her from crumbling to the floor.

"I loved you from the moment you were born. Please don't hate me," Gara whispered, her voice cracking with rare true emotion.

Before Pet could confirm or allay her mother's fears, Babs came up behind the group and saw the dangerous situation above. "Grandmother!" she exclaimed without thinking.

"For the last time, don't call me that!" an angry Myrtle yelped. She lunged toward the group below, throwing Gara off balance and setting off a chain reaction. Gara slammed into Nolan; he dropped the knife and was thrown against the railing. He teetered for a long moment, and plunged off the catwalk to the concrete floor below.

The gathered witnesses gasped in horror at the sight of Nolan's final moments. There was complete silence for many moments while they remained stunned by the shock.

"Serves the bastard right. Is it my fault he didn't hold on like Vera Miles did when I did the same thing to her back in 1964?" Myrtle croaked.

The police handled the situation in the most circumspect manner possible, befitting a death which had occurred during a charity gathering attended by royalty. Most attendees weren't even aware that it had happened. (The royals left as soon as the film was over; Princess Anne commented on the screening with a succinct, "Most charming," while Prince Edward couldn't resist an impish, "Surely no one ever bounced on an out-of-control pogo stick in a movie quite like Miss St. James.")

Gwyda snapped into control of the situation, daring anyone to think about apprising the police of the truth behind Nolan's death. As far as they were concerned, he had fallen while stringing streamers along the railing for a surprise backstage party to celebrate Gara's triumphant evening. (A resourceful Binky supplied the necessary shiny accessory from his one-of-a-kind Judith Leiber pink diamond clutch designed in the shape of male genitalia. "I've got more than you know packed in my balls," he cracked.)

Everyone maintained Gwyda's story to the police. Albert followed the family line but was inconsolable in the wake of his father's death, and was only comforted by Mina's presence.

Louise and Willis were relieved the children hadn't accompanied Babs in her dash to the party. Cliff and Carolyn, still attired in rock 'n roll finery, had sobered from the high of their club performance and held hands the entire time.

Barbara had Binky fix her manicure (ruined by flicking on the unfamiliar light switch), while Didums attended to a ripped hem in Gloria's gown with his trusty portable sewing kit. Both men kept a spare eye on

Myrtle, as their mothers had failed to keep the woman out of trouble. Fortunately, Myrtle proved to be easily babysat now; despite the evening's horrors, she fell asleep on a couch in the lobby.

Gara complained about the inconvenience she was enduring. "I can't believe I gotta deal with this now. I didn't even get to appreciate my movie like I was planning to do. And on top of this, that awful Caddy up and left me high and dry. He didn't bother defending me against that crazy bugaboo, and he didn't finish writing my book for me! All he left behind was his notepad," she gestured toward the tablet in Peony's devoted hand. "What am I going to do with this?"

An intrigued Babs snatched the notepad from Peony. "I might have an idea," she offered with a conspiratorial smile.

On the other side, Pet took her mother's hand in her own. Gara, at first worried that Pet would never forgive her, finally saw the adult her child had been for a long time. She teared up and began blubbering against Pet's shoulder in a scene that had played out many times before. Their roles as mother and daughter would continue as it had for decades even with a major change in its basic construction. It was as if Stella Dallas and her daughter Laurel had found a way to relate to each other after a particularly harrowing therapy session on *Dr. Phil*.

Many hours later, they were allowed to leave by a discrete back entrance. They returned to Brownmoor with little to say. Last night's incidents had left everyone more than a bit shell-shocked. Pet and Gara retreated to the older woman's room for a long heart-to-heart talk, but not before Pet gave Albert and Mina fierce hugs full of affection and gratitude. The couple retreated as well with only Sophie for company. Willis and Louise similarly decamped with their sons.

The others seemed unable to separate from each other, bonded by the bizarre incidents in which they had shared, like the shipboard passengers bound for heaven or hell in *Between Two Worlds*. They awkwardly settled in the study with Gwyda in the position of power at the desk. Impeccably brought up and uncomfortable with graceless quiet, Gloria cleared her throat and offered brightly, "I don't know about you, but after being up all night and most of the day, I'll fall dead asleep tonight!"

There were a few groans and Barbara sighed, "Gloria, dear, you must stop feeling this need to speak whenever there's an awkward silence. Didn't Miss Burns teach us that once?"

Gloria snapped, "Well, blame me for trying! I suppose we should stay quiet, or maybe we should just bring everything out into the open. I guess we all know now what it was Laddie wanted Gara to keep secret, according to his will. So maybe Mother Lamont should be taking up this time with her secret-keeping."

The others looked from Gloria to Myrtle, who had settled onto a settee with Binky adjusting the portable oxygen tank for her. "I'm not saying a word without Matlock here to protect my interests! He's the best lawyer on TV!" she squawked.

"You don't need to say a word, Mother," Barbara advised. "The check hasn't even gone through probate yet!"

Babs cleared her throat. She realized her hopes for using last night's evidence for a book would not pan out, as her affection for the kids overruled her quest for success. But a renewed sense of right and wrong inspired her even further. "Perhaps I shouldn't admit this, but the kids and I discovered Laddie's journal in which he confessed everything, the truth about Pet, and – something else."

"That's quite impossible," Gwyda glared.

"Don't say another word!" Barbara threatened her daughter. "I've got my own attorney on speed dial. Your brother will get that silver gravy boat instead!"

"I don't know if we can stand any more truth," Carolyn sighed.

"Are you saying it's impossible because you burned it?" Babs confronted Gwyda.

The older woman fixed her eyes on the American upstart. "You shouldn't accuse me of doing anything without evidence."

"Like this?" she responded, pulling burned remnants of paper and a green leather-bound volume from her handbag.

"You had no right to snoop! How dare you involve the children in these ridiculous schemes!" Gwyda raged.

"What exactly are those things?" Archie asked.

"We found these burned remnants in both Laddie's and Gwyda's rooms. Yes, perhaps we shouldn't have snooped. But we wouldn't have found this book hidden behind a sliding panel in Laddie's room."

"I searched in those and destroyed the diary I found!" the dame blurted out too quickly.

"There was one you didn't know about," Babs said with a raised eyebrow.

"I swear, if you blow this wad of cash for us," Barbara swooned as Gloria fanned her with jazz hands.

"Cool it with the theatrics, Barbara, it didn't impress Richard Burton and it's not impressing anyone here. You know you're not an actress," Myrtle croaked, pushing the oxygen mask onto her forehead. "These people can't grab my cash back now. They don't want what happened last night getting out, and they wouldn't want what I know getting out, either."

She grabbed the mask and took in some oxygen, and continued holding court. "Laddie told me this in a fit of passion on our honeymoon. We almost peeled the wallpaper off the walls that night!"

Carolyn wasn't the only one in the room responding with a brief shudder, but for once she decided not to voice her disapproval of lascivious behavior.

"We felt so close after achieving the best orgasms ever, so he told me he wanted to tell me about something he'd done, something he was ashamed   of."

"More shameful than that?" Gloria questioned Barbara.

"It happened back in 1941. He'd been carrying on with that chorus girl, that Winnie Potter, while he was still married to that cold fish Alice."

"Alice Asquith Bottomly was a fine woman. We were at an event not twelve hours ago to aid the fund she created," Gwyda huffed in defense.

"Yeah, and not twelve hours ago, your nephew tried to turn me into steak and kidney pie," Myrtle sniffed, taking a hit of more oxygen. "Where was I? Oh yeah, so Winnie had a baby, a girl she named Evie. She thought this would force Laddie to divorce Alice and marry her, but he wasn't having it. Then she kept soaking him for money rather than go to the tabloids with the story. He got sick of her grasping schemes and decided the only thing to do was get rid of her permanently."

"Permanently?" Cliff gulped.

"That's what I said. He planned it down to the last detail. He lured her to an address in London where he had planted explosives."

"You've got to be joking," Archie stated.

"Does it look like I'm joking? The city was under curfew and the blitz was still going on. He knew there was an excellent chance it could be blamed on air raids. But he didn't plan what happened. It turned out that stupid Winnie brought the child with her, and she left the kid there for a minute to run around the corner to a pub to fortify her courage with a beer. She couldn't leave the booze alone, that's what eventually did her in. Anyway, she went to the pub that night and while she was gone, the explosives went off, and Evie was killed."

"I don't believe this," Gwyda shook her head.

"I'm afraid it's exactly what Laddie wrote in this journal," Babs averred. Archie took the book from Babs's hand and read the page Babs had marked with her finger. Incredulous, he read in silence and nodded at the others.

"There *was* an air raid that night, and the explosion wasn't investigated," Myrtle continued. "Of course, he was sorry the child was killed, he hadn't wanted that. It probably explains why he wanted Ysabel to have Pet later on. Anyway, Winnie wasn't completely stupid; she knew Laddie had had something to do with it. So she ended up increasing her demands for cash and wasn't too discreet when she was drinking, bragging to pub pals about soaking a rich member of the House of Lords. One of those friends spilled the story to a tabloid writer and that's how the affair came out."

"But why would he admit to such a thing to you?" Barbara asked.

"Are you kidding? You know all – well, *most* of the things I did to help your career along! I bragged about a couple of things to Laddie to impress him. Like the time I threatened Harry Cohn that I could make the L.A.P.D. think he had something to do with the Black Dahlia murder if he didn't give you a part as Rita Hayworth's stand-in. Or the time I made Zanuck –"

"Mother, no one's interested in those funny stories right now," Barbara laughed a bit too loudly.

"Well, anyway, he wanted to impress me in return. And as a wedding gift, he gave me the deed to that same property in London to show how much he trusted me. It's a shame the marriage didn't last, but that little trump card I held ensured I got a good settlement and a promise for a cash payoff in his will. Was it my fault he underestimated me? I had to look out for myself, not to mention my untalented daughters."

"Yes, it's a miracle Athole had a career of any kind," Barbara agreed, preferring to ignore her mother's harsh assessment of her own stage and screen expertise.

"I'm going to rest in my own room," Gwyda said, rising from the desk. "I need some time away, especially if I'm expected to share any more meals with you people."

Dinner was uneventful, with perfunctory verbal appreciation for the meal and long stretches of silence (Gloria resisted the urge to engage in light, charming conversation). Albert remained quiet and ate little, but he acknowledged the obvious concern and attention from the new women in his life, Mina and Sophie. The girl shared friendly glances with Miles (and a wink or two from Henry).

Those who had not been present for the latest revelation had been apprised of the latest development, but they all agreed that there was no reason to let the children know the disturbing truths of the last twenty-four hours. At their tender ages, it was best they didn't realize everyone in the family was clinically suspect on some level or other.

Mrs. Dutton had also apologized to Pet. She admitted she hadn't known exactly what Hannah and Barnaby had been up to, but had seen them on more than one occasion exiting the passageway to the barn and suspected whatever they were doing, it was better to remain oblivious and quiet.

"There's nothing to forgive," she had assured the woman and gave her a comforting hug.

Their eyes met during dinner when the housekeeper carried the coffee service into the room. Mrs. Dutton's look was tentative, but Pet gave her a reassuring look.

A sudden draft caused one of the candles to flame out. Gwyda didn't wait for the servants to remedy the situation and pulled a matchbox from her pocket. Even with only one arm, she struck a match with practiced deftness and relit the candle herself.

She moved her eyes from the candle to Mina, who stared at her with a strange expression. And with that look, Gwyda knew that one more shocking revelation would be known before the evening was through.

STRANGE INTERLUDE 13

John McCain might have survived the Hanoi Hilton, but he wouldn't have survived the Venus de Milo Arms!

Starlets Hall of Fame opens in Texas by Scotch Linsell, *Classic Images*, April, 2002

The Starlets Hall of Fame opened in Dallas, Texas on February 27, 2002, to a throng of enthusiastic film lovers. Film historian Samuel Witherspoon has been collecting movie memorabilia of feminine stars his entire life, and is pleased that the public can enjoy his artifacts.

Witherspoon held a grand opening with some special hostesses in attendance: Mamie Van Doren, Gloria Prescott, Yvonne Craig, and Lori Williams were honored to attend the event and view the fantastic items on display.

"Look, one of my Batgirl costumes!" Yvonne enthused as Lori examined a still of costar Tura Satana from *Faster, Pussycat! Kill! Kill!*

Gloria studied a rare uncensored movie poster of *A Sharp Knife Can Be Dangerous*, a noir thriller starring Barbara Lamont. "Why did the censors insist on airbrushing in a higher neckline on Barbara's dress and removing that ad line calling her a 'sexy mattress-tester'? Everyone would want to see *that* on the big screen," Gloria commented as Mamie surprised her with a hug.

"Mamie and I go way back. We've been friends since that impromptu civil rights sit-in at the Coconut Grove," Gloria reminisced as she returned Mamie's affectionate embrace.

"Sam is wonderful to preserve all this film history," Mamie said as she unveiled framed nipple prints she was happy to donate to the museum.

The work of architect Eleanor Fountain-Black, while respectful to their subjects, have maintained a sense of humor. "The Divorce Paper Archives take up a significant portion of the Hall of Sorrow," Eleanor says, pointing out a niche with a portrait and candles lighted for the hall's patron saint, Elizabeth Taylor.

A marble portico resides on the property's western end next to a reflecting pond. The Calendar Girl Rotunda, as it's christened, offers bas-relief images of starlets April Stevens, May Britt, and June Blair. "But it's intended as a tranquil reminder of all the calendar girls: past, present, and future."

Star on Walk of Fame destroyed by Millicent Lillas, *Los Angeles Daily News*, November 30, 2003

Gara St. James's star on the Hollywood Walk of Fame was removed by unknown persons, officials reported on Tuesday.

"They just left a big hole out there," said Hollywood's honorary mayor Johnny Grant, who also oversees the star-unveiling ceremonies. "It appears somebody went out there with a pickax and chopped it up!"

This is not the first star to disappear since the Walk's inception in 1960. Stars honoring Jimmy Stewart, Kirk Douglas and Gene Autry disappeared after they were removed during construction projects (the stars for Stewart and Douglas were later recovered).

St. James's star was sponsored by her friend, former First Lady Nancy Reagan, in the 1970's. Gara's film credits include *The Ungrateful*, *Whatever Happened to Shprintzel?*, and *A Funny Thing Happened When I Sat Down in the Synagogue*. She has appeared on television programs such as *It's Gara's Show!*, *Arse of Nick in Old Lace*, and *Hora Hour* (a Jewish *Dance Fever*).

A police spokesman said a witness saw women in cocktail dresses with champagne bottles about 4:00 a.m. in the area. "He thought they looked familiar, like they had been on TV or the movies. But you know, all kinds of people come out to look, and a lot of them dress up like the stars. Heck, a group of drag queens show up at Marilyn Monroe's star once a week," Marcus Fields stated. The matter remains under investigation.

Actress provides proof of Bush on duty? by Daniel Chen, *The Washington Post*, March 15, 2004

Despite the White House's insistence that President George W. Bush fulfilled his military duty while in the National Guard in 1972, no one has stepped forward to corroborate the President's claims. Until today, that is. Actress Gara St. James claims she witnessed the President on duty in Alabama during the Vietnam War.

Ms. St. James asserts that she entertained the Montgomery National Guard in 1972 for the U.S.O. "It was part of my act to pull a young soldier onstage to participate in a musical number. He would play the bongos that were strapped to my bottom while I sang 'Heat Wave.' It was more tasteful than it sounds," Gara cautioned, aware of recent indecency charges tallied against Janet Jackson's Super Bowl performance.

"I pulled a nice conservative Christian from the audience, as I always did. George was game to play along with the gag for the appreciation of his fellow officers. He asked for my autograph, and I signed, 'To George W. Bush, with affection, Gara St. James.' I remember this because I had a wee drinkie and was a little tipsy. With poor judgment, I almost wrote a pun based on his surname, but good Midwestern morals prevailed and I signed my name like a lady."

Political pundits were quick to address her comments. Ann Coulter said, "There's all the proof we need. The testimony of a moon-faced Jewish actress is as reliable as if it had come from then-President Ford." When it was pointed out that the President in 1972 was Richard Nixon, Coulter responded, "Details, details, she's still a reliable old heifer."

Others weren't so quick to verify the claims. Both Commander Dwight McEntire of the Alabama National Guard and Carla Dean-Hamilton, a historian with the U.S.O., stated that according to their records, no such show ever took place.

Ms. St. James pooh-poohed these claims. "We all know you can't rely on people to fill out paperwork properly. This has been a problem with the government whenever a Democrat was in the White House."

When it was pointed out that the President Nixon had been a Republican, Gara said, "You didn't understand what I meant. I meant that the missing papers must have been misfiled by a subsequent Democratic administration."

Gara St. James: Out-of-control rage-a-holic? by Chloe Gonzalez, *The Star*, June 20, 2005

People are talking about actress Gara St. James, and what they're saying isn't pretty. At the Disney Studios lot, she got into a fight with Lindsay Lohan on the set of *Whazzup, Pippi?* (an update of the children's classic *Pippi Longstocking*).

Onlookers stated Gara (as Pippi's foil, Mrs. Bumblegloop) instigated the altercation by edging Lindsay out of a scene. When director Mark Waters corrected Gara, Lindsay smirked in amusement. During the next take, Gara knocked Lindsay off the stage and set off a melee of shoves and punches between the actresses and their handlers. Both stars were hustled off the set, and Gara left the studio lot for the day. What was intended as a one-day cooling-off period has extended into a set shutdown, and Disney execs aren't laughing.

Studio reps are keeping their mouths shut, but others in Tinseltown are talking about the incident. It's opened a floodgate of outrageous tales of Gara's behavior on- and off-set in Hollywood, and people are going on the record about it (practically unheard of in celeb gossip).

Harry Hamlin, who worked with Gara on the '80s miniseries *Beau Fauve*, stated, "She was a headache from day one. She intimidated Morgan [Brittany] to no end. When her character set fire to the plantation, we were *all* terrified that she was really going to set the place ablaze!"

Golden Age filmmaker Myron Elanbaum, who directed Gara in *Bride of the Golem*, stated, "I originally wanted Piper Laurie for the part, but I let the producers persuade me otherwise. Big mistake ... *huge* mistake!"

Kim Basinger, who played Gara's daughter in the 2001 straight-to-DVD farce *Nick & Tom Pitch a Tent in Central Park*, said it was a relief to finish the film. "She was a monster. She belched throughout my big scene on purpose! Gara makes my ex look like a real charmer."

Even Gara's friends are speaking up. The dancer Bahamia said, "I've said all along what a nutcase she is, but people thought I was joking. Well, nobody's laughing now. And baby, it *still* ain't my problem!"

Studio insiders expect an announcement of Gara's dismissal from the film. "Let's face it, Lindsay's the star, any old broad can play Gara's part. She should've been glad she was still getting roles all these years later."

If this mood grows, Gara may find parts harder to come by. She recently met with Queen Latifah's production company to discuss appearing in her upcoming remake of the Bette Davis classic *Dark Victory*, to be retitled *I'm Blind, Fool!* There was no comment from Latifah's camp.

News for Gara gets worse by Walter Halpern, *Movieline*, August, 2006

The Walt Disney Company filed suit on July 5 against actress Gara St. James after an incident on the set of *Whazzup, Pippi?*, caused the studio to shut down the production.

News of the lawsuit has reignited talk among Hollywood insiders. Golden Age hairdresser Hibiscus (just out with his memoir *If My Comb Could Talk*), has tended the tresses of every great star, including Gara. "She wasn't an angel like Lana or Liz, I'll tell you that. Sydney [Guilaroff] hated dealing with her. I dyed her hair from brownette to blondine for *Underwire Heiress*, and she asked if I minded making sure the carpet matched the drapes! I admit, I had done that procedure for a top star or two whose names I won't divulge, but no way was I going to do that for Gara. Let's just say that not everyone believes in that old adage, 'Cleanliness is next to Godliness.'"

Entertainment reporter Ted Casablanca said in a recent column that

Hollywood has changed since Gara's heyday and she hasn't kept up with the changes. "She's such a has-been, no one even does her for Halloween anymore."

Lindsay Lohan, who was starring in *Whazzup, Pippi?*'s title role, is at loose ends with the lawsuit until she can begin another project. She's currently making the rounds of L.A. nightlife with her new BFF, Paris Hilton.

Emmys honor winners, but Gara provides shock for viewers by Kerry McMahon, *Los Angeles Times*, September 19, 2005

There were the usual winners and some surprising upsets at last night's Emmy Awards. The biggest shocker also happened onstage, though it didn't involve the winning of an award.

Actress Gara St. James made a spectacle of herself onstage while introducing the nominees for outstanding variety, music or comedy special. (And at an awards telecast known to inspire vulgar fashions and wacky acceptance speeches, making a spectacle of one's self is a real accomplishment.)

The actress has been the recent source of unflattering news in the entertainment media, and called in a favor to be added to the slate of presenters. (Doris Roberts was the original presenter. "That old cow is sure to win again [in her comedy category], so she'll end up onstage anyway," Gara argued.)

The audience knew something was wrong from the moment she stepped onstage. She stumbled as she walked across the stage and bumped into the microphone stand. St. James threw her arms out and cried, "It's great to be back at The Palace once again! You're the best audience a girl could hope for." She then slurred the lines to "On the Atcheson, Topeka, and the Santa Fe" before host Ellen DeGeneres and presenter Jason Bateman emerged to escort Gara offstage.

She resisted their efforts, insisting, "My fans paid for a real show, and I'm gonna give it to 'em!" She threw her arms open again, this time knocking Bateman to the floor and causing her gown's bodice to expose her bosom to shocked viewers. Hugh Laurie and Mariska Hargitay joined the onstage rescue effort but she managed one last outburst: "Don't forget to buy a Baby Gara doll in the lobby on your way out!" (Technical problems kept the control room from stopping the debacle from airing to a TV audience of 18.3 million.)

Gara's spokesperson, Peony Lipschitz, insisted the actress was neither drunk nor on drugs, and stated that the star had devised a vaudeville comedy routine to honor the category she was presenting but hadn't run it by the producers. "If she hadn't been interrupted, it was going to end with Gara doing the splits onstage and pulling a rubber chicken out of her wig. Now that's comedy gold," Peony asserted.

The Emmys organization did not issue an official statement, but those in attendance had plenty to say:

Blythe Danner: "What a shame that happened. Hasn't she ever heard of double-sided tape?"

Jason Bateman: "How old is she, anyway? She's got a mean right hook!"

Gloria Prescott: "She can't even be trusted to read a teleprompter! Why didn't they call me? I know the right time and place to flash someone, and the Emmy Awards isn't it!"

Sean Hayes: "*My* gift bag didn't have a Baby Gara doll! Where can I get one of those?"

Barbara Lamont: "Three words: Bitch. Is. Crazy."

Rosa Parks praised as "one hell of a maid" by Ricki Oppenheimer, *The Onion*, October 26, 2005

Actress Gara St. James, who appeared in films as a child star known as Baby Gara before later films as an adult star, praised Rosa Parks on Tuesday as "one hell of a maid."

The civil rights icon, who died October 24 at age 92, was known worldwide as a symbol of the struggle for racial equality in the American South. "She's as important a symbol as Aunt Jemima and Uncle Ben, symbols you can find at your local supermarket," St. James praised.

The actress spoke at a political rally staged at a San Fernando Valley strip mall in support of President George W. Bush. The President's popularity has continued to fall in the face of an unpopular war, multiple White House scandals, and poor economic indicators.

"Fifty ... uh, thirty years ago in Montgomery, Alabama, this devoted maid stood up to injustice when she was told by a bus driver to move her can. The truth of the matter was that she was weighed down with my dry-cleaning, and couldn't stand up if she wanted to. But it's just nice that it all worked out so well," St. James beamed from the small dais, which threatened to cave in under the excessive strain.

"So this story should remind us all that even if things don't seem to be working out great for some people, that's no reason to drop plans mid-stream. Let's support our President as surely as those civil rights people did back then and inspired a young singer named Martin Luther Vandross."

All well in Gara's world? by Tisha Mosely, *Entertainment Weekly*, October 28, 2005

Gara St. James, the subject of unflattering headlines due to an onset altercation, an ongoing lawsuit with Walt Disney Studios, and a scandalous Emmy Awards appearance, didn't avoid the spotlight in an attempt to quash negative publicity. She attended the premiere of the Charlize Theron film *North Country* in Westwood and defended her bizarre actions at the Emmys as a "comedy routine."

The Emmys organization issued a statement two weeks ago, mentioning their admiration for Gara and wishes for her continued success. However, insiders whisper that St. James will never appear on an Emmys telecast again.

A contact with the organization would only speak on condition of anonymity: "In a town overrun with crazy Jews, that woman takes the cake. Literally. She stole a four-tier chocolate torte when she left the auditorium, a cake that was meant for the head table at the Emmys banquet later that night. She's always been one for a free handout, but now she'll find this town isn't so forgiving. The studios may look the other way if one of the *Desperate Housewives* or a *CSI* star makes demands, but they won't tolerate that from someone on the decline."

Gara wouldn't comment on rumors of Emmy discord, but mentioned her interest in updating a '70s anthology TV series for today's audience. "I think *Love, Conservative Style* is a great idea. But even though it's on the moral high ground doesn't mean it'll be stuffy. I'll add some 'aw-ights' and 'schizzles.' I'm sure my pal Bahamia knows the latest lingo."

Bahamia, fresh off a Broadway stint in the recent *Sweet Charity* revival, had these amusing comments: "Oh, she wants some lingo? How about these words?" The still glamorous dancer mentioned a few words unprintable in most media outlets.

Histrionics on display in court for Gara by Tanille Ebbens, *People*, March 16, 2006

Judge Howard Markham was astounded by what was described as a "three-ring circus" in his court last week and demanded actress Gara St. James be held without bail for 24 hours on a contempt of court charge after breaking into a string of profanities while in court to defend herself against breach of contract charges filed by Walt Disney Studios.

During a recess, Gara was seen crawling around on the ladies room floor gathering the spilled contents of a medicine bottle. Upon her return to the courtroom, her behavior turned increasingly bizarre. She began tapping her foot and humming as the Disney legal team introduced documents into evidence. She then jumped onto her chair and began singing, "Don't Rain on My Parade." When the judge banged his gavel and demanded Gara sit down, she stopped singing and began a string of obscenities.

"I've seen a lot of things in court, but never have I seen someone hike up her skirt and tell me to 'stick the roll of quarters where the sun don't shine,'" one of the security officers commented.

The final shocker was Gara's grabbing Judge Markham's gavel and threatening to "give him a whack for every birthday he missed giving her a present." It required six court officers to restrain the actress, who sat out her detainment before being picked up by her assistant, Peony Lipschitz. They left by the underground security exit and avoided the press.

"Miss St. James was tired, between preparing to defend herself against Mickey Mouse and not getting enough to eat. She gets low blood sugar if she doesn't eat every hour. All she'd had all day was a little piece of toast, maybe a pancake or two. A Denver omelet and turkey bacon, a bagel and cream cheese, some pickled kosher tripe. A star of Gara's width can't subsist on a lettuce leaf, you know."

"This is another example of her unprofessionalism and strengthens our case," said Edwin Fleesom, a member of the Disney legal team. The lawsuit stems from Gara's dismissal from the set of *Whazzup, Pippi?*, which was to star Lindsay Lohan before the entire project was shelved. Disney is trying to have the entire cost paid by Gara, who maintains the studio broke the contract first when she was unfairly fired, and therefore owes the studio nothing; she has also counter-sued for wrongful termination.

Lindsay was briefly unable to report to another movie set because of the legal issues. During that time, the young star began to endure negative publicity herself due to excessive partying with the likes of Paris Hilton and stepping out of limos *sans* underwear.

Excerpted entries from *Politics and Hollywood Celebrities: The Conservative Connection* by Franklin Butterworth, *Chapter 14: Gara Knows Best*

Terror threats: "I was at a diplomatic dinner in April of 2001, and anytime I approached George or Condi or Colin, they were muttering something about 'terror.' I cornered Laura to give her some advice on dealing with her wayward daughters, and when I left, I overheard her ask an aide, 'Can't someone do something about that terror?' So obviously the fight against terrorism was on this administration's agenda from day one."

Hurricane Katrina: "Bush cut his vacation short to make sure everyone was on top of things. He told 'Brownie' he was doing a heckuva job. How can anyone say that Bush doesn't care about black people when he's telling 'Brownie' that? And why did the liberals get all up in Barbara Bush's grill for pointing out how good things were working out for them? Bar was only pointing out a fact. Those people will have opportunities in Houston to find good jobs, like train porters or hotel maids."

Approval ratings: "I'm appalled that anyone would rate our President so low. These numbers have been baked by the biased liberal media. What, did they call 500 of the Clintons's closest friends, or a bunch of limousine liberals in New York City?"

Gay marriage: "Homosexuals need to realize that they are already free to marry whomever they want to, just as long as those boys marry women. They're helpful when you get a rip in your dress or need your hair done, but does that mean they should be allowed to marry *each other*? Lots of single ladies would love to get married. I hear a woman has a better chance of being hit by a terrorist attack than to get married. If we allow gays to marry each other, then the terrorists have won."

C.I.A.: "What's the big deal about somebody spilling that woman's [Valerie Plame] identity? Someone probably called for a work reference, and Human Resources just did their job. Why do the Democrats want to keep progress from happening?"

Christian conservatism: "Just because I'm a good Jew doesn't mean I can't appreciate smart Christians, who abide by what God and our elected officials tell us. Even some Catholics are all right. I tried to visit Pope John Paul in 1987 but was told I should have made an appointment. I thought that was rude. My *bubee* always said to keep your door open for visitors and keep a nice coffee cake on the table. Even when I did manage to meet him in 1988, he didn't even offer me communion wafers. But he blessed me and gave me a vial of holy water, which came in handy later in the day when I was tired and thirsty from shoe shopping. Why are all the streets in Rome done in cobblestone? Concrete is more practical."

Second amendment rights: "Liberals always want to take people's guns away. Why are they always trying to chip away at people's rights? Everyone should be allowed to bear arms wherever they choose, be it an awards show, a church service, or a peace rally."

Secrecy: "If Bush thought we needed to know more, he'd tell us, but sometimes they have to do things behind people's backs. I've done the same thing myself from time to time! If they need to spy on Americans and tap some wires, I don't see what the fuss is all about. How come when my friend Bahamia taps out some dance steps, everyone applauds like trained seals, but if George and Dick need to tap some wires, then all of a sudden there's a problem?"

Economy: "I don't understand where anyone's getting the idea Bush is bad for the economy. What looming inflation? *I'm* doing great!"

Military interrogations: "I don't know where people got the idea waterboarding constitutes torture. I've seen young people hanging out at the beach and riding the waves, when they should all be working instead. How can *that* be considered torture? I've got torture for you, try sharing an apartment with three backstabbing bitches trying to steal your career. John McCain might have survived the Hanoi Hilton, but he wouldn't have survived the Venus de Milo Arms!"

Minute of silence observed for Bottomly by Kevin Easton, *The London Evening Standard*, 7 June, 2007

The House of Lords observed a one-minute silence yesterday in respect of Lord Lindale "Laddie" Bottomly, who passed away yesterday at the age of 107. The funeral has been postponed a few days in order to accommodate the arrival of family and friends from Europe and the United States. He is survived by a son, Nolan, and a daughter, Pet, as well as one sister, Dame Gwyda Glasscock.

Laddie died at Brownmoor, which is where he was born in 1900. Brownmoor, at one time famous for parties and jet set visitors, was once dubbed "Bottoms Up" by locals. The theatrical air of the estate was well-suited to a family whose ancestral line includes two losing their heads on the block (one for aiding in a plot to overthrow the King, the other for pilfering blackberries from the Queen's Royal Bush). The castle survived the German blitz during WW II, but lost one wing and several out-buildings on the grounds in a fire 40 years ago.

Laddie leaves behind a legacy of racy scandals and newspaper headlines which titillated readers for decades. As a boy, Bottomly (then nicknamed "Little Flush" for his fascination with the privy), became interested in the theatre when the great Sarah Bernhardt visited. Bernhardt was the first in a long line of crushes young Bottomly was to have for actresses, showgirls, and the like.

Quite the gay blade at weekend parties, he was unmarried until the age of 38, when he wed Alice Asquith, daughter of tin magnate Humbreth Asquith. The couple divorced nine years later after reports of Bottomly's affair with chorus girl Winnie Potter made the tabloids. Rumoured to have fathered Potter's daughter Evie (who had been killed in a bomb fire in 1941), he later fled to Hollywood.

It was there that Bottomly was tapped by Columbia Pictures to appear in films, but a possible career petered out from lack of interest from both Bottomly and the general public. His time in the film capital resulted in a short marriage to Myrtle Dempster, the mother of actress Barbara Lamont.

He spent the next decade enjoying the jet set lifestyle in Hollywood, Buenos Aires, Monte Carlo, and other exotic locales. His 1961 marriage to actress Gara St. James resulted in the birth of a final child, a daughter named Petal. (A fourth marriage, to magician's assistant Jenny Menzies, ended in her drowning death in the Irish Sea.)

There were nasty whispers that Laddie wasn't Pet's father because of the child's dark complexion. Gara St. James only confronted the rumour once during a *Barbara Walters Special*. "Jesus Christ, people, I'm Jewish! God led us out of Egypt a long time ago, so once upon a time, we all had nice tans and nappy hair. Plus, the Bottomly family is not all that white. Their estate is called Brownmoor. Hello? Doesn't anyone remember *Othello*? Moors are black or dark brown, so there's obviously something back there in the family history."

Any tributes in Laddie's memory should be sent to the Asquith-Bottomly Health Care Coalition, which was started by Laddie's first wife. Members of the Asquith, Bottomly, Glasscock, and Fotheringay families continue to sit on the organization's board, which has done much to aid London's poor residents over the decades.

CHAPTER 14

In my hatred of one horrid bitch, I thought I had caused a terrible tragedy.

Mina had expected the knock on the door as soon as everyone retired for the evening. She took a deep breath and opened the door to Gwyda.

"Is there anything you or Sophie need tonight?" she asked.

Mina found herself resenting Gwyda's fake pleasantry, and she blurted out, "Didn't you come here to talk about something more important?"

Gwyda flinched, not expecting Mina's boldness. She recovered and nodded. "Yes, I think there are some things we should discuss."

"But not here. Sophie's asleep in the next room and I don't want her disturbed by overhearing anything."

"Then let's repair to my sitting room," Gwyda suggested, and Mina followed her to the older woman's suite.

Gwyda closed the door behind her and indicated the settee. "I believe I'll stand," Mina stated. A resigned Gwyda sat down in the preferred throne-like chair beside the small table. She looked down, smoothed the skirt of her robe, and faced Mina.

"I knew from the look you gave me this evening that you know the truth. I don't know how you know, but ..." Gwyda let the statement hang in the air as she raised her palm in a conceding gesture.

"Yes, I know the truth about the fire now," Mina said, her voice dull and heavy. "I didn't make the connection as a child nor in all these years. But being in the house again stirred up feelings I couldn't identify. And when the kids found that cigarette holder in the ruins, I knew there was something about it I couldn't put my finger on. It wasn't until you took those matches out and lit the candles that it came back to me."

Gwyda raised her head and looked at Mina. "You came back to Gara's room that day, didn't you?"

Mina nodded. "Yes, I saw what you did. There were two fires that day ..."

"I want the beads! Let me try on the beads!" Mina pleaded with Pet.

"Okay, okay, hold on, let me put on the bracelet first," she insisted, sliding an assortment of gold and silver circles up her arm. She handed the pearls to her cousin and picked up the sable jacket. "Do you want the brown fur or the blue one?"

"I like that one, can I try that one on?" Mina eyed the beautiful jacket.

"Sure, I'll wear this one." Pet threw the dyed mink stole around her shoulders, its adult size almost engulfing her. She giggled, sputtering as she pushed the fur out of her face.

"We are too, too fancy for this place," Mina laughs, putting a pair of enormous diamond-studded sunglasses on. They fell, and she pushed them back up and raised her head high to prevent them from falling again.

"Oh, darling, you are too, too divine!" Pet gave Mina fake "air kisses" as she'd seen her mother do dozens of times.

"And you are too, too marvelous," Mina responded, and the pair dissolved in giggles.

Playing with Aunt Gara's dress up "play pretties" was a rare treat for Mina. She and her parents had made the trip to England for the last three summers, and Mina so looked forward to spending time with her cousin, who was like a little sister. Pet was so pretty, with a dark tan and unruly curls. But she was just as rambunctious as she was girlish. Playing with dolls or climbing trees, it didn't matter, as long as the two of them laughed, screamed, and played the summer away.

Gara had been in the room earlier while the girls played. She didn't seem to like it so much when the girls became loud with their play. "Dears, dears, not so loud, you can be beautiful and quiet!" she bellowed. They'd become quiet for awhile, then the noise had started again.

Gara harrumphed and started to discipline the girls again, when Pet turned and gave her mother a dazzling smile. Gara's heart melted. "You girls have your fun, I'm going to take a long, hot bath." With that, she swept out of the room and into the enormous bath suite. The girls soon heard the gentle roar of the water and the muffled sound of music. Even with the closed door, the thunderous strains of Gara vocalizing with the music carried into the next room.

"What's she doing?" Mina asked.

"She's thinking about making a record and wants to get her voice in shape again," Pet explained.

They listened to the jarring notes through the door. "It must be awful hard to get your voice back in shape," Mina remarked, and they returned to their play.

Mina picked up a slender, black tube on the dressing table. It was so pretty, shiny and painted with silver flowers. "I like this. What is it?"

"It's one of Momsy Womsy's cigarette holders," Pet explained.

"How do you use it?"

Pet hesitated. *"Maybe we shouldn't mess with it. Momsy doesn't like me to touch those."*

"I'm not going to hurt it. I just wanted to see how it worked," Mina said, a hurt sound in her voice.

A sensitive Pet didn't want to disappoint her cousin, so she opened the table's drawer and removed the open pack of cigarettes. She fished a bit further and found the cigarette lighter. Momsy had warned her never to touch them, but she did want to be important and show off for Mina. And if she didn't touch it for long, maybe Momsy wouldn't be mad.

She placed the cigarette in the holder's end and showed Mina how to display it in her hand. *"Momsy Womsy does it like this,"* she said, holding it to her lips, waving it around, and pretending to flick ashes into the porcelain tray on the dressing table.

Mina grabbed the lighter and struggled with it. *"How do you work it?"*

Pet hesitated before taking the lighter from her cousin. With a shaking hand, she ignited the end. They watched the lit cigarette for a few moments before Mina took it from Pet's hand and imitated the same gestures her cousin had performed. *"Oh, darling, I'm so divine!"* she giggled.

The bedroom door suddenly opened and the girls froze. There stood Gwyda in all her formidable presence. Mina was a little frightened of her. Even if she'd had both arms, she still would have looked scary. She was as tall as a redwood and resembled a human vulture.

"Just what are you girls up to?" she demanded in a frosty tone. *"You girls know you shouldn't be playing with this, it's dangerous. You could start a fire. Where are your mothers?"*

"Momsy Womsy's taking a bath and Auntie Margaret's in the garden," Pet replied softly, hoping that Aunt Gwyda wouldn't dole out a punishment herself.

"Mina, put that cigarette out now. You girls have played long enough in here. Why don't you go outside and play with Albert and Willis," Gwyda suggested.

"Yes, Auntie Gwyda." Mina flicked the cigarette into the ashtray and both girls removed the mounds of jewelry and furs. They scooted out of the room and headed for the great hall.

They were almost down the stairs before Mina noticed she was still wearing a diamond brooch. *"You go ahead, I better put this back in your mommy's room,"* she told Pet.

Mina arrived at the room and discovered the door ajar. She started to enter and stopped short. Gwyda had returned to the room as well, or maybe she'd never left. The child watched as she withdrew a box of matches from the pocket of her dress. Deftly she managed to strike the match against the side of the box and held it to the cigarette lying in the ashtray. The cigarette reignited and Gwyda placed it in the *trashcan beneath the dressing table.*

Mina couldn't move. Gwyda stood there a few minutes and watched the trash catch fire. Gwyda then crossed to the bathroom door. The strains of music and Gara's singing were still coming through.

Gwyda pulled an enormous keyring out of her pocket. She found the wanted key and as stealthily as possible, slipped it into the bathroom door's lock. She turned it softly and extracted it from the door, then gently tested the handle, satisfied the door was now locked.

Mina turned and raced back to the great hall's gallery. She wasn't sure what had happened, but even a child's intuition told her it was something she shouldn't have seen.

"I know you hated her, but enough to kill her?" Mina asked.

Gwyda pursed her lips and closed her eyes for a moment. She looked up and nodded. "Yes, I did. I still do. You can't even imagine the fury she inspired in me the years she was married to my brother. An absolute beast. To think I'd sacrifice my home, a centuries old castle, for the opportunity to do away with her ..."

She paused and collected her thoughts. "You must think I'm a horrible person to have done such a thing with the hope of killing your aunt."

"I've wanted to throttle her myself on many occasions. But not enough to kill her."

Gwyda paused again before speaking. "My entire life has been ruled by two things: honor and intellectual curiosity. To spend that many years with an uncouth lummox who has neither was more than I could take. I thought of many ways to get rid of Gara but I always held back. And for whatever reason, I saw that cigarette and thought, 'How easy it would be to blame her death on her own carelessly unattended cigarette.' And I did it, plain and simple as that. I didn't think of the consequences.

"I thought everyone else was out of that wing and believed the fire brigade could minimize damage to the house, if not damage to Gara. But the fire proved much deadlier than I anticipated and didn't result in the death I wanted. Gara managed to escape while Hannah and Barnaby died."

"But –"

"Yes, I know now, I didn't set the fire that killed them. But for forty years, I've lived with the terrible guilt of believing their deaths were my fault. In my hatred of one horrid bitch, I thought I had caused a terrible tragedy. Perhaps it's what I deserved." Gwyda swallowed and raised her head, fixing her eyes on Mina. "And I suppose we'll have to report these matters to the police now."

Mina didn't speak, letting Gwyda's statement hang in the air for a few moments. Then she said, "I don't think that's going to solve or change anything. Yes, my initial reaction to remembering what I'd seen was to make this a police matter. But now, forty years later, I don't think that's the way to deal with it."

Gwyda stared at Mina, wondering just what the younger woman had in mind. In a halting tone, Mina continued, "I don't think this should go beyond this room. You wanted to kill Gara, and didn't. You believed you killed Hannah and Barnaby, but didn't. And you lived with guilt you shouldn't have had all these years, but had no guilt for what you'd actually done. Somehow, I think it all evened out."

Gwyda seemed stunned by this turn of events. She lowered her head and Mina could see tears staining her cheeks. She seemed even older now than Mina had ever seen her, and the younger woman realized that Gwyda was close to the end of her days. To have spent the last forty years of a long life clinging to some twisted honor credo ... Gwyda had stuck to a desperate notion of superior righteousness for so long, she didn't realize her own behavior more closely corresponded to the animal kingdom she had devoutly studied for decades.

Mina turned to leave. There was nothing more to do or say.

STRANGE INTERLUDE 14

These old gals are the best supporting players a star could hope for!

Scientist Dame Gwyda Glasscock passes away by Gene Dehner, *The Times of London*, 12 November, 2008

Dame Gwyda Glasscock, the celebrated zoologist, passed away yesterday in Flemshire. She was in poor health the last few months, due in part to her advanced age and sorrow over the deaths of close family members.

It was in June that her only brother, Lord Laddie Bottomly, passed away. Shortly thereafter, Laddie's son, Nolan, died in an accident at a charity event. The family has hardly recovered from these losses and now they must grieve the loss of their matriarch.

Dame Glasscock was born in 1910, the youngest of four children. (Her sisters Audra and Maida passed away in 1944 and 1971, respectively.) Even as a child, she was fascinated by the local fauna. She attended Imperial College London and obtained her graduate degrees from Royal Veterinary College.

Colleagues described her as fiercely competitive in her studies. Her most celebrated moment occurred in 1960 when she killed a rare subspecies of bear in pursuit of her work; she lost her arm in the struggle, but refused to give up. The following autumn, she read a paper condensing her studies before her peers at Royal Veterinary College and received a standing ovation of unprecedented length, both for her exquisite work and her amazing courage in returning to an active life of research and teaching.

She married Mortimer Glasscock in 1929, heir to a silversmithing fortune; they were married for 58 years until Mortimer's death from blood poisoning. (His breathtaking collection of vintage thimbles is on permanent exhibit at The Museum of Silver and Metal Goods in west London).

She was created Dame in 1974. She is survived by a son, two grandchildren, and two great-grandchildren. The family requests that any tributes in her memory be sent to the Asquith-Bottomly Health Care Coalition or Royal Veterinary College.

New Bottomly Gallery opens by Aileen Marquez, *The New Yorker*, May 19, 2008

The Bottomly Gallery of London has opened a branch in New York in Chelsea at 532 W. 25th Street, and its recent opening was a star-studded event. The crowning debut was the unveiling of the restored *Lady of the Tayto Crisps* by British portraitist Sir Ralph Musgrove, which depicts actress Gara St. James in regal splendor. The portrait has been unseen in public for many decades and with a resurgence of interest in Musgrove's career, the Bottomly Gallery has made a timely splash in its U.S. art scene debut.

The owners, Lord Albert Bottomly and his wife, Lady Mina, promise exciting future shows and a revolving slate of artists gracing the gallery offerings on both sides of the Atlantic. Next up will be an exhibit featuring rare Spanish art and sculpture, some of which belonged to Bottomly's mother, '60s songbird Mirabelle Peña, and have been unseen for years.

Also announced is a pair of photographic exhibitions celebrating renowned photojournalist Pet Bottomly. The first features a timeline of newsworthy photos from Bottomly's impressive journalism career; the second is an intriguing exhibition of rock star portraits, including Sting, Mary J. Blige, and Joel and Benji Madden. The centerpiece includes intimate portraits of Dietrich Seeking Garbo lead singer Bingham Lamont, and will be accompanied by an avant garde fashion show with stage garments designed by Didley Musgrave.

By staying on top of the latest trends and keeping an eye on the classics, The Bottomly Gallery NYC will surely be delivering some intriguing shows in the future.

Latest celeb autobio raises the bar (and eyebrows) by Joan Sanderson, *U.S. Book Reviews*, November 12, 2008

Most celebrity autobiographies are boring, self-reverential tomes that promise to spill the beans but never do. Here's one that reveals the truth and then some.

The Unbearable Toughness of Being Great: The Gara St. James Story is the autobiography (co-written with Babs Lamont) of the longtime star. Childhood stardom, lean years of failure, rebirth as an adult starlet, films and international headlines, life as an English Lady, symbol of the final years of Hollywood's Golden Age ... She's lived through all of those things, and what she has to say about it all is fascinating in a way most celebrity autobios aren't.

She's candid about the lean years between stardom as Baby Gara and her resurgence in the '50s. "I had to take whatever scraps I could to survive during those years. I had a family to support. So what if I had to stoop to the lowest level of show business to make money – unbilled work as a studio extra?"

Not many huge stars could admit such a humiliating experience. But Gara is outspoken and guileless, and celebrates both the highs and lows of her lengthy career.

She talks about her many romances, including Jory Plummer ("He was St. George *and* the dragon rolled into one, and I should have married him at least once"), Laurence Harvey ("He was so uptight, he'd practically write me a formal thank you note after a *schtup*"), and Lex Barker ("That shitheel never knew how to treat a woman. Someone who'd treat three of the most beautiful women in Hollywood – me, Lana, and Arlene – like that is a *putznasher* [a Yiddish word meaning cocksucker]!").

Despite tabloid tales of discord with her third husband, Lord Lindale Bottomly, Gara has only kind things to say about the father of her only child, the photojournalist Pet Bottomly. This is a woman who has learned life's lessons and is eager to share the wisdom that comes from a thoughtful reflection on one's place in the world.

Babs Lamont, the writer daughter of Gara's longtime friend, fellow actress Barbara Lamont, has helped shape Gara's saga into an entertaining book sure to be the book of the upcoming holiday season. We'll be reading more from Babs in the future; her first piece of fiction, due next year, will be *Hoors on the Moors*, a modern reimagining of classic literature from the Brontë sisters, and similar in theme to recent literary remixes like *Pride and Prejudice and Zombies*.

News channel announces photojournalist addition by Carrie Eisley, *USA Today*, January 15, 2009

CNN has announced photojournalist Pet Bottomly has been signed as an official correspondent for the international news channel. She is expected to host occasional specials advancing a unique take on photographic- and video-based moments in history and technological advances in media.

Pet has appeared as an expert guest on several CNN shows over the past year, and it's believed the network may begin searching for a high-profile permanent program match for the rising star. "I'm enthusiastic about this opportunity and hope to bring a different perspective to news analysis," she said as part of yesterday's press conference.

Bottomly is an award-winning photographer with a career spanning more than twenty years. She was honored last year with a nomination for Photo of the Year from the Global Press Initiative, for her photo of angry U.N. interpreters engaged in fisticuffs. She has an international pedigree as the daughter of an English Lord, the recently deceased Lindale Bottomly, and actress Gara St. James.

The ladies of summer by George Henning, *Entertainment Weekly*, June 5, 2009

The Memorial Day weekend, traditionally the start of the summer movie season, opened with a surprising bang last weekend. The expected blockbuster, *Elongated Man* starring Jason Biggs, tanked at the box office. Despite some interest from teen males familiar with the DC Comics character, lack of momentum and bad word of mouth spelled doom for the big budget, special effects-laden extravaganza. (The film earned only $4.5 million, a tiny portion of its reported budget of $379 million.)

The lesson of Summer '07, when *Huge Miscalculation* (despite a press frenzy in the wake of the stars's affair) opened and bombed, doesn't appear to have stuck in Hollywood's memory. So what *did* win the holiday weekend at the box office? Would you believe a film adaptation of a TV series starring four senior citizen actresses?

The Golden Girls: The Movie opened at #1 with a reported box office take of $63 million. With a modest budget of $19 million, this looks to be the success story of the summer. Starring Bahamia, Barbara Lamont, Gloria Prescott, and Gara St. James (an asterisk denotes the billing is "in alphabetical order") in roles made famous on TV by Rue McClanahan, Betty White, Beatrice Arthur, and Estelle Getty, the film delivers laughs and is delighting a diverse audience of fans nostalgic for '80s television, fans of Golden Age (pun intended) starlets, and young movie-goers curious to know what the fuss is all about.

Bahamia maintains her ageless appeal as the always horny Blanche and displays marvelous comic timing, whether she's bantering with her roomies or trying to snare a hunky millionaire. Barbara Lamont plays clueless and addlebrained Rose with terrific ease; her delivery of frequent St. Olaf stories is spot-on and sets off waves of laughter.

As Dorothy, Gloria Prescott raises her head imperiously and turns her head sharply (Prescott credits her MGM studio training with acting coach Lillian Burns) to deliver withering putdowns and sarcastic asides. And as Sophia, Gara St. James has the best time onscreen, skewering the foibles of her roomies and insulting anyone who crosses her path.

The four stars have known each other for many years; indeed, they were once roommates back in the early '50s. This familiarity helps sell the movie's silly contrivances (though set in the new millennium, the characters still dress in the '80s excesses of enormous shoulder pads and unstructured jackets in tropical prints, and more than one joke is made about the ladies wearing heavy sweaters and overcoats in Miami). And with top-notch supporting players, everyone's in fine form.

Fans nostalgic for stars from an earlier era are delighted to see Robert Conrad as Stan, Margot LeMora and Danielle Kusnal as Blanche's sisters, and Timima Bossi as Dorothy's sister. And today's film fans are amused to see Alicia Silverstone, Elizabeth Banks, and Ryan Phillippe among the stars playing the adult children of the women.

"I still look great in stretch pants and oversize sweaters!" laughed Bahamia when the stars were recently interviewed on *Good Morning America*.

"It was tougher than I thought it would be. It's not easy to appear stupid *and* believable," Barbara revealed.

"At first I wasn't that crazy about playing the unglamorous part of Dorothy. What sold it for me was the thought of Gara having to play my mother!" jokes Gloria.

"Ya mama! Ha!" Gara cracked. "I've gotta admit, I didn't think I'd get along with these girls. Back when we lived at the Venus de Milo Arms, I was the peacemaker, but I didn't know if I was up for it again. But let me tell you, these old gals are the best supporting players a star could hope for!"

With the enormous weekend opening gross and projected weeks looking healthy, they're already negotiating with the stars for the sequel. The studio might well be telling these women, "Thank *you* for being a friend!"